LINDSAY WONG

* * *

SIMON PULSE
New York London Toronto Sydney New Delhi

〰️

SIMON PULSE

An imprint of Simon & Schuster Children's Publishing Division
1230 Avenue of the Americas, New York, New York 10020
First Simon Pulse paperback edition May 2020
Text copyright © 2020 by Lindsay Wong
Cover photograph of girl copyright © 2020 by Nabi Tang/Stocksy
Cover photograph of toy tiger by Gabrieluskal/iStock
Cover photograph of skyline by bingdian/iStock
For information about special discounts for bulk purchases, please contact
Simon & Schuster Special Sales at 1-866-506-1949 or business@simonandschuster.com.
The Simon & Schuster Speakers Bureau can bring authors to your live event. For more
information or to book an event contact the Simon & Schuster Speakers Bureau
at 1-866-248-3049 or visit our website at www.simonspeakers.com.
Cover designed by Laura Eckes
Interior designed by Tom Daly
The text of this book was set in Cormorant Garamond.
Manufactured in the United States of America
2 4 6 8 10 9 7 5 3 1
Library of Congress Cataloging-in-Publication Data
Names: Wong, Lindsay, author.
Title: My summer of love and misfortune / by Lindsay Wong.
Description: First Simon Pulse edition. | New York : Simon Pulse, 2020. |
Audience: Ages 12 and Up. | Audience: Grades 10-12. | Summary: After a series of disastrous
choices and rejections, seventeen-year-old Chinese American Iris Wang is thrust into the
decadent world of Beijing high society as her cousin's English tutor.
Identifiers: LCCN 2019035425 (print) | LCCN 2019035426 (eBook) |
ISBN 9781534443341 (hardcover) | ISBN 9781534443365 (eBook)
Subjects: CYAC: Conduct of life—Fiction. | Family life—China—Fiction. |
Chinese Americans—Fiction. | Love—Fiction. | China—Fiction.
Classification: LCC PZ7.1.W6359 My 2020 (print) |
LCC PZ7.1.W6359 (eBook) | DDC [Fic]—dc23
LC record available at https://lccn.loc.gov/2019035425
LC eBook record available at https://lccn.loc.gov/2019035426
ISBN 9781534480704 (Canadian export paperback)

This book is dedicated to the very best
and worst disaster that I know: myself!

And also to anyone who has ever felt that they never
belonged to any particular people, purpose, or place.

I see you and I salute you and I promise
that you will be 85 percent okay (one day) in this scary,
tumultuous, and glittering world.

xoxo.

L.

Flower-Heart

I, Iris Wang, was born to be unlucky.

This is because I was born in the Year of the Tiger, and everyone in our Chinese family knows that girls born in Tiger Year are bad luck.

A flower-hearted Tiger girl, such as yours truly, means that I'm destined to pick loser boys and never listen to my parents. A flower-heart is someone who shows up hungover to her SATs and half-asses her college admission essays. She's also addicted to Starbucks lattes, expensive makeup, and super-fun parties.

But a Tiger son born into the family is supposed to make a lot of money and bring honor to his family name. Total sexist bullshit, am I right? Maybe that superstition existed in China in the time of Confucius, but not in twenty-first-century America, where Siri and iPhones practically run our lives.

Can I tell you an embarrassing and hideous secret?

When I was born, I was covered with thick, abundant hair all over my entire body, like I was an actual tiger cub. According to my parents, I even had coarse hairs growing on my chin, forehead, and cheeks.

My mom likes to joke that I looked exactly like a hair ball spat out by a designer cat.

My dad says that two weeks before I was born, he dreamed that my mom had given birth to a tiger cub, but he's deeply superstitious. He's the kind of guy who checks with a feng shui master before buying a painting for the house or making a new friend. My dad was born in the Year of the Goat, so he believes that anyone who isn't a farm animal, like his Tiger daughter—i.e., me—brings him bad luck. Before he could propose to my mom, who is a Zodiac Dog, he consulted the Chinese almanac. Then he hired a Chinese monk to work out the math and interview his future bride.

When my mom told him she was going to give birth to a Tiger, he was extremely worried. "A Dog and Goat for parents are no match for a Tiger!" he exclaimed.

When he found out that his tiger cub was going to be a girl, I think he actually cried from anxiety.

Anyway, I was lucky that a lot of my facial hair fell off by kindergarten. But it doesn't explain the gross, extremely long mustachelike hairs that sometimes appear when I'm super stressed. These hairs sprout above my upper lip and even grow out of my ears. I swear, those hairs are like, my whiskers. Thank god for the invention of hair wax and affordable laser treatment.

Without deluxe Nair Wax Ready-Strips, I don't think I could ever be seen in public during times of great personal duress.

That, and I have to blame my bad luck on my sometimes too-loving, overprotective parents. As soon as I was born, they took me to a famous fortune-teller who was visiting from China to ask her how to fix my life trajectory.

It all went wrong from the very beginning.

You see, the fortune-teller, Madame Xing, found a funny-shaped mole under my right eye and said it looked like a tear-drop. Like I was born to be permanently crying.

"This flower-heart is no good," she announced to my parents after a quick examination. My mom and dad were probably horrified and praying that they could send me back to the hospital and switch me for a Tiger boy.

It also didn't help that I was one of those babies who was always crying and puking everywhere. My mom said that I just barfed on Madame Xing's mink fur and she got flustered and started cussing nonstop. My dad swears that this was bad luck, as it offended a powerful fortune-teller, who must have put a double curse on me.

After our first and only fortune-telling session, Madame Xing cryptically said, "Keep both eyes on your Tiger daughter. If you take one eye off, she will bring shame on your family with her weak flower-heart."

Whatever she said was true. Since I was born, I guess I was destined to be a flower-heart. I have a weakness for terrible choices and terrible boys.

This brings me to my current situation.

Earth to Iris

Why am I panicking? Why is my throat constricting like I have a supersize packet of spicy ramen noodles stuck inside it?

It's okay, don't panic, Iris. Don't panic. Everything will be totally fine. It usually is.

Gasping, I take a swig of my extra-sugary latte and happen to glance down at my half-gnawed fingernails. I wince. The edges look super raggedy, like I've been clawing at the insides of my own personal coffin. I desperately need a manicure, even though I got one three days ago, and I also probably need another Venti-size Starbucks refill very soon.

But my iPhone dings again like an annoying reminder, and I sneak a peek at the screen.

It's still there.

The alert hasn't changed; it's still the same automated message that has been dinging me for the past few weeks, updating me on my spending habits. I was hoping it would just magically stop. It's an ongoing automated text message from the credit card company. Last year, my parents gave me an American Express card so I could easily pay the fees for online college admissions applications. Since the beginning of junior year, I've been using my credit card all the time. It's so easy to buy anything and everything when all you have to do is tap or swipe. It's like playing a real-life game of *Sims*, except that you get to physically touch and wear all the new clothes in your wardrobe.

Ding!

AMERICAN EXPRESS

Hello, this is a friendly alert to help you manage your spending. As you requested, your credit card statement is currently $6,512.96. Please call 1-800-746-3211 immediately if you suspect credit card fraud. Have a great day!

I let out a tiny, panicked whimper. But how can I have spent $6,512.96? It makes absolutely no sense. I think back to my spending for the month, and that Venti-size cup of black coffee, mixed with panic, surges up my throat. When was the last time I used my credit card?

This whole thing is a mistake. A scam for unsuspecting old people and desperate high school seniors.

I have been a victim of criminal fraud. How do I report this to the police?

How do I even tell my parents that I was scammed?

Then I finally remember, the guilt crashing through me like ill-timed nausea. My surprise plane tickets to Paris for Peter. Those were expensive, $850 each. Peter couldn't go on the tenth-grade Europe trip a few years ago, and he always talked about how much he wanted to go to Paris with me after graduation. And I was going to surprise him tonight. But how could two economy tickets cost $6,512.96?

Did the online booking site steal my credit card number?

Then I also remember.

I bought flowers this morning, a pretty bouquet of soft purple irises for Peter. I was planning to give him my namesake flowers and present the plane tickets as his birthday/early graduation gift. It was going to be an incredibly romantic surprise.

Oh yes, and then there was the sparkly Vera Wang prom dress from Nordstrom that I needed to buy. I had to have those matching silver heels from Saks; desperately needed that glitter gel manicure from the new spa down the street, and basketfuls of makeup from Sephora.

I mean, what was I supposed to do? Not buy a single product? The lady who gave me my free makeup trial for prom had been incredibly nice.

Actually, come to think of it, I never wear eye shadow, so why did I buy six nude-colored eye shadows and three pairs of mink eyelashes? Who needs fake lashes that I can't even glue on without poking myself in the eyeball? I can return the makeup, but where did I put the receipt?

And then there were all those super-late-night dinners with Peter at the Cheesecake Factory. I had paid for them, since he said he was super broke.

My right eye twitches. It has been doing that a lot lately.

I must be talking out loud because my best friend, Samira Chadha-Fu, looks up. She's sprawled, catlike, on my bed, unsuccessfully trying to apply a spiderly-looking false eyelash onto her eyelid.

Oh right, I gave Samira my $35 real mink eyelashes to try out. I don't think I can return them half-used, can I?

"Dude, are you okay?" she asks.

Samira has been trying to attach the eyelash for half an hour. She's holding a little compact mirror with one hand and tweezers and another broken eyelash in the other. It looks like she's trying to perform minor surgery. White glue oozes around her eyelid. Ew. She blinks, getting more goop on her brow area. The lady at Sephora had tried to teach both of us—small wingtips, followed by fluttery false lashes for old-school Hollywood prom glamour. Makeup tips to make our Asian eyes look bigger.

"Everything is perfect!" I say brightly. Samira shakes her head, her mouth twitching with amusement. She knows me too well. We've been BFFs, practically psychically linked, since the second grade when she moved to New Jersey from Singapore.

"Ughhhh," she finally groans. "These lash-things are impossible to put on."

With one last attempt, she ends up smearing more glue across her cheek, and then she drops the overpriced eyelash onto the floor. Rolling her goop-covered eyes, she ambles to my walk-in closet and begins trying on outfits. My parents are away this week in Honolulu, and we're having a fun spring-fling party at my house tonight.

Another terrifying ding lets me know that I have new email. So far, I have 52 unread texts and 361 unread emails. I'm too scared to check my inbox since colleges started sending out notifications three weeks ago.

"So . . . party? What are we wearing tonight?" Samira announces with her usual cheerleader enthusiasm. She rummages through my walk-in closet until she comes across the Vera Wang Swarovski crystal-beaded dress from Nordstrom. "This is gorgeous, Iris!" she squeals, looking very impressed, and I can't help but feel a little blush of pride at her approval.

"How much did this cost you?!"

"It was on sale," I lie.

But Samira is right. My designer prom dress with the extralong detachable skirt is amazing in every way. I don't even want to think about how much the dress cost, but luckily, I still have the tag on it. Honestly, I thought I was saving money because it's technically two dresses in one. I can wear the short, sexier version tonight, sans gauzy red-carpet train, and then return it at the end of the weekend after prom. Nordstrom closes at seven p.m. on Sundays, which gives me plenty of time.

"Oooooohhh, you left the price tag on," Samira says. And then with her perfectly manicured hand, she yanks the tag off, crumples it, and tosses it casually to the floor.

!!

I want to scream, but instead, I let out an involuntary squeak. My friend glances over again, and I force my lips into a frozen smile. I must look deranged. I can't even think about the cost.

As I'm feeling incredibly nauseous, my phone dings again. I decide to block the terrifying credit card number.

Done.

All better.

Ding! Another email. Shit.

I feel my smile vanish. I can't think about college or my credit card bill, especially when my parents find out. My mom will freak; my dad will be devastated by my lack of control and what he calls my reckless "bad American behavior." All of a sudden, my face feels rashy and hot, like I'm having a severe allergic reaction.

Is it possible to combust from the inside over a nonreturnable, super-expensive prom dress?

The answer is possibly-maybe-yes.

The answer is most-probably-yes.

Definitely yes.

Samira is still gabbing away about possible themes for our upcoming graduation party next month. "How about K-pop?" she asks. "Or something Bollywood? Sexy Disney?"

I force myself to pay attention, but I keep thinking about the dress. A spasm of worry churns through my stomach.

"So like, I think tonight . . . hello, Iris? Earth to Iris?"

Gulping at the sharp sound of my name, I nod with false enthusiasm and decide to toss my iPhone into the bottom of my underwear drawer. Who needs scary, real-world reminders when there is an amazing spring-fling Friday night party to host?

Crash Landing

As we wait for guests to arrive, we sit at the kitchen counter and share a huge joint that I got from my super-fun, incredibly sweet boyfriend Peter. Slowly, I toke, while Samira mixes us gigantic rum and Cokes in beer mugs and we play our favorite game: If you had ten million dollars, where would you visit in the world?

Anywhere But Here is our made-up fantasy exchange to help pass the time. Samira and I always play it before every party or school dance. There's no clear winner: we just try to outdo each other by naming fabulous destinations. We imagine suntanning naked on a private beach in Belize or taking selfies with the Great Pyramids of Egypt. In the boring, sprawling suburbs of Bradley Gardens, New Jersey, there's usually nowhere to go except for the mall and Chipotle.

"I want to go to Bali," Samira says, taking her fourth long toke.

"Hmmmm-hmm," I say. "You always say you want to go to Bali."

"I don't care as long as it's hot!" she says. "Where do you want to go?"

"Europe," I say without hesitation. "I loved our trip in tenth grade! Remember the Eiffel Tower and how we insisted on climbing all the way to the top even though it was super windy and rainy and everyone in our history class was afraid?"

"YES!"

She giggles, as if suddenly remembering the fun.

That's when I decide to tell her my plans for surprising Peter tonight. I think she'll find them exciting and deeply romantic.

But instead of sounding even a little bit happy for me, my best friend is weirdly quiet. Like she doesn't know what to say, which is super odd for Samira, since she's always so extroverted and chatty. Everyone is always saying that Samira would make a popular talk show host, which is why she is applying to college for journalistic broadcasting. I'm the total opposite: no one has ever told me what I'd be good at. Instead, they compliment my Miss Congeniality personality and tell me that I'll find my life purpose one day.

"I'm taking Peter to Paris for his birthday," I say again, in case she didn't hear me.

"Wasn't his birthday six months ago?" Samira asks, sounding surprised.

I shake my head. "Nope, it's June."

"It was in January," Samira insists.

"Dude, I'm pretty sure I know my own boyfriend's birthday."

Samira shrugs and doesn't say anything. She takes a long swig of her rum and Coke. She wipes her mouth with the back of her hand and belches. I'm in the sweet happy space between high and content, the credit card bill nearly forgotten.

From my closet, Samira has finally decided to borrow my favorite black first-date dress and strappy black heels.

"It looks way better on you," I say genuinely, changing the subject. Samira looks really pretty in lace cap-sleeves and her party makeup is flawless, without being too fake. "You should keep it!" I say.

Samira looks oddly touched. Another strange, half-sad, half-meditative expression crosses her face. I can't explain it, but I chalk it up to senior-year sadness. We might not see each other that much after high school is over.

"No, Iris, I really can't accept this—"

"Yes!" I insist, hugging her tightly. "I want you to have it. Dude, you're my best friend in the whole world."

Samira says nothing, and I take it that my gift has been accepted.

Peter hasn't shown up yet. When he gets here, I'll surprise him with the bouquet of purple irises and international plane tickets. He'll be so excited. He'll be so grateful. I'll win a trophy for best girlfriend in the world.

It will be the most wild, amazing, completely unsupervised vacation ever. The beginning of great romance into our real adult lives.

"Let me know when Peter's here," I say to Samira as I get up to fix myself another drink and say hi to some kids at school who have just arrived. "Be right back!"

"Is that dress from *Teen Vogue*?!" a girl I vaguely know from algebra class calls at me in the kitchen. I flash a grateful smile at her, thrilled that she noticed.

"You're the coolest, Iris Wang!" someone else shouts, high-fiving me.

I smile enthusiastically, wave like a nonplussed pageant queen, and make the social rounds. I'm not extremely popular at Bradley Gardens Public High School, but a lot of juniors and seniors know me enough to come to my parties. Freshmen and sopho-mores definitely come with the contents of their parents' liquor cabinets, and I don't mind. Freshman boys usually try extra hard to be nice, though, and sometimes I'll even accept a beer or two from one of them.

There's extra-loud rap music and some good-looking people and dancing.

I down another rum and Coke. Then another, and then another. Is it my fifth? I've completely lost count. It's all going so well. Credit card bill forgotten. SUCCESS. I get caught up in some pleasant chatting with some kids from study hall that I sort of know. We cheers loudly, clack our plastic cups, and then as if it's all predestined, a very drunk sophomore spills beer on my gorgeous Vera Wang dress.

I swear, this dress is cursed to the exponential of ten thousand.

How am I supposed to wash pee-colored beer off white Swarovski crystals?

How am I supposed to even wear it to prom next month?

Swearing loudly, I stomp back to my bedroom to change. Beer has trickled down the front of my dress. I'm worried that my night (like this gown) will be a stained, nonrefundable disaster.

Pathetic sophomore, I think angrily. *Pathetic dress. Pathetic party.*

That's when I hear nonstop giggling, and a familiar girl's voice is saying, "Not here, not here, not here!"

Positively giddy and almost feeling better immediately, especially with the prospect of having juicy gossip to tell-text Samira, I throw open my bedroom door dramatically, expecting to be half-annoyed, half-amused at the couple making out on my bed.

"Surprise!" I say.

Like in a bad romantic comedy, my best friend sits up, looking dazed. Samira is practically half out of the slinky black dress I gave her; her bra is showing. Peter, practically pantless, jumps off her. Samira and Peter are in my bed.

Peter at least has the decency to look ashamed.

What. The. Hell. Is. Going. On.

"Um, Iris! Hi!" he says, choking on his words. Samira has turned a hideous hue of rose-pink and is letting out a series of very undignified shrieks. Finally, she charges past me out of my bedroom. I'm stunned. I don't know exactly what to say.

Meanwhile, my right eye starts to wink uncontrollably at Peter, followed by the left one. This can't be happening right now.

Eye twitching has got to be the most annoying nervous tic on the planet.

"Iris," Peter says, as if I've forgotten my own name.

"I know my name," I say. "Thank you for reminding me, Peter."

"Iris—"

"How long has this thing been going on?" I manage to sputter.

"Please tell me that this THING, whatever it is, just randomly happened."

He looks rather taken aback.

"Last month . . . when you were in the city with your parents."

"And you didn't tell me?"

"We . . . I . . . I . . . I . . . just couldn't. Samira wanted to."

I can't breathe. I can't believe it. I can't believe it.

"Um, is your eye okay?"

"What?" I say. Is he joking?

"Your eye is . . ."

I touch my right eye and I can feel the eyeball spasm, like a pulsing monster, underneath my palm. Like it's a living organ, suddenly alive and determined to embarrass me.

"It's fine," I lie.

"Iris, you know how I feel about you, but . . ."

Peter pauses, like he's choking on a burrito. His face reddens into the shade of ungainly salsa. He fidgets.

"I'm . . . what?" I yell-ask. "Spit it out, Peter."

He blinks.

"You're . . . really boring," he finally says, looking deeply uncomfortable. "You're superficial, self-absorbed, and you kind of think the world revolves around you."

He's staring at me. My left eye has begun to twitch violently.

"You're narcissistic, Iris. And vapid. You just try too hard."

"What's wrong with that?" I say, not understanding. How can I be all these things? I'm just one person.

He pauses, then says, "I just don't think you ever really liked me as a human being. Do you even know my actual birthday?"

"Yes! It's June twenty-fourth. I got us plane tickets to Paris right after our graduation ceremony." I accidentally blurt out the surprise, devastated. Why does it feel as if my heart and stomach and brain are strangling each other?

"Iris, my birthday is in January! I've told you a million times. And why would you think we were going to Paris after graduation? I told you that I was going camping with my brother."

I pause. How did I not know that he was going camping with his brother?

"But I thought you said you wanted to go to Paris!" I protest.

And how can I be self-absorbed? What is Peter even talking about? I'm the most selfless person on the planet, after Gandhi and my parents.

Peter stares at me with the utmost disbelief.

"But I was taking you to Paris!" I shout at him again, spotting the Nordstrom shopping bag hiding the flowers and card and tickets. I grab the bag and then wave the bouquet in his face.

He backs away.

"Do you even know Samira's birthday?" he says. "Do you even know anything real about the people around you?"

My heart *thump thump thump*s. I stop listening. If my heart could be an actual living flower, it feels like it has been killed with weed killer.

Peter Hayes, loving boyfriend of two years, is dead to me.

Grabbing my purse, I run out of my bedroom and barely manage to make my way down the spiral staircase before I start heaving into the kitchen sink. I retch for what feels like the length of three movies until someone mockingly calls out, "You're a lightweight, Iris! Asian red-face!"

"Shut up!" I yell-slur miserably.

It's my kitchen sink and I can be sick if I want. My vision flickers in and out, like I'm having multiple seizures.

Being dumped would have to happen, tonight of all nights. At my own party.

But betrayal hurts more than being dumped. I mean, Samira, of all people? The last time I felt this shitty was when I was hungover and then I had to take a three-hour SAT.

The garage is the safest place, the most private place I can think of. I grab the car keys and sit in the driver's seat of my parents' two-month-old white Mercedes-Benz. It was a gift from my mom to my dad for his fifty-fifth birthday. I put my hands over my flaming cheeks. I squeeze my eyes shut.

Don't panic, don't panic. Everything will be all right, I think hopelessly. *It always is?*

I just need air. Lots of cool, fresh air. I just need to think.

Anywhere, I think, *but here.*

But why does the car seem so claustrophobic all of a sudden? It's like being trapped inside a tiny balloon of hot air. I inhale. Exhale. Inhale. I tell myself that things will get better.

They don't.

My heart hurts, and so does my reeling head.

I can't decide which one is worse.

Heartbreak or indulging in too much weed and alcohol.

Sobbing uncontrollably, I somehow accidentally rev the engine on. It's like my entire body is on autopilot, and I'm too distressed to notice that I've put the Mercedes in reverse. All I can think about is Samira and Peter. Samira in my favorite black dress and Peter in my bed. Samira and Peter. The world must be ending. In what horrible, clichéd universe would my best friend and boyfriend be cheating on me? And why didn't I even notice? Am I honestly that self-absorbed?

Denial combined with spurts of anger hit me like little fireworks. Maybe I imagined the whole episode. This is all a nightmare, right? A drunken hallucination?

At first I don't understand what happens next and I think that I am seriously dreaming. The *CRASH* is so loud and frightening that it doesn't seem real. A sharp, metal clanging noise roars in my eardrums. Like a special-effects sound in an action movie that gets closer and louder in volume and speed. I don't understand what on earth is happening. I didn't even notice that the car was moving. I don't understand the strangeness of it all. And that's when I decide to glance in the rearview mirror. And I *gasp*. All the feelings of surprise, shock, and horror fall out of my mouth, like a super-size Gobstopper. My dad's Mercedes has just rolled backward into the garage door. The car has rammed into one of our three newly painted garages and plowed an entire door off its hinges. I glance in the rearview mirror to check again. I'm not imagining things. I was never the best driver, but this is the worst car accident in all my life.

Holy shit.

This can't be happening.

I've just knocked the entire garage door off and smashed the trunk of my parents' $50,000 luxury car.

I wail loudly. What choice do I have? It's not like I can make any other sound. And it's not like I can pretend that nothing happened to the car or to our missing garage door. It's not even like I wrecked the backyard fence or broke a small window. A garage door is a very important focal feature of a house. It's always the first thing that you notice on a real-estate brochure.

A bunch of kids come running out at the sound and look super confused. A few of them point and take photographs with their cell phones.

"Oh my god!" someone exclaims.

I think I see Samira, but then her shell-shocked face disappears into a frightening gray-black blur.

"Is that Iris?" someone else is yelling.

My stomach churns again. *No more puking!* I think. My vision flickers in and out. *Please don't let me puke again.*

Instead of vomiting this time, I gratefully pass out.

Broken House

My mom always said it was best to avoid beautiful movie-star boys, much like avoiding ice cream and cheddar cheese if you're severely lactose intolerant. She always said good-looking boys would stomp on my fragile flower-heart. But I never listen. I always insist on eating my delicious ice-cream cake from Dairy Queen, and then I have to elbow whoever is in front of me to use the bathroom.

Lactose intolerance is no joke.

"Choose someone uglier than you to romance," my mom would always say, before heading to work at her firm, where she is both the CEO and senior electrical engineer.

But she wasn't right: it wasn't a beautiful boy who stomped on my fragile flower-heart, but just Peter Hayes. Freckled, messy-haired Peter, who played the drums completely off-beat, liked food and pot as much as me, and was average in intelligence, height, and weight. If you asked me to describe Peter Hayes, I'd say he was pretty much unremarkable. We definitely had a lot of fun, fooling around in his dad's old Toyota when we were both supposed to be at school. On weekends, when I was supposed to be in ACT and SAT class, he'd pick me up and we'd drive around the suburbs, smoking and listening to indie rock bands on repeat.

"Iris, he's not right for you," my mother would always say whenever Peter came over to pick me up. "He doesn't love you. Why do you always pay with your allowance money when *he* invites you to dinner?"

Despite the fact that Peter always smiled and made polite small talk with my mom and dad, my parents just didn't like him.

But I would continue to defend him. "You just don't like Peter because he's American! You want me to date a geeky, boring Chinese dude!"

"Your dad is not boring!" my mom would say.

"I'm not boring," my dad would echo, joining the conversation. "In fact, I'm very exciting!"

Peter Hayes was the source of many ongoing screaming fights. We'd fight about Peter after school and on weekends. He was the most popular topic in our household besides college applications and the FIFA Cup.

I hear a voice calling me gently.

When I open my eyes, a concerned face is asking me if I can hear her.

"Can you tell me your name?" a woman says, and checks my wrist for a pulse. "I'm a paramedic."

At first, I don't understand, but then I remember.

Someone must have called 911. An ambulance and a police

car are here. A broken house and a broken sports car. Underage drinking. This does not look good.

There's nothing to be done about the garage.

"Honey," the female paramedic says. "We're taking you to the hospital."

I try to slur out something rational, a word that sounds suspiciously like "garage."

"Shhhhh," she says reassuringly. "You've had a bad accident and you're in shock."

I start crying nonstop.

Loser

My parents come back ASAP on the first flight from Honolulu. They pick me up from Hackensack Meridian Health Emergency Room, frantic with worry. Even after I reassure them that I'm totally fine, except for my headache and bad hangover, they insist on one more checkup and my mom and dad yell that they love me over and over again.

"You could have been killed and wouldn't be able to go to college!" my mom and dad take turns screaming after the emergency room physician and the nurse confirm that I'm definitely going to live.

My mom's eyes can't stop tearing up as she hugs me tightly. "Iris! Do you understand what you just did? One bad decision and it could have been game over! No reset button!"

"We would never see you again!" my dad says. "How can you be so selfish?"

"I love you guys," I sniffle, and then I start crying from intense guilt. My dad is right. Not even realizing that the car engine was on was probably one of my most terrible, riskiest life mistakes. More careless than when I accidentally shaved off an eyebrow, and way more dangerous than when Samira and I didn't have any cab fare after a two a.m. party. Instead of calling our parents, we decided to hitchhike on the side of a near-empty highway. Luckily, no one picked us up and we found our way to the bus station.

My parents are so worried about me that I dread driving home with them. I won't even know how to apologize for the destruction and mess. I'll see the extreme disappointment and I'll feel like a bad daughter.

The drive home from the hospital is uncomfortably silent; normally, I'd ask them about their trip, and they'd tell me about the hotel and their waterskiing excursions and describe their meals in Food Network detail. They might even ask me about Samira and Peter. My mom has always liked Samira as much as she's liked Peter. "She's not a nice girl," my mom would always criticize when Samira came over to hang out with me. But she always tolerated her because Samira's parents went to the same country club as her and my dad.

Maybe my mom was right all along about Samira. A blister of worry bubbles in my gut and I accidentally belch from nervousness. Thinking too much about life is bad for the digestive system.

When we turn into our cul-de-sac, I see my mom stiffen like a zombie, and my dad actually looks horrified. His mouth plops open and closed like a dying fish. Their new car is still parked askew, the trunk completely wrecked, and our beautiful house is missing a garage door.

"What happened?" my dad yell-asks. I can see his face transform into the color of morgue gray. "We thought you had a car accident! Not a house accident!"

"It was a mistake," I say in a hushed voice.

We go inside. And then there's more shock and disappointment to fill the entire state of New Jersey.

Normally, Samira and Peter help me clean up the bottles and crumbs of crunched-up potato chips and dirty plastic cups. Inside my parents' house, though, is really a mess. A dumpyard in our typically pristine living room and marble-countertop kitchen. Mounds of garbage and shards of broken glass everywhere.

Someone has even left a pile of orange-gray vomit in our stainless steel sink.

Oh wait, that was me.

"You had . . . a party?" my mom asks, incredulous. "We said you could have friends over, but what is this mess?"

"I didn't mean for it to happen," I say miserably.

"We trusted you!" my mom shouts. "How could you do this?"

"What happened?" my dad says, looking stunned. He sits down on the floor and touches an empty bottle. He sniffs his fingers, almost disbelievingly. Like he doesn't want to admit that his seventeen-year-old daughter had a party in his house. "Is this . . . beer!? Alcohol? You drink alcohol, Iris?"

"Of course she drinks!" my mom snaps. "Our daughter is obviously a deviant. Iris, go to your room this instant. The damage is coming out of your allowance!"

Slinking to my bedroom, I spend the rest of the day crying until my eyes are red and puffy and swell to the size of golf balls. For once, I don't care that I resemble a monster. I hear my parents arguing downstairs; my mom is on the phone nonstop with the insurance company.

I spend all of Saturday and Sunday in my room. Except to scold me endlessly about my life choices, my parents don't really bother me until early Sunday afternoon.

I keep waiting for an attack of stress-induced facial hair.

Nothing comes.

Just a bulbous Rudolph-size nose zit.

It makes me hopeful that I've outgrown my childhood affliction.

Later, I don't know what time, but my mom doesn't even knock when she interrupts my sad-girl crying. Despite still being furious and disappointed at me, she seems to not be able to help it when she prances in like she's Samira with some hot gossip about a first date or some random boy that she's been crushing on. She's holding a giant pile of envelopes. Her mouth twitches, like she's not sure whether to scream in anger or with roller-coaster excitement. I hope it's the latter.

"Iris?" my mom finally yell-asks. "Have you checked the mail? College letters have arrived! Mrs. Chu at the country club was just asking me last week about what colleges you got into. I said I was sure that you got into all of them! You know her son *only* got into Harvard and three other Ivies?"

For a moment, she seems genuinely pleased and expectant. It's almost as if she's completely forgotten about the wrecked car and house. She's still clutching the envelopes like they're a winning lottery ticket for a brand-new house and luxury SUV.

Oh.

"I don't feel well enough to be opening letters," I lie. My voice is small and sounds funny.

And here I thought that by ignoring emails sent from colleges, I could actually pretend that I never received any of them.

I mean, who actually uses the United States Postal Service anymore?

I thought snail mail was practically an urban legend. An American myth.

My mom calls my dad to come upstairs.

"Iris has some very big news!" she shouts.

My dad actually looks excited when he hurries into my bedroom. "I have been waiting for this moment for seventeen years!" he announces, clapping his hands. He looks like I'm about to perform some well-rehearsed magic trick.

If I can get into a top-tier college, I know my parents might eventually forgive me for the humongous mess downstairs and our busted garage door. Since I'm their only child, I am practically their main responsibility, so they will never be able to fully forget when I go away to college (unless they replace me with some kind of medium-size pet). But if I get into one of the Ivies, they might stop lecturing me about how "irresponsible" and "unbelievably reckless" I am.

Which part of the country will I even be in next year? Who will be part of my ever-expanding entourage? TV shows and movies always show that characters who make it to any type of postsecondary education suddenly become smarter, better-looking, and less average than who they once were in high school. If this transformation is true, I'm seriously excited about the future.

Okay, admittedly, the SATs were a bit difficult to finish in my semi-drunk, practically comatose state, and maybe I should have asked my tutor to proofread all those application essays. Maybe I shouldn't have just randomly clicked the SUBMIT button on the Common App and then raced downstairs when Peter picked me up for a drawn-out make-out session.

Holding my breath, I open the first extremely thin envelope from NYU.

A horrible flulike feeling overcomes me, but I force myself to ignore it.

If I think positively enough, the letter could possibly say that I've been accepted into NYU with a generous financial aid package. In fact, the amazing, prestigious scholarship that I'll win means my parents won't even have to pay a single cent for four entire years. The letter could possibly include a nice congratulatory note from the dean of admissions, who will want to meet me for a fancy lunch on campus, and he or she will even ask me to give an inspiring speech at freshman orientation. I already know what I'll be wearing. I bought my sleeveless floral knee-length dress from J. Crew and matching cream-colored sandals ages ago.

I gasp.

> Dear Ms. Iris Weijun Wang,
>   The Admissions Committee has completed its review of your application. I am very sorry to tell you that we are unable to offer you admission to New York University this fall.

Please understand that this is in no way a judgment of you as a student or as a person, since our decision has more to do with the applicant pool than anything else—many of our applicants are not offered admission simply because we don't have enough space in our entering class. This year we had nearly 19,000 candidates for fewer than 1,600 offers of admission, from which will come our 1,100 freshmen. Since all of our decisions are made at one time and all available spaces have been committed, all decisions are final.

I wish you the very best in all of your future endeavors.

Sincerely,

Dean Sandy P. Schmill

My fingers tremble.

My lower lip wavers.

The nauseous, flulike feeling tunnels through me again, this time at full force.

I want to believe that this is some mistake. Another Chinese American girl called Iris Weijun Wang received my actual acceptance letter. It's a straightforward case of mistaken identity, easily proven when I show up on the first day of classes and show them my driver's license and passport.

I tear open the rest of the envelopes, fighting my mounting disbelief. These are all addressed to me, but not one of them is an acceptance.

I, Iris Wang, am a real victim of twenty-first-century identity theft.

"What is it?!" my mom gasps, and picks up each dropped letter.

Then my dad practically grab-wrestles a letter from my mom, and I can literally hear him stop breathing. Is this the moment where I accidentally kill my parents from utter shock? Is it considered murder if both of them suffer from heart attacks simultaneously?

All of the thin envelopes hold polite rejections from Rutgers, UCLA, San José State, Fordham, Sarah Lawrence, Kenyon College, and my obvious hard-to-reach schools like Stanford and Berkeley. Forget the Ivies and baby Ivies. When I get to my safety schools . . . wait, I didn't apply to any safety schools. Rutgers *was* supposed to be my safety school.

"Did you . . . apply to any other colleges?" My dad starts turning purple-orange-blue, all the colors of a supersize pack of Tropical Skittles. "Are there any more . . ."

I freeze, then shake my head no.

"How could this happen?" my mom asks. "This makes no sense! You went to SAT class and we hired so many expensive tutors!"

I don't know how to respond. I haven't been going to my lessons.

"Does this mean she's not going to Yale, Amy?" my dad finally asks my mom.

"Of course she's not going to Yale," my mom sputters. "She's not even going to community college. Let's face it, Jeff. Our daughter is going to be a loser."

American Failure

I can't believe my life is over.

I just didn't think it would happen like this.

Peter's words keep playing in my mind, like a broken iPod shuffle.

Am I *really* self-absorbed? What does that even mean? Mom says that if you have to ask, that means the answer is always yes. Mom is a supersmart electrical engineer who met my dad while studying in her sophomore year at City College in Manhattan. Dad was a not-so-smart mechanical engineer who dated my mom to help him pass his classes. Eventually, I think they fell in love for real when my dad guiltily confessed his intentions for dating her, and my mom said that she admired his pragmatism. While Dad cooked and cleaned and raised me, my mom earned her PhD in engineering at Johns Hopkins. Despite her penchant for math and electricity, my mom loves my dad so much that she puts up with his superstitious beliefs about the Chinese zodiac.

Unfortunately, I take after my father in the brains department. I'm not particularly gifted at anything. Shopping and spending exorbitant amounts of money don't count.

Am I boring? Ouch. I wish I could ask Samira, but I'm currently not speaking to her.

I don't even know what "vapid" or "narcissistic" mean. They weren't on the SAT vocabulary lists, but then again, I didn't really study.

I hear a loud, familiar buzzing and then I remember my iPhone is in my underwear drawer.

Ten missed calls from Samira.

Twenty-two texts from her.

Please call me! I wanted to tell you.

I'm SORRY!

The same texts but in different variations. Fake concern.

Are your parents home?

You okay?

I miss you. <3 <3 <3

But zero messages from Peter. Not a single apology text.

But what did I expect? He was the one who dumped me. If I text or call him, would that make me the pathetic one in our broken, one-sided relationship? I don't know anymore. I don't know what makes someone hurt and lie to a person that they supposedly care about. What makes a smiling boyfriend or bestie look you in the eyeball like you're an adorable guinea pig while they are rolling a joint and telling you that you are literally the best thing that has happened to them besides discovering weed? Peter always said that I was just like cotton candy, while Samira compared me to a bag of assorted gourmet jelly beans. I just don't understand! Does comparing me to a sugary treat make me less human, like it's somehow okay to use and throw me away?

My heart stings and throbs like a three-hour visit to the dentist after the anesthetic has worn off.

Nothing can be worse than this, so I finally check my school email and there are three emails marked *Urgent! Please Respond!!!* from my high school guidance counselor. What could be so important? For a second, I feel giddy, light-headed. Is she telling me that I've been voted valedictorian? Maybe even salutatorian? Oh my god. Am I prom queen, finally? I have been exceptionally nice toward my classmates this year, and I'm always there to comfort a crying freshman or hold the door open for the school secretary.

Yes, this must be the actual good news that I so desperately need.

I click on the email eagerly.

But the news is spectacularly bad. In fact, the WORST news of my entire weekend. Not even counting my eight-plus college rejections.

I've just failed Algebra II.

And AP Economics.

And World History.

And English!!!

How does one even fail English? It's my first and only language. I thought I performed spectacularly well on all my in-class essays. To prep for AP Lit, I watched *Death of a Salesman* and *Heart of Darkness* twice on Netflix. But come to mention it, when was the last time I bothered to go to class? When was the last time I've even read a book? Does rigorously reading *TV Guide* on the toilet count?

Then there's even worse news at the bottom of the email: the guidance counselor says that I won't be graduating this year.

We need to talk about your options ASAP, she has written.

I can't focus.

My vision blurs.

Like someone has rubbed suntan lotion on my eyeballs.

Please come see me.

I blink hard.

Then, to make things worse, a more recent message from my counselor, dated Friday afternoon.

I'll be calling your parents Monday morning if I don't hear back from you. This is serious, Iris. We really need to have a meeting.

This can't be happening, I think.

The only good thing to come out of reading my ignored emails is that my eyelids have finally stopped twitching.

Chinese Banishment

"I have some news," I announce at the dinner table.

My father looks hopeful. "Yale?" he asks.

My mom shoots him a withering stare, which she then turns on me. I frown and dig my completely chewed-through, nonexistent fingernails into my palms.

"What is it, Iris?" she says matter-of-factly. "It's better to deal with it today than wait until it's too late."

Angrily, she dumps three large pork chops onto my plate and then adds a messy scoop of overcooked broccoli and mashed potatoes.

I fidget, like I'm suddenly five years old again.

An ugly, spud-size lump forms in my throat.

I force it to go away by ignoring it.

My mom glares at me.

Inwardly, I shrink. I apologize nervously.

My dad doesn't even notice.

But I can't bring myself to say that I won't be graduating this year, so I finally forward the email from the guidance counselor to my parents' email accounts. Their iPhones ding simultaneously and the noise makes me shudder. Text alerts are like recurring nightmares. I never want to read a text message again.

"Check your email," I say slowly. My vocal cords sound strangled.

I wait for their reactions.

No one speaks.

"Just check your email," I say again in a flatter tone.

I touch my cold, sweaty upper lip, and I can feel new three-inch hairs growing from stress. Normally, I'd be upset about the recurring distress-mustache, but I almost don't care. My horrific Tiger curse. I guess I haven't been cured of my weirdo problem.

I can see my parents rereading the email over and over again.

More silence. The bad, suffocating kind.

I can't breathe.

"Dinner is over," my mom finally says. She leaves the table abruptly, her food untouched.

I turn to my father, hopeful.

His eyes are moist.

"Iris, go to the car," he says.

This is not a suggestion but an order. I slink to the green Volkswagen because the Mercedes is in the shop for repairs. My father has never taken that tone with me before. He has gotten aggravated, certainly, and sometimes he'll take on the loud repeated bleating sounds of animal-like annoyance. My mom always says that he is a true Goat. But since my mom was born in the Year of the Dog, she is the noisy barking one and usually does all the disciplining.

Usually when my dad has something serious to discuss with me, like the time when he wanted to tell me about his early stage II colon cancer, we take a field trip to this discount salon in a strip mall and get pedicures. He always says he finds the public bustle calming when he wants to share shitty news.

We park and then slowly walk toward the salon entrance. It's more like a sidestep shuffle, really. I count to one hundred and stare at the cement ground. I don't look at him.

At the salon I choose a sad-looking lilac color, and a pretty Korean lady examines my toes. My dad soaks his feet in the bubbling tub and lets out a remorseful-sounding sigh. Another Korean lady begins to vigorously file his wide, hoof-shaped heels.

I don't know what will happen. My heart is beating in triple time, filling my hollow chest, mouth, and head with extra-fiery heat. The technician clucks in sympathy over my calloused feet.

"I spoke to my brother this morning," my dad announces slowly. He sounds like he has a severe toothache. "He offered to help with your situation. We are sending you to Beijing to live with him and his family."

"What are you talking about?" I say. The way my dad is saying "situation" is almost like he is saying that I am secretly pregnant.

Although come to think of it, me getting pregnant would be so much less shameful than not getting into college on top of failing senior year. All my life, my dad has always wanted me to be "smart like Mom" and my mom has always wanted me to be "smarter than Dad."

"Why are you doing this?" I ask, shocked and hurt and baffled. Hearing his news is like devouring a 32-gallon Slurpee and brain freeze is spreading, slow-motion, through every major organ. Is this what happens before turning into a human-size freezie? You feel every spiky, stomach-churning, chill-inducing emotion as you simply stop existing.

"Your mom and I only want you to be better than us," my dad says, staring at his hands. "We immigrated to the US so you could have more opportunities. We wanted you to be semi-professional at one or two things. Iris, you tried synchronized swimming, country dance, and even a candle-making class. You always said it was too hard and quit."

I don't know how to respond. This is far too much responsibility on someone who can't even remember to vacuum her room! How can I be better than both my parents? It's unfair because their IQ combined functions like unlimited 5G LTE internet. Despite what my dad is saying, I still feel betrayed and hurt that I am capable of causing so much melon-size disappointment.

To their credit, the spa ladies keep paying attention to our feet.

I am suddenly even more confused. My dad's story actually makes zero sense.

"But I thought you were an only child. You told me your parents were dead!" I protest instead.

"My half brother," my father says, as if that answers my question. "My dad, your grandfather, had an affair, but it had to be a secret because of the shame that it brought on the entire family."

What the hell is my dad talking about?

"We have relatives in Beijing?" I interrupt, not caring if I'm being loud or rude. I'm so done with this whole politeness-in-public thing. "I have grandparents living in China?"

No response from Dad.

More silence.

"Your grandparents are dead."

"Does Mom have family I don't know about too?" I finally yell-ask.

"No, her parents and brother are all in Flushing."

"Are you sure?"

My dad says nothing again for a long time. He looks deeply uncomfortable. Like he's just ingested an unlimited amount of dairy. Our entire family suffers from severe lactose intolerance, but it doesn't stop us from regularly ordering ice-cream cakes from Dairy Queen. Dad looks like he's just eaten six slices of ice-cream cake by himself.

"Your uncle and I never spoke until this year. He was the one who asked a lawyer to send me an email, and we have been talking regularly since. I have been telling him about you for two months. He thinks we can help each other."

"Why are you sending me off to TOTAL strangers?"

"He's not a stranger. We've already video-chatted many, many times. Sometimes even twice a day! And he has one daughter called Renxiang. Her English name is Ruby."

So I have a random uncle, aunt, and some girl cousin called Ruby? What is my life coming to? What else has my dad been lying about?

"You can't stay here," my dad continues. "Your mother is worried about talk at the country club."

"Who cares about the country club?" I'm practically screaming now. The woman filing the dead skin off my heel has stopped filing.

"Should I come back?" she asks hesitantly.

"Yes!" I say, while my dad shouts, "No!"

The Korean nail technicians, who aren't even pretending to scrub our feet anymore, exchange superlong meaningful glances. I wonder if they are used to witnessing family drama or if we're the first ones to ever have embarrassing heart-to-hearts over double mall pedicures. Either they are accustomed to CW Network–style soap operas or else we'll give them something to gossip about later on.

"Your mother cares very much about you," my dad continues. "But all her friends are bragging about their children who are ALL going to Harvard, UPenn, Princeton, Yale . . ."

His voice catches and then trips over Yale. Yale has always been his Ivy League dream for himself and then me. I was six years old when he took me to visit the campus for a family vacation. I've never been to Disney World, but I've visited Yale three times.

"Can't I just stay home and do my GED online?" I plead. "I'll take classes at the community college!"

"Iris, we have given you everything," he says, as if almost talking to himself. "We tried to be the best parents, but look at what happened to you. We love you, so we are sending you away."

Inconsolable guilt overwhelms me. So much shame. So much shitty decision-making. Tears leak out of me like snot.

My dad's expression is also a combination of horror and shame. Then he begins half crying. I don't think he ever expected this nightmare scenario of having a failure daughter to happen. When he finally stops crying, he says, "Your uncle would like to meet you. Your uncle would like you to teach your cousin proper English. She will be a good influence on you."

"How old is my cousin?" I ask.

He ignores my question.

"Too much partying, too American," he finally says, staring at me with such heavy-hearted disappointment. "You will go to Beijing next week. You will think about your mistakes. End of discussion."

"I've never been to Beijing! I don't even speak Chinese!" I protest, even though my dad knows all this about me. My voice seems shrill and tinny-sounding.

"You'll learn to be Chinese," my dad says matter-of-factly.

My dad has never spoken so forcefully before. I don't recognize his tone. What the hell does "learn to be Chinese" even mean?

"How long do I have to stay there?" I whimper.

No response.

"When can I come home?" I say again.

Zero response.

"I can come home, right?" I'm practically yelping now. I sound just like my mother when she freaks, exactly like an oversize Chihuahua.

True, desperate panic eclipses me, like I'm about to fall off a roaster coaster ready to derail. How can this even be possible? How can my dad be kicking me out of my home and sending me to live in a strange country with strange people???!!

I have so many questions, but my dad has picked up a random magazine and he's flipping through last month's *Teen Cosmopolitan*, as if he's fascinated by the articles and glossy photos. I don't think he's even reading about eyeliner or summer beach bronzer, but he won't look up.

Zodiac Goats are not supposed to have secretive personalities. They can be stubborn, but they are usually gentle, docile farm creatures. So how can my dad have kept his entire Beijing family a secret? Who exactly is my dad? And who is this uncle I've never heard of?

Most importantly, what will happen to me?

Who Am I?

"Don't you love me anymore?" I ask my dad in the
nearly empty parking lot of the strip mall.

He looks a little bit taken aback. It should only take a few seconds for him to respond in the affirmative. After all, I'm his only child. That I know of.

"Answer my question!" I shout like a malfunctioning surround-sound speaker. Due to the tragic absurdity of the past seventy-two hours, it could actually be that I'm a contraption made out of metal, lip gloss, and wires. I don't know who or what I am anymore.

"Don't you love *me*??!" my dad bleats back in the strip-mall parking lot, his eyes twitching agitatedly.

At least I know where my involuntary eyelid spasm comes from. I must have learned this truly shitty habit from my dad.

"You answer my question first!" I yell. How hard is it for him to say YES??!!

In automatic response, my right eye suddenly winks excitedly back at him. Like I've told a very funny, parent-inappropriate joke. I'm horrified and devastated that my dad can't answer this simple question.

A car driving out of the parking lot honks its horn angrily. Someone sticks their head out the window and shouts at us. Apparently, we are blocking the entrance of the parking lot. We quickly move to the side, and a Ford Buick nearly backs into us. If one of us were to get hit by a car, would Beijing still be a possibility?

"Why are you winking at me?" my dad asks as we stand safely beside our Volkswagen. "Is it because you don't love your mommy and daddy?"

"Why are *you* winking at me?" I shoot back. "You started it!"

"I did no such thing!" my dad exclaims.

He looks as if I've just insulted his favorite baseball team, the New York Yankees. He pauses. Both of his eyes blink enthusiastically this time, like they're having a nonstop dance marathon. Is that what I look like? No wonder Samira ran away. No wonder Peter looked so scared of me.

No wonder no one loves me, including my own father.

Finally, my dad says, "Iris, just get in the car! We are going home NOW."

"Fine," I say, "but to be clear, are you sending me to Beijing because you don't love me anymore?"

Silence.

"Get in the car, Iris."

I need to figure out how to change my dad's mind about Beijing. Is blackmail an authentic possibility? Tears and guilt-tripping don't seem to be working. Jumping into the passenger side, I slam the door. I start sniffling again and passive-aggressively blow my nose into my father's extra jacket, which is lying on the floor at my feet.

As we drive through the suburbs, I sneak a quick sideways peek at my dad. He looks both shocked and red-faced at the same time. He's gripping the steering wheel and driving a little bit too recklessly. Normally, he'd be anxious about running a four-way stop, but I don't think this is the time to mention it.

In reflex, I check my reflection in the passenger mirror and gasp. I don't even recognize myself. I look blotchy and Shrek green. My dad and I both seem to be exceptionally ugly criers. We're never cried in tandem before! But at least our hands and feet look amazing for a discount combo mani-pedi of $24.99 each. I can't help admiring my new lilac-colored nails. Maybe I should have gone with Fresh Minty Green to match my new permanent complexion.

My dad's left eye twitches, and I'm suddenly furious at him again.

If he loved me, how could he have not told me about my China relations?

If he loved me, I wonder how many other times he would have lied to me in the past seventeen years?

Eyes, nose, and mouth watering, as if I've ingested an entire jar of chili peppers, I side-stare angry-intently at my dad. His knuckles grab the wheel tighter and tighter, and his face is pale and scrunched up like a Shar-Pei's neck. And that's when I realize that it all makes sense now. I must not even be his biological daughter!

Both my parents are tall and freakishly hairless, while I am somewhat petite and excessively hairy, particularly under times of duress.

All my life, I knew that I was supposed to be born to rich, famous, jet-setter parents. I've always known that my real mom must be a socialite or a renowned beauty queen. And my dad must be a famous actor or an aristocrat of a small to medium-size country.

Then a shocking thought occurs to me: What if I'm not even Chinese? I could be Korean, Malaysian, or even Thai royalty!

What if I was kidnapped at birth and my actual parents are still scouring the globe for me? The thought of my real mom and dad missing me brings actual tears to my eyes. I begin sniffing from the fact that I could be bringing deep, authentic pain to the people who birthed me.

Hearing my messy, snot-waterfalling sniffles, my dad makes some kind of barn animal grunt in return, but he still doesn't speak or look at me. I wipe my nose and stare closely at his features to see if there is any resemblance.

Rain starts splashing nonstop across the windshield. The suburbs look small and depressing as usual, but with another pang, this time across my chest, I realize that I suddenly don't want to leave New Jersey. I've always said that I wanted to leave my gray neighborhood of matching McMansions, but I've never traveled out of the country by myself. I was supposed to spend the summer gallivanting around Europe with my boyfriend. We were supposed to live off true love, perfectly rolled blunts, and music festivals. I was not supposed to be exiled to a strange country that I know nothing about.

Self-pity hurts more than lactose intolerance, pink-eye, and tooth decay combined.

Don't be pathetic, Iris, I tell myself. *You caused this mess. Now you have to fix it. You just need to find your real parents.*

When we finally reach our house with the missing garage door, my fake dad suddenly slams on the brakes. I lurch forward in surprise and nearly bash my head on the dashboard. Luckily, I pull backward before any real damage is done.

"Who are you, Iris Wang?" he asks. "Who are you and where is my daughter?"

"Are you even my real dad?" I shout back, and he looks so shocked by my outburst. I've never used such a harsh tone with him so many times in one night. I'm honestly surprised by it myself.

I pause, as if choking on my own tongue.

"What if I'm not actually made for Yale? What if I'm not made for college?" I continue.

My words are like stomping on his American dream with my imaginary five-inch $3,000 Jimmy Choo stilettos. The most expensive, glittery pair that I dream of owning one day. For seventeen years, I've been his only life purpose. But how do you tell your dad that his sole reason for living is a friendless, hopeless mess with massive credit card debt?!

Suddenly, my dad's face crumples like a red-and-purple balloon. Both of his eyelids start winking at triple speed. Mine start imitating him on automatic. Soon it's like an Olympic ping-pong competition between my right and left eye.

Which eyelid is winning?

And in an epic staring contest against my father, would I win?

Frustrated, I leap out of the passenger seat. I'm so upset that I barely notice the shiny white BMW parked beside us. There's a sharp ferocious scraping sound of metal digging into metal as my door screeches across the other car. It sounds irreparable. It sounds expensive. Two wrecked luxury cars in less than seventy-two hours. Shit. Why am I never careful around motor vehicles?

"Iris Weijun Wang!" my dad exclaims. He also runs out of the car to examine the damage. "Whose car is it?"

"Does it matter?" I yell. "Are you going to send it to China too?"

I'm way too afraid to look at the damage, so I run inside to the kitchen and nearly collide with my mom, who is making a fresh pot of coffee.

"I don't know how to fix it," I wail at my mom, almost too distressed to notice the coffee and that she's wearing her third-best cashmere cardigan and matching pearls on a Sunday night.

All I can focus on are my head and heart aching with the horrible, churning news that she wants to send me away. I thought that being unwillingly sent abroad for cultural immersion only happened to adolescents in old-fashioned, pre-internet days. In medieval times, disappointing young people were sacrificed to find new lands and win world wars. But in the twenty-first century, isn't it just cheaper and safer to learn about one's ancestry through a home DNA testing kit?

"I'm sorry for everything," I blurt out. "I'm so sorry!"

Instead of commiserating or apologizing in return, my mom shushes me. But her face softens, like cream cheese at room temperature. She looks genuinely taken aback by my tears and reaction. She looks like she's struggling with what to say: confusion, heartbreak, regret, sadness, and terror flash across her features like a three-episode miniseries. Can she forgive me and just let me stay in New Jersey?

"What are you doing home so early?" she whisper-yells instead. "Samira and her parents are here. They have very big college news to share."

9

Selfie!

For a moment, I can't think. I can't breathe. Is it possible for my head to combust from stress, shock, and fatigue? I can see the headlines on social media: *17-Year-Old Girl's Brain Explodes from Bad News. Too Much Stress Caused a Nuclear Reaction. Government Passes Law in New Jersey that Bans College Season.*

I heard that small children can die of fright, so why can't teenagers drop dead from an overload of shitty, tragic news?

After all, our brains and bodies are still developing too.

"Why is Samira here?" I manage to whisper. "Couldn't they have called instead?"

"Bragging is always better in person," my mother replies, rolling her eyes. "Chinese people invented the sport."

"Fantastic," I grumble.

My voice catches in the back of my throat, like a bug in a chemical trap. I don't remember how to talk or properly breathe. Then I hear my dad's voice calling loudly. "Amy! Amy! Iris thinks we don't love her anymore! Also, you need to see this! Our daughter dented someone's BMW parked in our driveway."

Quickly, my mom shushes him. "Jeff! Samira's parents are here to share the wonderful news about Samira's college acceptances."

My dad shoots me a look of raw, actual panic. College season is bragging season with my mom's friends at the country club. Everyone has to compare and contrast college acceptances, like they're showing off end-of-season purchases from the big designer outlet Woodbury Premium Outlets. It's what Samira and I used to mockingly call Asian Brag-and-Tell. It's more holy and prestigious than Lunar New Year.

Not only do parents post thousands of photos of their children's college acceptances online, but they like to take family selfies, of everyone holding the acceptance letter.

The letter is then framed and hung in the living room for the purpose of showing guests.

Rejection letters are shredded and never shared with anyone, even if no one outside the extended family and friend group actually cares.

"This can't be good," my father moans. "What do we do?!"

"Iris, hide!" my mom finally hisses. "We don't want anyone to know about your situation!"

I spiral into panic mode.

It's way too late to run upstairs to my bedroom or charge into the basement or lock myself in the hallway bathroom. Our living room is in a prime entertainment location. That's why my parents bought our house and renovated it: for the sole purpose of showing off to their friends.

I hear Samira's familiar high-pitched laugh. I can't hear what she's saying, but I hear my name being mentioned once or twice.

Iris this, Iris that.

It must be a normal Pavlovian response, where hearing my name makes me feel warm and fuzzy inside. Despite my best efforts to hate her, I suddenly miss my best friend. It makes absolutely no sense. If we could rewind to the party, if she could sincerely apologize for Peter, we might be able to save our friendship.

"Jeff! What do we tell everyone about Iris's problem?" my mom says in a low, low voice that makes me feel so ashamed. I have never felt so insignificant. I have never felt so useless.

"Iris, hide in the closet and stay there," my dad suddenly says.

"What?" I say.

My dad is not joking.

He points at the kitchen pantry.

I shouldn't be surprised. First he's exiling his only daughter to China, and then he's forcing her to hide inside a tiny closet for dry goods? Treating his offspring like a can of tuna should be illegal. But admittedly, I understand his point—there's nowhere else to hide unless it's under the kitchen sink.

Quickly, I shut myself in and crouch-sit on a 20-pound bag of jasmine rice. I'm surrounded by cans of baked beans, SPAM, and digestive cookies. My parents' favorite snack when they first immigrated to America. They can eat rolls and rolls of these cookies slathered with globs of unmelted butter. I have no idea why, when sliced bread is so readily available at any supermarket. My elbow bangs into a jar of tasty Nutella.

I stop myself from yelping.

I want to laugh and cry from the absurdity of the situation.

Suddenly starving, I open the jar and start scooping the spread with my fingers. Nutella has never tasted so creamy, nutty, and delicious.

What else am I supposed to do when I'm stuck in a kitchen closet?

What else am I supposed to eat? Certainly not cold, greasy SPAM!

The sound of braying laughter and Mr. Chadha-Fu's overly cheerful newscaster voice blares in our living room. This closet has some shockingly amazing acoustics. It's like being in my own VIP theater. If I had known about it growing up, I would probably have spent 75 percent of my childhood eavesdropping in the pantry. Think about how much blackmail currency I could have collected on my parents and their friends.

"Where is Iris?" a voice booms enthusiastically.

I hear the crystal clink of my parents setting down cups of coffee. Mr. Chadha-Fu is also known as Mr. NPR (National Public Radio) in Bradley Gardens, New Jersey. His nickname is because he broadcasts all the official and unofficial gossip in our neighborhood. He knows everything from boring lawn maintenance to the most mundane fundraising event at our school to little-known international celebrity news in over three continents.

For a parent, he's not boring. He's a tabloid magazine disguised as a middle-aged dad.

My mom says that if you want everyone to know about a new mole or your latest failure, you just have to accidentally tell Mr. Chadha-Fu. Samira's dad is a successful stockbroker with two toy poodles, yet he still manages to out-tweet and out-text all of us every day.

The Chadha-Fus can't find out that I'm a two-time failure.

"Iris is—" my dad says. The unmistakable sound of a clanking spoon.

"Volunteering!" my mom finishes.

"Volunteering?" Mrs. Chadha-Fu says. "Yes, Samira has been volunteering at the Salvation Army and the local newspaper. She wrote at least two dozen articles on global warming and the refugee crisis recently."

I didn't know Samira volunteered.

I didn't even know Samira was capable of writing news articles. If I were asked to write on such serious, unimaginative topics, I wouldn't even know where to start. If I'm being completely honest, I don't even really understand what global warming is, even though everyone is always talking about it, like it's an extremely important brand of face cream.

Shamefully, I realize it's because I haven't been paying attention to anything current-events related. I've just been focused on me and Peter, but mostly, my own personal development.

My own personal enjoyment.

Was Peter right?

Self-doubt crawls uneasily across my skin, like a tragic case of ringworm.

Why don't I know anything real about Samira?

"Anyway, we came here to share the great news!" Mr. Chadha-Fu announces as if he's a celebrity host of a game show.

There's a dramatic pause.

I lean my neck forward, wondering what the news could possibly be. Then he shouts, "You won't believe it! But we got into PRINCETON! Samira is going to Princeton!!!"

This is followed by the unnaturally shrill squealing of Mrs. Chadha-Fu and Samira. From my closet, they sound like excited seagulls. Then I hear a mixed cheerleader chorus of "We got into PRINCETON! And NYU, Brown, and Cornell! PRINCETON! PRINCETON! Samira is going to our first choice! Princeton!"

My heart tumbles into my stomach.

Due to so much unexpected news, this fist-size organ can no longer support its own weight.

I didn't even know Samira was applying to Princeton.

I didn't even know that Samira was actually book smart. Sure, she seemed like she would get into college . . . but then again, *I* thought I'd get into one of my first choices.

"Congratulations," my mom finally says, sounding like she has a horrible case of acid reflux. My dad says nothing. I hear him excuse himself to go to the bathroom. Luckily, the Chadha-Fus don't seem to hear the zombie awkwardness because they are too busy chattering and making plans. But then Samira asks, "Do you know when Iris will be home?"

"Probably very late," my mother lies. "Can I get you anything to drink?"

"Seltzer, please," Samira says, and I hear my mother asking if anyone would like more coffee. Mr. Chadha-Fu requests another cup with sugar and cream, while Mrs. Chadha-Fu wants to know if we have any pastries.

"Do you mind taking a family photo of us?" Mrs. Chadha-Fu suddenly calls out. "We want to show all our relatives in Singapore, India, Australia, and Malaysia that Samira got into Princeton! It's not every day that your child gets into an Ivy League school! It happens only once in a lifetime, unless they go on to be a doctor or lawyer!"

I hear my mom say that she'll bring out some cookies. There's more chattering, but the delicious Nutella has turned into a soggy cardboard-tasting mush in my mouth. Samira will be attending Princeton in the fall. Samira even has *my* boyfriend. She now owns *my* favorite first-date dress, and it would be horrible manners if I asked for it back.

If I don't know who my former best friend is, how can I know myself?

Aren't we 99.9 percent defined by our loved ones?

Aren't we supposed to be identical reflections of our friends?

Looking at Samira was always supposed to be like staring at myself in a Saks Fifth dressing room. We wear the same clothing size and used to share everything, including bras, bikinis, and mascaras. And now, apparently, we share boyfriends. Since the second grade, I have relied on Samira to tell me who I was, but I suddenly realize that I have never known her as a person.

Don't be self-pitying, I tell myself firmly.

This is only a temporary setback, like something the genius Steve Jobs would face before founding a multi-billion-dollar company named after a fruit found in a supermarket.

I'm on the verge of discovering a great, fantastic new life venture. Being royalty is a legitimate career path. Did Meghan

Markle wake up and decide that she would one day marry royalty? From a young age, she probably knew in her bones that it was her destiny.

Once I find my real aristocratic parents and determine my birthright, not getting into college will seem unimportant.

That's when I hear whispering. Someone is laughing girlishly again. Samira. Maybe it's the acoustics of the pantry, but I never realized that her laugh sounded like a donkey imitating a hyena.

"Which colleges do you think Iris got into?" Mr. Chadha-Fu asks.

Mrs. Chadha-Fu laughs. "Iris? College? That's an oxymoron."

I suddenly can't breathe. My lungs have disappeared.

This is because most of the people that I once cared about are gossiping about me. In my living room!

"She's a very nice girl," Mr. Chadha-Fu announces helpfully.

My face grows jalapeño-hot.

Samira laughs quickly. "I'd be shocked if she got into any. Iris . . . just . . . doesn't have a very high IQ."

Her words cause me to gasp out loud.

"She has never been good at anything that is important."

The Chadha-Fus laugh.

I drop the jar of half-eaten Nutella. It makes an unreasonably loud clatter. I try to catch it, but my elbow knocks over stacks of canned tuna and boxes of macaroni and cheese. I accidentally smear Nutella all over the pantry walls.

I don't know why I'm so shocked by Samira's words. For some reason, her second betrayal hurts more than the first. I have been nothing but kind and generous to Samira.

Heat floods through my neck and prickles across my face like an unrelenting rash. How could I have wasted ten-plus years of gifts and gossip and texts and phone calls and friendship on her? The pantry suddenly feels like a radioactive sauna. Black dots, like chocolate chips, scatter across my corneas.

Is my brain combusting?

Tears are leaking uncontrollably from my eyes. I can't help it. Maybe my parents are right that I'm a complete, uncategorized disaster. Hurricane Iris, Category 10. A national danger to myself and others.

Suddenly, I don't care if everyone knows I'm home.

I don't care anymore.

Bursting out of the pantry and stampeding into the living room, I barely care that globs of Nutella are smeared all over my hands and mouth. I don't care if I look like a deranged, snack-deprived vampire. I whip out my iPhone.

"How dare you say these things about me!" I sputter. "Here's your shitty photograph!"

Samira's smirking mouth drops open. Her entire face transforms into a hideous sweet-and-sour-pork-chop red, and the Chadha-Fus at least have the decency to look ashamed. They avert their eyes and stare at the leopard-print rug on the floor. I quickly take their shame-faced picture. Mrs. Chadha-Fu is holding the college acceptance letter in her lap.

"Get out of my life!" I shout at Samira, whose mouth hasn't closed yet. "First you steal my boyfriend and then you talk behind my back! You're right about me not being smart. I trusted you!"

My mom and dad suddenly appear in the living room. They look queasy and horrified, like they both have food poisoning simultaneously. My dad is actually clutching his abdomen and staring at the wall behind the Chadha-Fus. Is he praying to the wallpaper or Buddha?

"I think you should go," my mom says firmly to the Chadha-Fus, who stand up and race to the door, as if there is a sample sale at Prada.

"Don't worry, I'll text you your photo!" I shout at them.

Tears are falling onto my iPhone like there is an actual typhoon inside my eyeballs. But I manage to press SEND and wipe slimy Nutella off the screen at the same time.

How is it possible to feel so abandoned and hurt and alone all at once?

It's like I've accidentally swallowed a whole tube of Nair's extra-strength hair removal.

This kind of internal pain should not be real.

Suddenly, Beijing looks a tiny bit more appealing than staying parent-less, boyfriend-less, and best-friend-less in Bradley Gardens. If you had to choose between a broken kneecap and a fractured elbow, which one would you choose?

It's a game of which location would be worse.

Forbes Asia
Top 30

I can barely sleep on the 15.5-hour plane ride to Beijing.

Even though I'm terribly sad and disappointed in everyone and myself, I have a plan.

In front of me, in addition to my usual magazines, I have bought a special-edition *Forbes 30 Asia*, which profiles the richest women and men in Asia. Like the Ivy League student that I should be, I'm flipping through it, making a list of potential parents on an airplane napkin. As I passed Hudson News in Terminal 1 at JFK, I had a brilliant last-minute thought that I could be a descendent of some Bill Gates of China.

Whoever said that I couldn't think outside the box?

I'm determined to prove that my genius has been hiding deep inside me for seventeen years.

Forbes has done all the research for me, and it's just up to me to narrow down the candidates. Math is so easy when genetics and inheritances are at stake! If this question were on the SATs, I'd have aced it.

Anyway, I've successfully vetted the billionaires by eliminating the people who are either too old or young to be my parents, like the whiz kid Cai Teng, who is only fifteen.

At the top of my napkin parent-list is Penelope Xia Xu, who is Shanghai's #25 billionaire in clothing manufacturing for several lingerie stores in America. She seems like she could be my mother. Her forehead is large and sloped, which is what my fake dad believes indicates abundant success in one's career. But I'm not sure if Penelope Xu looks fun and spontaneous enough to have a love child with a movie star. She's so . . . stern-looking. But sometimes the most unexpected people have the biggest, juiciest secrets. Like my Goat dad.

Then there's also a tall, slender man called Xie Fei at #12, the head of a big data research organization, and #16 Dai Feng, a short, balding dude who built his own startup construction company. Both of them are average-looking, but they're the perfect age to be my parent.

I also tried eliminating people based on their facial features. But then I realized, what if some, if not all, of these gazillionaires had plastic surgery? I can't eliminate that possibility, can I?

So my final parent list is at fifteen.

Fifteen out of thirty. That's not bad, is it?

After my fake dad drove me to the US consulate to get my tourist visa for China approved, my fake mom took me to Macy's to buy "thank-you hostess" gifts for my uncle, aunt, and cousin. I found a pretty pink beaded fringe scarf from H&M

and super-fun, humongous hoop earrings for my cousin. Then my parents and I headed to Macy's makeup counters to buy my aunt a deluxe Clinique moisturizer gift set that has twelve tiny vials of face and hand cream. We even found a nice blanket-soft leather Coach wallet with double zippers for my uncle.

"Listen to your uncle," my fake dad said in a monotone at Air China's counter at JFK. He sounded hoarse because he had been talking to my guidance counselor and principal for hours about letting me leave school a month early before graduation. At first they were seriously concerned about my lack of a diploma, but my dad promised them that he would make sure that I received my GED online. At this point, my dad had argued, it was better to "completely throw away a burned holiday dinner and start all over again." I didn't exactly understand what he meant, but the school administrators agreed.

"Listen to your aunt and uncle better than you listen to us," my fake mom said stiffly.

And that's all they said to me. It was as if a week of disappointment and not-talking about the whole incident had suddenly turned them into robots from a sci-fi movie. At JFK, I was expecting someone to have a moment of true realization: *We love our only daughter, Iris, and we just can't bear to send her away!* Instead, there was no goodbye hug or heartfelt apology. They were almost acting as if they were relieved to be sending me far, far away.

This lack of concern at the airport could undoubtedly prove that they are not my real parents. How does my fake dad even know if this is my real uncle??! For all I know, the lawyer making the overseas introductions could have made a horrible mistake and found the wrong person. Isn't Wang one of the most popular surnames in the United States?

I check my list of Asia's Richest carefully, then take a photo of it with my iPhone for safekeeping. I feel a gigantic, fizzling rush of adrenaline, like I'm a detective who is on her way to solve an incredibly important personal life mystery.

When the flight attendant comes around with water, I beam at her and hand her my empty soda can and the crumpled-up napkin. My list is safely stored on my iPhone.

Despite being sent a billion miles away from everyone I know, I do want to look my best and make a semi-good impression. For the first time, out of nervousness, I can't focus on an in-flight movie. I flip open one of the five fashion magazines that I bought at the airport. But I'm too anxious to concentrate on a quiz in *Allure* about first-date makeup. Who cares about eye shadow when I'm about to become a bazillionaire heiress?!

I also don't know what my father told my uncle about me.

Already I'm imagining scenarios where they think I'm some horrible, spoiled teenager who is some combination of a McDonald's cheeseburger and suburban shopping mall.

I love plane rides because it means there's possibly new adventures and glamorous people waiting when you land. I not-so-secretly love being suspended in air with nothing but movies and magazines and free cookies. It's also impossible to get work done in these ridiculous cramped seating spaces, so no one expects you to study or read anything serious while flying. I suddenly remember that my mom stuffed a pillow-size GED preparation book into my luggage, but I won't think about it now.

GEDs aren't for geniuses who have figured out how to find their birth parents by reading *Forbes* magazine.

As I fiddle with my earphones, I can't help but nervously apply my lip gloss and mascara and shimmery blue eyeliner over and over again.

"Why wearing so much makeup?" a voice says.

I flush and turn to a disapproving Chinese lady sitting in the aisle across from me. She's a bit older than my mom, wearing a gorgeous peacock-print silk scarf. Blushing furiously, I check my makeup in my compact. No one has ever criticized my makeup before! Not even my mom, who always approves, and thinks that unmade-up women are just lazy. What if I shouldn't arrive in Beijing with a full face of makeup? What would my uncle and aunt and cousin think if I arrived looking like one of the Kardashians?

"Is there something wrong?" I ask hesitantly.

The woman shakes her head sternly at me. "Too young! Too much makeup!" she says again. But she has a full face of powdery white foundation and garish Santa Claus lips, so she shouldn't be complaining. But maybe teenage girls don't wear a lot of makeup in Beijing. What if everyone is boring, uncolorful, and plain-faced? I desperately want to fit in.

That's always been one of my biggest problems.

I have wanted to match others since my first day of kindergarten. I've always wanted to be liked. If I'm not included, well-thought-of, and accepted by others, then who am I? What happens if not one single person likes me in Beijing? Will I simply disappear?

Nervously I excuse myself to go to the bathroom.

Rummaging into my purse for my makeup-remover wipes, I

suddenly realize that I've forgotten to pack them. I splash cold water on my face, but mascara leaks all around my eyelids, leaving splotchy streaks. Horrified, I continue to stare at myself in the mirror. Time freezes, like someone has pressed pause on an especially terrifying horror movie. I don't know how long. I don't recognize the girl staring back at me. I'm paralyzed by her anguished expression. Her feral Tiger features. Her uneven mascara stripes. I want to scream.

I grab toilet paper and rub my face until someone raps on the door.

"There's someone in here!" I shout.

Honestly, people are so impatient. I've only been in the bathroom for less than twenty-five minutes!

"There's a line," the voice calls, rapping again.

"Someone is in here!" I shout back.

Don't they know I'm having a personal emergency?

Seriously, what if I was having nonstop diarrhea?

It could very possibly happen, since everyone knows that air travel is full of germs and airplane food leads to salmonella.

But the constant rapping on the door makes me flustered.

I swivel too fast in the very cramped bathroom, and *clang!* I somehow knock the contents of my purse—a tube of MAC lip gloss, mascara, iPhone, passport, toothbrush, tweezers, and wallet—into the toilet bowl. I freeze. If food drops on the floor, there's a three-second rule, but what happens if all your personal belongings fall into a public toilet?! How long until it's considered too hazardous to retrieve them? Twenty seconds? A minute? Two minutes and thirty seconds?

What do I do???!!!!

Should I flush it all away?

Shuddering, I let out a wail and decide to try to save my iPhone with its life-changing list. My destiny is on that phone. But it's drenched with blue chemical water and I don't even want to touch it.

The knocking on the door escalates.

"Are you . . . okay?" the voice asks. "Do you need assistance?"

I exhale loudly. How many more hours to Beijing? Can I somehow ask them to stop the plane? Does a toilet blockage constitute an international emergency?

"I'm fine!!!" I mumble-shout.

The cramped plane bathroom makes me claustrophobic and dizzy.

I touch my forehead and tell myself not to panic. For a second, I think my forehead is expanding horizontally, and looking a bit like Penelope Xu's, top 30 billionaire. Upon closer inspection, the girl in the airplane mirror looks extremely hungover. A messy doppelgänger of the usual super-confident, put-together, and highly optimistic Iris Wang. I don't even recognize myself. I stare closer at my reflection. That's when I see it: new hairs, long and spidery-looking. Tiger whiskers.

Groaning, I tell myself that I'm just overexhausted, overheated, and probably hallucinating. It's just shitty PMS and not my Tiger curse, which seems to be spiraling out of control lately.

Reaching into the toilet bowl, I pluck the remaining items out. Like a present for someone you don't care about, I clumsily wrap them in a wad of extra-flimsy airplane tissue paper. Surely my iPhone and personal items will be dry by the time we land in Beijing.

Chauffeur

Nervously I collect my luggage and trudge to the waiting area.

There's an overriding smell of fast food, stale airplane air, and imploding excitement. It feels like I'm on a giant cruise ship.

Admittedly, it took a long time to get my bag, as the Beijing Capital International Airport at the start of summer vacation is like two JFK airports crammed into one. Imagine if the population of New York City were all fighting to claim their luggage. Or if a bank were suddenly just handing out stacks of free money to all their customers.

Sleep-deprived and on autopilot, I had to dart around multiple hugging families shouting enthusiastically in Chinese. I maneuvered elbows, flailing arms, and Louis Vuitton bags just to swing my bulky suitcase off the rotating carousels.

"Excuse me!" I hollered, but no one seemed to hear me. I felt a little bit sad and pathetic. Just like the mismatched, orphaned shoe at a Nine West outlet. I always wondered what happened to those shoes. Do they get thrown out or sent back to the manufacturer?

I actually don't even know where I'm supposed to go. Everyone is running toward someone or *something*. In fact, I notice that airplane passengers are running up to signs. But I don't see one with my name on it. But then I also don't read Chinese. Would my uncle make a sign for me? My dad also didn't say if my uncle would bring my aunt and cousin with him. I feel quite left out. I just want to race up to an eager, smiling person holding up my name. I want to be claimed, like overseas luggage.

What I want is to feel normal, but also special at the same time, which is what my mom always says is "Iris's biggest life problem." My dad insists it's my flower-heart and shitty Tiger curse. But I honestly don't see it as a problem that my inner life goals do not align with theirs. Mine seem to be flexible. Mainly driven by my peers and advertisements on social media, while theirs are about being hardworking with the purpose of affording super-nice cars and vacations. I like all these things, but the difference between me and my parents is that they seem to find school and hard work ridiculously easy. Their brains never seem to malfunction. Their wet-eyed disappointment hurts because they think that I'm a four-star restaurant in Manhattan, when I'm really just a box of Kraft dinner.

I really don't know how to be better than I already am.

With a sudden pang, I realize that I should be here with my parents. Even if they aren't my real ones, they should be visiting Beijing with me. The fact that I'm alone in a strange country terrifies and paralyzes me.

I can't help but take being sent to China personally.

Before I left, we tried to talk about my dad's decision. In our family, usually Mom makes everyone's executive life choices, but Dad kept insisting on the trip and booked my one-way plane ticket. He has never seemed so certain of anything. Each time I tried to nervously bring up failing high school, everyone just started trying not to cry-yell and talking hysterically about what was for dinner (Panda Express).

Needless to say, the whole not-talking about my impending banishment was a Level 10 national disaster.

Eventually, I realize that I've been wandering around the International Arrivals section in Terminal 3 for a while. My arms ache from pulling my rolling luggage, and my sneakers are squeezing the sides of my feet. I just want to lie on the ground and possibly sleep.

My dad assured me that my uncle would pick me up at the airport, but I realize that I don't even know what my uncle looks like. Am I supposed to look for a younger version of my dad? Am I supposed to stand on the escalator and scream my Chinese name over and over again? (The only Chinese words I know.)

To be honest, I am not even sure I know how to properly pronounce my Chinese name. It was just something that I never asked my dad.

I try to turn on my iPhone to text my dad to ask him how to find my uncle and how to say my name again in Chinese, but it still isn't working. Disgusting toilet. I read somewhere that you're supposed to resuscitate a wet phone by soaking it in a tub of short-grain rice or baking it in the oven like a ginormous brownie. I'm not sure what the proper advice is. I don't know where I'm supposed to find a giant sack of rice at the airport.

Finally, I lug my suitcase up an elevator and then perch near a faux-gold-topped temple with potted ferns and silk lamps. I'm so relieved when I spot a Starbucks, I practically start sob-crying with relief. I really need another cup of black coffee and maybe a tasty piece of frosted lemon cake to make me feel better after a long, horrible flight.

But that's when I see it. Near the Starbucks, there is a mobile phone booth. They can probably fix my phone! Aren't Apple products made in China? My iPhone and I were originally manufactured in China, and it's like now we're coming home. With renewed determination, I grab my suitcase and head over, elbow-jostling through a crowd of a senior-citizen tour group.

The young pimply dude at the counter greets me in Chinese: "*Zǎo shang hǎo!*"

"Hello," I say politely. "I dropped my phone in the . . . sink . . . and I'm wondering if you can fix it."

"Chinese?" he asks, looking very surprised.

"No, um, English only."

"Why?" he asks.

I don't know. That's actually a good question. I never needed to learn Chinese in New Jersey. Practically everyone speaks perfect English.

"I'm American," I say.

"Chinese," he says, sounding confused.

"I'm from the United States," I say again.

"No, you Chinese." He points to my face, then back at his facial features. We look nothing alike!

"I'm Chinese American," I say to the cashier.

"Chinese!" he insists, looking puzzled. "Why you not speak? What is your problem?"

"No problem," I say, suddenly exhausted. "Can you please just fix my phone?"

He's extremely confused about my ethnicity, but at least he tinkers with the ON button, and tries to plug it into his laptop. He presses another button and fiddles with more wires.

The screen remains dark.

Shit.

"No fix," he declares, shaking his head.

Oh god, I can't afford a brand-new iPhone. That's a mega expense that I didn't predict. It's almost the same price as a round-trip ticket to Paris or Beijing. And I don't think my parents will want to buy me another one, especially since I've wrecked the garage and their most expensive car.

"New cell phone," he suggests, pointing at the rows of assorted boxes behind me. Never mind that I know nothing about cellular devices that aren't smartphones. I feel lost without Siri.

"I'll take one!" I finally say, desperate to have access to technology and Google Maps. But then I realize I don't actually know my uncle's phone number.

"How much is an all-inclusive long-distance plan?" I ask.

"Seven hundred eighty-eight *yuan*," he says. I hand him my American Express card and then, to my dismay, it's declined.

"Try again," I beg, wondering why it isn't working, and then

I remember that I still haven't paid the exorbitant bill, which is collecting interest. I fish around in my purse for Chinese money, and finally locate the envelope that my dad handed me from the bank. I sort through the various colored bank notes, but then I realize I also don't know my parents' phone numbers. I've always just relied on my contact list. I do know the area code of New Jersey, thankfully, but what are the four or eight numbers that come after that?

The only number I've memorized is Samira's, but I'm not going to call her.

"You want phone?" the cashier says, watching me. He looks slightly uncomfortable. Distress seems to be radiating all over my features like I'm a giant Wi-Fi signal, and he's picking up on it.

I don't know which phone I want. I don't know which long-distance plan. I don't even know which number to call.

What would happen if I dialed 911 long-distance from the airport?

Just as I'm about to wail in frustration, someone taps me on the shoulder. I whirl around, expecting to have to argue with another impatient customer telling me to hurry up. But it's an extremely tall man in an elaborate black-and-gold-striped driver's uniform. He's wearing a matching chauffeur cap like he's from an old-fashioned movie. He's also holding up a phone with what appears to be my photo.

Is this a prank on a reality television show?

Otherwise, why would a man dressed in what looks like a Disney World costume from Main Street, USA, of all places, want to talk to me? Why would he even have my photo?

Of course I recognize myself instantly. I'm hugging my mom outside Six Flags Great Adventure and we're laughing hysterically because my dad was too scared to go on the seven-story-high Cyborg thrill ride. He turned leprechaun-green and forced my mom to ride with me. In the photo, it's windy and my hair, like a napkin, is stuck to my lip gloss. My mom looks genuinely happy, and for once, she's not worried about me, my dad, or her work. A stab of overwhelming sadness hits me like nausea from binge-smoking weed and devouring nachos. I suddenly miss her.

I miss both of my parents.

I don't know the time difference, but right now, my mom is probably running to work, thermos in hand, looking slightly flustered. And my dad would still be sleeping with his white noise machine set to Rushing Water, which honestly reminds me of a nonstop flushing toilet. Peter would be honking the horn to let me know that he had the engine running in the driveway. And instead of driving to school, we'd go for a long drive/smoke, missing first and second period.

I seriously regret Peter. But mostly, I regret being the kid that my parents were so horrified by, and so utterly disappointed in, that they had to ship me, like an overnight parcel, in economy class to a foreign country.

How do I make my parents forgive me for such a colossal mistake?

How do I make myself forgive them for sending me to a non-English-speaking country?

Most of all, how do I even forgive myself when all I feel is a gigantic Jolly Rancher of shame and resentment stuck in my throat? Honestly, why can't three-way forgiveness be as easy as picking a set meal from a Japanese restaurant menu? I never have any trouble choosing Bento Box B with one brown rice California roll, a side of crunchy edamame beans, and sixteen pieces of fresh salmon sashimi.

Blinking, I force myself back into reality.

The man in the driver's outfit proceeds to show me more photos of me as a child. I nod eagerly. I'm actually supercute. In one of them, I'm dressed as a black-and-orange tiger for Halloween, posing with my dad, who is dressed as a Super Mario Brother. There are more Christmas, cruise, and beach vacation photos. I'm being shown an Oscar-worthy photo montage of my life!

"Uncle?" I ask excitedly. I did not know my uncle was a professional driver. I wonder if he owns his own limo company or if he is responsible for regularly dispatching a fleet of luxury cars. I wonder if he'll chauffeur me around Beijing first-class, or better yet, if he'll let me drive my own convertible.

Imagine speeding down the exotic countryside of China with my own luxury sports car.

Then I realize that I don't actually know my uncle's name, and due to the frantic packing for this trip, my father forgot to tell me. My dad and I have just been calling him "Uncle." Of course, I never bothered to ask.

"Thank you for picking me up, Uncle!" I babble.

Enthusiastically I attempt to hug him, but he steps sideways. I try to hug him again, but this time, he literally long-jumps backward. My uncle looks like he's been electroshocked. Confused, I stare up at him. I decide to try one more time. Family is always worth trying to overcome social awkwardness. After all, like no-fee checking accounts and Visa cards, aren't they supposed to forgive you?

But the man in the fancy costume shakes his head and says something long and explanatory in Chinese. He bows twice. Am I supposed to bow back? He continues talking. It's like I'm watching *Star Wars* without any of the subtitles. My dad loves the franchise and makes my mom and me watch it with him, even though I don't understand what's going on. When I fail to respond in a familiar but foreign language that I don't know how to speak, the man impatiently tries again.

I glance at the cashier, who asks the man a question in *Star Wars*–like Chinese. They speak for a long time, gesturing at the photos.

"He pick you up," the cashier translates, looking suddenly impressed. "You are Wang Weijun?"

"Yes!" I say, instant relief bubbling inside me, as if I've just taken a swig of Pepto-Bismol to combat nausea. "That's my Chinese name! I'm Wang Weijun. Uncle, I'm your niece. My name is Iris Wang. I'm from America."

I can't stop babbling because I'm so relieved.

I'm finally saved. I won't have to stay in the airport until my parents discover that I'm missing and call the US Embassy and the Chinese police, which could take ages. It could literally be a week before anyone finds me in this messy, swarming crowd. By that time, I could be extinct. That's probably what happened to the dinosaurs. First, a broken promise by a beloved family member, and then they were kept waiting.

All I can think about right now is changing out of my day-old airplane clothes and relaxing with Netflix and a Diet Coke and a humongous bag of salt-and-vinegar chips.

"He say your uncle gave him picture," the cashier continues. "He drive you to meet him."

"That's great!" I exclaim. Then I add, a teensy bit embarrassed, "Can you please ask him what my uncle's name is, and where he'll be taking me?"

12

Ruby

The chauffeur ushers me into the back of a gorgeous black Porsche with tinted windows. Soon we're creeping at turtle speed through a winding highway and then we are somehow in the fast, pulsing circle that is Beijing. There's so much thick smog, concrete, and traffic. It's like sneaking into a two-star nightclub in New Jersey. You can't even see the person who wants to make out with you. Instantly my sinuses clog up. I cough ten times. I was expecting a modern and ultra-high-tech city like Paris or New York City.

Never mind what I expected.

Because through the fancy car, it's like watching a commercial for humidifiers on high-definition TV!

I'm sure that everything would look different if I were watching the city through the back of my parents' boring Volkswagen.

I just knew that all my positive thinking would pay off! The universe is rewarding me for all my good deeds. For instance, I even found a clear bottle of extra-strong liquor in the back of the car, and I have been helping myself.

This is the first day of my brand-new life. Uncle Dai is the name of my dad's half brother, and this man, Mr. Chen, is supposed to take me to my uncle. That's all I got from the cell phone clerk, who looked disappointed when I ended up not buying anything. I felt kind of bad for him and gave him a wad of *yuan*. He looked so shocked that I think I might have accidentally given him a lot of money. I'm not entirely sure how many *yuan* is worth a dollar, even though my mom explained it. I'm supposed to multiply or divide everything into American dollar signs, except I forgot what the equation is.

What I love about traveling to foreign countries is that the fun, colorful money and coins don't feel real. It's like playing an interactive game of Monopoly. When you go shopping, it's not like you are actually spending real money. In fact, foreign money is the opposite of American money. You see, American dollars are all one color and incredibly no-nonsense-looking, which discourages you from doing any serious spending at all. That's why I only ever use my American Express card, which is made out of shiny red plastic. Money should look friendly and fun, otherwise there could be serious repercussions for the economy.

My uncle Dai must be excessively generous with his company car. My parents are comfortable suburbanites, but they'd never send a chauffeur to pick me up at the airport. If they couldn't make it, they'd just tell me to hop on public transit.

Eventually, we stop in front of a hotel. Not just any hotel, but the Shangri-La. I gasp involuntarily. It's the same chain, almost exactly like the one from my Paris trip planning! The Shangri-La is a four-star hotel with luxury suites and several penthouses for rent. The only reason that I know all this is I actually spent a ton of time imagining what it would be like to spend a romantic vacation in one of their deluxe honeymoon rooms.

Why would my uncle want to meet me here?

Maybe Mr. Chen needs to pick up another passenger? This is possibly an elite ride-share, which actually makes sense. But as I wait for another passenger to climb in, Mr. Chen opens the back door. It turns out we're actually stopping in front of the Shangri-La. Maybe Mr. Chen needs to use the bathroom? But he takes my luggage, and I'm ushered inside the lobby and greeted enthusiastically by many hotel staff, and then someone else efficiently wheels my bag into the elevator.

Everyone is looking very excited to see me. As if I'm a famous celebrity or well-loved toy poodle. I can't actually tell what category they think I belong to.

What is going on?!!! Why aren't we stopping at a conference floor? Does my uncle work in hospitality?

A horrible thought passes through my mind. Is this a case of actual mistaken identity? I just know it is when I'm led into a penthouse on the sixty-sixth floor.

I inhale.

I blink.

The suite is immaculate, with beige lacelike wallpaper and gold leafy embroidery everywhere. It's like I've wandered into the living room of Versailles or a Disney movie. Imagine a crash pad of a medium-deal celebrity or a really old person who has spent their entire life aspiring to be French royalty.

Impressed, I can't help but let out a tiny squeal when I see the focal point of the room is a ginormous *Beauty and the Beast* chandelier. It's made of millions of sweeping pink and white Swarovski-looking crystals, like cherry blossoms on an origami glass tree. The chandelier is literally the size of my parents' wrecked Mercedes-Benz.

I suddenly understand what my AP English Literature teacher meant by *symbolism*. The chandelier is hanging above me, just like a shimmery metaphor of my life, practically within arm's reach!

There's even a spiraling glass staircase that reminds me of a sculpture of Cinderella's shoe, which leads outside to a rooftop terrace. I feel like I'm inside a movie. I race up the stairs, almost slipping, and push open the balcony doors. The sun in Beijing is bright and light and the sky is glittery with dense fog. I cough and sneeze for at least six minutes. My allergies are flaring up.

Despite my watering nose and eyes, I force myself to survey the view, but everything looks so surreal from the sixty-sixth floor: the whizzing cars, the ant-size people. It's like I'm watching tiny people inside a snow globe. Giddy, I'm already wondering how many people I could fit on this roof for a housewarming party.

I prance back inside. But I don't know which room is mine, so I decide to leave my bag in the middle of the living room. I need to go relax by the pool ASAP, followed by a hot steam in the sauna and a full-body massage. If my new residence is in a hotel, does that mean room service is free?

But first, I really have to snoop.

I may never have this amazing opportunity again.

The first bedroom isn't locked and it looks like it belongs to royalty. I find myself running, as if magnetized, to a walk-in closet that is practically the same size as my bedroom at home. I need to see what's inside. Suddenly, I've been transported to Nordstrom department store. My own miniature boutique. Are these racks of expensive clothes and boxed-up shoes and handbags for me?

I just knew that all my good deeds would pay off.

Before I can begin fully checking my (hopefully) new closet, I notice a whole pyramid of humongous trophies and gold medals in a display case and framed certificates on the walls. At first I think it is just part of the home decor, but the whole room is covered with shiny awards. All the trophies have titles and names on them. *Number 2 in Creative Dog Grooming Contest, Shenzhen* and *Number 1 in Colorful Animal Cutting Champion, Shanghai* and *Number 10 in Jungle Animal Competition, Netherlands*. What is all this???!

Mostly, I'm fascinated by the shiny poster-photos of a thin, giraffelike girl posing in one couture dress after another, standing proudly beside various matching pooches in costumes. But what's stranger and cooler and more exciting is that all the chow chows, golden retrievers, and poodles have these wild, fabulous haircuts. Some of the pooches look like stuffed animals of pandas, gorillas, or lions. A border collie even looks identical to Lady Gaga.

I have never seen anything like this. In another glossy photo, the same girl is dressed as the yellow-hoop-skirted Belle, and a Newfoundland is the shaggy Beast from the cartoon Disney movie. Then in another, the girl is strutting on the stage as Ariel from *The Little Mermaid*, and a terrier is dyed and styled as Sebastian the red crab. It's like a beauty pageant starring dogs with their humans as giant accessories. What event is this? And how do I participate?

Why didn't my parents ever enroll me in matching animal and beauty queen pageants?

I simply must find out who this bedroom belongs to.

At first, I think that I'm just going to take a peek in the closet. I tell myself that a little oohing and aahing isn't going to hurt anyone. In fact, looking and making loud appreciative sounds could be considered multiple compliments at once. My dad and I make these sounds all the time, resembling background singers, especially when my mom buys a $4.99 roast chicken from Costco and pretends that she baked it.

I gasp. Then I *ooooooh* and *aahhhhhh* for the longest time.

Amidst a rack of boutique dresses, there's a gorgeous sequined ball gown with what look like gold ostrich feathers and a pink beaded tulle skirt, perfect for when I meet my real parents. The dress honestly looks like something out of a runway in *Teen Vogue* magazine. My mouth drops open, and it takes a while for me to be able to close it again. If no one is home and not a single person actually ever finds out, it's okay to swathe it on my body for two minutes, right? All I have to do is unzip and jump in like I'm diving into a pool of tulle and silk. It's just like having a quick romantic rendezvous with Peter whenever my parents left the room.

I hesitate for the brief moment that it takes to send a tweet to my 300+ followers. Self-control has never been my strong point. Like a horrible itch inside the brain that I need to desperately scratch, I have never been able to refuse my impulses. I have never been able to say no to several helpings of dessert, an overpriced handbag, or even an annoying favor asked by an acquaintance. Ignoring my nagging inner voice, I find the strappiest, most sparkly pair of matching open-toed heels and a diamond-studded clutch.

Before the owner (hopefully me) is back, I must try on all these clothes ASAP. I push the worry of being discovered away. If I'm quick about it, no one will ever know about my terrible self-control. People try on clothes all the time, right?

As I attempt to zip the dress, I notice that it's very small and usually when I shop, most clothes are way too big. Whoever designed this dress has all the proportions wrong! There's no room for my rib cage, shoulders, or lower back. But I just know, in the center of my gut, that this dress has been waiting for me its whole life, so I literally suck in my stomach. I will myself to squeeze into this dress, which has not been designed for a human being. I wonder if I'm actually wearing the costume that belongs to an extra-thin greyhound. But isn't the train too long for one of the grinning canines in the photographs?

Clenching my teeth, I use all my determined willpower to make the zipper go up three-quarters of the way, and for a magical mystical moment, it does.

In the closet mirror, I stare at myself in shock. The dress is absolutely stunning and Best Actress Oscar–worthy. I feel exactly like the girl in the pageant dog photos. My eyes have become larger, my legs have gotten longer, and I suddenly have developed an hourglass figure.

I'm 60 percent more attractive in this dress.

If I could wear this gown to an event, I'd be known as the long-lost Chinese American princess in the nameless couture dress. It's perfect for my future role as a serious and devoted heiress!

I pose in the mirror, and just as I begin to admire myself from various angles, I imagine Samira and Peter seeing me in this dress, once I'm crowned princess of a small to medium-size country. "Resist me now!" I imagine yelling at Peter. The poor boy wouldn't be able to run away.

Grinning like a crazed corgi with a bone, I swivel to examine myself from the side. But panicked shouting in Chinese suddenly bursts through my eardrums. At first, I think it's my mom yelling and I can't breathe. I spin around, embarrassed that someone has seen me posing and waving and making irresistible royal-canine faces at the mirror.

I don't know what to say.

The only Chinese I know is my name.

More nonstop yelling from a girl who looks like she could be my age.

I don't understand why she's shouting.

Plus, I don't understand what she's saying at all. Sometimes I can understand a few words like "hello," "school," "dinner," or "bathroom" when my parents speak, but the girl is speaking way too quickly. Like the cell-phone clerk with Mr. Chen. They're speaking Chinese way faster than my parents. Chinese fast-forwarded X 2000.

"This isn't what it looks like," I say awkwardly, waving my hands at her. The girl stares at me for a long time before yelling in Chinese again.

"I'm sorry, but I don't speak Chinese," I say, but the girl looks even more unimpressed. Finally, she purses her glossy ketchup-colored lips and looks like how I look when I pluck a very spiky hair from my mustache.

She waits for me to respond, tapping her rose-gold Apple Watch impatiently.

"I don't speak Chinese," I say again.

Her surprise interrogation makes my cheeks flame. Like I've just ingested six vodka tonics in a span of thirty minutes and blurted out a very dirty secret.

Upon closer inspection, I realize it's the same girl from the shiny photographs minus a very dressed-up dog. The girl facing me is definitely America's Next Top Model material in real life. Her refrigerator-white skin looks practically photoshopped, and if I didn't know any better, I'd assume she was a robot. Her bleached white-blond hair is long and rope-straight. She's also wearing a nightdress that is both fluffy and magazine-editorial-looking and science-fiction all at once. It's one of those amazing garments that reminds me of a very expensive but fabulous futuristic chicken.

Because I can't help it and I have limited self-control, I reach out to pet the material. It's like grabbing a handful of multi-colored cotton balls. It's absolutely fantastic, and I want to own it immediately.

"Your pajamas are amazing!" I say, hoping that she will somehow hear in my tone that I'm friendly and worth befriending.

But the girl yelps like she's been electrocuted.

Then she picks up her phone and begins dialing frantically. Is she calling hotel security? The Beijing police?

I have to convince her that I'm not actually a thief.

Also, how do I tell her in pantomiming and English that I have a seriously real and emotional connection with this dress? How do I explain that the dress was practically begging me to try it on?

"I am so sorry," I say, hoping that she will stop shouting and accept my apology.

The girl stares at me, flabbergasted. Then she continues shouting and I begin nervous-talking. She doesn't seem to speak English, so it doesn't matter what I say. I just want her to hear my calming tones. Aren't you supposed to make loud, reassuring noises and dramatic hand gestures when you encounter wild animals and scarily angry people?

I start waving frantically while making what I think are soothing noises. "Oooh! Ahhhhhhhhh," I say, feeling ridiculous.

Why did I even try on that dress? Couldn't I have found the exact same one somewhere online and gone to the store to try it on?

My gesturing and noise-making works, because she suddenly stops yelling in Chinese and begins speaking in heavily accented English.

"Who are you? Why are you in my room?" she asks.

"I'm supposed to be here," I say quickly. "I didn't know this was your room."

She points to the photographs on the wall.

"Are you involved in some sort of beauty contest?" I ask.

"This is the Creative Dog Grooming Contest," she snaps, looking offended that I don't know who she is.

"Huh?"

"I'm the second-best creative dog groomer in China!" she says.

"What?" I say, astonished.

The girl looks quite paralyzed by my response.

"Don't you recognize me? I'm a top-ranking national champion of the dog and human show!"

She does not look impressed when I stare at her blankly.

"Turning dogs into other animals is a competition," she insists, frowning at my lack of understanding.

"What do you mean?" I ask.

"I groom dogs into pandas or gorillas for pageants," she says.

"That's amazing!" I say, and I mean it. But I don't exactly know what she is talking about. Are dog-grooming pageants a recognized sport in China? I smile encouragingly at her to continue, but she stares at me without blinking. She's still in shock, so her eyes bulge a bit like a bug and I am honestly not sure where to look.

But after a few moments, Mr. Chen arrives. I'm so relieved. I want to hug him again, but I doubt that he will let me.

For a moment, he speaks with the girl and they argue frantically. He pulls out his iPad with the beautiful assortment of photos and points at me.

"Yes!" I say enthusiastically. "I'm Iris Weijun Wang! That's me!"

Then it hits me. This Girl in the Cotton-Ball Pajamas must be my cousin Ruby. My dad said that we're practically the same age. It did not occur to me because we look nothing alike. For one, she's taller than my dad. And her face is stiletto-thin and angular and cheekboney like she's on a cover of a magazine. But once she realizes that I'm her long-lost American cousin, she'll know that this has been a gigantic misunderstanding and we'll automatically be BFFs.

Family can always forgive and find each other.

At least that's what I have always strongly believed.

And my instincts, so far, have been 85 percent correct.

But for some reason, instead of immediately embracing me, the girl looks stunned. She blinks for a long time. Then she says in a snooty voice, "The dress you are wearing is for my upcoming dog show."

"I'm really sorry," I say again, thinking that an excuse would be totally unacceptable at this point. "You must be my cousin Ruby. I'm Iris. Hi!"

She ignores me. "It's for MY competition."

My expression indicates that there is something wrong with me. In fact, I have no idea what she's talking about. She points to another closet, which I had completely missed. "These clothes are for wearing. These ones are just for showing."

I stare at her. Is she kidding? What's the point of owning fabulous dresses if you only wear them for dog shows?

For a moment, we just look at each other, taking each other in. Her glossy upper lip curls upward. "That dress you are wearing is from Paris Fashion Week. There's a reason I'm number two in dog competitions in China," she says, as if it explains my transgression.

"Oh," I say, unsure of how to respond to her statement.

She stares at my dehydrated airplane hair, my unmade-up face, my sweatpants and sneakers, and her mouth starts to twist in almost comical revulsion. I hear a small hissing sound, and at first I think she's passing gas. It takes me a while before I realize that it's actually a noise of disapproval.

"I don't understand you at all," she says, frowning. "Why don't you know any of this?"

I don't understand YOU, I want to retort. *And I don't know anything about your life in China.*

Instead, I stare at her, my mouth opening and closing like a socially awkward golden retriever.

No one my age has ever *not* liked me before. If I were a product or a business on Yelp, no one in my generation would ever give me less than four stars. My average rating, if you factor in parents, teachers, and tutors, might actually be 3.5.

"Listen, I'm so sorry," I apologize again, wincing.

She points at my gorgeous dog-show dress. Her dress.

Smiling nervously, I struggle with the zipper. To my horror, it won't budge.

"Can you—can you please help me?" I stammer. Mortification, in the form of an aggressive allergic sneezing fit, hits me. Ruby's face turns murderous pink. The same shade as the dress and the chandelier.

13

New Family

Hotel services are called, and several maids all try to unzip me. It's like an international fashion emergency.

"Move right," someone says.

"Raise arm," another person says.

"Suck in tummy."

We try everything.

But I've accidentally stuffed myself into this doggy-pageant gown like a Thanksgiving turkey. I'm like bulging pork filling in a delicious deep-fried dumpling.

My willpower is so strong that it cannot be undone.

This dress has claimed me, and it won't let me go.

Finally, the manager of guest services at the Shangri-La decides to call in the hotel seamstress. She's an older lady with a bad perm who constantly humphs and growls with annoyance and then finally grabs a pair of sewing scissors from her kit. I can't believe that my spontaneity has resorted to the destruction of a brand-new dress.

"No!" I shout, at the same time Ruby yells something accusatory in Chinese.

The older lady looks at both of us and speaks urgently to Ruby. They sound like they're arguing. I don't understand what they are saying, but I agree with my cousin that under no circumstances can my coronation dress be destroyed.

All I can hear from the conversation is "Valentino!" which makes me more determined that I will just have to keep this dress on. I will wear this dress for the next decade until it magically falls off. Maybe this is my karmic punishment for buying a prom dress that I could not afford, and then wrecking it with spilled beer. *Iris Wang, at 102 years old, finally dies in a tattered Valentino ball gown. She could never be free of her designer garment, as it refused to come off her.*

But despite my protests, the old lady starts to cut me out of the dress. A hotel maid gathers the extra-long folds of the skirt, while someone, a clerk, helps hold the dress in place. Honestly, I've never had so many strangers' faces pressed so close to my backside. I wonder if we'll all be close friends and sisters after this mess.

As the magic dress finally slides off me, Ruby and I both gasp.

"NO!!!" we both wail in a duet.

It hurts so much that I can feel the dress's disappointment in me. Is it possible to betray a gown after feeling so wholly connected and invested in it? I'm finally free, but I feel so horrified at ruining such an expensive piece.

After all, I was supposed to wear this dress to my crowned princess of a small to medium-size country ceremony.

It's practically dark out by the time all the staff leave us alone with the wrecked gown, which Ruby says is "unfixable." I don't know how the hotel seamstress will stitch it together again. I could offer to pay, but I don't know how much it will cost. I also doubt that I could even afford to pay for it.

"Listen, um," I begin to stammer, "I'm really sorry—"

Suddenly, the alarm on her watch beeps, interrupting me.

"Dinner," Ruby says abruptly. "Time to go."

"Where are we going?" I say.

"I just told you," she says again. "Time to go."

"Are you getting changed?" I ask as I rummage through my luggage to find something appropriate to wear. I pick a cute floral romper and a gray cardigan. I want to appear conservative and modern when I meet my uncle and aunt for the first time. Quickly, I slather on mascara and gloss to match Ruby's made-up face.

"Why?" she asks.

Is she serious?

"You're . . . wearing pajamas," I say, trying to sound polite. Maybe dinner is at home, and I'm overthinking it as usual. Maybe people in China wear silk blanket pajamas to dinner? From the side, it looks like she could be wearing a poncho? Maybe it's something that everyone in our family does, for the sake of having a weird practice.

It could be true that excessively rich people adopt eccentricities like multiple charities. I make a mental note to find myself a strange habit and an important social cause. I don't have any quirks, but how hard can it be to learn one?

She scowls at me.

I pause, but only for a second. I can't let Ruby know that I have discovered her eccentricity, which is obviously like her super-power.

"This is a very expensive jumpsuit," she says with what looks like an evil eye. I can't be sure because it looks like one eye is closing, and the other one is ogling me with distaste.

"I totally knew that," I say, winking. I almost sound like I mean it.

If my tone is enthusiastic and well intentioned, does it cancel out a white lie?

The answer, in this case, must be yes.

It's always yes if it involves someone potentially liking you.

"This suit cost 67,448 *yuan*," she says, shooting me another look of disdain.

"It's . . . very nice," I say, but I still have no idea how to convert *yuan* into American dollars. "Do you use it for dog shows?"

Ruby doesn't smile. She humphs and folds her arms across her chest.

I ask her more about her dog grooming, and slowly, she looks as if she is about to warm up to me, despite her misgivings.

"I practice ten hours a week during school at a grooming salon," she brags. "For the summer, I do eight hours a day. Then I meet with a costume designer in Paris for outfits. What do you do in America?"

"Shopping mostly," I say.

"I mean, your professional interests. Do you play any sports? Have you played at Carnegie Hall yet?"

"No," I say, taken aback. "Do you?"

"Yes, of course. I play first violin, tennis, and I'm on Beijing's youth fencing team. I'm also in debate and Model UN. I'm actually scheduled for a solo concert at Carnegie Hall next fall. You mean you don't do ANYTHING?"

I stare at her in disbelief. Shopping is a hobby and a serious interest. It takes up at least ten-plus hours of my busy school week.

Ruby blinks. "Do you paint or draw or sculpt?" she finally asks.

"Um . . . no."

"Robotics and programming?"

I shake my head. How would I know how to program anything?

Incredulous, Ruby asks me, "You have a full-time job, then? Last summer I worked part-time at my dad's friend's cafe in Taipei as a waitress for work experience.

"You must have won awards in *something*," she insists when I don't say anything.

"No," I say, feeling foolish. To be honest, I have never won a single trophy or plastic medal. In elementary school, I couldn't even finish Sports Day without needing multiple hot dog and blueberry Gatorade breaks. I spent so much time resting that I didn't even earn a participation certificate.

At my response, Ruby sniffs like one of my mom's disapproving country club friends. Dismissing me with a rapid roll of her eyeballs, she resumes texting on her phone.

I gape.

Is this what it feels like to have disapproval from your peer group? Like you have bad odor plus horrible middle-aged man breath? By not having any noticeable talent, am I suddenly not worthy in Beijing? The shock is more uncomfortable and uglier than discovering that you contracted head lice from trying on headbands at a high-end department store.

Half an hour later, Mr. Chen drops us off at the back of Jing Yaa Tang, a four-star Chinese restaurant, and a waiter ushers us into a private banquet room. We wait thirty minutes. Then forty. My stomach rumbles with hot, gassy hunger. I haven't eaten in nearly twelve hours. That's practically half a day.

"Is your dad coming?" I ask, listening to the angry tiger growl in my stomach.

No reply.

Ruby is texting furiously on her phone. I wonder if she is dating anyone. Maybe this question will finally get her to warm up to me and tell me her deepest and most meaningful secrets. I'm an excellent listener and relationship-advice provider.

"Who are you texting?" I finally ask when my curiosity gets the better of me.

She doesn't seem to hear me.

"Do you have a boyfriend?" I ask. "Girlfriend? A new crush?"

She glances up, then furrows her brow.

"You're still talking," she comments, then returns to her texting.

"So . . . um . . . when is dinner?" I ask.

I know I'm being annoying with the interrogation-type questions, but I just hate this awkward silence.

I'm not used to being ignored. It's like I'm boring background music—the kind in a hotel elevator that people under the age of twenty-five never care about or listen to. It's a bit rude, really.

I tap her on the shoulder. "Is your dad even coming?"

Ruby looks seriously annoyed. Is this what it's like to be unpopular?

"Is it normal to ask so many questions in America?" she asks, staring at me.

"It's always encouraged," I say. "No question is a waste of time, right?"

I don't know what I'm doing wrong. It's like talking to a busted, unresponsive Siri on my iPhone. Like voice activation hasn't been programmed yet. The dress incident was horrible, and the fact that she disapproves of my professional hobby of mall-hopping is completely disheartening. I am just hoping that first cousins are genetically programmed to forgive and forget. It's in our blood.

"Listen, I'm really sorry about your dress," I say again, trying to apologize. "How can I make it right?"

Awkward, uncomfortable silence.

"My dad is coming," Ruby finally says, sounding a bit defensive. "He's just working."

"What does your dad do?" I ask. I almost say "our," but I catch myself. I wonder if she suspects that we could be sisters. But she shrugs, as if not caring.

I sip the syrupy-tasting jasmine tea and examine my own

broken iPhone, which is sadly beyond repair. I open the menu, but I can't read it. It's all in Chinese, but the photographs look amazing. The filleted black cod on a bed of green shallots and black beans. Shredded potato wedges with crispy pork slices in a steaming, sizzling wok. My stomach rumbles. I'm absolutely starving. I could literally eat the cloth napkins for dinner, so why hasn't a waiter come by to take our order? There must be appetizers in Beijing. What do Chinese breadsticks look like?

Just as I think I'm about to faint from hunger, a pudgy man rushes in, followed by a kind-looking, friendly-faced woman. They look frantic and worried. Behind them, there are three boxy security guards who are amazing at blending into the restaurant's lush floral wallpaper. At first, I don't even notice them. Who exactly is this family? They have more security guards than a Top 40 pop star.

"Weijun!" the man says, looking relieved when he sees me. "Your dad call me many time. We just fly back from late business meeting in Hong Kong. Your dad say you don't call him. We are so worry!"

"Uncle?" I ask. "Auntie?"

The man looks very familiar, even though he looks nothing like my dad. They're supposed to be half brothers, but this man is short and round, exactly like the wealthy dude from the game Monopoly. Despite being bald, he has a fantastic toothbrush mustache that seems very familiar. I stare at his features without fully understanding. As if suddenly waking from a shitty, twenty-four-hour hangover, I realize that I have seen him before. I have literally memorized his face.

I stare closer and gasp.

Number 16.

Number 16 in *Forbes Asia*!

That means *I am* related to an Asian tycoon!!!

I'm practically extended royalty.

I stare at my relative, both shocked and delighted. My uncle smiles broadly. I smile back. Enthusiastically, I embrace both my uncle and auntie, and they timidly hug me back. Actually, they both stiffen and my uncle and aunt pat me on the shoulder, twice. Yikes. Do people not hug in China? Does this side of my family not like physical affection? Was I supposed to offer them a handshake instead? A curtsy? A bow?

What do very rich people do when greeting relatives?

"I am Uncle Dai," my uncle says to break the awkward silence. "This is Auntie Yingfei."

My aunt, who literally looks like Mrs. Claus's kid sister, smiles sweetly at me. "Sorry. I not speak English well."

My instincts have been correct all along. This is the universe's way of rewarding me for all my horrible luck in the past week. Great things usually result from immense suffering.

"Why you don't call Daddy?" my uncle says.

"Oh," I say in a tiny voice. "I broke my phone."

I pull it out and show him the dead screen.

"No problem!" he exclaims. He plucks my broken iPhone from my hand and then tosses it into the tray of a passing waiter who is carrying a pile of dirty dishes. He just chucks my one-year-old iPhone away like it's a used napkin.

I pause, a little shocked.

An iPhone costs a lot of money.

I know I'm generally wasteful, but I'd at least try to exchange it at the Apple Store for a new one. What would my mom and dad say about this waste? Do I tell them that I carelessly dropped it into the toilet, so my uncle threw it away?

Before I can say anything, Uncle Dai hands me an iPhone from his suit pocket. "Keep," he says.

For a moment, I stare at the latest model. It looks practically new.

"Are you sure?" I say, shocked by his wastefulness and his generosity. A brand-new iPhone is at least a thousand dollars.

"Of course! You are my niece and we have many extra international phone."

"Oh," I say. "In that case, then . . ."

Quickly, I set up my new iPhone and log into WeChat. My dad said that iMessage might be spotty in China.

Thirty-five unread texts. Yikes.

WECHAT GROUP (Wang#1Family!!!)

Mom: Iris! We have been so worried! Call us back!

Mom: We are SORRY

Mom: Dad is also SORRY for everything

Mom: IRIS!!!!! Did you land in Beijing? Please respond.

IrisDaddy: Why aren't you picking up!

IrisDaddy: We know we were harsh at the airport, but ignoring us is not the answer.

Mom: Dad checked and the airplane didn't crash. So why aren't you picking up! Please call/text us back!

IrisDaddy: We can talk more about this.

Mom: IRIS THIS IS NOT FUNNY. Be responsible for once in your life!

IrisDaddy: Are you okay?

IrisDaddy: Is everything all right?

IrisDaddy: CALL US BACK.

Mom: IRIS!!!!!!!!!

IrisDaddy: I am calling your uncle if I don't hear back from you in 30 minutes. IRIS!!!!!

"Text your daddy," Uncle Dai says.

I'm okay, I send my dad a quick message. **I just broke my phone. I'm with uncle and aunt and cousin now.**

He responds immediately. **Glad you are okay. Your mom and I are very worried. We thought you got lost!**

I'm fine. We're eating now. Talk later.

To my stomach's gurgling relief, dinner is served quickly. Uncle Dai chats rapidly with the waitstaff, who all seem to know him, and then, within a few minutes, a platter of hot, crispy Peking duck is brought out. I love Peking duck, but we have it only when we're in Queens with my mom's family for fancy Chinese banquets. This dish is literally the best duck I've ever eaten.

"This food is AMAZING," I exclaim, and dump tons of sweet-spicy sauce and green onions into a thin white tortilla, then roll it up. Like I'm eating miniature tacos, I swallow ten of those delicious Chinese tortillas within minutes. I lick my fingers excitedly.

I've honestly never tasted such fresh, crispy, and delicious cuisine in my life.

I have no idea how I've grown up never eating real Chinese food. My mom and dad are excellent cooks, but we eat a fusion of ready-cooked supermarket Chinese, American, Thai, Indian, Italian, and Mexican food. We also eat a lot of takeout and frozen Costco meals.

My uncle and aunt beam at me.

They're looking at me like I'm their long-lost daughter! Their eyes are watering nonstop, but I don't know if it's because the Peking duck is really spicy. It could also be the smog situation outside. What allergy meds is everyone taking?

"You don't know how to use chopsticks?" Ruby asks, staring at me with mild shock. It's almost as if she finds this fact to be more scandalous than me not winning a single award.

"Yeah, of course I do," I say smoothly, and grab a pair of ivory chopsticks, but the Peking duck is small and slippery, especially when slathered in goopy red sauce. I drop my food onto my plate multiple times. More trouble comes when the waiter brings slivers of spicy Sichuan chicken with crunchy snow peas and cashews, pan-fried cod covered in a light crispy batter, scallops the size of gigantic campfire marshmallows, and sautéed pork wrapped in a thin, flaky pastry. All followed by heaping plates of zesty green bean noodles.

And forget about picking up the noodles in a dainty bowl.

The strings keep sliding off my chopsticks.

I've always just eaten Chinese takeout noodles and spaghetti with a fork and Western spoon. I don't know how to properly eat with chopsticks, but I can't exactly ask for a fork now, can I? I glance around, trying to copy my uncle and aunt, who seem to be coordinating food from their bowls to their mouths so well. They can talk, eat, and smile effortlessly! Why did I tell everyone that I know how to use the utensils of my cultural birthright?

In Bradley Gardens, I never needed or wanted to learn how to eat with chopsticks. I laughed whenever my mom and dad tried to teach me. Nervously I wonder if I can google *how to use chopsticks* under the table when no one is looking.

Suddenly, it feels like I've signed up for a dance recital and I don't know the steps. Sweat slides down my back like a waterfall. Even my hands feel like I've slathered them with Vaseline. I just don't know which finger wraps around which stick or how to balance two chopsticks with one hand. But I'm determined to prove that I can learn the choreography or at least improvise. Is eating with chopsticks like tweezing facial hair?

What would my new family say when I explained to them that I needed a fork and spoon?

"Do you want order different food?" Uncle Dai says, looking at me with concern.

"It is fantastic!" I say, and even Auntie Yingfei looks anxious, but begins scooping more scallops and green bean noodles into my bowl.

Quickly, I attempt to use my chopsticks by gripping them like a tube of lip gloss. As a clump of crispy, sauce-laden noodles plops onto the white tablecloth, Ruby snickers. "Good job," she says softly.

No one seems to hear her.

My cheeks burn, and the muscles in my neck seize up.

Fed up, I pick up my bowl and cram as many noodles as I can into my mouth. I'm too hungry to care about bad manners. The best I can do is to anxiously shovel and slide the noodles into my alligator-wide mouth by tipping my bowl. But I'm too enthusiastic and half the noodles fall from my mouth into my lap.

Shit.

I try to smile to cover up my awkward embarrassment. This has never in all my seventeen years happened to me before. How are my table manners suddenly equivalent to a five-month-old Labrador? What's wrong with me?!!

By now, Ruby is gaping at me like I'm a human-size cockroach.

I try my best to grab the fallen noodles with a cloth napkin. But embarrassment continues to tunnel through me like a $5.99 McDonald's Big Mac Meal with large fries and a Coke. My newfound uncle, aunt, and cousin are watching me like I'm some sort of trashy reality television show. Uncle Dai has an amused expression on his face.

"Are you even Chinese?" Ruby asks, looking genuinely baffled. Uncle Dai shushes her.

But she's right. What kind of Chinese person am I? In New Jersey, I never even made an effort to learn. It never seemed to matter. In Beijing, I can't even eat my dinner properly and prove that I belong to this family. Ruby's question about who I am is even more humiliating than growing thick Tiger whiskers on my very first date with Peter. It's more embarrassing than when we slow-danced at an outdoor concert, and when he squeezed me like a tube of half-empty toothpaste, I accidentally farted. Luckily, Peter laughed at my jalapeño-faced embarrassment and still made out with me, but no one is smiling now.

Why is everything so incredibly hard in Beijing?

Why are group dinners painfully difficult?

And why aren't utensils universal?

If we all ate with our fingers like back in Neanderthal days, I swear we'd eliminate at least 60 percent of all our cultural problems. The United Nations would have a much easier time dealing with misunderstandings, and history might have fewer world wars. AP World History would even have far fewer dates to remember.

Is this why my parents have always tried to encourage me to be more Chinese? To avoid future embarrassments when meeting other Chinese people who didn't live in North America?

Luckily, before I can spill even more food, a waiter brings out a bottle of Dom Pérignon. I've only had champagne once, when it was Samira's sixteenth birthday and her parents let us have a tiny sip. Instantly, I cheer up.

Uncle Dai instructs the waiter to pour us all a full glass. I'm shocked.

"Drink, Weijun, drink!" he says, smiling proudly.

"Great!" I say, forgetting about the noodles.

I take a sip and it's sweet and bubbly and as delicious as I remember it. It's like inhaling helium. It's like getting high with your friends before a super-fun party . . . no, I can't think about Samira and Peter now.

I down my glass in a gulp, and Auntie Yingfei pours me another one. I swallow that one quickly too.

"Happy family," Uncle Dai says, raising his glass. He beams cheerfully and so does my aunt. We clink glasses, and I'm truly speechless and a little intoxicated but also moved by this warm welcome.

"Happy family!" I enthuse.

The only person who isn't paying attention is Ruby, who is furiously checking her phone and ignoring everyone.

I peek over her shoulder, but the texts are in Chinese. I'm so curious! I wonder if I took a photo and ran it through Google Translate, would I be able to understand the gist of it?

"You're not drinking?" I ask her, and Ruby shrugs and resumes texting like it's a global emergency. What could possibly be happening in her world? Is that why my mom is always complaining when I text at the dinner table? I'm physically there but not really present.

Honestly, it feels so strange to be excluded. Even if I don't know what exactly I'm missing out on.

Wanting my new family to like if not love me, I grin excitedly and swig down another glass down in less than twenty seconds. Ruby is so strange. Doesn't she care about downing a delicious glass of bubbly? After all, it's not every day that you get to drink champagne while meeting missing family.

"I'm so incredibly happy!" I gush to Uncle Dai and Auntie Yingfei, who nod and beam back. Uncle Dai starts crying full-on, and I start tearing up too.

After a dessert of warm coconut jellies and chewy tapioca pearls in a cold, clear soup, Uncle Dai calls for the check. Then, as we head out the private back entrance, a photographer snaps a photo. Another person follows suit. Someone rushes up to Uncle Dai and asks him questions, but then the restaurant's manager steps in. Uncle Dai's three security guards quickly usher us away.

Who is my uncle, really?

Why are people taking photos of him exiting the restaurant? I want to pose for an impromptu photo shoot, but I have no time. Mr. Chen has pulled up and we're all piling into the backseat of the car and we're speeding back to the Shangri-La. The security guards are following us in three separate vehicles.

As we drive through the downtown district, I can't help but grin at the bright, smoggy city. I keep pinching myself to make sure I'm not hallucinating.

It's a billion times better than what I had imagined prom night to be.

"You have good time in Beijing, okay?" my uncle says. "You make Ruby good at English, okay?"

"Yes, yes, of course," I babble, not fully listening.

"Most important I want Ruby to have big sister," he says. "I don't have brother growing up and I wish I had. You only understand how important family is when you are older. When lawyer tell me that my brother want to be family, I was very happy. So Weijun, we are all so happy you are here."

"Uncle very happy he cry," Auntie Yingfei says, smiling. "He more happy when he hear he has niece."

I nod, tearing up despite myself.

Looking serious, Uncle Dai reaches into his wallet and hands me a black prepaid Visa card. Ruby scowls and mutters something in Chinese. Auntie Yingfei quickly shushes her, glancing at me furtively.

I ignore the deep flush rushing across my cheeks.

"She can't understand Chinese," Ruby says in English, and pouting, she crosses her arms across her chest.

Uncle Dai says something scolding to Ruby. Then he and Auntie Yingfei smile apologetically at me.

"She just grumpy," he says, smiling widely.

"She broke my dress for my dog show," she says, scowling.

"Weijun just make easy mistake," Uncle Dai says, sighing. "Beside, you have one hundred dress. If you have ninety-nine, no different."

"I have one hundred and six," Ruby says.

"I'm so sorry, Ruby," I say. "It was an accident."

I genuinely mean it.

"Weijun already apologize," Uncle Dai insists. "No more talk of dress now. It is very silly to cut dog hair. Why don't you practice violin for big concert?"

"She broke it," Ruby hisses.

"Iris is your cousin," Uncle Dai says again. "In America, economy is bad and maybe they have shortage of nice dress."

He looks at me expectantly.

"Um . . . yes," I say, thinking of my own wrecked Vera Wang gown. "It's very possible there is a dress shortage. For instance, I only have one nice dress."

"See!" Uncle Dai says, nodding at Ruby, who glowers at me. She mutters something in Chinese at her dad, which actually sounds like a small lizard hissing. He shushes her again. Auntie Yingfei lightly pinches her arm and whispers back something in Chinese.

"Be friend with cousin," Uncle Dai scolds her while checking his phone. "I found you sister, Ruby. You can help each other better. That is what family do. We always help each other."

Ruby gives me the stink eye.

It's worse than my mom's.

My stomach feels heavy, and it's not from eating third and fifth and seventh helpings of all the amazing, melt-in-your-mouth Beijing food. It's not the champagne that is giving me a slight migraine. It's Ruby's disdain and her constant eye-rolling that makes me uncomfortable. Older sister? I'm an only child. I always thank my parents that they didn't give me the additional burden of a younger person to shape and inspire.

"We were given you, and then we decided that we couldn't handle more," my mom said when I asked her why she didn't have a second kid.

"You're just too exciting for a first baby," my dad said.

I stare out the window to avoid eye contact with my smiling aunt and uncle, and scowling cousin, focusing on the few glass skyscrapers and the sprawling concrete buildings. They remind me of the gray LEGO spaceship structures that Peter kept as models in his room. I tell myself a hundred times that I'm not in a prison.

As we drive, I decide to distract myself with this amazing gift of a prepaid Visa card. I wonder how much money is on it. Is there a special Chinese etiquette for spending your relations' money? Are you supposed to spend 60 percent on yourself and 40 percent on presents? And is there a limit at all, if your uncle is super China-rich?

Feeling homesick, despite being still furious and hurt at my parents, I decide to send them a quick message. It can't hurt to check in, right?

WECHAT GROUP (#1WangFamily!!!)

Iris: If Uncle D gives me money, is it okay to spend it?

Mom: How much money?

IrisDaddy: Thank him and give it back.

Mom: Are we talking like 20 bucks or 200?

Iris: I don't know.

Mom: What do you mean you don't know?

IrisDaddy: They could be very poor and might just be giving you money to save face. Make sure you give it back.

Iris: They're not poor.

IrisDaddy: Your uncle never brought up money in our conversations, which means that money could be an issue for them. You should thank him nicely and give it all back. Besides, we gave you the equivalent of $6,000 US for the whole summer. I'll wire your uncle some money later for food and housing. How much do you have left??

Belonging

Even though Ruby and I both say NO, Uncle Dai insists that I take Ruby's gorgeous store-display bedroom.

"Where will Ruby sleep?" I say, worried that we'd have to share a room. What if we have to share a bed? Shouldn't this penthouse suite have a guest bedroom? I'll happily take the couch in the living room if it means not sharing with someone who hates me more than I detest Algebra II.

I'm honestly disappointed that Ruby seems to have graduated from strongly disliking me to showing me open disdain. It stings that she thinks I'm such an international loser. Is this how an adored Bernese mountain puppy feels when she grows up and her family no longer lets her sleep on their stomachs anymore?

"I'm not sleeping in the maid's room!" Ruby says. "Iris is a spoiled American. Make her do it. She has never even had a real job."

"She is guest, Ruby!" Uncle Dai admonishes her. He looks

flustered, as if embarrassed by his daughter's outburst. He smiles at me apologetically.

They argue heatedly in Chinese for a while.

Spoiled? What on earth is Ruby talking about? She lives at the Shangri-La and has a personal driver! The nicest hotel that I've ever stayed at is the Marriott Suites in Miami with my parents, who had a corporate discount through my mom's company.

The thought of sleeping in the maid's quarters causes Ruby to turn the same color as the expensive washed-out wallpaper. She looks scandalized.

"I can sleep in the maid's room," I offer quickly. "It's totally fine. I don't mind. Besides, this is Ruby's room."

My cousin nods, agreeing emphatically with me.

She points at me like I'm a ginormous insect.

Feeling flustered but also annoyed, I roll my eyes.

She rolls hers in reply.

I feel like we could bond over our synchronized eye-rolling, but my cousin doesn't seem to have a sense of humor.

And here I thought that humor was supposed to be inherited. Not something that people agree on.

My dad and I frequently laugh like hyperactive monkeys at the same jokes; even my mom can giggle with me.

What's wrong with Ruby?

Then an anxious thought slithers across my mind. "Where will I sleep?" I ask, concerned.

"No maid," Uncle Dai replies. "We have many hotel staff already. Twenty-four-hour desk help. I promise your daddy I take care of you, Weijun." Then he adds, sounding slightly anxious, "Do you need maid? We can get one for you."

"No," I say quickly, feeling shell-shocked.

"You want to bring from America?"

"Twenty-four-hour desk help is enough."

Despite our protesting, my uncle insists that Ruby move to the empty maid's room, which is a medium-size room with its own marble bathroom and decent-size porcelain tub. It's as immaculate and fairy-tale-like as the rest of the luxury rooms in the penthouse. Just smaller. Shocked, I don't understand what my cousin is complaining about. I'd be perfectly happy here.

When Uncle Dai and Auntie Yingfei say good night and go to the master bedroom, I help Ruby move her clothes into the smaller room, while she mutters nonstop under her breath. I have no idea what she's saying, but it all seems very angry and directed at me. Like she's passive-aggressively silent-tweeting me.

"I'm sorry for everything," I say.

I am genuinely sorry, but Ruby doesn't seem to care.

I read in the autumn issue of *Cosmopolitan* that you're supposed to communicate sorry-ness with your eyes by widening your pupils and making sure that your arms aren't folded across your chest, to convey authentic intentions. You're also supposed to show people your palms. I make sure to open my eyes as wide as possible and roll my shoulders backward like a baby gorilla. Then I show Ruby the backs of my unmoisturized hands.

"What's wrong with you?" Ruby asks. Then she slams the door, causing me to jump and blink. I hear her mutter insults in Chinese and English as I turn to leave. "Horrible . . . spoiled . . . *ChineseChineseChinese* . . . spoiled brat!"

"I'm sorry!" I shout again through the door. I have no idea what to do.

"Spoiled American!" she yells back. "What was my dad thinking, letting you live here?"

"Listen, I'm really sorry," I say again, but Ruby doesn't respond.

I glance anxiously at the closed door. Why does she blame me for being American? I have never felt so confused about someone not liking or at least tolerating me before. How do I make Ruby understand that I'm not a supremely shitty person? I'm sure really amazing, well-meaning people, like Ellen DeGeneres and Lady Gaga, made one or two medium-size mistakes when they were teenagers too. Anxiously I try to knock on her door again. If I knew Morse code, maybe it would make it easier to apologize.

No response.

Finally, I retreat to Ruby's bedroom, determined to show my cousin during the next twenty-four hours that I'm a fabulous and extra-generous person.

After passing out facedown with my clothes still on the next morning, I find a basketful of flaky doughnut sticks and sweetened soy milk, shrimp wontons, bean juice, gloopy wheat porridge, and breadlike buns stuffed with pork and veggies laid out on the kitchen counter. There's also strong-brew coffee and sliced tropical fruit. My whole head, unfortunately, is slightly throbbing, but I tell myself that I'm just not used to being spoiled with rich-people food and drink.

I wonder if everyone left the apartment already. I dump four packets of sugar into a mug of hot, delicious coffee and begin stuffing my face. It's like I'm at a Cinnabon buffet at the mall and can't stop myself. I shove an entire bun in my mouth and feel light-headed. Everything is freshly made and intensely delicious-smelling.

"Why are you late?" a voice asks, in a disbelieving way.

I look up, my cheeks full of soft, juicy chicken. It's Ruby again, dressed in the same identical pajama-looking jumpsuit, but it's a slightly different color than yesterday. Pale yellow like rotten milk. Yesterday I thought her couture suit looked like expensive poultry, but today I think she looks like an unripe banana. Is this a costume in our family? Do I get one too?

"Are we going somewhere?" I say, confused.

I thought my cousin was still angry at me, but we're hanging out? Did Uncle Dai plan a family outing that I forgot about?

She ignores me as she texts nonstop on her phone.

When I continue eating, she looks at me with an incredulous expression. "Let's go?"

"Where are we going?" I ask.

No answer.

I tap her on the shoulder. It's like touching furniture. She doesn't even move. Is my cousin a store mannequin?

"Where are we going?" I ask again.

"Store," she says without looking up. "Time to go."

Sighing, I grab a couple of savory pork buns in a cloth napkin and follow her out the door. Never mind that I'm still wearing the same clothes from lat night's dinner. Groaning, I sniff myself. *Eau de* leftover stir-fry noodles with an undertone of spicy Peking duck. Not bad for an American-Born Chinese (ABC) in high-society China.

Mr. Chen drops us off at the Oriental Plaza, and immediately I feel myself tense with adrenaline. I'm so excited to use this beautiful piece of plastic from Uncle Dai! But then I remember what my parents said about returning it.

But my problem has always been that I just want to accumulate as many items as possible. It's like a weird itch in your armpit that you shouldn't scratch in public but you always do. Also, I don't know what they sell in China's malls, but I do know that everything is made in this country and then shipped to America. This could possibly be the most thrilling discovery of my shopping career. China is like the flagship store of the United States.

I follow Ruby, who is still text-walking on her phone, and then as if by magic, a gaggle of three chauffeured girls are dropped off individually. Are these her friends? They all look like identical chickens with matching dyed hair and gold Fendi purses and five-inch platform sneakers. If I want to fit in, do I need to buy a uniform too?

I try to introduce myself, but none of the girls acknowledge me. In fact, they look at me for a brief, revolted second, then resume their animated conversation. Has Ruby told them that I'm her non-Chinese-speaking cousin with zero awards and zero talents? Are these her champion-doggy-pageant friends? By now, I'm almost getting used to being ignored and belittled. I sigh and follow them to the mall's ultra-modern entrance. There are so many people rushing around—it's like Black Friday at Nordstrom.

Inside the mall, I realize that I'm in the motherland of high-end fashion.

I can feel all my senses light up, like I've developed ESP. Each nerve is electric, and I feel this wonderful, warm tingle running from my head to my toes. Then it occurs to me it's because I have to pee, so I shout at Ruby that I need to use the bathroom. Of course she doesn't hear me, but I can't wait. I rush toward the yellow toilet signs, like I'm winning a year-end sales race.

After I hand the man a wad of *yuan* to use the toilet, I squeeze into the tiny bathroom stall and at first, I think there's something wrong with the bathroom because it's missing a toilet. I rub my eyes hard and then I see that it's located on the ground and I don't know how to use it. I wish I could ask someone how to use the toilet. Isn't there an instructional video around?

Wincing, I decide that I really need to pee anyway, so I pull down my pants and it's honestly an awful mess. Wrapping my gray cardigan around my waist, I slowly panic. My vision gets blurry and I wonder if I should try to call Mr. Chen for a ride home. I feel like I'm seven years old again when I wet the bed at Samira's sleepover and I was so embarrassed that I covered it up with a fur rug and never told anyone.

Leaving the bathroom and slinking self-consciously through the mall, I'm thrilled when I see Esprit. I rush inside and quickly find myself a new pair of underwear and jeans. I end up buying several pairs of ripped jeans because the shop people are so enthusiastic that I cannot bear to leave without buying five. After I make the first purchase, it's like something flips off inside my brain and my metaphorical underarm itch returns with intensity. I just can't help myself. A voice in the back of my head keeps saying, *Enough, Iris, enough,* but I ignore it. It's like a strict Asian mom saying that you can't have the third slice of greasy pepperoni pizza or smoke that fifth joint. It's the same nagging, scolding voice-over that told me to study for the SATs, and not to party the night before the exam. *Oh shut up*, I tell my conscience.

When I see a salon, all self-control dissolves. I decide that I must have a seaweed facial, a full-body massage, and a new sparkly leprechaun-green gel manicure and pedicure. Never mind that Ruby has ditched me on my first full day in a foreign country. Who cares if I'm lost?

Somehow I manage to convince myself that my parents have sent me to Beijing to enjoy the finer privileges in life.

It hits me later on that I've spent quite a bit of money at the mall, in total, and bought a lot of really nice leather handbags and shoes. I stopped counting after the twentieth time the cashier swiped the prepaid Visa card. Guilt-ridden, I plop down on a bench to think. The horrible sick feeling crashes down on me again, and I feel as if I'm on the tiniest plane plummeting to the ground. Actually, I don't really need four pink purses, do I? But I guess I can give one to my mom, and the rest save as presents, whenever someone has a birthday, so I don't have to continue shopping. I'm actually being economical and saving a lot of time by thinking ahead. Maybe I should have kept the money for emergencies or travel, but I can't think about that now.

More quicksand feelings of shame engulf me. My parents will seriously scream at me over video chat. Will Uncle Dai be upset with the amount?! Will he and my dad gang up on me? He didn't explicitly give me a number, but what if he was just being polite? It also doesn't help that all the shopkeepers are so enthusiastic and friendly, offering me piles and piles of clothes. They're like cute designer dogs offering me their favorite toys. How can I possibly say no to anyone who looks so happy to see me?

When I'm tired from thinking, I buy a strawberry bubble tea at the food court, and the lady at the stand pours a delicious cream cheese froth on top of it, which tastes like I'm actually drinking an entire cheesecake that has been put into a blender. To stop spending more money, I decide to wander outside the mall, and then I see a street vendor who also looks so thrilled to see me. Of course I just have to buy a plate of steamed dumplings, *xiāo long bao*, which are fat and juicy and squirt hot broth when I bite into them. They're like little doughy firecrackers! The food is so Food Network–good that I order another bamboo tray and sit on the sidewalk, slurping and eating. I don't care if anyone sees me, since I don't know anyone here. I also don't know where Mr. Chen is, but it doesn't matter because today has been one of the better days of my life. In fact, it's been such a wonderful day, I buy another six *xiāo long bao* from the vendor, who grins at me. I can't help but grin back.

I'm so stuffed from steamed dumplings that I seriously need a nap.

That's when I see it: a billboard over the Oriental Plaza. It's a giant photo of my uncle, who is looking down over the entire boulevard. He's grinning like he's won the lottery. Like he's a ginormous Rich Uncle Pennybags in a game of real-life Monopoly. Underneath the Chinese lettering of the board, I see the English title: FENG CONSTRUCTION CORP. Does my uncle own this mall?!

I have so many questions. Like how many luxury malls and properties he owns. And if he is actually my biological father.

I decide to hail a taxi, but the driver, a middle-aged man in a baseball cap, doesn't speak a lot of English.

"What wrong with you?" he demands. "Why you not speak?"

"I'm American," I say, irritated. Normally, I would be polite and explain that I'm from Bradley Gardens, New Jersey, but I'm honestly a bit cranky from always having to justify why I don't fit in. Since I arrived in Beijing, I'm tired of explaining why my outsides don't match my insides. It's like asking a doughnut why it doesn't have jelly filling.

"But you look Chinese," he argues. "Why you not speak?"

"American Chinese," I say, hoping that he'll stop interrogating me about who I am. How is the concept of being born Chinese in a different country so foreign to Beijingers? Just because a Skittle is a teensy bit misshapen doesn't mean that it isn't still a Skittle. If I can't be an exciting fusion dish, a bubbly and bold blend of two countries, where do I belong? I mean, why do I have to be only Chinese or American? Can't I just be delicious, MSG-infused chop suey?

Sighing with annoyance, I show him the photo of the Shangri-La on my phone, and he nods, like he knows where the hotel is. But we drive in a full circle for forty-five minutes, and he seems to be hopelessly lost. We seem like we're heading in the wrong direction. Office towers, concrete buildings, highways, and steel factories pass by.

Finally, he stops the car at an abandoned street full of old, deserted traditional Chinese houses. There's no one here. I panic momentarily. I've seen *CSI* and *Law & Order* before, and I know when something horrible is about to happen. You never want to be the girl alone with a stalled cab. The character always ends up on the nightly news, whether or not they find her body.

"You pay me six thousand *yuan* or you get out," he says, turning to me.

Is he kidding?

The cab driver scowls.

Would this even happen if I spoke a minimal amount of Chinese?

I'm scandalized but relieved that he's not going to kill me (at least, not yet, anyway).

I won't pay a scammer 6,000 *yuan*, so quickly, I hop out of the taxi and start running back to the main road. Pant-jogging, I have no sense of where I'm going, but I continue in one direction. To my relief, he doesn't chase me with the car. I hide behind a dumpster in an alleyway to make sure that no one is following me. For an hour, miserable and blurry-eyed, I wander around until I somehow find myself at Xidan Commercial Street market. Around me, there are crowds and stalls of colorful clothing, socks, and cheap electronics in plastic bins.

Stress-panting like a Doberman on the way to the vet, I'm eventually able to speak to a small shop owner of funky-smelling herbal medicine, and she helps me flag down another cab and negotiate a fee of 87 *yuan* to the hotel. Never mind that the shopkeeper charges me an additional 35 *yuan* for her help.

Then I realize that I've forgotten all my purchases in the taxi's backseat. I've never lost a whole day's purchases before, and I've used up nearly half of my dad's envelope of cash on travel and customer service.

I want to cry from such a horrible ordeal. What would my dad say if I told him that Beijing is ridiculously expensive and I had to spend all his money on emergency assistance? Would he blame me if I told him that I got scammed by a taxi driver?

When I finally get to the penthouse, sweaty and panting, I discover that my suitcase is missing. All my clothing, makeup, underwear, and my toothbrush are gone! This can't be happening. I look everywhere for my belongings. I check the entire penthouse suite.

Maybe housekeeping accidentally took my bag away and stored it in a closet.

Maybe I'm in the wrong suite.

But when I go into my en suite bathroom (not a squat toilet, thank god!), I see a note on a piece of paper: *GO BACK TO AMERICA. NO ONE WANTS YOU HERE!*

Ruby. I sigh with anger. *So passive-aggressive, right?*

After my shitty day, her note makes me feel almost as horrible as a monthlong stomach ulcer. Furious tears begin splashing down my face, and I do my best to wipe them, but they keep monsoon-raining from my eyeballs. I don't know how to stop crying from the hurt and frustration. Nothing I do in Beijing is working.

I know I did a supremely shitty thing—trying on Ruby's clothes was rude, and then I also made her doggy-pageant gown unwearable. I ruined an expensive dress by not thinking and being completely disrespectful.

But how do I show her that I'm genuinely sorry?

Nothing in my social skill set from America is working.

I can't possibly replace her dress, and even if I could, I am not sure how we could start over. How do you show someone that you are generally well-meaning and harmless? I'm practically a cute mosquito, not a termite.

And that's when I see it: all my clothes strewn in the bathtub full of water. And the presents that I haven't yet given to my uncle, aunt, and cousin thrown inside too. My cheeks become wasabi-hot. My throat constricts, like I'm choking on a sticky candy wrapper. When I bend closer and grab a few items, I realize that the scarf that I got for her had been cut into threads.

Even my favorite Victoria's Secret bras have been snipped in half right through the center strap! What am I supposed to do? Walk around covering just half my chest?

Then I find one of my Converse sneakers, half-drowned, in the toilet.

Ruby did a very thorough job.

My eyes water for real this time. I hyperventilate. Anger bursts through me. How dare she wreck my things? Ditching me, ignoring me, and then shredding my clothes?

With hot, horrible shame, I realize that she's not just blaming me for wrecking her beautiful gown. She wants me to go home. It's her form of petty revenge, yes, but it's more than that. These were my belongings. All the things that I brought with me from home. Anything to make me leave her penthouse apartment.

Suddenly, New Jersey feels very far away.

I unplug the bathtub. It gurgles, but then it gets stuck. I try again. It gets stuck. I can't even unplug a bathtub in China. I start sobbing again and sound strangely like the gurgling drain.

Why don't I fit in yet?

Why does being born in a different country, in a strange culture, make me such a weirdo?

And why does it make the simplest things across the world so difficult?

Being American Chinese in China is like accidentally showing up in old gym clothes to a black-tie wedding. It's realizing that you have no clue about *where* you belong or *who* you belong to.

I'm interrupted from my erupting frustration when the phone from Uncle Dai rings. Even my iPhone, my old self, has been erased. I don't even recognize the tone, but I pick it up anyway. Who would be calling me in Beijing?

"Weijun!!!" my uncle says, sounding relieved. "Mr. Chen say you and Ruby are not at store. Where you?"

I pause.

"I'm totally fine," I say, hoping that he doesn't hear how upset I am. "I just got back to the hotel."

"You are home?" he says, sounding a bit incredulous but also relieved. "Ruby with you?"

"I'm here, but Ruby isn't."

"Okay, please stay in hotel until Mr. Chen back."

He hangs up the phone. I wonder what to do with this humongous mess. None of my clothes are salvageable unless I want to sew together a giant soggy past-life Iris quilt.

I start raiding Ruby's closet.

Normally, I would never dare aggravate someone who is already so upset with me. As an only child, I've never fought a family member my age before. Even Samira and I, while growing up, have never had a horrible fight, only minor petty disagreements about crushes and clothing styles. I once spilled soy sauce on her white cotton knit sweater, and she once lost my favorite polka-dotted Kate Spade bag when I asked her to hold it for me while I went to the bathroom at Pinkberry. For twenty minutes, I was angry, and then I instantly forgave her. My mom was fifty times more angry than me. "I bought you that bag for Christmas!" she shouted. "Iris, how can you be so irresponsible? It cost two hundred fifty dollars on sale."

But I don't care anymore.

I am so furious that I almost don't care anymore if Ruby will ever like me.

Angrily, I respond to my parents' texts as I haphazardly throw piles of beautiful designer clothes on the bed, sorting them into outfits that I could possibly wear. Then I feel super, super guilty and put all the clothing items back on their hangers and in plastic bags and fold them neatly in the drawers and pray that Ruby will think that the maids moved her stuff. It takes me at least two hours to tidy up.

I don't belong in Beijing.

I just want to go to my boring, familiar home in New Jersey.

WECHAT GROUP (#1WangFamily!!!)

Mom: How is Beijing?

IrisDaddy: How is everyone? Are you getting along with your cousin?

Iris: Fine . . .

IrisDaddy: Uncle D is taking care of you? You give him back the money, okay?

Iris: Uncle D is a fricking billionaire.

Mom: What are you talking about?

Iris: He's super rich. Like movie star rich.

Mom: Huh?

Iris: Like crazy, crazy Asian rich. They're CRAs (CRAZY RICH ASIANS)!!!

IrisDaddy: How do you know???

Iris: He lives at the Shangri-La. The hotel . . .

Mom: That's probably why he just sent a message about not wanting any money for Iris's expenses.

IrisDaddy: Tell him that we cannot accept. Give the money back.

Iris: I spent most of it already . . .

IrisDaddy: Okay, I'll call him and pay him back. How much did you spend?

Iris: Don't know.

Mom: ?

Iris: A cab driver scammed me and I lost all my things.

Mom: WHAT?!! Did no one teach you about strangers?

IrisDaddy: Are you okay??

Iris: Fine . . .

15

Job Interview

Deciding that I need to relax ASAP, I find a fluffy neon-pink Hello Kitty house robe and matching bedroom slippers in the bathroom. There's a mouse-colored clay horsehair face mask in the cabinet, so I smear it on my skin and wait for it to settle.

The air is suffocating in Beijing, and I need all the help I can get for my clogged-up pores.

I find a notepad that belongs to the hotel. Despite being furious earlier, I don't want to make a permanent enemy of someone who lives with me. It's not in my easygoing, fun-loving nature. Because what if I never make a friend again?

Does everyone hate me?

I don't know how to backtrack to Day 1 in Beijing and not touch Ruby's dress. If I had sat there in the living room and pretended to be furniture, I wouldn't be in the mess that I'm in now. It's my nonsensical lack of control that has led to all of my current apocalyptic life disasters. How can I stop stuffing down the fifth scoop of double-fudge gelato when I'm ridiculously full? How do I stop myself from becoming a popping champagne bottle of nervous energy and making really shitty, regrettable decisions?

I tell myself—if I can befriend Ruby, I can befriend anyone, and I'm not, after all, a social pariah.

I'm sooo sorry about your dress. Can we please talk?

xoxo.

Iris

Sighing, I slip the note under Ruby's door in the guest bedroom. I don't know if she'll respond, but it's worth a try. I don't know how to remedy this situation of a botched-up, unwearable dress. How can I make this better?

With Samira or Peter, it would be one ounce of sorry-weed, a gallon of Rocky Road ice cream with marshmallows, or even a sixteen-inch vegetarian pizza with extra cheese—but how do teenagers in China show remorse? Is this a cultural faux pas dropping a note under someone's door? Apparently, I'm just not Chinese enough. How can I be both eccentric and trophy-winning to gain Ruby's approval? In Beijing, being below average is not in vogue.

Flopping on the couch in the living room, feeling miserable, I try to watch TV, but all the channels are in Chinese. I finally settle on the Shopping Channel because at least I can look at the models wearing tons of purple jade jewelry and holding leather handbags like survival kits.

Thank god Shopping is a universal language, something I at least understand.

Normally, watching a clothing catalog would soothe me, but there's a funny, deeply unsettling feeling inside me, which I attribute first to homesickness and second to culture shock. I just don't understand how Ruby could hate me, especially when we are related. I have never had a sister before, let alone a cousin. Why won't Ruby accept my sincere apology? How long do people in China hold grudges for? What's the proper etiquette?

Even though my aunt and uncle are kind and everyone looks exactly like me, I don't fit in. Beijing is just like watching the Shopping Channel; you can touch the beautiful sale items on the television screen, but you are separated by four inches of glass and colored pixels.

I stare at the flashing images on the big-screen TV: sandals, a silver crystal-studded watch, an orange infinity scarf, dangling beaded hippie bracelets. I know that this could be an opportunity for self-betterment, but I honestly don't know how to start. I have no idea what to do with myself when left alone. I try a search engine: *how to make friends in China*, but there's nothing helpful.

But that's when I see it: a model holding a bright new red handbag to make me feel better about myself. It's only 20,000 *yuan*, and it could replace all the ones that I lost in the taxi. I could buy one for my mom, my aunt, and even Ruby.

With a sharp spasm of relief, I'm just incredibly glad that I put her belongings back in her Doggy-Pageant Closet ASAP. On the screen, I can feel the shiny bags calling to me. Gifts are tokens of friendship, and isn't fire-hazard red supposed to be a lucky color?

What if I offer to help Ruby with her professional hobby? Maybe she needs an assistant? I know nothing about dog grooming, but how hard can it be to wash and cut hair?

The telephone number keeps flashing across the screen like a benevolent call-alert reminder.

The narrator is reading out the numbers in Chinese.

What is the purpose of having a Visa card and not using it? Then I remember that the card is not actually mine. But the voice nagging me is saying that at least I'm being an asset to China's expanding economy. How can I not want to participate when the TV seems to be calling specifically to me?

Just as I begin to dial the shopping phone number, the telephone in the penthouse rings a few times. Then Uncle Dai's phone buzzes. I ignore it. The phone rings again. It seems incredibly urgent. Luckily, my no-self-control itch is interrupted when I finally decide to pick up.

"This is the front desk," a woman says in lightly accented English. "Miss Wang, you are needed in the conference room on the third floor immediately. Everyone is waiting."

"I don't understand," I say. "Who's waiting?"

"Please hurry," she says.

Sighing, I rush outside the apartment and head to the elevator.

In the open-window conference room, there are exactly ten young people dressed in boring black suits and clutching briefcases and what look to be fat résumés. Panting and pacing like nervous hamsters in a cage, they appear to be college students who are applying for a first-time internship at a bank. One of them freezes when he sees me. Another one stares with zero embarrassment. A girl with thick glasses frowns at me. Then the entire group pauses; someone, pop-eyed, quickly looks down at the floor. What's wrong now? Do I have food stains like chicken pox on my face? Is there lunchtime dumpling meat stuck between my teeth?

I smile awkwardly. Then I hear someone laughing; there's a dude, relaxing on one of the fancy conference room sofas. Everyone else is standing except for him. I would have missed him, since unlike the others, he's wearing a navy-blue grandpa-cardigan, the same color as the couch upholstery. While everyone else appears nervous, he looks comfortable and supremely confident in a quiet way. He has one arm draped casually around the back of the couch, a folder on his lap.

Upon closer inspection, the dude has a broad, distinctive face, unbelievably high cheekbones as if he's wearing highlighter, and the most sculpted nose that I have ever seen. I can't stop staring. It looks like he should be auditioning for a reality television show instead of a corporate job. He's movie-star handsome! He catches my eye again and tries to suppress his amusement. Confused, I stare at him. Why is he laughing at me?

Before I can say anything else, Uncle Dai rushes into the room and beelines over to me, beaming.

"You sleeping, huh, Weijun?" he asks. "That is why no one pick up the phone?"

"Huh?" I say, confused.

"You taking nap? The jet lag?" he asks.

"No," I say, astonished.

He gestures at my outfit. Then, with a shock of embarrassment, I realize that I'm still wearing a fluffy pink house robe and Hello Kitty slippers. And I'm not wearing anything underneath!

I still have my clay face mask on! I forgot to get changed. I forgot to wash off my face. Luckily, the robe is large and long and thick enough to cover me. I flush deeply, but no one can see my inflamed face under the concrete superhero mask of horsehair.

Is this a group job interview?

Are these all of Uncle Dai's aspiring interns?

Do they all want to be like him in some capacity? This must be some sort of board meeting, and I have been accidentally summoned to participate. Before I can ask to be excused to go back to the suite to change, he indicates the conference table.

"Interview now," he says.

"For what?" I say. "Am I being considered for a job?"

He bursts out laughing. "Helper for you," he says.

I'm even more confused.

Everyone quickly takes a seat around the conference table, and it slowly becomes apparent that Uncle Dai is hiring someone. A thick stack of résumés and folders is in front of him.

"This is my niece, Wang Weijun. All the way from America. She need the help."

The group of students politely applaud.

Uncle Dai whispers at me, "Chinese business manner. You have to clap back."

Awkwardly, I clap and smile at them.

"Louder," Uncle Dai says.

I clap a few more times, like I'm a teacher trying to get a kindergarten class's attention.

As if we're playing some kind of game of Uncle Dai Says, they all applaud again. But this time, the clapping is much louder, as if I'm a prima ballerina or even a dancing bear performing at the circus and this is my final encore.

I'm slightly flabbergasted.

No one has ever clapped for me before. Is this applause because I am Uncle Dai's niece? Am I going to be given a personal assistant/shopper/servant? I sit up instantly, almost forgetting that I'm in a neon-pink housecoat and I have clay and horsehair smudged all over my face like toothpaste. I have always known that I was worthy of someone to fetch me low-fat lattes and answer my emails.

He points at the first person on the right of him, a nervous-looking boy with a sweating problem. "Zhao-Ru," Uncle Dai barks. "You are number six in class from Fudan University. What can you teach Wang Weijun?"

The boy nods. He jumps out of his chair, knocking it over as he attempts to bow awkwardly. "I can help her find success with mathematics and statistics."

The boy glances at me and bows, hands clasped in front of him.

Should I stand up and bow back? Just like the clapping?

It seems as if everyone is waiting for me to say or do something, but I can't be sure. How does a hiring manager behave in Beijing?

When in doubt, isn't it best to imitate the behavior of those around me?

Isn't life just a fun game of charades?

Jumping up, I attempt to bow back, but as I lean over, I realize my house robe has come undone. The nervous boy reddens. Shit! I knew I should have shaved this morning.

Quickly, I attempt to hide myself and luckily, no one else seems to notice because they've all averted their eyes. To cover my stumble, I attempt to curtsy, but I have never curtsied before except when I was four years old and my dad enrolled me with him in a preschool parent-and-baby tap dance. In my fumbling attempt to cross my legs and half curtsy, I almost lose my balance and fall on my face.

"Weijun, sit down now, we have next person," Uncle Dai says, looking confused.

I scramble to take my seat, nearly knocking over a pitcher of water in my hurry.

Uncle Dai continues on to the girl with the glasses. "Tingwei. Number three at Peking University. You study psychology? Very good. Why you want to teach Weijun?"

"This will be a good learning experience for me," the girl says, examining the ground. "I want to be a teacher."

"Why teacher?" Uncle Dai says, sounding perplexed. "Teacher is very poor. You should get MBA at Stanford."

The girl flushes and agrees with him without hesitation.

It becomes apparent that this is not a position for my personal assistant.

When my parents were hiring me tutors, we looked on Craigslist. We asked friends who recommended reputable teachers or smart older siblings. We checked the advertisements in the Bradley Gardens local paper. In China, it appears that hiring a personal tutor requires fancy business suits, three-page résumés printed on embroidered paper, and a formal group interview.

"Okay, next question, Yurao of Peking University." He points at a baby-faced kid with acne and a humongous nose. "What is life goal after Bachelor of Engineering degree?"

"I want to get to an MBA at Stanford!" the kid exclaims eagerly. "I want to be a CEO like you, Mr. Feng."

Uncle Dai humphs in what seems like approval.

Finally, it's the boy in the navy-blue cardigan's turn. He's the only one who looks like a model posing as an old-person librarian, not a wannabe stockbroker. He catches my eye again and winks. Blushing slightly, I catch myself winking back. Not on purpose, I tell myself—my eyeball twitch seems to be returning due to nervousness. I want Mr. Pageant Dude to succeed. Then I can at least find an excuse to get his number.

"Chaoren!" Uncle Dai barks, pointing at him. "You went to Beijing Normal University as math major? Number ten?"

Frowning slightly, the dude who was previously laughing at me shakes his head.

"Mr. Feng, my name is actually Liao Faxian. Frank Liao," he says confidently, correcting Uncle Dai. "I'm a classical English and Chinese major at Tsinghua University. Number one in my class."

Nervous, frantic stares are exchanged around the table. Everyone looks like they've eaten too many slices of greasy pepperoni pizza and deep-fried jalapeño cheese sticks. I get a feeling that my uncle is not someone who is contradicted often, if at all.

I'm impressed by Blue Cardigan's fearless attitude.

I don't think my uncle, however, is impressed.

Frowning, Uncle Dai turns to me. "Weijun, we are finding you good Chinese language tutor. I promise your daddy to help with school. So I have assistant find you best smartest student in China. You have question to ask them?"

"Will there be homework?" I say, but no one laughs.

Why doesn't anyone have a sense of humor in China?

Why is everyone so serious?

Except for the boy in the cardigan, they all look as if they're on an airplane, waiting to find out if there is going to be an emergency crash landing into an erupting volcano. You'd think that Uncle Dai was Godzilla.

At the end of the question round, there is a two-hour essay component to test their English and Mandarin writing skills. As the students begin furiously scribbling in booklets, Uncle Dai turns to me and beckons for us to exit the conference room.

"We are done now," he says.

"What?" I say.

"I already pick tutor for you," he said.

"So fast?" I say, stunned.

I don't even try to hide my disappointment.

I didn't even have time to get the good-looking boy's number.

Admittedly, I just want a friend so badly in China that even the nervous, sweaty boy would do. Anyone who understands a medium level of English, anyone friendly who isn't of Uncle Dai's age group. This is the longest that I have gone without texting Samira and Peter. I don't understand what people without human companions and all-inclusive long-distance plans do in their spare time. Who do they constantly talk to?

"Shouldn't we get to know my future tutors better?" I ask, gazing around the conference room hopefully. Everyone is writing intently in their booklets, eyebrows scrunched, lower lips stuck out in concentration. Honestly, if all job interviews are like China, I would be permanently unemployed. Don't college students relax during the summer holidays?

Sighing heavily, I follow Uncle Dai out of the room, leaving the eager students to finish their essays. At the front desk of the hotel, he picks up a heavy package. It looks suspiciously un-fun, and I give it the stink eye.

We take the elevator back to the penthouse suite. Uncle Dai and I settle on the couches in the living room. A maid has left out strawberries, pineapples, sliced kiwis, an assorted plate of elegant cakes, and a fragrant pitcher of mango fruit tea on a table. Eagerly, I help myself to a passion-fruit swiss roll, a decadent slice of black sesame chiffon cake, and some purple potato and cheese bread.

"Weijun, I have big favor to ask," Uncle Dai says seriously.

"Yes?" I say, confused. I put down my plate reluctantly. Can't Uncle Dai wait until I've taken my first bite?

He continues, sounding worried. "Weijun, you are not like Ruby. She always afraid. She hiding behind silly dog show, but she is smarter girl and I want her to work at my company. Ruby doesn't like to talk to people. I want her to be friendly and always smiling like you. As parent, you always want next generation to do better. You want best for them."

A door slams. Is Ruby home? Is she eavesdropping on our conversation?

Gulping, I stare at my uncle. First, I'm still in shock about hiring a tutor. Does he actually expect me to do homework on my summer vacation abroad? And what does Uncle Dai mean about Ruby? Is this a lost-in-translation issue? Or does he actually think his daughter is shy like some kind of cute-looking rodent that has secretly sharp teeth?

"Ruby is very sensitive girl, Weijun. You be her friend, okay? I worry a lot about her because she never have friend. Your dad said you have opposite problem. Too many friend."

Loud Mandarin pop music begins to blare from the maid's quarters. My cousin is definitely home.

"Ruby!" Uncle Dai says in a loud voice. "Stop practicing for show. No waste time! Please play violin instead!"

Nodding firmly, Uncle Dai glances at me and continues. "Please spend time with your cousin. Take care of each other. Influence each other to be better."

The dance music from the speakers pulses louder.

Incredulous, I stare at my uncle. Is he asking me to teach Ruby not to be a bully? They have school psychologists and counselors for that in America. Is there somehow a shortage of specialists in Beijing?

"Ruby!" he calls again. "Come out and talk to your cousin, please. Weijun come all the way from America to visit."

Uncle Dai says something long and lecture-sounding at her in Chinese. He sounds a lot like my mom when she's telling me not to go out on a weeknight, to be honest. For some reason, lecture voices sound eerily similar to my guilty conscience. The volume of the music causes the apartment's walls to shake.

Then it suddenly stops. A sullen Ruby appears, clutching a large stuffed dog animal. Apparently, she has been practicing for a doggy pageant.

"Help Weijun study, okay?" he says, beaming as he hands me the package. "I make important phone call before dinner. Then I have good news surprise to tell Weijun later."

Uncle Dai presses the remote on a surround-sound system. Chinese opera, soft and classical, fills the suite. It's the kind that people in nursing homes dress up for and drive to concert halls to spend a small fortune on. I suppose it's helpful for studying.

Ignoring her dad, Ruby switches the music back to her upbeat pageant routine. She stretches and begins prancing around, holding the large stuffed dog that she says is supposed to be a mastiff. Apparently, the theme for the year-end international competition is *The Muppet Show*, and the mastiff will be groomed to look like Miss Piggy. Ruby will be dressed as Kermit the Frog and has ordered a bright green jumpsuit from Italy.

"That's amazing," I say, and I'm actually impressed by her dedication to the show's theme.

Ruby glances at me suspiciously.

She continues strutting around the living room, holding the dog as a prop.

I don't know what else to say to my strange cousin.

But then, as if the universe has heard me yelling SOS, her phone rings, and as she answers it, her face falls with shock. Rapid Chinese. Arguing for fifteen minutes. Pleading for five. Pink-faced, she scowls and slumps on the couch dramatically.

I wait for my chance. This almost reminds me of Friday

afternoons with Samira, when we would lie on her bed like an old married couple and make a long list of our life complaints and boy problems, while sucking down chocolate ice-cream floats and slurping Cheese Whiz straight out of a spray can.

"What's wrong?" I ask when she hangs up. "Seriously. Maybe I can help."

"Why?" she asks, frowning at me. Ruby chews her pinkie.

"We're cousins," I say. "Isn't family supposed to help?"

"What about . . . your clothes?"

A look of unmistakable guilt flashes across Ruby's features.

I wince.

She sees my pained expression, and she looks ashamed.

We both stare at the immaculate marble floor.

"It's fine," I finally say, laughing awkwardly. "It's a good excuse to get new ones."

Forgive and forget, right?

The problem, Ruby reluctantly explains, is she needs someone to pick up a practice Tibetan mastiff that is being flown from a temple full of monks in the Himalayas. She can't change the day of her dress fitting in Milan. Uncle Dai won't let Mr. Chen watch her dog because he thinks that "dog grooming very silly." But she's going to fly in a different mastiff every four months since it takes a year to practice for the international competition. The rented dogs will be groomed and fed and then returned to the temple. Then the one with the best temperament will be paraded as Miss Piggy for the show.

I stare at her, absolutely delighted. She's flying in dogs from Tibet?!!

"I could get the practice mastiff for you," I offer, "while you get fitted for your costume in Italy!"

How hard can picking up a dog at the airport be? I have no idea what kind of breed a Tibetan mastiff is, but aren't rich people always carrying them around like tiny wallets? Ruby hesitates and looks doubtful.

"I would love to help!" I repeat.

"You would help me?" she says.

"YES!" I enthuse, remembering what Uncle Dai said. I say again: "That's what family is for!"

Uncle Dai peeks his head out of his office at my enthusiasm. He gives us both a thumbs-up sign, which makes me laugh. I give him one back. He is acting exactly like my dad, always goofy and thrilled when someone in the house sounds like they are having fun. Ruby stares at me curiously. Uncle Dai said that I was supposed to hang out with Ruby to teach her people-skills, but Ruby seems to only care about dog shows. This is the perfect opportunity to show my cousin that I'm not an awful human being, and I could win a trophy for best dog-sitter of the year.

Ruby nods hesitantly.

"YES!" I say, incredibly eager to please. "You won't regret it."

With a weird gravitational lurching in my tummy, I finally open Uncle Dai's package. It consists of three cushion-size GED prep books and a *Mandarin Language Beginner Guide*. Wrinkling my nose, I open the first book and there is a list, which is surprisingly easy to read. Then I realize that it's just the Table of Contents, and there's even more text to follow! Long paragraphs of numbers and equations and diagrams and I swear they're not even written in English. Math was obviously designed by Pictionary-obsessed aliens who had access to robots to help them understand extra-sophisticated concepts. As I try to understand an equation, another horrible, panicky feeling rushes through me. I have never felt so much anxiety from learning before. Is this how teenage babysitters in slasher films feel when they get the scary phone call from the murderer who's already hiding inside the house?

Studying feels exactly like a horror movie.

How do you even get your mind to focus?

Recoiling, I wrap the books back in their packaging and stuff them underneath the bathroom sink.

Out of sight, out of mind, right?

The saying was specifically invented for me.

Ruby has gone back to practicing her doggy walk in the living room, almost hopping like a frog. I start giggling again and pretend that I'm yawning whenever Ruby catches me quiet-laughing.

I finally remember to scrub off my horsehair face and end up watching Ruby practice with her stuffed dog, which is far more interesting than the Shopping Channel.

Sibling Rivalry

This time for dinner, Mr. Chen drives us to Opera Bombana, a fine-dining Michelin three-star Italian restaurant, and even more paparazzi than last night line up to take Uncle Dai's photo. Five scowling security guards stand impressively around us, while reporters shout nonstop questions at Uncle Dai. A few people are even holding hand-painted signs and yelling passionately. I wish I understood Chinese so I could understand the fuss. Is Uncle Dai some kind of local celebrity?

"What's going on?" I say as Auntie Yingfei puts her arm around me and smiles sweetly.

"We build hotel," my uncle says, while my aunt nods with excitement.

"Not malls?" I ask hopefully.

"Just hotel."

"Shopping centers?" I ask.

Uncle Dai shakes his head.

"How many hotels?" I finally say, trying to hide my disappointment.

"Twenty-five in Asia," Uncle Dai says proudly. "This one in Beijing will be biggest one. Seven-star."

They have seven-star hotels? Are seven stars for real? Then why are we staying in a lowly four-star Shangri-La? Math might be my worst subject, but even I know three stars is a staggering difference.

As if reading my mind, Uncle Dai says, "Shangri-La owned by friend. He give us big discount."

"Oh!" I say.

Billionaires like discounts too?

I don't know how to respond to that.

Uncle Dai and Aunt Yingfei smile warmly at me.

"Weijun is taking interest in our company, Ruby," Uncle Dai announces, nudging his daughter. "Maybe now you will pay attention too."

In response, Ruby says nothing as we are escorted to a private dining room at the restaurant. She still hasn't said anything since I offered to help pick up her borrowed mastiff. I smile at her encouragingly, but she doesn't look me in the eye. What just happened? I thought we were starting to become friends. Before we left for dinner, since my clothes were still sopping wet, Ruby lent me an ankle-length dress made out of orange bath mat material with swaths of pink organza sewn onto it. The dress was supposed to mimic a romantic Caribbean sunset. Ruby assured me that the garment was supposed to make me feel "like modern art," but my skin seems to be allergic. Inadvertently, I scratch myself.

Rather than chat with me, Ruby sighs and keeps texting someone on her phone.

To be honest, no one warned me about lukewarm, standoffish girls in China, but I just assumed my cousin, like everyone else, would automatically gravitate toward my Type B, cheerleading persona. Compared to America, China has a long, unbelievable history of fighting wars, and Ruby could certainly be an expert in making my life as difficult as possible. Isn't it enough to offer to help her pick up a dog?

I scoot closer to her, but she moves away. As if she's afraid to get too close to me.

It's like she doesn't even want to be casual acquaintances, and yet there are moments when she seems okay.

In America, everyone used to run *at* me, but I don't know what happened after Samira and Peter. It's like I have suddenly developed horrible, eye-watering, nose-stinging BO. People in Beijing are now running away!

Panicking slightly at the thought of smelling like fermented tofu and aged cheese, I lift and sniff my armpits to check for odors. Ruby, Uncle Dai, and Auntie Yingfei stare at me, looking shocked.

Scowling, Ruby says something in Chinese and her dad quickly replies, "America is opposite of China."

"What is wrong with you?" Ruby turns to ask me when her dad and mom seem to be busy chatting with each other.

"Why are you so angry?" I ask her quietly.

Ruby looks uncomfortable for a moment. Her brows knit together and she makes a series of small choking sounds, like she has swallowed too many bubble-tea tapioca pearls at once. Like she doesn't even know how to respond. Like she's not used to talking about her feelings.

What exactly am I doing wrong?

"You are okay, Weijun?" Uncle Dai asks, interrupting our conversation.

"I'm fabulous," I say.

Ruby doesn't say anything. She just avoids looking at me.

Honestly, my stomach has been hurting a lot since I shoveled down two plates of *xiāo long bao*. Maybe I shouldn't have drunk that strawberry bubble tea too. For once, I'm glad that I did not indulge in any of those fancy desserts after the group interview. At dinner, I politely sample a tiny bit of focaccia bread, a bird-size portion of spaghetti Bolognese with veal cutlets, which is absolutely delicious, and then a teaspoon of double-chocolate gelato.

More paparazzi after dessert. Ruby strikes a ridiculous pose outside the restaurant, but Uncle Dai and Mr. Chen yell at her. A security guard jumps in front of her, as if to protect her from a camera lens. Another guard ushers her away. I suppress a snicker. Although I do want to pose with her. I just feel incredibly queasy.

In the car, Uncle Dai announces his "good news surprise for me." I expect that it's more textbooks or tutors, but he shocks me by asking if I would like to "work travel" with Auntie Yingfei to Europe at the end of the summer.

"Auntie go to Paris, then Italy, and Spain for work but need good helper. Weijun, you want to go?"

I stare at him. Is he serious?

"I want to go to all these places!" I say, gasping loudly. Uncle Dai has no idea how I spent my entire senior year plotting and dreaming about Paris. Trip planning had been essentially my full-time job.

"It is lots of work, all day long, you helping Auntie," he warns. "You must go to meeting and answer phone and talk English all day and take many note."

"I can do all these things!" I say with excitement.

Auntie Yingfei smiles and starts applauding at me like an enthusiastic seal at Sea World. Her hands are absurdly close to my face. Remembering what Uncle Dai taught me about Chinese etiquette, I imitate her and applaud back energetically in her face. Soon we are all clapping (Uncle Dai and Auntie Yingfei, at least), as if competing with one another on who can be the noisiest in the back of the chauffeured vehicle. I can't help but giggle at the absurdity. For a moment, I forget that being sent to China wasn't even my choice. For a moment, I forget that I was even homesick for an entire afternoon. As I applaud, I remember that these kind and generous people are my recently found family. I'm so pleased and ecstatic. It's almost like being around my parents again, pre–college admission disaster, and feeling exactly like I belong. My aunt and uncle are beaming at me like I'm a newborn kitten.

Suddenly, Ruby bursts out, "But *Máma*, I was supposed to go with you!"

The clapping in the Mercedes-Benz SUV stops.

I quickly put my hands in my lap.

Ruby's features have turned the color of rotten milk.

Quickly, Auntie Yingfei shushes her, and Uncle Dai says, "Ruby, we talk about this many time already! Your cousin probably never go Europe before. You go Paris shopping many time. Beside I need you to help me at work. You are old enough for summer internship at Feng Corp."

"Bàba!" she whines like a small child, her expression looking puzzled and hurt. She looks different than the surly, eye-rolling girl from yesterday. And way more different than the confident girl who was prancing a few hours ago as Kermit the Frog. It's like I'm seeing the real Ruby for the first time.

"Enough!" Uncle Dai says. "Every business student in China want my internship, and you don't want? Why?"

"I . . ."

"You must grow up," he says sternly to Ruby. "Life very hard outside of China. Not just all about grooming dog. You ask Weijun. Everyone, including college graduate, cannot find job inside the America. So many of them have no life purpose after Harvard."

Uncle Dai looks at me, as if expecting me to agree. He taps his fingers on his leg impatiently. A nervous tic disguised to emphasize a boardroom order. To be honest, he sounds exactly like my mom: a CEO parent who has no time for inefficiency. They both run their households like they're head Olympic coaches.

"Um, yes," I stammer, not looking at Ruby. "It's very hard to have no life purpose."

And I mean it.

Uncle Dai doesn't know how absolutely right he is. I have no clue what to do with myself or my future. All I know is that I could be treading water in a shark-infested lake. I don't know who I am or where I belong. Because when I find these small, beautiful moments with family, they quickly evaporate. And when my feelings of being accepted are released into Beijing's pollution, all I have left is triple the anxiety that I'm trying to slurp down like a bowl of hearty beef noodle soup.

Ruby stares at me, her lips upturned. She hisses something harsh and undecipherable in Chinese, but she doesn't speak for the rest of the ride home. Is this sibling rivalry? I have no clue, but her behavior stings me personally.

I can't help but think that she'll never forgive me for replacing her at the end-of-summer trip with her mom. Can't we both just go to Europe? She can take my place if she's bull-angry. A summer internship at Feng Corp doesn't sound horrible. We could swap.

As expected, I don't receive a reply to my note left under her door.

17

Grooming Practice

I should be delirious with joy about escorting Auntie Yingfei to Europe, but all night, I sweat and toss with stomach-churning insomnia. I think it's just heartburn or the stress of not automatically becoming BFFs with my cousin. I have no stomach for breakfast, even though it consists of delicious-smelling rice porridge with heaping piles of pickles, boiled eggs, dried fermented meat, and roasted peanuts. There's also a side dish of deep-fried doughnut sticks and puffy sheets of steamed bread to be dipped in super-hot steaming soy milk.

Also, my eyes and nose have been watering constantly. It seems to get worse every time I go outside. I don't know if I'm having seasonal allergies or if I'm coming down with a red-eyed flu. I sip my coffee hesitantly. Somehow, even black coffee with my double dose of four packets of sugar feels nauseating today.

The ache in my stomach won't subside. Nausea backwashes even when I try drinking water. Gross.

Since the dress from last night makes me itchy and I have no wearable clothes, I decide to wake up early to see if I can borrow a maid's uniform from the hotel. But my alarm doesn't go off, and Mr. Chen is already waiting for us. Nervously I grab one of Ruby's cotton-ball jumpsuits. I know she'll undoubtedly be upset, but maybe I can convince her to let me wear it until we get to the mall.

It's not like her parents are home and I can ask to borrow one of Auntie Yingfei's Hermès business suits. I assume both Uncle Dai and Auntie Yingfei are at work because whenever I wake up, they aren't home.

"What are you doing?" Ruby demands when she sees me dressed in her garb from her regular day-to-day closet. I was hoping that she'd remember that we sort of bonded before her parents told her that I would be going to Europe with her mom. I've put on one of her jumpsuits that looks and feels exactly like a dramatic poof of pink cotton candy, and I look and feel fantastic. I can see why Ruby wears this garment as her everyday costume. Even though my stomach is cramping nonstop, new clothes can make me feel better. The jumpsuit is exceptionally tight around the waistline, but it doesn't matter. At least I can half squeeze into Ruby's baggiest outfit.

I am too exhausted to respond. Instead, I stir more sugar into my coffee.

My phone buzzes. A WeChat message pops up.

SuperPrincessQueenRuby8421: You're wearing my dress! wtfff

SuperPrincessQueenRuby8421: Take it off

Iris: I don't have any wearable clothes

Iris: Can I wear it until we get to the mall?

Iris: You wrecked mine, remember?

SuperPrincessQueenRuby8421: Just stop!

SuperPrincessQueenRuby8421: Isn't it enough that both my parents are taking care of you and sending you to Europe?

Iris: ?

SuperPrincessQueenRuby8421: I was supposed to go with my mom

SuperPrincessQueenRuby8421: We go every year

SuperPrincessQueenRuby8421: This was supposed to be our summer

SuperPrincessQueenRuby8421: They are using you to punish me, can't you see? They never think i'm good enough

SuperPrincessQueenRuby8421: You're not better than me

SuperPrincessQueenRuby8421: My parents just feel sorry for you. They can't see that you just take everything for granted. You actually don't care about anything. I actually try really hard.

Iris: What are you talking about???

SuperPrincessQueenRuby8421: That's what i mean. You just don't get it. I can't believe you're so dense.

Iris: Get what?

SuperPrincessQueenRuby8421: Everything. just go home!!!

SuperPrincessQueenRuby8421: No one wants you here

Iris: Ruby, I'm so sorry

Iris: I'll talk to your mom and dad

SuperPrincessQueenRuby8421: Like you care

Across the kitchen table, I glance up from my phone. Ruby's face reddens to the color of a sour Caesar—my least favorite cocktail but my dad's favorite drink. Ruby's messages make me feel more nauseous and angry. How is any of this my fault? Why does she think that I'm deliberately ruining her life? I feel humiliated for repeating the words "I'm sorry" so many times in a week. "Sorry" isn't resonating with Ruby at all. "Sorry" to Ruby is like trying to teach me how to find *x* in an algebra equation. It won't work.

Then, to make matters worse, I sneeze unexpectedly. A wad of snail-gray snot lands on my borrowed dress.

Ruby's mouth drops and for once she doesn't roll her eyes. My cousin makes a choking sound as I scrub at the stain frantically with a napkin. My allergies have been getting worse, and my nose, throat, and ears feel congested. The morning smog is particularly overbearing. I sneeze violently again. More gray snot. What is happening to me? In America, my snot was white or yellow, but in Beijing, it has become the same prison color of all this sprawling concrete. Like a mutant, is China somehow changing me biologically on the inside, as well as on the outside?

Mr. Chen escorts us to the car, barely looking up from a video of a meowing kitten on his iPad.

I expect that we're going shopping again and I'm all prepared to buy a new outfit, but Mr. Chen drops us off at a hideous oyster-colored skyscraper building. It doesn't look like a mall, but I'm instantly intrigued. Is this an illegal warehouse for cheap designer purses and shoes?

"Where are we?" I ask Ruby, who doesn't even look at me. She seems nervous, even preoccupied.

Then I see a sign: HANYUAN LANGUAGE SCHOOL. Why are we even here? Does Ruby take English lessons? Are we picking something up?

Real slasher-movie fear overcomes me.

Since kindergarten, learning has always made me extremely nervous. I have never done well in a classroom setting, and I just don't understand how I'm supposed to absorb so much knowledge inside my brain. If you think about it, the brain already has to be responsible for eating, sleeping, talking, and muscle memory, so how can I absorb various facts and multiple equations? These numbers are not applicable to real life. Languages are impossible to learn. Plus, I have a C-plus average in Spanish and French, and even though my parents tried to teach me Chinese all these years, I could never understand it.

I once told my guidance counselor at school that the SATs have way too many different sections, which expect one to be able to multitask efficiently. Afterward, she looked at me funny and asked me to list my hobbies and any alternate career paths.

"Sephora isn't a hobby and Yale isn't a job," she told me, but of course, I wasn't listening. I was too busy planning my valedictorian speech and searching for inspirational quotes on the internet. I was going to pretend that I was Mindy Kaling giving her brilliant commencement speech at Harvard.

Confused, I follow Ruby into the building and we walk into a long gray hallway. I start hyperventilating because we're in an actual school. With classrooms, desks, lockers, and very few decent-looking male students.

"Ruby, Ruby, Ruby," I whisper, trying to get her to stop walking. Sweat begins sliding off my fingers, and I can feel my Tiger whiskers start to sprout on cue. Just by being inside a school, my body is beginning its change for the worse. I could actually be turning into a mutant feline.

Still furious, Ruby ignores me until I grab her chicken-leg arm. She sees my panic-stricken face and pauses for just a millisecond.

"I honestly can't be here," I panic-whisper. "You won't understand because you like learning, but I'm seriously terrified right now."

The shock of failing senior year is suddenly raw, fresh, and real. I shoved the bad news into the back of my brain like an overdue credit card bill. I never wanted to deal with it again. In real life, failing high school actually means that I could be a permanent adult failure for the remainder of my jobless, friendless, boyless, no-fun, no-luxury-shopping life. The fear is too unmanageable, like the time that I accidentally used nail polish remover instead of eye makeup remover and burned my own cornea. At the emergency room, the doctor looked at my red swollen eyeball and said, "You need to be careful, young lady! You could have permanently blinded yourself!" That has always been my metaphor for my life: mixing up makeup removers and never wanting to deal with the terrible, unfixable consequences.

"What are you saying?" Ruby says, seeming distracted. "Iris, I never understand you! Speak English, please!"

Her Apple Watch beeps.

She's apparently in a hurry to go somewhere.

"Please," I say, clinging to her arm like an annoying child.

I can't help it. I feel so useless in this sprawling LEGO city. I never understood Peter's fascination with his models, and I somehow suddenly feel claustrophobic and queasier in this dense landscape than I was at breakfast. I feel like I'm inside a gigantic, rocking spaceship in *Star Wars*.

"Fine," Ruby hisses. "You can come with me."

She beckons at me and says that she isn't planning to attend private summer school. The teachers don't care, she says. Apparently, they don't get paid enough to take attendance or teach students.

Eagerly, I nod.

Anything sounds better than being stuck in a scary classroom that looks like a spaceship.

This time, we get into another car, a DidiChuxing (Uber) hired privately by Ruby, then another Didi, and this one drives us in the opposite direction. It's all very mysterious and a bit alarming when we transfer cars and seem to be driving in circles. What sort of illegal business is my cousin into? Finally, we go under a concrete bridge, passing more ugly smog-colored skyscrapers and hordes of busy-running people in fashionable business suits who seem to be going to the office. Street vendors selling fresh durian juice, brown curry fish balls, and sautéed chicken skewers fill the chaotic streets.

I'm relieved that this time we seem to be heading to a heavily populated area. After what feels like eternity, we're in the bustling heart of Beijing, and there's another warehouselike prison building and a sign that says SOHO XU-RHEN DOGGY SPA AND HOTEL PAMPER. Suddenly, I'm incredibly relieved. Are we just having a nice visit with some pampered pooches?

"You can't say anything to my dad," Ruby insists, frowning. "He doesn't know how much I practice."

Grateful not to be in school, I nod, as if Ruby's paranoia makes total sense.

I'm excellent at keeping secrets, except when they're too juicy for just one person. Secrets lead to gossip, and in order for human evolution and biology and future societies to continue, someone needs to be willing to share newly acquired knowledge.

For instance, if my dad had simply told us that he had family in China and would send me away if I misbehaved, I would have known never to piss him off. As a result, he would probably have had better parenting results if he had told me that exile would happen if I did poorly at school.

Knowing your extended family should be search-engine knowledge. You just *need* to know that you were born with a half uncle. There are consequences for not sharing information. I swear, that's how Atlantis was lost. It's the only real explanation for how we could lose an entire city in the whole ten-thousand-year history of our solar system. And since I don't seem to know anything about my world, am I more at risk of vanishing?

How many more days on Earth do I have left?

Confused, I reluctantly follow Ruby to the top floor of the building and into a fancy pink-and-white-curtained room. I pass sour-looking pugs receiving nail clippings and snooty poodles getting complicated French braids. There are even a few yapping Pomeranians getting acupuncture and massages by professional staff in hospital-looking uniforms. It all looks amazing and wonderful. Just seeing the soft doggy beds makes me want to be an exotic canine breed owned by very wealthy people. I want to be anyone or anything but impulsive, out-of-control Iris Wang.

I want to lie down and take a long, peaceful nap.

In a private spa room, there are seven sheep-size stuffed animal mannequins with spiky yarnlike hair spread over different workstations. Ruby's coach, the mustached owner of the fancy salon, Master Hui, has set up cutting stations around the room. Ruby needs to be able to groom and train a Tibetan mastiff into the perfect Miss Piggy within a six-month time frame in order to become a finalist in the international competition.

"You mean . . ." I trail off.

"These are my practice until my real practice dogs arrive at the airport," she says enthusiastically.

I gawk.

Ruby is skipping summer school to cut hair on fake dogs. No wonder Uncle Dai is always upset with her. It's like me never showing up for AP Economics whenever there's a sale at Saks.

"While I practice grooming, why don't you try making one of these mannequins into Winnie the Pooh or something?" she says, handing me a large pair of shearing scissors and a thick booklet of instructions. "Eeyore is very easy too."

After fifteen minutes, it's clear that I have no talent for dog grooming. My stuffed animal is patchy and looks nothing like a cartoon bear. In many places, it even looks bald. From a distance, my mannequin could best be described as a plucked turkey.

Ruby has already finished two of these practice models. All of them look stunning and distinct, each Miss Piggy better and more thought-provoking than the last. Ruby's even working on color theory; her creation will be dyed thirteen different shades of ombre pink using all-natural organic beet juice imported from the UK. She's already ordered her dog's wardrobe from Japan.

I tell her that I need a break.

"Keep an eye on the time," she warns me as she shaves off the right side of her doggy mannequin. "We need to leave at fourteen hundred hours, before Mr. Chen gets to the school."

"Sure," I say, but I'm barely listening. Fourteen hundred hours? What is Ruby going on about?

Stomach rumbling, I still feel nauseous. I tell myself that I'm just having a normal reaction from having been inside a school. In the privacy of the bathroom, I finally check my Instagram feed. It seems like a waste of time not to do so. For some reason, I see Samira's post pop up first. She and Peter. Someone's throwing a really fun party with keggers. First date at the Cheesecake Factory. Little hearts. Kissing pics?!!!! Samira's Facebook status says *In a relationship with Peter Hayes.* <3

My heart and stomach cramp simultaneously. Both from displacement, betrayal, and slow, internal poisoning.

Instagram is making my condition worse.

Samira and Peter are officially a social media couple? It hasn't even been a full two weeks.

I check my DMs. Twelve messages from Samira. As I read through them, I start to feel giddy and light-headed. Am I going to pass out?

Samira Chadha-Fu: Iris my darling, are you around for a shopping day? Stop avoiding me. I know you're dying to visit Nordstrom.

Samira Chadha-Fu: Okay, how about a quick toke, girl? Coffee? Drink?

Samira Chadha-Fu: Listen, you can't stay away from me forever. What will you do if you don't have your BFF around? You need me. We're a dream team.

Samira Chadha-Fu: What are we going to do about prom? I hired a limousine. Parents are throwing me a big party for getting into Princeton. Where are you going to be at next year?

Samira Chadha-Fu: Iris, come on. Msg me. I miss you. <3 <3 <3

Samira Chadha-Fu: Okay, Iris . . . everyone is talking about why you're not in school. There are rumors that you are getting plastic surgery in Korea or you're doing rehab in a spa in Switzerland or that your parents exiled you to Canada. Tell me it's not true!!!! If you're at a spa, can I come visit?

Samira Chadha-Fu: Giving me the cold shoulder isn't your style, babe.

Lavalike anger rises in me and I stop reading her messages. How can she still not be apologizing for stealing my boyfriend and then shit-talking me in my own home? How can she expect me to respond to her casual indifference? Since she came over with her parents, she has never bothered to beg to meet me face-to-face for an apology and a chance to explain. She could have had the decency to at least FaceTime me if she was busy.

But Samira is half-right.

I'm so lonely in Beijing that I am tempted to send her a text. Just to say a quick hello. Despite being badly hurt, hating her, and missing her, I just want to feel accepted again. Honestly, if Peter texted me and wanted me back ASAP, I might even be tempted to make up with him, too.

Does that make me extremely forgiving or someone who is a sad, desperate pushover when it comes to besties and shitty boys? Even though I know the answer, I can't help but want to talk to my former best friend. I want to imagine that just messaging Samira will temporarily soothe my heartbreak. Like putting a Band-Aid over an expanding wart. No one tells you that your best friend, whom you swore to love through college and take on the role of spunky, joyful maid of honor at her wedding, can also tear up your already fragile flower-heart.

Through the walls, I hear Ruby happily singing the Muppets' theme song to herself. She's completely off-tune, but she's obviously excited and super focused. The snip-snip sound of her shearing is almost as loud as her singing. The spa's owner comes in occasionally to check on her cutting technique and evaluates it on a 10 scale. So far, Ruby's average is 8.5.

I wish I could be as content and focused as she is. Ruby seems genuinely passionate about her professional hobby.

I distract myself with a perfectly timed WeChat message from my dad.

Hopefully, he'll have some exciting news from home to share, or he'll send some goofy selfies and videos of himself and Mom trying to sexy-Hawaiian-dance in the kitchen. They used to go to a weekly community center class together, with mostly old retired people, before Mom got too busy. My dad even took Peter and me with him one time so we could practice the easy swaying choreography with him.

There's a YouTube video of me hiding in the back of the class, in the very last row, oddly out of sync with the rest of the students, feeling absolutely humiliated and thinking that being recognized was the worst possible thing that could happen to me. Peter, shockingly, is in the front row with my dad, thoroughly enjoying the steps. He and my dad are laughing like baboons, moving their hips as if they're at a real-life luau, and they are actually getting along. We're all wearing matching green grass skirts, and even then, I remember that I cared so much about what everyone thought of me. I just couldn't have any fun. And no one except ten retired people in the class ever saw the posted YouTube video.

I just want Ruby's joyful confidence to pursue whatever she wants. But most of all, I want to know exactly what I'm good at, and like Ruby, what I want to devote my life to. If I had an aptitude for it, creative dog grooming wouldn't be so bad.

But instead of a casual text checkup, my dad is all-business, no-bullshit.

WECHAT GROUP (#1WangFamily!!!)

IrisDaddy: How is Beijing?

Iris: Fine.

IrisDaddy: Everyone nice to you?

Iris: It's fine.

IrisDaddy: Are you learning Chinese?

Iris: No.

IrisDaddy: You know you can't come home until you know basic conversation.

Iris: Why are you being so hard on me? Are you still mad?

IrisDaddy: We are not mad anymore. Just very disappointed and sad.

Iris: Don't you want me to come home?

Iris: And what do you mean by basic conversation?

IrisDaddy: . . . . . .

Iris: How many phrases?

IrisDaddy: When your uncle tells me you are learning enough.

Iris: What does that mean????!

IrisDaddy: He will decide.

Iris: What if I don't ever learn Chinese?

IrisDaddy: Then I guess you have to stay in Beijing forever.

Iris: Gtg. Bye.

Why is my dad making the most ridiculous demands? Doesn't he care about my feelings, which are as soft and messy as Jell-O Pudding Snacks? Most of all, I just want validation from someone my age. Ruby is too busy practicing for her competition. And even then, she wouldn't understand how school is so terrifying and impossible for me.

Hesitantly I type a message to my ex-BFF.

Iris: Hey, what's up. I'm in China. Long story.

Samira Chadha-Fu: WHAT???!!

Iris: Yeah . . . it's been interesting.

Even though I'm not supposed to tell anyone that I'm in China, I can't help it. Samira is like a really bad habit. She's like picking your nose on public transit or smoking a jumbo-size joint between classes. Samira and I always share very awkward details, from radioactive acne in embarrassing places to gross, unsatisfying encounters with boys. She used to be my only confidante and powerful female ally. How can I suddenly stop talking to her? How can I not tell her that I'm stuck in the black hole of China?

Soon we're engaged in our usual lighthearted banter and an hour practically flies by. I almost miss Ruby telling me that we've forgotten to phone our private driver to pick us up. Mr. Chen will almost be at Hanyuan Language School by now.

"We have to go!" Ruby says, sounding breathless. "Weren't you paying attention to the time?"

Running to the hired Didi, we barely make it because the rush-hour traffic is terrible. The driver honks at least five times. We nearly collide head-on with a bicycle, but thankfully, no one is hurt. No damage is done to the car, just our throats from screaming so much. On the way back to summer school, Ruby looks incredibly anxious, fidgeting with the thousands of yellow cotton balls on her jumpsuit. She accidentally plucks one off.

"Iris, just don't tell my dad, okay?"

I promise that I won't.

Ruby looks at me with incredible relief.

"My jumpsuit looks good on you," she admits.

"Thanks," I say, smiling.

Nervously Ruby tries to smile back, but only the corners of her lips twitch, like they're superglued shut.

Listen to Iris

I wake up at three a.m., thirsty, nauseous, vomit-y and achy all over. I barely have time to stumble to the bathroom before I pass out. Auntie Yingfei finds me unconscious and calls for Uncle Dai. Instead of calling an ambulance, they carry me back to bed and tell me, "Help is driving."

Dr. Xiāo is the family doctor who pays house calls. In this case, he caters to families in the most elite hotels in the city. He works 24/7, and all I have to do is phone him and he'll come running. That's what Uncle Dai says, anyway. Ruby once had the Hong Kong avian flu at five a.m. on a Sunday before the China National Youth Debate Championship, so Auntie Yingfei called Dr. Xiāo to give her experimental meds and hook up a personal IV into her arm to combat dehydration.

He looks like a businessman in a baby-blue Prada suit rather than a doctor. Glancing at me quickly, Dr. Xiāo explains that I have "traveler's diarrhea."

"What does that mean?" I say.

Traveler's diarrhea sounds like a made-up, bullshit name for food poisoning.

"Foreigner cannot eat street food like local," he says.

He then hands me some marshmallow-colored powder to mix with water for dehydration and says the sickness will pass within seventy-two hours. I hope he is right because I cannot seem to leave the toilet. Luckily, the penthouse has three bathrooms, not including the toilet in the maid's quarters.

"You want IV, too?" Dr. Xiāo asks. "How is sleeping?"

I reassure him that I'm absolutely fine and he looks a bit disappointed. I wonder how much he's paid to be a private hotel physician.

"Here is pill for nausea, and I will give you more when you finish," he says, before exiting the penthouse.

Uncle Dai and Auntie Yingfei are extremely worried about me. They keep glancing at me and asking me if they need to call Dr. Xiāo again, even though he just left an hour ago. Uncle Dai excuses himself because there is "emergency at work," and he's needed at a new hotel construction site. He stares pointedly at Auntie Yingfei, who exchanges rapid words with him in Chinese. She looks upset.

I wonder what could be the problem. It's six a.m. Don't my aunt and uncle ever sleep?

Auntie Yingfei kindly says that she has already "order new clothes" for me. I nod, embarrassed and grateful. I fell asleep wearing Ruby's pink cotton-candy jumpsuit with the cotton balls and admittedly, when I got sick, I puked all over it. The jumpsuit is wrecked.

Of course, Ruby does not take the news well. The second garment that I have destroyed. Then it doesn't help when Auntie Yingfei leaves for work, not before ordering Ruby to help me study.

"Why don't you just go home?" Ruby asks me, openmouthed. She crosses her arms and looks seriously aggravated.

"I can't!" I say.

"I'll pay for your ticket back," she offers. "No one asked you to be here."

"No one asked me if *I* wanted to come here," I say. "I didn't even know you existed until a few weeks ago."

"How do you think I feel? No one told me about you coming here until your flight landed. My dad wanted to surprise me with a cousin my age. I used to beg him for a sibling to play with when I was a kid, and he thought I would be happy when you came along. I just can't believe we're related."

Incredulous, I stare at her.

Her eyes twitch.

I sigh. We're definitely related.

No wonder Ruby is so angry and disappointed with me. She's still reeling from the news. I didn't take it well either when I found out that she was a long-lost family member. It somehow made being Chinese more like a Wikipedia fact, having this instant weirdo connection to Beijing, whereas my cultural identity had previously been Sephora and Nordstrom department store. Chinese was just a type of late-night take-out food: greasy, gassy, but always delicious. Suddenly, my dad's stories and superstitions about zodiac animals and people with flower-hearts seemed REAL. My parents never once mentioned their past lives in China. They never talked about going back "home."

Poor Ruby.

Poor me!

"Well, when are you going home?" Ruby finally asks in a resigned voice.

"My dad says I have to learn how to be Chinese," I say miserably. "It might take a long time."

Like a ravenous water buffalo, Ruby lets out a huff of unceasing frustration.

I want to join her too, but I don't. Howling out loud would make my stomach hurt more. My insides already feel as if they have been trampled by a herd of overzealous elephants.

Seeming to recover from her anguish, Ruby finally speed-dials housekeeping to help her dispose of the suit. She won't even touch it. I don't blame her. The Shangri-La sends two chambermaids and a well-dressed manager with rubber gloves and tongs to dispose of the garment. When the staff all see me again, they sigh deeply.

Afterward, Ruby disappears into the maid's quarters and shuts the door.

When Uncle Dai and Auntie Yingfei come home at lunch to check on me, they insist that I drink more tongue-scalding herbal tea and ingest more chicken broth. I honestly have no appetite. Every fifteen minutes, I run to the toilet. The powder doesn't seem to be helping. Neither do the pills.

"Doctor say you are okay!" Uncle Dai says. "So now you can help Ruby with English. Time for language exchange."

I stare at him. Is he kidding?

He's not.

I should know by now that people in Beijing do not have a sense of humor. At least the people that I have encountered so far.

"I'm not feeling well!" I say in a meek voice.

"Nothing wrong with your mind!" my uncle says cheerfully. "Just stomach problem, right?"

I keep staring at him, horrified. Who makes someone work when they have fainted from some mysterious illness called "traveler's diarrhea"?

I know that I'm definitely not related to these obsessively studious people at all when he forces Ruby to come out of the maid's quarters and makes her hand me a twenty-page typed paper on Proust. The font is practically unreadable. It's so tiny. Like little polka dots. I squint.

"You need your glasses, Weijun?" Uncle Dai asks.

Glasses? What is my uncle talking about?

"Oh! I have 22/22 vision," I say proudly, and bring the paper close to my nose. This is ridiculous. Is the font somehow smaller in China? Do people have super eyesight in Beijing?

"Proust? What country is that?" I say, not understanding what I'm reading. I flip through the pages anxiously. "Is that a new name for Persia?"

Geography is always changing. I can't keep track.

Ruby stares at me.

I try again.

"So, what country do they speak Proust in?" I ask. "Is that a region in the Middle East?"

Uncle Dai looks at Ruby. Like he's asking her a question.

"Joking!" I quickly say, and Uncle Dai starts laughing.

"Weijun is very funny," he says, patting me on the back.

He suddenly gets an important phone call and exits the living room. I stare at the paper, and I can feel my mind turn to mush. Surely this isn't English literature?

Marcel Proust was one of the most profound and influential writers to come from France. He is the father of modern letters . . .

Immediately, I start yawning nonstop. It's like my mouth won't stop making noises of angry protest. I know I'm being rude, but I honestly can't help it. I get through the first sentence and realize that I've fallen asleep when Ruby taps me on the shoulder, like she's furiously texting me another rant-message. She has to literally whack my shoulder a few times for me to even wake up from this boring hallucination of reading about someone I don't know.

If a paragraph is longer than 142 characters, it's hard for me to pay attention. It's like my brain disconnects from my body and I have an out-of-body experience. I have no idea how I will ever master Chinese, a brand-new language, when I failed AP English Composition and AP English Literature.

"You were sleeping!" Ruby accuses me.

"I was not!" I say.

"Yes, you were!" she says.

"Sometimes when I'm concentrating, I just zone out!" I say.

"Well, what do you think of my paper?" she says.

"It's excellent!" I say brightly.

"Do you think the thesis statement needs to be refined more?"

I have no idea what Ruby is talking about.

"Is it too general?" she persists, frowning.

"How can an essay be too general?" I ask, feeling smart for knowing the answer to her trick question. "Essays should be about one subject."

Uncle Dai and Auntie Yingfei overhear us and walk over to the couch, carrying more cups of strong-smelling tea for us. I take a sip; it tastes like jasmine, nectarines, and walnuts. I take another. It's wonderfully soothing and delicious.

"Ruby is good at English?" Uncle Dai asks, looking pleased.

He doesn't see his daughter's exasperated but hopeful expression. The way that she wants her dad to approve of her, just like how I want my peer group to appreciate me.

"Yes," I say, even though I haven't read the paper, but grudgingly, I have to admit that it seems that my cousin is above-average smart based on the opening sentence. Ruby is definitely more advanced in English writing than me.

"Auntie Yingfei and I are studying English word too," he says.

"What 'acute' mean?" Auntie Yingfei asks me. She pulls out a fat book labeled "Engglish Vocabularley."

"Oh, it means adorable!" I say, proud to be able to be useful. "Like, that's 'a cute' purse or 'a cute' dog."

Uncle Dai and Auntie Yingfei nod enthusiastically. "Weijun, we are so glad we have native English speaker here!" Uncle Dai exclaims, clapping me on the back. "We hope Ruby will be smart like you. So much to learn from American cousin. Ruby, you must ask Iris lots of question."

Ruby looks up, horrified. "It doesn't mean that!" She pulls her face into an indignant expression.

But Uncle Dai doesn't seem to hear her. She actually looks genuinely hurt. Like she wants to say more about how she feels. I also want to say something about me not being smart and failing senior year, but I'm not sure if it will even help in this situation. It's like her dad is completely underestimating her mental abilities, while my dad constantly overestimates mine.

Why does my dad think I'm smarter, better, and more capable than I am? Why couldn't he just think I was a humongous loser and none of us would even be having this shitty conversation?

The truth feels slimy, a lot like eating potato salad that has melted in the sun.

My heart collapses.

Our dads' perceptions of us as real people, to be honest, kind of suck.

Don't they know that expectations can lead to multiple and long-lasting disasters for future generations? How selfish can they be?

"Weijun, your daddy tell us to be careful because you are Tiger," Uncle Dai says, interrupting my downward spiral of gloomy thoughts.

"Oh," I say, frowning.

"But I told him not to worry because Auntie Yingfei and I are powerful Dragon. We can control wild Tiger."

I laugh nervously. Chinese superstitions make me nervous. Do they have more power to come true in China?

"What is Ruby?" I force myself to ask.

"She is Monkey," he says, frowning.

He looks at Auntie Yingfei and they seem to exchange worried looks. Then they speak together in long strands of rapid-fire Chinese.

I don't know what it all means. Are they all absurdly superstitious like my dad? I'm seriously worried that means Ruby and I are about to set off a double curse. If I'm flower-hearted, what is she? Her heart must be made out of stainless steel or concrete. Maybe my cousin is a clockwork monkey or just a heartless glass figurine. What type of monkey-heart is she? I just can't seem to figure it out.

Ruby says something complain-y to her parents, but Uncle Dai shushes her.

"Listen to Iris! English is her first language!"

"Iris doesn't know what she's talking about!" Ruby says, sounding frustrated.

Uncle Dai frowns, staring at me. I wonder what he sees when he looks through me. Does he see me as a potential Ruby?

Then I remember that I need his approval so that he can decide when I'll go home. I've never wanted to go back to Bradley Gardens so badly. I want to wake up in my own bedroom; my dad goofily singing Broadway musicals, making cheddar cheese, bacon, and chive waffles on Sunday; my mom reciting, like a personal mantra, which top-tier colleges all her friends' children were applying to for early admission. All of that I would have found supremely annoying once upon a time, but it would make me feel less lonely and homesick now.

"English is my only language," I finally say, nodding wisely. I inhale my nutty tea like water and feel more worldly and wise. Like some newly named prophet. At least I know my English vocabulary words. Proust was too foreign.

"Okay, Ruby teach Weijun Chinese now," Uncle Dai says, clapping excitedly. "I tell your daddy that you will learn Chinese by end of summer, okay? Starting today."

Isn't it enough that I'm apparently a genius at English?

The deadline to learn a brand-new language is incredibly fast.

"I promise your daddy that your uncle Dai is always right."

Ruby snorts and turns to me. "Of course, since you are great at English, learning Chinese shouldn't be hard, right?"

"Absolutely!" I say, taking another swig of tea, then reaching for Ruby's, since she hasn't touched hers. She quickly slaps my hand away, like I'm a fly-size annoyance. I wince.

"Okay, I go to work now. Ruby teach Weijun and Weijun teach Ruby. Everyone learn new language or no more allowance."

He laughs at his own unfunny joke. Then he stares at us seriously. "No more shopping, no credit card if you both do not show improvement. Ruby need A-plus in English paper. Iris need finish reading all textbook and pass beginner Mandarin test. If I can talk English, Weijun can talk Chinese. Okay?"

Quickly, in response, I make a face and clutch my stomach, saying that I need to go to the bathroom. I don't do well with deadlines or ultimatums. Being told what to do causes sharp, fearful spasms inside me. For Iris Wang, expectations are like sweaty long-jump meets or hurdles. They usually mean falling on my face and chipping a tooth because I can't meet or surpass them. Since kindergarten, I don't remember ever excelling at anything.

Even my macaroni necklaces were subpar. If I fail Uncle Dai's demands to finish an entire Chinese beginner book, will he no longer like me? Will he exile me and Ruby to a Proust-speaking country?

Pretending to flush every fifteen minutes, I fake moan: "Owwwwwww! Oh my god, I think I'm dying! Ughhhhhhhhhh!"

I sound like one of those bad special-effects machines in a haunted house at a carnival, but it seems to work.

No one bothers me afterward.

Anxious and afraid, I stay in the bathroom until I hear everyone go to bed.

WECHAT GROUP (#1WangFamily!!!)

Iris: Hey, what does it mean if someone is born in the Year of the Monkey?

IrisDaddy: Normally, a Monkey is a smart animal, but it is a Tiger's worst enemy. Do you know a Monkey? Why do you ask?

Iris: No reason.

IrisDaddy: Okay, but be careful of the Monkey. Not a Tiger friend.

Iris: Ok.

Mom: Don't listen to your dad. It's all nonsense. How's your stomach?

IrisDaddy: Are you learning Chinese? Hope you are studying.

Chinese Parent Approved

Since I am too sick, I am allowed to stay home.
I hope this is an indefinite leave of absence from studying and summer school. Auntie Yingfei, who apparently works at a very important international bank, cannot take a day off and asks Mr. Chen to babysit me. Mr. Chen watches a football game on his iPad, so I end up scrolling through my social media feeds.

At least six people have commented on Samira's relationship status. *Are Peter and Iris really over? What happened?!!!!*

My heart lurches. I still can't believe that Peter broke up with me.

Social media suddenly makes it *too real.*

It's not official until it's been posted on at least three different social media sites and retweeted and shared six times. To make matters worse, despite us recently reconnecting as DM "friends," Samira has tagged me in ten new photos of her and Peter. They're touching each other's arms and legs in every single shot. Samira has even taken photographs of all the presents that Peter has given her: flowers, concert tickets, and Blu-rays of movies that he and I used to watch together.

Peter Hayes always said that he was "way too broke" to buy me nice things.

Come to think of it, he never bought me anything, not even on my birthday.

Suddenly, I want to throw up.

Samira has hurt me again, and I let her. Why did I even respond to her messages? Why didn't I just block her?

I'm seized by intense homesickness again, the shitty kind I had when I was in eighth grade at summer camp in Connecticut. Of course, I was sharing a cabin with Samira and six other girls, but when I wasn't making friendship bracelets, I was thinking about getting pedicures with my dad. Despite his lying and all his secrets, I really miss him. I even miss my mom, and all her unrealistic expectations.

That's probably why their abandonment hurts the most.

In the twenty-first century, it's like getting rid of a beloved pet by giving her to another home. No one ever asks a guinea pig or a gerbil whether they want to relocate. Anyway, I thought that being an only child meant that I was automatically the favorite, and exempt from parental punishment. I just never thought of my parents as actual people who could make earthquake-size decisions for me.

I've been too preoccupied with my own shock, anger, and sadness to realize how much I took their love for granted. Even though they sent me away, they would never hurt me so casually like Samira and Peter.

Until now, I never understood why my mom expected so much of me, but maybe I should have tried harder to listen to her, like how I try Olympic-athletic-hard to be well-liked in any social situation. I always assumed that my mom was being overly picky, but maybe she just saw who my ex–best friend and ex-boyfriend were from the beginning: soggy, leftover Doritos that no one else wanted.

"Iris, I don't understand why you never listen to me," she once said, frustrated, when I waltzed out of the house to meet Peter, surprising him with a brand-new T-shirt from an indie band that he liked. Or even when I rushed over to see Samira after midnight because my best friend had an emergency favor to ask me. Never mind if I had an exam the next day and overdue homework.

"You want me to have no life like you," I shouted back. "You don't want me to have any fun!"

"You keep inviting termites into your house and there will be nothing left," she said, sighing. "Why do you want these insects to like you? How is having bugs in your house fun?"

I never understood what she was talking about. I just assumed that she was referring to our ongoing home renovations. I was just grateful that there were two additional people, besides my parents, who said they liked and needed me. At least that was what I had honestly thought.

My parents would never betray me in real life and on social media, would they?

WECHAT GROUP (#1WangFamily!!!)

IrisDaddy: We have very bad news :(:(:(

Mom: We saw Samira and Peter today at the mall.

IrisDaddy: You know they are holding hands? Acting like boy-friend and girlfriend!!!

Iris: . . .

Mom: Good riddance to such bad people.

Iris: . . .

IrisDaddy: You can do better, Iris. Remember you are a Tiger. King of the jungle! Better than them.

Iris: Thanks, Dad.

Iris: I'm sorry for everything . . .

Iris: I'm really sorry for how I behaved.

After chatting with my parents, I feel even more teary-eyed and heartbroken. I want to go back to my old life with the boring suburbs and parents who criticize my shitty life choices. I just want to hop on the next return flight. If I had known I would be banished to Beijing, I would never have *not* studied for the SATs. I would have even proofread all my college applications twice.

A knock on the apartment door interrupts my soft-crying rev-erie. Mr. Chen is absorbed in his football game. So I wipe my wet, monster-red eyes and answer the door, wondering if it's house-keeping. There's a random dude in the hallway in a blue cardigan, and for a second, I don't even know why he's here. Normally, I might send him away like I do with door-to-door salespeople, but then I remember the unbelievably good-looking tutor at the interview who laughed at me in my housecoat and face mask. He puts his hands together and bows briefly.

Should I bow back?

Up close, Blue Cardigan is tall, polite, and handsome, the complete opposite of all the usual dudes who come looking for me. He's better-looking than all the boys in Bradley Gardens, and in comparison, way hotter than all the tutors that my parents have ever hired.

He starts talking to me in Chinese.

When he sees my confused expression, he quickly switches to English. "Weijun, I'm Frank Liao? Your uncle said that I was supposed to tutor you to help you catch up in school."

"Wrong person," I say, quickly closing the door.

Then I regret that I didn't just ask him for his number before pretending that I didn't know who he was. For a millisecond, I almost wish that I wasn't so severely allergic to learning.

I hope Frank doesn't actually recognize me without the horsehair face mask. What a lucky coincidence I decided to prioritize self-care after being scammed by a cabdriver! A facial scrub is better than any superhero costume. I have always wondered why bank robbers on TV don't just get classy spa masks as substitutes for goofy cartoon ones.

I wait for my new tutor to leave, and half an hour later, I decide to take the subway. The penthouse seems too congested. I need to hop on a train or a bus—to get anywhere from here. Mr. Chen is too busy shouting at his live-streaming game to even notice.

All those years of sneaking out to see Peter have paid off. I'm an expert at stealth. Ask any teenage girl of strict Chinese parents what her superpower is, and she'd say it's sneaking away or telling believable white lies. I don't have a skill in inventing plausible alternative scenarios to my parents because I usually feel so guilty that I have to suddenly confess. My dad says it's a Tiger trait: it's noble not to lie.

I guess Goats are great liars.

But a Tiger is excellent at stealthily running away.

Of course, I can't find the same Oriental Plaza from the first day.

As soon as I leave the lobby of the Shangri-La and bow enthusiastically to the doormen, I don't know which direction to wander in. I pretend to be supremely confident, like I'm strutting down a runway at a Victoria's Secret fashion show, as I follow what I hope is a sign to the subway. It doesn't resemble transit at all, and the logo looks like Gucci and Chanel merged as one multinational Chinese company. Is this a sign to a clothing factory? But I'm proud of myself for at least getting somewhere.

When I see the subway station, I whoop and congratulate myself. I always knew that I was destined for foreign travel. But I get hopelessly lost after I buy a subway ticket. There are so many rushing people, and I don't really understand which train to get on. All I know is that I'm at the National Library metro stop. I ask a girl my age for directions, but she ignores me. I ask a woman who could be my mother, but then our exchange turns into a nonstop lecture about why I don't speak Chinese.

"You look Chinese," she says, staring suspiciously at me. "Why you not understanding?"

Why don't Beijingers get it when I say I'm from the suburbs of Bradley Gardens, New Jersey?

"What wrong with you?" another man asks.

At his question, I glare at the stranger, and I feel a bit shitty for doing it. He doesn't understand how language can be lost when your parents leave the homeland and work hard to adapt to a foreign culture. He doesn't understand that I am the most important product of their decades-long struggle. My dad, who is not as smart as my mom, told me he took ten years to be able to speak English fluently, and another five more before he could compose a decent-sounding email. Both of them forced English down their throats like a hangover-cure smoothie of raw eggs, licorice root, and tomato juice. Teaching me Chinese was not their priority. Making me happy was what they cared about most.

"I'm American Chinese!" I holler at the retreating back of the man. He begins to jog-run, as if he is actually scared of me.

Eyes watering and sneezing nonstop from the smog, I get even more hopelessly lost at the station. I'm also not feeling better when my stomach cramps relentlessly and I realize that I still have my unruly traveler's diarrhea. This made-up bug has obviously not exited my system.

Someone taps me on the shoulder.

Shit.

Involuntarily I jump.

SHIT.

"I saw you leave the hotel." It's Frank in his blue grandpa-cardigan. He looks serious but also slightly amused. His lips twitch at the corners, as if he's afraid to fully smile. But then he winks at me, like he knows why I am running away, and for some reason, my breathing and my heart stop completely. It seems that my flower-heart is officially malfunctioning or working too well in China.

Physical attraction isn't supposed to be dangerous to your overall health. How can finding a boy attractive cause disruptions to one's major organs?

As if on cue, my stomach rumbles. The sound of undigested thunder. And every shitty soundtrack to a slasher horror movie.

"I promise I'm not stalking you," he continues.

I'm barely listening.

"Do you have small change, I mean, six *yuan*, for the bathroom?" I blurt out, embarrassed that I lied but needing to use the bathroom more. To my surprise, I'm thrilled that I might at least have some company, if not some serious boy-candy to soothe my aching eyeballs. But first, bathroom business. I continue, almost not caring that I look slightly panicked, "It's an emergency. I'll pay you back."

Fumbling for his wallet, Frank hands over some spare change, and then I remember just in time that I need a bit extra to buy toilet paper. He obligingly hands over a few more crumpled *yuan*.

"Everything is okay?" he asks when I return.

He smiles politely and hands me a bottle of mineral water.

I nod.

My heart is literally thumping hard, and I'm not sure if it's because I've been getting a leg workout from crouching with my traveler's diarrhea or if I'm dehydrated and just delirious. I gratefully glug the water down, not caring that I spill most of it on my sweatshirt and the ground.

"So famous Wang Weijun, favorite niece of Feng Construction Corp, all the way from the United States, how do you like Beijing so far?" he says, grinning. He gestures proudly at the steel structures around him, like he's responsible for their particular creation.

"China is . . . interesting," I say, not sure how to explain my last seventy-two hours of misadventures. Would he care that I'm a cultural misfit? Does Frank know anything about being homesick, which is like having mono and a weekend hangover at the same time? Has he ever been banished to another country with strangers who all look like you but everything you say and do is strange and unrelatable and leads to confusion?

"It's really, really lovely to finally meet you," Frank says. Genuine warmth seeps into his words, and he sounds like he actually means it.

For a second, my body temperature suddenly feels hotter than Las Vegas. I gulp more water, unable to look away.

We shake hands. And I can't stop staring at Frank's incredibly symmetrical features. I'm actually jealous. He makes me feel a bit intimidated, to be honest. My mom's advice keeps looping in my head like an annoying pop song: *Never date dudes who are better-looking than you*, I find myself repeating. *Otherwise they will football-smash your heart.* She also said not to be BFFs with better-looking people, but look at what happened with Samira and Peter, who were really average-looking. "Boyfriends and best friends are not like shopping for fruit," she once explained. "In this case, a rotten apple is not rotten. Find your ugliest fruit."

I never really understood what she meant.

I just really miss her confusing advice. I hope she is thinking about me right now and feeling guilty and worrying about her only child. (I'm pretty sure that I don't have a sibling that I don't know about. I'd be so bummed if I was suddenly replaced.)

Besides, it's not like I have to be romantically involved with Frank. I just want someone to talk to in Beijing. Bonus points if he's an extra-beautiful specimen who looks like he takes care of himself.

"Sorry I lied earlier," I say. "I just don't like being tutored, you know?"

He looks baffled. "Why?"

"Because it's work," I protest.

"It's more work for me," Frank says. "Sometimes I have to tutor people who don't put in any effort."

I laugh nervously.

Back in New Jersey, tutoring seemed like a waste of time when I could be with Peter. But in Beijing, there's honestly nothing better to do.

Taking my elbow, Frank walks me to a nearby coffee shop in what he calls the "tourist district," and he orders our drinks. "Do you take cream in your coffee?" he asks.

"No thank you!" I blurt, thinking about the bathroom situation.

Frank says that after the group interview, Uncle Dai's secretary immediately hired him, congratulating him on passing the rigorous hiring process. Uncle Dai thought that Frank could probably teach Mandarin to an opinionated American and help me pass my GED with moderate effort.

As he talks, I notice that Frank's English has a soft, flat British-Mandarin accent. Sipping his coffee, Frank explains that he has been studying English since he was five years old, and that he's an English literature and classical Chinese literature major at Tsinghua University.

He proudly says the name "Tsinghua" like it's Harvard University, but I honestly haven't heard of it before.

Confused about why someone would want to spend their whole life learning a language and giving up their summer holiday to work, I want to ask Frank about his life in Beijing. But he finishes his coffee, and I'm disappointed when he immediately opens an SAT book and begins discussing the verbal component.

I nod and pretend to be interested.

He keeps talking energetically about multiple choice, like he's narrating a red carpet event at the Oscars. How can anyone find fill-in-the-blank vocabulary as glamorous as designer evening wear?

"So let's try some verbal reasoning . . . ," he says, at the same time that I ask him about his hobbies.

I just want to know more about Frank. I don't care about unpronounceable words with more than four syllables.

But he ignores my question and continues discussing strategies and word choices. I don't know any of the vocabulary that he's referencing, even though English is my first language and English is his second. I thought I would be some prodigy at English when I arrived in Beijing. But people who are second-language learners seem to know more thesaurus-sounding words than I do. How is this possible? Isn't English vernacular something you absorb through the osmosis of peers and social media celebrities who slowly replace your parents?

Inevitably I yawn several times and pretend that I'm stretching my lower jaw. I hope my yawning will signal to him that he should change the conversation and tell me more about himself. What does he like to do for fun in Beijing? Who are his friends?

Frank nods and looks unfazed.

I raise my hand. I cough, like I have something very urgent to announce. As if I'm captain of an airplane about to announce a crash landing over a major metropolis. The thought of meeting Uncle Dai's ultimatum of finishing the entire *Mandarin Language Beginner Guide* is absolutely terrifying. How can Frank be so calm about learning?

"Can we take a break?" I ask politely.

Frank stares at me, looking astonished and confused. I can't tell if he's laughing at me like he did in the conference room or if he's having a seizure. "But we're only ten minutes into our lesson," he says.

"Is that a yes?" I ask.

With a meaningful expression, I glance at the coffee shop's display case of cheesecakes and flaky pastries. I spot a cream puff with matcha-green filling. Slices of puffy, yellow sponge cake are arranged on a tray. "How about a snack?"

"No break," Frank says firmly. "We need to finish the chapter."

He resumes his long explanation about strategizing. How can test-taking be this complicated? There are only four possible answers (A, B, C, D). Does he not know that SAT multiple choice only requires a 25 percent chance of intuition, genius, and good fortune? You have more of a chance getting an answer correct than winning one of my dad's scratch-and-win tickets.

Frank's mouth is moving, but I can't help thinking about the too-symmetrical shape of his lips, which is like a geometry lesson in itself. The way that he overpronounces his words and nibbles beautifully on his lower lip when he's concentrating. It's adorable and fascinating. Almost like watching a quirky but intelligent chipmunk.

Most importantly, I am also thinking about Ruby and how I'll be able to get out of this "learn to be Chinese" situation. If I learn enough conversational Chinese to fake it, maybe I can convince Uncle Dai that I am authentically Chinese on the inside, so that my parents will let me return home to my former life of Chipotle and malls? Maybe they'll let me come home early and finish my GED and I won't have to stay in Beijing anymore. But how do I stop being a full-on banana who has to magically transform into one of those impossibly delicious yellow sponge cakes at the counter?

"I am going to fix this!" I accidentally blurt out, and Frank gives me that strange, quizzical look again.

"It's a name of an American TV show," I cover up quickly. "Speaking of movies, have you seen anything life-changing lately?"

Frank ignores my generous social cue to change the subject.

Instead, he keeps talking about planning and strategy (so many steps to answering one question). How will I ever finish the verbal component of the SAT when he claims there are multi-steps and multi-ways of thinking about a problem?

If Frank were discussing something exciting about pop culture or Beijing hair trends, or had some semi-interesting anecdotes about his life as a college student, I might enjoy listening to him. I want to know the fun, dirty secrets on campus. What happens at university parties? What's Beijing's drug scene like?

But having a lesson with Frank is like watching an hour-long show on PBS when it should be the CW. I just want the fun, winking dude from my interview back. It's my duty to distract Frank from his tutoring lesson.

There's a shift in tone, and then I really don't understand what Frank is saying. Then I realize that he's speaking Chinese to me!

"Sorry, I don't understand Chinese," I interrupt, confused.

"I've been waiting to see when you'd notice," Frank says. "The correct term is Mandarin, and I've been speaking it to you for at least three minutes."

"I noticed," I lie quickly.

Honestly, there's absolutely no difference between speaking the Chinese language and listening to the SATs.

"Have you ever thought about what your ancestors would say about you not speaking their language? What if they showed up at this coffee shop right now and you couldn't talk to them?" Frank asks.

"Not really," I say, fidgeting. "I would just assume that a ghost would have access to Google Translate."

"What?" Frank laughs loudly.

He thinks I'm making a joke, but I'm dead serious.

I flush.

"You wouldn't want to talk to your ancestors?" he says, sounding incredulous. He looks incredibly excited by the prospect of communicating with dead people. "You wouldn't want to ask them questions about your history or find out what they are like as individuals?"

"Probably not," I say, shrugging.

Frank looks astonished. Then he finally relents at my lack of curiosity. Truthfully, I wouldn't want to speak to a ghost, even if they were related to me. What if they were just like my cousin Ruby? What if they were a million times worse?

"Okay, but can you just *please* pay attention during our lesson?" Frank asks.

His emphasis on the word "please" somehow strikes me as boyish and charming. There's also something weirdly appealing about his hyperfocused personality. Combine that with photoshopped good looks and extra-polite manners. His whole presence seems to make me feel slightly strange and woozy. I fan myself with a paper napkin. I've never had this sort of physical reaction when I was with Peter or any of my ex-boyfriends whose names I don't actually remember.

Smiling brightly at Frank, I nod with overly fake enthusiasm. Should I clap? Or would that only encourage him to talk more about the SATs?

But so far, Frank doesn't need more encouragement. He launches into verbal reasoning. He's being the perfect mannequin tutor who seems immune to my exciting EQ, which means that my parents would love him. My dad would definitely date him. Frank is a perfect CPA (Chinese Parent Approved) boy to woo and marry and reproduce two to three offspring.

Because I spend so much time trying not to listen to the SATs, I almost miss a glimpse of that bold, radioactive personality that emerges when he reaches the analogy section. A sneaky grin, a barely heard chuckle that instantly makes me wish we were somewhere more stimulating than a coffee shop. When he looks at me, my face tingles like I have been bitten by a mutant spider with magical boy-attracting powers.

Why am I staring so much at my CPA tutor?

Oh god.

Am I turning into my parents, who have the weirdest taste in boys?

I tell myself that it's because I've been recently dumped and have not met any hot male twentysomethings since landing in Beijing. This is just a symptom of my wild, beating flower-heart.

It's my unpredictable Tiger curse.

Finally SAT class is over and I want to leap up to the counter for a coffee (I deserve a mocha with extra whip and multicolored sprinkles for learning), but charming robot tutor Frank pulls out another humongous textbook from his backpack and he insists on teaching me how to greet someone in Mandarin. He also hands me a study schedule that has math, chemistry, physics, economics, and American history printed on it.

Rubbing my face, I yawn pointedly and stare at the schedule.

He wasn't kidding, was he?

"*Nǐ hǎo, nǐ hǎo ma,*" he says. "Hello, how are you? Let's look at page three."

It's honestly both terrifying and boring learning a brand-new language. I have no idea how my parents both did it. Most of all, I'm so scared that Frank will think I'm a hopeless, unteachable mess if I don't pick up a few of the easier phrases within the next hour.

I try my best to stifle it, but I end up panic-yawning so much that I think I'm giving myself a self-induced TMJ disorder.

Frank doesn't even blink.

Dude is like a learning machine!

What he does try to do is make me practice the Chinese etiquette line two thousand times, like we're rehearsing for an audition for a television show. I absolutely refuse to practice.

What is it with all Beijing people and constant learning? When do they ever take a vacation? Learning about Frank's educational history, multiple choice, followed by a Chinese saying, was enough for a week.

I excuse myself to go to the bathroom, and when he isn't looking, I decide to hail a taxi to the hotel. This time, I carefully negotiate a fee of 67 *yuan* with the driver before I get inside the car. I even take a photo of the taxi's license plate in case he tries to scam me.

I'm learning, but very slowly.

Secrets

There's serious scream-arguing when I get back
to the penthouse. The kind of extreme soap-opera shouting that
reminds me of the fight that I had with Dad in the parking lot.
It feels like a lifetime ago, almost in another reality, with a completely different Iris Wang. Has traveling already changed me?

My body tenses up, either from a shitty association or from
the fact that I've never liked confrontation. I don't know whether
I should creep backward down the hall or make a nonthreatening
noise to let them know I'm here.

Are you supposed to politely cough or sneeze? Which one is
less obvious and more convincing?

I start to half cough, half sneeze.

It sounds like I'm choking on a Life Savers candy, but it causes
the two people to suddenly stop screaming.

At first, I think Auntie Yingfei and Uncle Dai were arguing,
but it's an older, tiny Chinese lady. She's wrinkled like a *Star Wars*

character and sobbing uncontrollably. She gasps in shock when she sees me. At first, I think she's horrified by my outfit, but she's looking at me like she's seen a real-life ghost.

She's actually so startled that she knocks over a vase of pink chrysanthemums and yellow night-blooming jasmine. *CRASH!* Glass shatters everywhere. I rush to help clean it up. This woman seems to be as clumsy as I am.

Uncle Dai turns the color of an unripe banana as soon as he sees me. "Weijun! I did not know you were home. Mr. Chen is driving around looking for you!"

The old woman starts crying even louder as soon as she hears my name. She grasps my arm and pulls me toward her into an awkward, one-armed hug. I am so shocked that I can't react. I still have the soggy wet flowers in one hand.

Normally, I'd polite-hug her back. It's not very nice to ignore an attempted embrace, especially from a senior citizen. The poor lady could be confused and mistaking me for someone else.

While the old lady keeps crying and trying to hug me, I stare at Uncle Dai for instructions or a clue. He looks as shocked as me.

Finally, he says, "This is your *nǎinai*, grandmother."

I stare at her. I drop the gathered flowers. I am literally being hugged by a ghost or a zombie.

I don't know how to react.

I'm not sure if I should keep letting someone who might not be real hug me, or if I should pull away. What is the proper Chinese etiquette here? My parents never mentioned what to do if someone who is supposed to be your long-dead grandma puts you in a headlock. I decide not to move until Uncle Dai explains the proper custom to me. I don't exactly know when I should clap or bow or run away. There are too many viable options to choose from.

"So I DO have living grandparents?" I manage to sputter after she lets me go. "Why did my dad tell me that my grandparents were dead? Why would he lie about it?"

At my words, Uncle turns even whiter. He says nothing. But he doesn't tell the woman what I said in English. At first, I wonder if Uncle Dai is confused. Is he mixing up Ruby's grandparents with mine? Wait, do cousins even have the same grandparents? How do family trees work?

The woman who is supposedly my undead grandmother starts sobbing again and speaking urgently to me in Chinese. Finally, she lets go of me. But she seems to be begging me, asking me a question I don't know. The only Chinese I can understand is my own name. As if she's pleading directly to me.

"What is she saying?" I say to Uncle Dai.

"It is not important," he says, slamming his fist into the counter. It makes a loud, horrific bang. He turns to my grandmother, his mother, and begins talking in a serious, urgent voice. My mild-mannered uncle has never seemed so terrifying before. His fist hits the counter in a series of loud, frightening bangs and I flinch.

If he acts like this in a boardroom meeting, I can see why the students vying for a tutoring job were so scared of him!

My grandmother stares at me, almost beseechingly. She turns to my uncle and then back at me. I keep hearing her say my name between bursts of tears and Chinese.

I don't understand. She keeps pointing at me. Does she want me to do or say something? Am I somehow being rude?

Am I the reason they're arguing?

Sobbing, she embraces me again and I feel her slip something into my fingers. I freeze. But only for a moment. What she hands me is smaller than a bill and lighter than a gram of weed, but I smoothly slip it into my high-heeled boot. My uncle starts speaking again and her face crumples, like an aluminum can.

Her pupils are wet and she's still looking at me, as if she's trying to communicate a message.

I stare at her, but unfortunately, I don't have ESP.

Are her eyes saying *Follow me*? Are they saying *I'm sorry*?

Is she saying that I'm hallucinating? I'm still in shock by this totally unexpected encounter.

My grandmother starts trying to say something important to me, but I honestly don't understand. Sobbing, she finally flees the apartment. The door slams.

I wish there were subtitles to this dramatic scene.

I wish I knew how to understand Chinese, at least! It would make trying to guess what everyone is saying or doing so much easier. It would make things way more simpler if I knew what my aunt, uncle, or cousin was really trying to say.

Reading facial features and body language isn't one of my greatest strengths.

Beijing has taught me that I definitely do not have powers of ESP.

Shocked, I pretend to be busy cleaning. But my mind spins like an Olympic figure skater who fails at doing a triple axel and lands facedown. I'm making myself dizzy from my own brain-boggling thoughts. How is that possible? I never overthink or cause myself to stress out. Baffled, I bend down and continue picking up the flowers and broken shards of glass.

Isn't my grandmother supposed to be dead?

My dad lied about having a brother, but why would he continue to pretend that the rest of his family wasn't alive? Does he not want me to actually meet my grandparents in Beijing? What is my father so afraid of?

Why should I be surprised by anything my parents say or don't say? My family members obviously cannot be trusted. Uncle Dai could be lying about my grandparents. I'm surrounded by a family of Dragons, Goats, Monkeys, and liars! Lying is apparently a genetic, transcontinental trait.

"Weijun, just leave glass for maid," my uncle says, suddenly sounding exhausted. He has stopped beating up the counter. He sighs deeply and surveys the room.

I continue pretending to be cleaning. Normally, I'm never so diligent about tidying my own room.

"Stop cleaning, Weijun."

I act as if I don't hear him. I scoop the glass into a large pile and half attempt to haphazardly sort the pieces by size and shape.

"Weijun!" he finally says, and I stop immediately.

His face is twisted into something painful and unrecognizable. At first I witness anger and indignation, and then his expression softens into fear and shame. Like how I felt or still feel about failing my entire senior year. How I feel about being a loser to my lying but loving and mostly devoted parents.

If I'm completely honest with myself, I don't even want to admit that I really don't know what to do with myself.

But I have never been remotely good at real life.

But this whole episode with my grandmother is just so terrifying, and I honestly don't know what to do. Seeing my panic-stricken face, my uncle relents and says in a softer tone, "Weijun, you can never see your grandmother again. Your daddy does not want you to see your grandparents. Please do not tell him what happen today."

I don't know what to say.

Suddenly, Uncle Dai grabs my arm. "Do you understand what I'm saying? This very important."

I say nothing.

"You promise, Iris?"

It's the first time that he uses my American name.

"It will break him," he says.

Break him?

Uncle Dai is looking very intense and serious, and I can't imagine what would happen if I didn't say yes. He no longer looks like a kindly Rich Uncle Money Bags. There's a fiery toughness in him that I don't recognize. A ferocious Dragon hiding under a benevolent Santa Claus disguise. Uncle Dai has actual teeth, claws, and scales underneath his Armani three-piece suit.

"Your father cannot EVER know that you saw your grandmother," he says.

"Why?" I say.

"He make me promise."

"Why?" I ask again.

"Stop talking," he says. "And promise."

"Sure," I manage to squeak out, but I keep my fingers crossed behind my back. It's not technically lying if I pretend to agree with him and then secretly find the truth out later. There's no rule about investigating after a promise. Why else would you cross your fingers? Isn't it for luck?

When Ruby gets home from "Hanyuan Language School," I decline eating dinner with them at Han Wa Ju, a popular Sichuan-style restaurant that is famous for mouthwatering dry-fried green beans and *Mapo Doufu*, a simmering spicy meat and ultra-soft tofu stew.

"Weijun not feel well," Uncle Dai tells Ruby, and they turn to leave. But not before he gives me a worried look and hands me a humongous wad of *yuan*.

Is this a bribe?

I excuse myself to use the bathroom and I stick my flaming face under the taps, cooling my cheeks with icy water. Three stubbly new hairs have sprouted above my upper lip, and one particularly thick one is struggling to emerge from my cheek. I grab my Nair Wax Ready-Strips and rip them away, feeling confused and uneasy. I still don't understand what is happening.

When I finally finish waxing, Uncle Dai and Ruby have not left the hotel yet. They are immersed in frantic, serious discussion. I pause, unsure if I should interrupt or just sneak past them. They don't notice me, awkwardly standing in the living room like a floor lamp. Should I fake cough? Loudly declare my presence by belting out a song?

But I notice that Ruby's face has turned into a full-on sneer.

She stomps her feet, like a hurt toddler. She's wearing neon-blue Louboutin sandals, and I'm honestly disappointed that she still doesn't like me enough to ask me what's going on. Instead, she erupts. I can see why Uncle Dai has a bad temper due to his Dragon nature, but Ruby is supposed to be an easygoing Monkey. A little mischievous, but not a chimpanzee having a full-blown meltdown. I don't understand why she's so wounded about Uncle Dai giving me more money. Is it because she already thinks I'm spoiled? She can have the money if it makes her stop yelling at me.

"What did Iris do to deserve it?" she says, starting to cry. "All she does is sit around and mooch off our food and spend all our money on ugly clothes. She doesn't know about our lives before Beijing."

Uncle Dai speaks sharply to Ruby in Chinese.

In English, he says, "It is my money, not your money. Please. No more talking."

"No!" she replies, sniffling. "I won't be quiet. You need to send her away. I don't want a cousin. My life has been terrible since you let her live with us. Why do you insist on being nice to a half brother who wanted nothing to do with us before? He never helped us, Grandma, Grandpa . . . he practically abandoned us."

"What are you talking about?" I interrupt, and both of them seem shocked to see me. Ruby flushes a deep burgundy-orange color, looking mortified. She wipes her eyes and nose quickly and refuses to acknowledge my question.

My mouth is dry like a fourteen-day-old chocolate cake. And my heart beats faster at this new development.

"Ruby, you talk too much," Uncle Dai says. "Go to car NOW."

"What do you mean my dad abandoned you guys?" I say, shocked. "My dad would never do that to family?!"

I feel a sudden protective urge to defend my dad.

"Weijun daddy is my brother, Ruby," Uncle Dai says. "It is all the past. Big mistake lead to bigger misunderstanding that last too many year. We already talk about it when I hire detective and lawyer to help find family in America. Problem over. Sometimes angry people make mistake. He say sorry, I say sorry. Enough."

"Your dad and you are ungrateful mooches," she says to me softly. "Just leave Beijing and go back to the United States."

My face burns. Like she's splashed a cup of scalding espresso on me.

I flinch.

I know when I'm not wanted or welcome.

"Just take money, Weijun," Uncle Dai interrupts, and slaps another huge wad of *yuan* into my palm. He doesn't say anything else to defend my dad or chastise Ruby for her nasty accusations. He just leaves the apartment, stomping like a war general as he exits. Head held high, Ruby follows him, not even looking back.

The hotel suite suddenly feels empty, dark, and silent. Homesickness overwhelms me like a three-month case of mono.

I feel seriously sick.

Anxiously, I painstakingly count out 8,000 *yuan*. 8,000??! What's a girl to do with so much money? I could run outside and go shopping and immediately forget about meeting the ghost of my not-dead grandmother. At least I think that's what Uncle Dai hopes I'll do.

I could even take the money and buy a return ticket home. 8,000 *yuan* could be a remedy to this truly shitty cultural experience.

Suddenly, like a horrible conscience, my phone dings nonstop. I can't bring myself to tell my dad the truth.

WECHAT GROUP (#1WangFamily!!!)

IrisDaddy: Everything okay today???

Iris: Yes.

IrisDaddy: Anything interesting happen???

Iris: No. Just learning Chinese.

IrisDaddy: Who are you and what have you done to my daughter?

Iris: Very funny, Dad.

IrisDaddy: Hahaha.

IrisDaddy: Study hard. We love you.

IrisDaddy: Do you love us too?

Iris: Yes.

IrisDaddy: Yes, what?

Iris: Love you guys too.

IrisDaddy: Oh, Samira's mommy and daddy came over with Samira today for a surprise visit. They brought over your favorite chicken samosas and coconut curry. They kept asking about you . . . They seem to think you are out of the country. Why is that?

IrisDaddy: They kept trying to ask which college you got into, and your mommy finally told them it was none of their business. They were shocked. We won't be talking to them at the country club anymore.

IrisDaddy: We really miss you.

Iris . . . .

Iris: Then why did you send me away??????

IrisDaddy: It was not an easy decision. You will understand when you grow up.

Iris: ???

IrisDaddy: We only want the best for you. A new place is good for a new personality.

Iris: You want me to get a new personality??

IrisDaddy: No, we want you to learn to work hard. Learn from your uncle, aunt, and cousin.

Iris: If I was miserable here, would you let me come home?

IrisDaddy: What's wrong??

Iris: Please let me come home!!! [Retracted message]

Iris: Nothing . . . just really miss home.

Iris: BIG question: why didn't you tell me that Grandma and Grandpa were alive??? [Retracted message]

Finally, I decide to stuff the 8,000 *yuan* inside my wallet so I can't see it.

If it's out of sight, I can ignore it, right? After all, my dad just said that he loves me. My dad can't be the bad guy in this family situation. Despite our recent problems, he's always understood me more than my mom has.

Curious, I take out the mystery item from my grandma in my boot. It's a tiny gold envelope for the Red Mandarin Hotel, the kind that clerks give you when you check into a hotel. There's a room number 33245 and a white plastic key card.

I stare at it, confused. Does my grandmother want me to go to the hotel? Was this an open invitation or a mistake? But slipping her room key into my hand seemed to be deliberate. I examine it for the longest time.

Unable to relax, I pull up high-res photos of the Red Mandarin Hotel, a spiraling glass palace in the shape of a flying dragon, on my iPhone and realize that it's one of Uncle Dai's famous seven-star hotels, built only a few years back for celebrities and the world's top 3 percent. The Red Mandarin Hotel is award-winning for hospitality and received Beijing's top architectural medal. I'm impressed that Uncle Dai is responsible for such a fantastic feat.

I realize that even if I found a way to the hotel, I wouldn't be able to communicate with my grandmother. How would she be able to tell me the truth about the past? No one told me that growing up and learning family secrets in another language would be practically impossible. I am honestly disappointed in myself, almost ashamed that I never tried harder to learn one simple greeting. I can't even say "grandmother" in Chinese. My fear of studying and failing means that I might never be able to speak to her. I keep seeing her stricken expression over and over again. Would my grandmother say that I wasn't Chinese? If I don't understand her, will she think that I'm not part of her family?

Not speaking Chinese has already made me an ugly centipede in my Beijing family of silk caterpillars.

All this unexpected sleuthing is making me ravenous, and I realize that my appetite is back. To cheer myself up, I order room service: strips of raw mutton to be instantly boiled in a cauldron of hot water, shredded pork tenderloin in green sweet-spicy bean sauce, and zesty soybean noodles piled with lightly stir-fried vegetables.

What would my parents say if I flew back to America? What if I told them that I just couldn't learn Chinese? That I tried to be ethnically, culturally, and politely Chinese, and I completely failed in every way possible? Nothing is stopping me if I used Uncle Dai's wad of *yuan*. They wouldn't legally be able to kick me out, would they? But then I imagine the shock, red-eyed fury, and nonstop disappointment that they would feel if I disobeyed them again. We might never recover as a family. I just want things to go back to pre-failing-senior-year days. I want us to be happy and normal and ordering seven-layer ice-cream cakes together from Dairy Queen.

I used to think being Chinese meant that I had to be a boring geek like my dad or a super-high-achieving CEO like my mom, but in reality, I just didn't know the definition.

But in this city, there seems to be more to being Chinese than politeness, hard work, and pan-fried noodles. Whether I like it or not, I am connected to a long legacy of real and complicated people who have ugly secrets. At the same time, I am not used to being an outsider, a hopeful loner, or an unlicensed detective who has to use her IQ to solve serious life problems.

Why does Generation Z have to solve the issues of all the past generational alphabets? Is it because there are no other letters after Z?

I take comfort in the fact that if we were still friends, Samira and her dad would be so wildly jealous that I have my own real-life soap opera.

Instead of watching TV, I surprise myself and find the Mandarin language textbook from Uncle Dai that I hid under the bathroom sink. Feeling determined, I flip it open and ignore the escalating panic that typically takes over my mind whenever I have to study. *"Nǐ hǎo, nǐ hǎo ma,"* I keep repeating, even though I'm not sure how to properly say it. *How are you?* I want to ask my grandmother. I practice saying it at least a hundred times, in four different voices (soprano, alto, tenor, and bass) because I'm not sure which tone improves my accent. And then I move on to *"Wǒ jiào Wang Weijun." My name is . . . "Wǒ shì nǐ de dà nǚ'ér . . ."* *I am your granddaughter.* There are at least a thousand phrases in the book. If I learn three a night, I could be fluent in Mandarin (I use the calculator on my phone) in 333 days. That's practically a whole year. Why does mastering a language take so long??!!

In one year, I could also find out that I have another identity and all this learning might have been for nothing. What if instead of Chinese, I am supposed to be learning Korean or something obscure like Latin?

If I am truly Chinese, shouldn't I somehow find learning Mandarin easier based on my genetic makeup? If I'm truly ethnically, culturally, and politely Chinese, isn't there a special cheat code to level up?

All night, my mind goes on fast-forward, images of my grandmother, Uncle Dai, and Ruby blending together in a confusing dream montage. *Wǒ jiào Wang Weijun,* I keep saying to everyone, but no one can understand me. Finally, nightmare Ruby tells me that I'm not Wang Weijun. I'm just an impostor who doesn't belong.

Wasting Time

"Are you paying attention?" Frank asks me. He doesn't say anything about me bailing on him yesterday. I want to make up creative excuses, but I'm too tired. Secret-keeping is exhausting. I don't have enough storage space left in my brain. Plus, he should be proud of me. I practiced three Mandarin phrases for almost half the night. But I can sense his disapproval with the crossed arms and nonstop frowning.

Honestly, I also don't know how my dad or Uncle Dai keep such complicated secrets. It's like I'm doing intense, invisible work with my imploding thoughts and getting zero credit. I must be an outdated iPhone with 8GB, but my dad and Uncle Dai are the latest model with unlimited storage capacity.

After only one day, I just want to blurt out everything to anyone who will listen. My dad kept the secret of his brother and undead parents for seventeen-plus years. Did he keep upgrading his memory? Installing new software?

I'm still furious at my dad for lying not once but twice. Is he trying to deprive me of all the family that I could know? What would happen if I asked him to produce a family tree? Would all the ancestors that are supposed to be dead be actually part of the living too? What the hell is wrong with our family? Do people not die when they're supposed to?

"Iris, are you even listening?" Frank is asking me a question. He waves his hand in front of me.

I blink.

We're at the penthouse and housekeeping has placed on the table an assortment of baked goods and multicolored macarons, fresh cream puffs, and trays of assorted Belgian chocolates. Distracted, I munch on a lilac-colored macaron. The taste of soft, nutty pastry melts in my mouth. It's honestly the best macaron I've ever eaten.

"Are you still here?" Frank says. "Can you *please* repeat what I said about the proper way to greet a stranger?"

"Hmmm," I say, my mouth full.

All I can think about is my grandmother. Was she a ghost? Was I sick and hallucinating? But I still have the hotel key. And her pleading expression is stuck to my eyeballs, like a frozen screen saver. Uncle Dai slapping the kitchen counter. Ruby's mean-girl parting shot about my dad being a shitty person.

I pinch myself to stay focused.

"So what am I supposed to be learning?" I ask Frank.

I give him what I think is my most prize-winning smile, and to my relief, he actually smiles back hesitantly. His annoyance disappears, and I decide that I actually really, really like it when

Frank smiles. He has the nicest, most genuine one that I've ever seen. The corners of his mouth move very slowly, and his eyes light up like those extra-giant Christmas trees at Macy's Herald Square. And this all makes him seem incredibly playful. Self-consciously, I twirl my hair, which is super dry from having been bleached more times than I have remembered to do my laundry.

"Your hair is nice," he says, "but let's focus on Chinese introductions, okay? The ones we've been talking about for the past hour. Have you been practicing our lessons?"

"Of course!" I say, even though I haven't.

I flash him another huge mega-smile, and then I realize that I have bits of macaron stuck between my teeth. Oops. Hopefully, Frank doesn't notice.

Suddenly, I have an amazing idea. If I focus extra hard, after all the studying I did last night, I might be able to understand Chinese within a faster time frame. I wonder if by my fully immersing myself in class, my 8G brain will magically start to understand the language of my genetic and cultural birthright. How long does learning a foreign language take with a tutor? It's not like I have to become fluent. I just want to understand what my grandmother was trying to say to me.

"Test me! I'm ready!" I say enthusiastically, leaning closer to Frank and propping my elbows on the table.

But after twenty more minutes of *Nǐ hǎo, nǐ hǎo ma*, it appears that, even with extra studying, I'm not going to pick up this language. How will I learn basic phrases by the end of the summer? I am not Jabba the Hutt or Yoda or Luke Skywalker—my dad's favorite *Star Wars* characters. I cannot make these complicated science-fiction sounds! My neurological center seems to have very slow Wi-Fi. I wonder about hiring a translator. But would my grandmother even speak to a stranger?

I ask Frank to take a break.

Shockingly, this time he agrees.

At the kitchen table, I dunk more lilac macarons into an Earl Grey latte. I chew thoughtfully. I have never been this stuck on a personal problem. I don't understand why old people and Chinese families are so complicated.

"I'm sorry to say this, but I don't understand you," Frank says suddenly. "I have never tutored someone who doesn't even seem to try."

I stare at him. "Excuse me?"

He stands up and begins gesturing at me with confusion. He's no longer smiling. Not even a little. He looks actually bewildered and worried.

Seemingly agitated, Frank runs his hands through his neatly trimmed hair and his plaid polo shirt and cardigan hike up, revealing a slice of the nicest, flattest belly that I've seen in the longest time. His posture and profile are super confident and poised. It's like the captain of the school rugby team borrowed a nerdy librarian's costume for Halloween. Where does he even find his clothes?

Then Frank begins to pace up and down in the kitchen, and that's when I notice his steady walk and backside. I gasp loudly. To be honest, everything about them are absolutely perfect, 250 percent pageant-worthy. Frank has the well-shaped buttocks of a prize-winning golden retriever and the legginess of a standard-size schnauzer. At least that's what Ruby would say.

And why am I even checking out my Chinese Parent Approved tutor in the first place and comparing him to different dog breeds? Oh shit. I've been hanging out too much with my doggy-pageant cousin. Beijing is actually turning me into a true weirdo, and I'm worried that Frank might start to think I'm creepy.

Of course, when he catches me full-on staring, I try to distract him by gesturing excitedly at the snack table. "Macaron?" I ask extra sweetly.

I blush slightly when he doesn't respond.

"They're really tasty," I try again.

No answer.

"Don't you care that your uncle is paying me to tutor you?" Frank says instead. He sounds super determined now, like he has an actual toothache or he's allergic to macarons. "He's giving me an extra thousand US dollars if you finish the beginner textbook in two months. He wants you to be able to hold a basic conversation."

"Well . . . ," I say, staring at him.

Doesn't he know Uncle Dai is a bajillionaire? A thousand US dollars is nothing.

"You and the other rich kids don't care about anything, do you? It's your horrible, spoiled attitude," Frank accuses me. He crosses his arms. Like he's genuinely offended by my creative approach to learning and spending money.

And what is Frank talking about? Of course I care! I always want to know what's going on in everyone's lives 24/7. I always want to know what everyone's thinking and what they are doing and what they are buying and why they choose to date your best friend instead of you. If anything, I care too much.

Can't Frank see that I check social media a million times a day?

More importantly, can't he also understand that I'm going through a difficult emotional dilemma? My eyes look Popsicle-pink and puffy from lack of sleep and crying. They are practically the same size as the cotton balls on Ruby's everyday jumpsuits.

I want to wail at a demanding Frank: *I have been betrayed by everyone I thought I loved, and I'm super distracted because I am carrying a horrible family secret.*

Frank is looking intently at me, and I resist the urge to blurt out what happened to me last night.

"What do you know about Beijing?" he insists. Frank flips open a page in his textbook and jabs at a paragraph with a tiny, unreadable font.

My mouth drops open.

What does Beijing have to do with me not trying? And why does everything have to be connected to a boring history lesson? *There are more things, like my family and social life, at stake!* I want to exclaim.

"I want to show you something," Frank says, shaking his head in what seems to be an extreme mix of frustration and disbelief. He seems horror-stricken. Like my dad when I explain to him how I still don't understand what's going on in the *Star Wars* or *Jurassic Park* movies. "What is not to get?" my dad always asked me, to which I said, "Everything."

The plot, language, and characters all seem incomprehensible.

Grudgingly, I follow Frank outside the Shangri-La and we take a crowded subway. Normally, I love crowds, but it's rush hour in Beijing and I feel myself become increasingly lost. Someone tall elbows me in the head, and then a harassed-looking woman accidentally stomps on my foot as she exits the train in a hurry. "Ow!" I shout, but she doesn't hear me or apologize.

How could I have thought that Beijing was better than my suburban teenage life in New Jersey? I am trying my best, but I don't know how to do better.

If I did, I wouldn't have been sent to China in the first place.

The subway takes forever, but we get off at Dongsi, and Frank and I are suddenly in front of the National Art Museum of China (NAMOC). I have no idea what we're doing here. I have always liked art, but I have never been to a museum before. Outside of school, of course.

Frank and I stand in the ridiculously long line, get our bags checked by security like we're entering an incredibly expensive store, and then arrive in a showroom full of dull red terra-cotta statues and white-and-blue antique vases. I tell myself that I love home decor. This will just be like shopping at Homesense with my mom. I glance at an English-translated plaque:

Magnificent Ming Dynasty vase with ornate blue-and-white dragon and lotus roots, Xuande period (1426–1435) . . .

Oh god. Is Frank trying to punish me for ditching him last class? Is he trying to give me a coma from boredom? These English words make absolutely no sense. Also, how will I know how valuable an item is if there is no price tag?

Does this mean that these items are not for sale?

Or does it mean that customers can bargain?

Frank scurries through a wing on Ming Dynasty art, and I reluctantly follow him.

After a while, I finally realize that no one is haggling and there are absolutely no price tags on any of the display cases or ink paintings, which means not even the richest person in the world can hand over their platinum card and purchase any of this collection. I've entered the most expensive, most boring shopping experience of my life!

He stops in front of a sculptural exhibit on twentieth-century Chinese nationalism.

"What do you know about Beijing?" Frank asks me again in a quiet, intense voice. "What do you know about our people, the language, the culture?"

"The smog is terrible," I say, checking my phone for messages.

Samira has tagged me again in a photo of her and Peter at Starbucks. She sends me a message. **Thinking of you. Hope you're well. Shopping date when you get back from the end of the world? xoxo.** A second later, she sends another one: **BFF, I seriously miss you. Hugs. <3 <3 <3**

Anger fills me. What the hell is wrong with Samira?

What does she gain by making me feel even more shitty about being dumped and not getting into a single college?

Somewhere, the answers to some of the most pressing questions of my life are floating out there on a weak museum Wi-Fi signal.

Frank taps me urgently on the shoulder. Like it's Morse code for "Pay attention." He honestly looks incensed and concerned by my inability to learn. His eyebrows furrow, and I feel like a moth trapped in a glass jar under his stare. For some reason, his gaze feels seriously outer-space-magnetic today.

I'm not liking or hating the feeling. But my mouth feels dry and raw and tingly.

Frank's still wearing the same navy-blue interview cardigan like a uniform, and he begins to nervously shove his hands in his pockets. His face is solemn, like he's seriously sorry for what he has to say. He paces back and forth like a German shepherd following orders. He squares his broad, basketball-player-shaped shoulders. What's the rush? Doesn't anyone in Beijing ever slow down?

"Iris, when you wake up, what do you even think about? Do you think that people like your uncle work hard so you can enjoy living in a hotel? Do you think that your grandparents and great-grandparents and great-great-grandparents *suffered* so you could enjoy yourself? Don't you get that you come from a culture and tradition and people that are several thousands of years old? And the wealth was not handed to them, but earned with hard work and sacrifice?"

Frank sounds scary-disappointed and also scary-sad at the same time. Like Uncle Dai confronting my grandmother, minus his Dragon Zodiac rage. And exactly like how my dad sounded when he first learned that I hadn't gotten into colleges. I force myself not to think about it, even though I feel seriously hurt by his tone.

Staring intensely at me, he continues, "If you don't care about anything, then what's the point of anything? What's the point of being tutored? Don't you care that you're wasting money and time?"

I say nothing.

"What *do* you actually care about, Iris Wang?" he continues. "Why do you even get out of bed in the morning?"

I don't know how to respond. "Breakfast" doesn't seem like the right answer.

Sometimes, denial is the best way to go.

Other times, I wish I was a possum and had an excuse to drop dead any moment that I faced something overwhelmingly difficult: the SATs, disappointed parents, and maybe a seriously hot college student interrogating me in a public space. The museum lights emphasize Frank's stark emotions, highlighting his confusion and sincerity. Is that why I need to have everything I see in shops?

Focus, Iris, I think. *Focus. You are a Tiger, not a possum.*

Frank continues staring at me, and I avert my eyes like a guilty terrier. Under his hyperfocused gaze, I start to feel like I'm suffocating. Suddenly, I'm so ashamed. His question confirms why no one (minus my aunt and uncle) seems to like me in Beijing. His question pushes me to think about *why* I was banished from America in the first place.

I don't know where China is in relation to America on the world map, but it feels like I'm falling off the edge of the world.

Frank is absolutely right.

I have never really tried in my life, unless it was related to fitting in and being liked.

I just don't know how to begin.

In the east wing of NAMOC, I sit on a bench beside the sculptures of the Heavenly Moon and Earth Goddess. Feeling horrible because I know Frank is telling the truth, I pull my knees to my head, and I start to cry. Not just a few sniffles, but a whole lot of messy tears. In less than six minutes, I am sobbing uncontrollably. My tears could fill the entire China Sea (the one that I just learned about from reading a plaque).

"Oh no, Iris," Frank exclaims, sitting beside me. He looks and sounds horrified as he tries to pat me clumsily on the back. "I'm really sorry. Please don't cry."

He's surprisingly awkward for someone who looks like he should know how to comfort a crying girl. It's like he's trying to soothe a heavily drooling chow chow but doesn't really like dogs. This makes me cry harder because I think that he doesn't like me as a human being but sees me as his lucrative summer job.

"Why is China all going so wrong?" I sniffle.

"What?" he says, looking startled.

"My cousin hates me no matter what I do," I say, sobbing as softly as I can. "Even you're disappointed in me." Words are dropping out of my mouth like Fruity Pebbles. With Frank, for some reason, I'm more conscious of my inability to control what I say.

Unlike with Peter, Frank's presence seems solid and no-bullshit. He takes up space with lionlike confidence, as if he believes whatever he says 150 percent. Also, I usually don't even understand at least 40 percent of what Frank is saying. I could probably understand a squirrel or pigeon better. But Frank is real and beside me. And he's gazing at me like how Ruby looks at one of her top-rated mannequin practice animals, like I'm at least an

8.5 Miss Piggy. I just wish he would hold me or take my hand.

"Why don't you like me?" I ask, averting my eyes.

"Iris, of course I like you," he says, sounding stunned. He tries to shush me, and his face reddens as he apologizes to a curious museum guard in Chinese. Frank looks guilt-stricken and confused for whatever reason. His expression makes me almost believe what he said.

"Shhhhhhh!" Frank says again when I open my mouth to speak.

"Then why do you keep telling me to study like you're my parent?" I ask, trying to use a softer tone.

"It's my job," Frank whispers, and finally stops trying to pat me on the back. "Tutors in Beijing are strict with their students so they can get better."

"I really don't understand how to get better," I admit. "I just don't know how to learn another language or study."

Overcome with emotion and unable to control myself, I eventually let out a huge wail of immense frustration, rage, and sadness. I swear, you could hear me all the way in Bradley Gardens, all around the world. Not just in China.

Everyone at NAMOC stares at me, looking shocked.

College students, parents, staff, security guards, families with young children, and international tourists. They all look at the sniveling, bewildered girl with gray snot pouring from her nose like soft-serve ice cream.

For once, I care deeply that I'm a hot, awful mess. Usually, I can always forget after a few blunts and beers. But Frank's accusations burn like too much Nair Wax on my upper lip. It really hurts that Frank thinks so poorly of me and identifies me as an outsider. Even though he is not related to me and was just hired by my uncle, he already knows that I don't belong.

Looking deeply uncomfortable, Frank pulls out a thermos from his bag, unscrews the lid, pours himself a cup of tea, and offers it to me. How is this helping? Angrily, I knock it away and brown liquid splashes all over the framed ink painting of two swallows diving headfirst into a lake. Tea slides down the glass like mud. The lid clatters noisily to the ground.

Oh shit.

I'm not even surprised when the NAMOC security guard asks us to leave immediately. Frank escorts me out with his arm draped around my back, looking thoughtful but relieved.

For the rest of the day, we actually make it through three whole chapters and I learn how to successfully apologize in Mandarin. "*Dùi bu qǐ, dōu guài wǒ,*" I can say slowly. *I'm sorry, this is all my fault.*

Hard Feelings

I don't have enough time to scream.

I have been spending all evening thinking about what happened at the museum, and my brain feels mushy like leftover red bean pudding. I am strangely quiet all through dinner at Shi Zhi Liu Qui Noodles, and everyone comments on my lack of appetite. Normally, I remember exactly what dish everyone ordered, but I don't remember taking even a fruit-fly-size bite. My mind keeps showing me repeat images of Frank looking incredibly stricken and horrified by my attitude. I'm so preoccupied by the fact that Frank thinks I'm a selfish disaster that I almost miss what's going on around me.

But it's real and scary, like a commercial truck driving straight into a tree.

As we wait for the Mercedes-Benz SUV after dinner, someone hurls a glass bottle through the air, striking Uncle Dai's head. The bottle passes me, but it sounds like a toy airplane, whooshing past my ears and landing on the ground. Grabbing his head, Uncle Dai shoots a panicked look at Ruby, Auntie Yingfei, and me.

"Get in car!" he yells at us.

Uncle Dai sounds absolutely terrified. His head is bleeding, as if oozing ketchup.

I gasp at his forehead, but he points at me to get into the car.

This might be exciting if it were happening on the big screen, but in reality, it's slow-motion and scary.

Auntie Yingfei and Ruby push me facedown into the back-seat, and I think this is just a bad party drug trip.

How could this be happening?

"Move!" Ruby screams, waking me up. She folds my legs like I'm a store mannequin and plops down beside me.

Suddenly, Mr. Chen is trying to speed through the chaotic traffic of the city, but the mob of protestors outside at Shi Zhi Liu Qui Noodles is blocking us. He tries to back up, but there are more shouting crowds. Uncle Dai is dialing frantically into his cell phone.

"What's going on?" I finally manage to say.

No one answers me.

Someone throws another glass bottle at the car. It shatters.

Ruby looks terrified. Her face has gone eggshell white, at least three shades lighter than her usual skin-whitening foundation. I examine my reflection in the window mirror. My own face resembles the color of milky iceberg lettuce. Together, we look like we're starring in our own horror movie.

Auntie Yingfei motions for us to get on the floor of the

backseat. More furious protestors are surrounding the car and then they are suddenly banging on the windows. What did we do wrong?! They're all shoving the car, as if they want to football-flip us over!

"What's happening?!" I manage to yell, terrified.

"They're—" Ruby says. Auntie Yingfei glances at her and speaks sharply to her. She looks at me. "It is okay, Iris. No worry."

Incredulous, I stare at my aunt. Is she serious? There are at least a hundred people outside who want to force us out of the car?!!! Have they gotten Uncle Dai's car confused with someone else's? Like a political figure? A war criminal?

As the protestors gather, we crouch on the floor for what seems like an eternity. My heartbeat fills my ears like July 4 fireworks, while Uncle Dai shouts instructions to Mr. Chen. He wraps his tie around his bloody forehead as a bandage. More extreme yelling in Chinese, and for once, I'm almost glad that I don't understand anything. The rocking of our car gets worse. I hear screaming sirens and then we are finally lurching forward. I breathe a heavy sigh of relief.

Ruby, Auntie Yingfei, and I stay huddled together on the floor until we get back to the Shangri-La.

No one says anything when hotel security escorts us to the suite.

I want to ask so many questions. I want to know why a screaming mob of people would prevent my uncle's family from getting home safely after dinner. How could we have gone from being photographed to being punished? Why are people so angry at us?

Dr. Xiāo is called, and he instantly attends to Uncle Dai's

bleeding head. Three stitches, special black-market Chinese Advil, and two drinks of strong liquid later, Uncle Dai seems to be absolutely fine. No one says anything when I pour myself a strong drink from the bar too. Auntie Yingfei is still shaking like a newly rescued frostbite victim. Ruby is strangely silent. No epic eye-rolling, sneers, or snide remarks.

Why isn't anyone saying anything? Is this normal in Beijing? To not talk about us almost being injured/killed? Why do the scariest things happen to me in motor vehicles? Is this a new summer Tiger curse?

Uncle Dai is suddenly on the phone, yelling maniacally in Chinese at someone.

He catches my worried expression and then shuts the door to his office.

I look at Ruby, who looks at her phone again.

Auntie Yingfei tries to smile at me, but it doesn't quite work. "No worry, Weijun, okay?" she says. "Not happen again."

"What should I do?" I wail.

"Go study," she says firmly. "No waste time."

Is she joking?

We could have been seriously maimed and she still wants me to learn a new language?

Ruby pulls out a textbook on eighteenth-century poetry and begins furiously taking notes. It makes sense that my cousin is a gorgeous robot with a 64GB brain and legs that are longer than a Great Dane's.

Hours later, after a tense silence in the suite, I receive an email from Frank, inviting me to a party tomorrow night at someone's apartment near Tsinghua University. It's a long, explanatory message about his angry lecture at the museum and an apology for his behavior, asking me if I want to meet his friends. **Let me make it up to you,** he wrote. **I didn't mean to be so patronizing.**

I type back: **What you said today made me really upset. It made me think a lot about myself. I know I haven't been the best student, but I honestly mean it when I say that learning is scary AF. You are right that I need to try harder, so consider your apology accepted. I'm also sorry for having a shitty attitude too.**

Maybe it's the word "party" in his invitation that causes me to almost instantly forgive him.

But I don't know what the interpretation of "party" is to Frank.

What if he actually means "study group"?

Astonishingly, Frank immediately responds and his message catches me by surprise. **I REALLY hope I see you tomorrow night.**

My heart leaps.

Does Frank mean it or is he just being polite?

I expect Uncle Dai to say NO to a fun gathering of college students, so I tell him that I need to "cancel my study group with my tutor because of the incident." I wonder if he will order us to never leave the hotel until the end of summer, but seeing my extremely worried expression, he insists that I attend "study time" with Ruby, who looks uncomfortable and surprised by his announcement. He will hire additional bodyguards to stand outside the study group building.

"You are going to a study group?" Ruby finally says, glancing skeptically at me.

"Yes," I quickly say. "What's wrong with studying languages in a group?"

"I don't need a study group!" she says.

We stare and try to out-eye-roll each other. Her eyeballs seem to reach the back of her brain. She wins.

Uncle Dai ignores us and touches his bandaged forehead. Like he has a serious migraine, which is probably true. "Auntie Yingfei and I have lots of work to do. Mr. Chen will drive you to party. Weijun tutor Frank is good serious student. Please go."

Despite the scary mob incident yesterday, I'm excited to be surrounded by my peer group. In the car, I keep checking my reflection in the phone's camera, wondering if I have any bits of food stuck in my teeth. Then I wonder why I care so much. It's just Frank. My tutor. He's seen me cry and spill tea in public before. Ruby is ignoring me as usual, reading and highlighting a passage on her phone.

Oh god. Is she still studying?

Whatever for?

The party is off-campus, at a tiny, cramped apartment where there are at least fifty students dancing and drinking. Strobe lights flicker on the ceiling, and everyone is practically elbow to elbow and shouting like they are separated by a whole continent. You literally can't move without smacking someone in the face. I hear super-loud Korean pop music and I suddenly relax. I'm finally in my element! How I miss parties and no-purpose socializing.

"Oh my god, I'm going to be okay!" I shout at Ruby, who stares at me.

"This isn't a study group," she says.

"I'll tell your dad about your Miss Piggy mastiff if you say anything," I reply.

In response, Ruby turns pink and purple, reminding me of saltwater taffy.

On the counter, I grab a couple of bottles of Tsingtao beer (my dad's favorite) for a nervous-looking Ruby and me, and then that's when I see Frank with his friends, who are all good-looking and interestingly dressed. They're wearing gold platform sneakers and stage makeup. Frank, of course, is the exception, but at least he's not wearing his boring plaid shirt and cardigan, thank goodness. He looks normal today: a black T-shirt and ripped skinny jeans.

Frank actually smiles charmingly when he comes over to greet me, and despite myself, my heart thumps extra fast. Not the scared fast that happened in the car with the mob, but an exciting roller-coaster rhythm. Giddy heart palpitations for my usually ultra-serious, no-nonsense tutor? Tonight Frank looks and acts handsome and not like a CPA (Chinese Parent Approved) boy. I swig down my beer, hoping it will calm my quivering insides when I interact with Frank. The beer tastes extremely watered down, so I'll need something else ASAP.

The insides of my stomach are literally shaking.

God, I hope it's just a case of mismatched physical attraction, not PMS hormones or food poisoning again.

I stand very close to Frank. He doesn't say anything for the longest time but keeps full-on staring. Is this what flirting is like in China? Just sexy, lingering eye contact, no talking? In Bradley Gardens, the boys hand you an unrefrigerated beer and herd you upstairs. In America, hooking up at parties is usually to-the-point, superefficient, and requires minimal eye contact.

"Iris! You made it," Frank finally exclaims when I'm beginning to wonder if I should apologize or even bring up the museum. "You look so, so lovely."

"Thanks," I say, pleased that he noticed that I'm wearing a new polka-dotted dress from Auntie Yingfei, which is red and white and I'm not entirely sure she didn't order it off Minnie Mouse from the Disney Store.

More smiling from Frank.

And more serious eye contact that feels like serious, unsubtle flirting.

"I'm really sorry again about yesterday," he continues. "I was out of place for scolding you."

"You're right," I say. "I just haven't been focusing."

"Beijing really hasn't been easy for you, has it?" he says, looking sympathetic.

I nod, for once wholeheartedly agreeing with him.

To my amazement, Frank absentmindedly runs his hand firmly from my bare shoulder and rests it on my forearm. Carefully, he touches and examines my wrist where I once started a small tattoo of a flower inside a heart and quit three minutes in because I was in such excruciating pain. I hadn't even realized that the ink wasn't temporary that time Samira and I went to some dude's sketchy basement in New Jersey. Luckily, the accidental tattoo is like a tiny outline that resembles a funny-shaped, zigzag mole, not even noticeable unless you look super carefully.

Frank takes my barely tattooed wrist in his, but he doesn't

ask me about it. I'm practically hypnotized. I should move my hand, but this feels way too nice. I haven't been touched by a boy since Peter dumped me. Frank flushes. And I notice that he's rabbit-chewing his lip. Is he nervous?

"You said something that really shocked me," I eventually admit, ignoring the fact that my heart is thumping and he is still holding my arm. "Honestly, I didn't realize I was coming across as a two-headed monster."

"I keep forgetting that you aren't Chinese at all," Frank says, frowning at my unfinished tattoo of a flower-heart.

"What are you talking about?" I say, confused. "My family lives in Beijing. You reminded me of my family tree at the museum."

Face burning, I pull away from his touch. I don't want to hear another lecture, especially at a party that he invited me to.

"You look Chinese, but you act different and think different from everyone in Beijing. Being Chinese is . . . always thinking about your past, present, and future. You're connected to your people. Americans tend to only think about what they want. It's very individual."

He sees my stricken face and quickly says, "It's not a bad thing. It's just contrary to what Chinese people believe. What I'm trying to say is, I'm sorry for being so hard on you."

"I think about people!" I protest. "That's literally all I think about when I'm not thinking about what to eat."

"I'm not saying you don't," he says. "You just view learning in the opposite way as someone who was born in Beijing. They feel that they have a duty to study to help their family. You view learning as a punishment, when it should be a privilege to be part of your culture. It's a gift to speak your ancestors' language."

My face quivers.

I don't know how to explain that I have never thought of studying as altruistic charity work to one's family and self. Frank might be right. I never thought that school and test-taking would be part of a gigantic quest to understand my own sense of purpose and reason for existing. From now on, I vow to work on becoming a less shitty and less lazy person.

"You're right, though," I admit grudgingly. "I really need to try harder. Tomorrow is a new day, right?"

Frank bows.

I attempt to half bow, half curtsy back. I end up spilling beer on myself.

Being told to my face that I need an internal makeover, I'm determined to show Uncle Dai and prove to my parents that I'm super worthy of my culture and a penthouse apartment at the Shangri-La. Frank reminding me that I have still-living people who care about me, but I can't communicate with them because of my own selfishness and lack of effort, is a serious wake-up call. I'm more than just a series of real-life catastrophes, broken dresses, and traveler's diarrhea.

Whooping loudly at my surprising realization, I help myself to another beer.

Frank then drags Ruby and me over to meet his university friends. They're all enthusiastic and already drunk. He introduces them by their English names, Emerald, Kitty, Alex, and Jason. Only Kitty speaks English fluently, and she winks at me. She's wearing a multicolored wig, fake neon-orange lashes, and some fabulous black lipstick. She introduces herself as a theater major and aspiring visual arts critic at Tsinghua.

"Feng Corporation, hey?" she says, smirking knowingly at both me and Ruby. We cheers beers and I laugh. She pours out some clear liquid into plastic cups for us. *"Baijiu,"* she says. "Careful, it's strong."

Eager to get more alcohol than the watered-down beer, I swig it down, accidentally burp, and ask for a second round.

Everyone laughs and whoops and claps me on the back.

I ask for my third. This Chinese liquor is nothing at all! It's like drinking water mixed in with a few drops of rubbing alcohol.

But Ruby flushes and looks extremely uncomfortable. When Alex or Jason, I forgot who, puts his arm around her, she jumps and looks shocked. Like it's the first time that a cute older boy is flirting in person with her. She stares at her feet and takes a tiny sip of her *baiju* and then she spits it back out. She doesn't even look up. Oh my god. I grin. Does Ruby not know how to talk to boys?!! Has she never been to a party before?

The *baijiu* is making me warm, excited, and giddy.

On WeChat, I quickly text my cousin.

Iris: You ok?

SuperPrincessQueenRuby8421: Of course. Can we go?

Iris: But we just got here!

SuperPrincessQueenRuby8421: What are we supposed to do?

Iris: Are you joking?

SuperPrincessQueenRuby8421: Do i just stand here?

SuperPrincessQueenRuby8421: What do people usually do at these things?

Iris: Just drink and talk and laugh

Iris: It's just for fun

Iris: It's really easy

SuperPrincessQueenRuby8421: That's it? I don't know what to do

SuperPrincessQueenRuby8421: What if someone talks to me? What do i say? People are different than talking to dogs

Iris: Say anything that comes into your head . . . What did you do today?

SuperPrincessQueenRuby8421: I wrote an essay on Freud

Iris: What is that?

SuperPrincessQueenRuby8421: ??!!!

Iris: What else did you do?

SuperPrincessQueenRuby8421: Practiced grooming

Iris: . . . .

SuperPrincessQueenRuby8421: So talk about Freud?

Iris: Omg follow my lead.

Iris: You'll do great!

Determined to have fun, I decide that we all need to relax ASAP and I ask Kitty if there is "anything besides alcohol." She keeps winking at a greasy dude wearing a hoodie with a large fanny pack. He finally comes up to us and asks if we want "anything extra" in a growly German accent.

"You want to study? Relax?" he suggests.

"How much is weed?" I instantly say, brightening at the prospect of getting high in Beijing.

"One hundred twenty-five *yuan* for a hit."

"Are you kidding me?" I ask. "That's so expensive."

The guy in the hoodie shrugs and holds up a tiny baggie of pre-rolled joints.

"How much is that in American?" I ask.

Ruby glances at me, looking a bit scandalized at my inability to do math. "That's approximately eighteen dollars US."

"That's way too expensive!" I say to the dude. "For a tiny, pre-rolled joint?"

"Hey, this stuff is hard to get here," he says. "I'll make you a deal. How about your pretty friend, the tall, shy one, come sit with me?"

I roll my eyeballs and frown at him.

Snickering, Greasy Fanny-Pack points and grins at poor Ruby, who towers over everyone at the party. She's seriously blushing lipstick red and looking totally horrified. Greasy Fanny-Pack might be someone that I might actually hang/smoke/laugh with in New Jersey, but he makes my cousin uncomfortable, which makes me strangely worried for some reason. After all, I brought Ruby to "study group."

"No deal," I say, moving in front of Ruby like one of Uncle Dai's security guards. "What else do you have for me?"

"You don't have to," Ruby whispers. "I have money."

"Your dad gave me money too," I say.

And yet, somehow, I know it's not my money to spend. Miraculously, my voice of limited self-control has somehow disappeared in my time of need. It's like I have no guardian devil of recklessness to guide me. Uncle Dai gave me that money after seeing my grandma in hopes of keeping me quiet, but I will give it back to him or save it for a real-life emergency like an earthquake or other natural disaster.

"How about you stand up, sing a song, and I'll give you three of them?" Greasy Fanny-Pack is sneering at me, as if daring me to catwalk away. He dangles the baggie of weed in front of me.

"Deal!" I say, knowing that he expects me to decline and pay the marked-up price. He looks surprised.

Normally, I'd be so embarrassed, but I don't know anyone in the room. Ruby looks mortified, but I already know what she thinks of me. Seeing Frank and his friends watch me with mild shock and a lot of unfiltered amusement, I smile nervously. Somehow, I don't care anymore. I've already done and said a trillion embarrassing cringe-worthy things in Beijing. What's one more item to add to my ever-growing list?

Greasy Fanny-Pack switches to extra-loud Chinese, shouting for everyone in the small apartment to be quiet, I assume. It takes a while, but the room hushes. He helps me stand on a chair. I wobble a bit in my red platform sneakers before finding my balance.

Everyone is looking at me. Someone catcalls and people start applauding loudly. I swig down another cup of watery-tasting beer and burp.

Both Frank and Ruby are staring at me in amazement.

Awkwardly, a cappella style, I belt out "The Circle of Life" from my dad's favorite musical, *The Lion King*. I don't even know half the words, but I make them up as I go along. Then I twirl a bit, and clumsily attempt the choreography from the sexy Hawaiian dance class that my dad took me and Peter to over a year ago. I sway my hips like a Tyrannosaurus rex and I hum along tunelessly.

Horrified silence.

No one says anything.

After a while, many people boo and hiss like the ostriches at the Bronx Zoo.

This is the most awkward, humiliating thing to happen to me in front of my peer group. Yet shockingly, I don't really care and I'm not even drunk. For some reason, I always thought that I would go extinct from embarrassment if no one liked me. Who am I? I don't even recognize this unselfconscious version of Iris Weijun Wang.

I ignore the booing crowd.

Jumping off the chair, I grab seven pre-rolled ones from gaping Greasy Fanny-Pack (one for each of my new best friends), who all look delighted. Greasy Fanny-Pack is too stunned to stop me. A flash of happiness blooms inside me. I honestly love to share things.

"You are amazing," Kitty says, smirking at me. "Frank, you found a keeper."

Frank flushes and I smile widely. Is my tutor blushing?

I make an it's-no-big-deal face and shrug casually. But on the inside, I'm incredibly pleased.

Alex, Jason, and Emerald are all nodding. Even Ruby's eyes pop a bit in shock from my super-awkward performance, but she looks impressed, if nervous. I smile at her, but she still looks incredibly scared, like she's about to throw up. How are parties frightening? Frank's friends are all incredibly interesting-looking in an artsy way and seemingly nonjudgmental. We go outside on the balcony and smoke. Ruby takes a hit and recoils. She starts coughing and mouths something that looks like *SOS* at me. I flash her a thumbs-up sign, but she looks like she's ready to leap off the balcony, screaming. I motion at a drink, and she instantly gulps it down, like it's a slushy strawberry bubble tea.

It's all going fantastic, I think happily.

When it's my turn with the joint, I breathe in deeply, and I stare at the hazy lights and the traditional architecture; the mix of old concrete buildings and rustic heritage houses with their triangular tiled rooftops. It's very gray but incredibly breathtaking. Like being in an international documentary with subtitles. The smog is so thick that it makes me think I'm watching the city through a series of black-and-white slides that they show you in American history class.

Frank gestures oddly at the neighborhood houses. "An end to our dream," he says seriously, and his friends all look solemn as they cheers plastic cups and clap each other on the back.

"Are parties as fun as this in America?" Kitty asks me, attempting to lighten the mood.

"Very close," I say, grinning.

For the first time since I arrived in Beijing, I actually fit in.

No one is asking me about learning Chinese and no one is talking about school or math or politics. I inhale and toke and drink like the old funny Iris. I laugh and tell silly stories from my former life. Jason or Alex is flirting with Ruby and finally, she begins to relax and giggle awkwardly and glances around, as if afraid to look the dude in the eyes. For a brief moment, I catch her stare and nod encouragingly. I point at her, to let her know that it's okay to talk about herself, but then I hear her mention the designer of her jacket. "Prada *ChineseChineseChinese*," she is saying, and Jason/Alex is nodding but looking confused. I honestly can't believe it!

After a while, we run out of drinks, so we go back inside and then someone brings out a guitar and then someone else reads a poem. Of course, it's all done in advanced Chinese and I can't understand anything. Then it's Frank's turn to stand up at the front of the room, and he reads a passage. I can't understand it either, but I have never thought that Mandarin sounded so beautiful.

"He's the best poet in our class," Kitty says to me.

"What does the poem mean?" I say.

"He's translating Li Bai's famous love poem. Shhhhhhhhhh!" Staring at me, Frank recites:

> *The autumn air is clear,*
> *The autumn moon is bright.*
> *Fallen leaves gather and scatter,*
> *The jackdaw perches and starts anew.*
> *We think of each other—when will we meet?*
> *This hour, this night, my feelings are hard.*

"Huh," I say, pretending that I understand. How can feelings be hard? Everyone knows that they are just side effects from ingesting too much alcohol or drugs, and sending regrettable two a.m. texts.

For some reason, I can't help staring at Frank, who keeps looking back at me. His eye contact is honestly alarming, and normally, I would find it creepy and not endearing.

As the night goes on, I down another watery beer, but then I notice Ruby can barely stand up. Her eyes are half-closed and she's starting to slump over. Her tongue lolls out of her mouth like an English bulldog, and I resist the urge to laugh.

Hugging Frank's charming and wonderful friends goodbye, I insist that it's time to go. It takes an enormous amount of effort, but Frank helps me bring Ruby to the curb, where Mr. Chen is waiting. He's just watching football on his iPad again, but he helps me push my cousin, who's stumbling slightly, into the backseat.

"That was really fun," I say to Frank.

He doesn't say anything.

"Thanks for tonight," I try again.

But Frank is super-staring at me with what looks like what Li Bai calls "hard feelings"—and what *Cosmopolitan* calls "bedroom eyes" in their latest issue—so I take his hesitation as an invitation.

Boldly, I lean forward and kiss him.

It's just a light smack on the lips. And at first, he freezes and I pause, unsure of what to do. I don't understand! I thought he liked me. But it's like kissing a celebrity's face on a poster. There's absolutely no reaction.

For almost an entire minute, he stares at me, looking shocked. Like I'm a shitty kisser (I'm not!). But my mom always said that she had to make the first move or my timid Goat-dad would never have gotten her pregnant. Without my mom's no-nonsense attitude to romance and dating, I would not exist at all.

I don't know if I'm supposed to apologize for kissing a boy in Beijing.

I don't know if I'm supposed to shake his hand before parting ways. What is the correct Chinese etiquette?

Mortified, I have never been so outwardly rejected on a first kiss before.

"Can we pretend that never happened?" I finally ask. Heat rushes through my face and neck like a severe case of alcohol poisoning.

"It tickles," he mutters. "Like a cat."

"What??!" I say.

Oh my god. I feel my face, which I thought was Frank's mustache, but it's actually mine. Frank's face is smooth and hairless. The Tiger curse that I haven't been thinking about. I must have grown more hairs yesterday during the scary mob incident.

"I'm going to go now," I say, biting my lip awkwardly and staring at my hands.

I don't know how many more times I can embarrass myself in this bad luck city.

But this time, Frank grabs my arm and I guess he doesn't mind my Tiger mustache because we kiss again, with lots of tongue, and it feels really messy and nice even though I suddenly can't help but think of uncaring, ungrateful Peter Hayes. Peter was the last boy that I enthusiastically made out with. As I try to focus exclusively on Frank, Peter dumping me feels more real again, even though I haven't thought about it since I checked my social media page hours ago.

Suddenly, kissing Frank is like kissing the ghost of Peter Hayes.

Frank tastes like *baijiu*, weed, and bitterness.

Frank is what happened because I failed senior year, bombed the SATs, and wrecked my chances of college.

Frank kissing me back is the ultimate result of my parents' spiraling shame and STI-like burning disappointment.

But also, the kiss reminds me of tomorrow and the brand-new possibilities that happen after getting a deep-pore exfoliating facial. Frank is someone that I would never have met if I hadn't been sent to live with my aunt and uncle. There's definitely something sweet and surprising about kissing a college boy in an alleyway. Like sneaking cookie dough from the freezer at three a.m. on a weeknight.

Mr. Chen honks the horn impatiently.

I guess we've been making out for too long to be appropriate. Even my mouth is getting tired. And even though I initiated the kiss, I'm not ready for another relationship. I tell myself it was just the booze and weed that made me curious enough to kiss my beautiful, movie-star-looking tutor.

But there is something undeniably real and raw and trance-like between us. Call it chemistry, hormones, or a momentary weakness, I can't pinpoint it. Frank and I are like two continents finally colliding at record-breaking speed after never having met before. It's North America and Asia having a brief but very sexy affair.

"You're not afraid of anything, are you?" Frank asks as I reluctantly pull away.

"What do you mean?" I say.

For a second, I feel light-headed and giddy and more internally beautiful but also messed up from our kiss. I just want Frank to slide his warm tongue back inside my mouth. Suddenly, my vision flickers. Maybe I'm drunker than I thought?

I look at the smoggy sky and try to pretend to look for stars, but all I see are different shades of pollution. Beijing is really like being on a different planet.

But Frank is still staring at me somberly. Like he's about to tell me that the end of the world is coming and it's prophesied that I'll be the only human being left (my worst fear!).

"You just say and do exactly what you're feeling," he says. "Most people are always hiding, but you aren't."

"There's no point hiding anything," I say, thinking of my dad and Uncle Dai. "Secrets always get found out."

"I admire you for being so real," he says.

"Are you saying I'm too honest?" I ask, puzzled. "No one has ever said that to me before."

"You're not scared to be yourself," he murmurs, gently cupping the side of my face. A fast, electric, otherworldly current runs through us. Frank is breathing extra-extra-hard and his eyes look glassy. I shamelessly think about all the amazing, magical possibilities of what could happen if I could just follow him back to his college dorm room. I just want us to take off all our clothes before one of us sobers up.

"Iris, I . . . ," Frank suddenly says in a raspy voice.

Mr. Chen honks loudly again, interrupting us, and I finally slide into the car.

In the backseat, Ruby drunk-mumbles and slowly wakes. We stop the car twice so she can vomit. I hold her waist-long hair back and accidentally pull off several dyed white-blond strands. Practically a fist-size bunch, to be honest. God, I hope these are hair extensions. Otherwise, she might blame me for male-pattern baldness in addition to ruining her life.

"You're helping me?" she says, coughing and looking surprised when she finally finishes puking up what could possibly fill every river and lake in China. Her eyes are frighteningly pink, and her complexion seriously looks the same color as a hot dog.

"Why wouldn't I?" I say, stunned. "I would never leave someone who was sick."

Groaning, she leans her head on my shoulder as we say good night to Mr. Chen and I help her to her room. I know I shouldn't be shocked, but her parents aren't home. The lights in the penthouse are off. Shouldn't Uncle Dai be resting after his head injury? I don't understand how he could just go back to work after what happened in the car. The thought of us almost tipping over . . . we could have died. At the thought, fresh fear slides through me immediately. The idea of dying on another continent without ever seeing my parents again and not eating Dairy Queen once more absolutely terrifies me. What sort of trouble is Uncle Dai in? Why didn't I notice all the extra security cars? How did I think that money and living at the Shangri-La would never have a host of problems?

For a moment, I close my eyes, shoving the feeling of extreme full-blown panic down, like an extravagant three-course meal that I'm too full to eat.

Ruby suddenly makes a retching sound. I grab a trash can for her and she vomits again.

"Are you going to be okay?" I say, worried. "Should I call your house doctor?"

"You are being so nice," she mutters as she finishes puking and falls sideways onto the bed in the maid's quarters. "But I've been so mean to you."

"Is that an apology?" I say.

"He is cute," Ruby mumbles suddenly.

"Yes, Frank's friend totally liked you!" I say with enthusiasm.

Her face flushes as I help her take off her gold thigh-high boots. I check the leather lining: GUCCI in large gold printing. I'm very, very impressed. How much did these boots cost?

"You and Frank are perfect for each other," Ruby says, slurring slightly.

As if she is reading my mind, I blush. Why should I care about what my cousin is saying about Frank? Tonight was a humongous mistake but admittedly a very nice one. At least I got to unwind at a super-fun party. My first one since I caught Samira and Peter in my bed.

I wait for Ruby to continue her thought, but she starts snoring loudly. Drool gathers on her lips and begins dribbling onto her pillow like she's a dainty Saint Bernard. I start laughing because it's so ridiculous.

The universe is so absurd!

Ruby's caninelike snoring suddenly stops.

I check to make sure that my cousin is actually sleeping. I check her breathing and wave my fingers under her nose.

No response.

She's out.

Then she sits back up again, her eyes snapping open like a zombie.

"Oh! I almost forgot. Can you still meet the mastiff at the

airport?" she says. "I'll send you an email with the details."

"Yes, yes," I quickly promise.

Then she notices me looking at the gold boots. "You can have those," she offers. "I have so many and those would look fantastic on you."

I gasp. "Are you sure?"

"Yes," she says, and falls fast asleep again.

I can't believe that Ruby and I are becoming friends. It feels as if a second ago we were arguing over a ruined dress.

Before bed, I try on my new Gucci boots and they fit like a pair of leather gloves. They're so soft and warm and glamorous. I stare at myself in the full-length mirror, and suddenly, my legs look twice as long, and I swear I've lost five whole pounds.

As I look in the mirror, I keep wondering: What if no one likes me for just being *me*? What if I'm someone without anything to offer anyone? And what did Frank mean that I wasn't afraid to be myself?

If he thinks that I'm open and authentic, it means that I'm seriously unraveling in China. There could be something very, very wrong with me.

23

Family Secrets

The next day, I agree to meet Frank at Tiananmen Square, where there was a violent and messy massacre many years ago. Admittedly, I don't know much about China's history, but even I have heard a bit about this important location.

While I was eating delicious vegetable *baozi* and brown gloopy *miancha* for breakfast, Frank sent me a message on WeChat saying that he was too tired to make our morning class, and he suggested that we meet in the early afternoon for a history field trip.

I shock myself by getting there fifteen minutes before Frank. Granted, Mr. Chen dropped me off, but I have never been early for tutoring before. In fact, in New Jersey, I'm always late or never even show up for lessons.

Frank nods stiffly at me when he sees me at the entrance of Tiananmen Square. Like a newbie pageant queen, I wave awkwardly at him, trying to smile. He doesn't smile back.

We pretend that nothing happened, and Frank seems way more

somber than last night. I'm almost glad when he launches into a speech about political activism and resistance and executions, where Chinese people were fired on by their own government. At least talking seems to animate him.

Also, it makes it easier to find him a little less attractive whenever he starts talking about learning.

But his half-moon smile.

And the way that he watches me when giving me a straight-up narration about the square.

I could literally observe him all day, but it's more than that. It seems like he can actually see through me, as cheesy as it sounds. None of the boys that I have ever hooked up with or dated have ever treated me like a real living person before. Peter and all the ones who came before him always mixed me up with the ATM machine.

How can I find a tutor nerdy, handsome, mysterious, and a bit alluring at the same time? Who am I? Iris Wang would never make out with one of her tutors back home. Pothead guitarists and intense partygoers were always my preferred boyfriends. These dudes were never 100 percent authentic Chinese, and they were always despised by my parents.

How can I be falling for a Chinese Parent Approved boy?

It literally makes no sense.

But Frank is someone who has a life purpose. He knows exactly who he is, and what he cares about. He's the complete opposite of Peter Hayes, who had negative zero direction.

In fact, Frank is the very opposite of me, which is probably why I'm so confused and repulsed and fascinated at the same time. Frank is like my first foray into eating braised fermented red bean chicken feet. When I ate my first clawed foot at a Chinese restaurant in Manhattan, it was slimy, terrifying, and tantalizing all at once.

For the former Iris Wang of small-town Bradley Gardens, New Jersey, Frank Liao would be the equivalent of falling in love with the narrator on the History Channel while using them to cure late-night insomnia.

Beijing time has truly messed up my understanding of romantic attraction.

Frank is still talking about political activism. He gestures at the walls and open space around us, pointing enthusiastically.

I can't help but grin genuinely at him.

He smiles back, like I'm almost as important as a historical landmark.

My heart beats faster. Like I'm about to parachute off a plane.

When is the history lesson over?

Don't get me wrong, Tiananmen is a really nice public meeting area, but where is the gift shop? I still have some leftover *yuan* to spend, and Tiananmen Square could totally benefit from more tourist spending.

Also, the boots Ruby gave me are a few sizes too small and the sides pinch my feet like passive-aggressive hermit crabs. Where can we find a bench to sit?

I do feel proud of myself, though, for enjoying a real-life cultural heritage site. I mean, the flagpole is nice for younger children playing tag, and there's even something called an Arrow Tower for a great view of the city (perfect for hooking up). There's also a Great Hall of the People, which I gather is a backup meeting place for citywide emergencies. In front of the entrance is where the Forbidden Palace is located, and there is also a full-size photo of a stern balding man that reminds me a lot of Uncle Dai.

In fact, I'm almost certain that the portrait is of Uncle Dai.

Is my uncle a major donor? Is that why Frank brought me to the square? Is Tiananmen Square part of Feng Construction Corporation?

"That looks exactly like my uncle!" I say, waving at the portrait.

No answer from Frank.

"You think your uncle looks like Mao Zedong?" Frank finally asks, sounding incredulous.

"Well, yes. Don't you see the resemblance? Who's Mao, anyway?"

I snap a selfie with the poster and try to take several where I put a leg up to showcase my new beautiful gold boots. These photos are definitely Instagrammable. Frank stares at me, looking stunned. As if he can't believe that Uncle Dai owns the entire square. As a matter of fact, I don't believe it either.

Suddenly, a security guard starts yelling in both English and Chinese, "NO PHOTO ALLOWED! What you doing, miss?"

I quickly apologize for the misunderstanding and scamper away. I worry that he'll make me delete the photos. It's a bit difficult to run, actually, since these boots are high with six-inch heels. It's honestly like walking on a pair of attention-grabbing gold stilts.

Frank bows and apologizes profusely to the security guard, who mutters something long and explanatory in Chinese as we leave.

As I continue to scan the area for a gift shop, I pretend that I don't see the National Museum of China in case Frank wants to go in.

After I accidentally compared Uncle Dai to Mao Zedong, Frank has said nothing for the longest time. But I'm glad when he agrees that it's time for a late lunch.

He hails a rickshaw, which is a bike pulling an old-fashioned carriage, and I honestly feel a bit bad for the skinny older man who agrees to haul both of us. We can't be very light, especially since there are two of us, and there is a lot of panting and huffing on his part, especially when we turn up a bumpy cobblestone road. Going uphill takes forever and each time we hit a pothole, I worry that we will flip over.

"Isn't this great?" Frank says, grinning.

He seems more relaxed now, as if able to put last night's "mistake" behind us.

I nod, but I keep worrying about how the rickshaw driver will manage to get us to our destination. I can't understand why I want Frank to like me when I see all my flaws and mistakes in his totally serious, opposite-of-Iris personality.

A shocking thought hits me: Maybe love, like family, isn't supposed to be just for fun?

What if the real reason for all my previous mistakes is that I'm horribly afraid of hard work? Come to think of it, whenever there is a pothole in the road, I find the nearest overpriced coffee shop and will my problem to go away with a fudgy pecan brownie and an extra-large caramel latte. I just don't enjoy problem-solving. I just don't want to figure out how much cement to use to fill a hole.

Honestly, I don't like to think about *why* or *how* something went wrong.

Despite the heavy factory smog, central Beijing slowly comes into view. The historical areas are well-preserved. There are long winding alleyways containing traditional houses with tiled roofs, and narrow streets that Frank refers to as *hutongs*, in their postcard white, reds, and grays.

"They're so beautiful!" he says, grinning strangely. "They haven't been bulldozed yet for commercial buildings like those big chain hotels."

On the streets, there are vendors and hustling people, but I'm still too worried about the man on the bicycle to fully enjoy the scenery. What if he has a heart attack while pulling us up this ginormous hill? Is it unfair of us to force him to carry our weight? He's not a donkey!

What if he needs what my dad keeps warning me about, a full knee and hip replacement due to overexercising, in his golden years?

Finally, we stop at Fucheng Food Market in the Haidian District, and I hand our driver a lot of Uncle Dai's money and don't even count it. This practically counts as charity work. The rickshaw driver grins at me, revealing stumps of blackened teeth. Yikes. He grabs my hand and shakes it, thanking me profusely in Mandarin. Despite my astonishment, I still manage to smile gratefully. Honestly, I love giving people money and making others happy. Maybe he can visit a dentist or go on a weekend vacation.

I'm surprised when we enter a street market, and at first I

don't want to eat anything until Frank insists that it's safe, since my stomach should now be accustomed to the food in Beijing. Street vendors are roasting fat ducks, geese, piglets, and chickens on spits. People are rolling large doughy pancakes and stir-frying plates of white onions, scrambled eggs, carrots, crushed tomatoes, and rice in gigantic, hissing woks.

The smell, all of it exotic and familiar, fried and fresh, saturates my nostrils. I sniff hungrily.

"This is local food," Frank explains. "This is the real Beijing. What you've been eating is the fine dining stuff that they think foreigners like. No authentic flavor."

Eagerly, I hand over some *yuan*, and Frank orders twenty of the fattest and juiciest *xiāo long bao* that I have ever seen. They're like the size of small helium balloons. They smell beefy and divine. At another stall, a dude rolls the sticky flour dough before yanking and hacking it into fresh hand-pulled noodles. He cooks the yellow shoestring bundles in bubbling water and then dumps them into a spicy, red-hot simmering seafood soup. He ladles green Chinese veggies on top. Last, we walk to a stall that has boiling vats of clacking lobsters, mussels, baby crabs, squid, and freshly shucked oysters. It's like food sample day at Costco. I want to eat all of these immediately, and a smiling woman hands me a generous portion of each in a bucket.

An actual-size bucket!

Like she thinks we're giant, slobbering mastiffs!

We sit down at an outdoor table and feast.

I'm too busy stuffing my face to make conversation, and then I notice that Frank is just watching me. He's not eating.

Is he not hungry? Is there something on my face? I touch my mouth and chin to make sure that no more hairs are popping up like weeds. Frank's staring at me intently, as if he has something important to say. Thankfully, he's not lecturing me and I can happily eat my food without listening to another speech on history.

Frank keeps staring at me.

I blush, averting my eyes.

Then I realize that he's studying me. Like I'm a no-price-tag art piece at NAMOC.

Was last night so horrible?

Then why is he looking at me like a fun new party drug that he wants to dissolve under his tongue but knows that he has to wake up early the next day for school? If I were him, I would just cancel all my obligations and follow the dangerous rabbit hole to wherever the drug led me. New friends, hot shocking hook-ups, and unforgettable adventures that could replace the horrible mundane memory of day-to-day life.

There's also a hungry longing in Frank's eyes, and I honestly hope to the gods of all the major shopping malls in the world that it's meant exclusively for me.

After he's been staring at me so much, I finally wonder if Frank is horrified by my inability to properly hold chopsticks or the fact that I'm using my fingers to eat seafood. Then I wonder if he's embarrassed about our wet and sloppy makeout session from last night. I did use Nair on my Tiger mustache this morning just in case.

Deliberately, I touch my bare knee to his under the wooden table.

We're skin to skin. And it's like he's paralyzed.

Hmmmm.

I've never had to make such a monumental superhero effort on a dude before. But I also don't want to move my knee away. It just feels so completely natural. We stay that way, interconnected like magnets, until a janitor clears our buckets. We don't speak. Frank's face is as red as the lobster that we have just ingested.

He can't stop smiling at me.

I can't stop grinning back.

It's like we're both stoned, but we haven't partaken of Beijing weed since last night. The same fantastical trance current from outer space is running through us. It's a powerful frequency because it's like being zapped by a falling constellation made of extra-fiery heat. Honestly, when I'm looking at Frank, it's like hurtling through the unknown universe and landing headfirst on Planet Earth for the very first time.

Winking at him on purpose, I lick my lips in anticipation of what could possibly come.

For dessert, Frank mischievously offers me a deep-fried scorpion on a stick.

I recoil.

"What the hell is that?" I exclaim, pushing it away.

"Don't tell me you're afraid," he says. He grins wickedly, as if daring me to try it. Some of the fun, spontaneous, pot-smoking Frank from last night's party is returning.

Suddenly, my tutor chomps off the head of the fried insect. He chews. Then he grins at me, like I'm the only other person who survived a zombie apocalypse. No one else matters except for me.

For a second, the hustling world of Fucheng Food Market tilts, fragments into itsy-bitsy pieces, and completely disappears.

Then I notice that Frank has a humongous chunk of scorpion stuck between his front teeth!

I thought that watching a boy you like eat an insect would be the scariest, most traumatizing thing in the world, but it's actually kind of hilarious. I double over and can't stop laughing.

"I thought you Americans were brave," Frank teases me. A bit of fried scorpion, like chewing gum, is stuck to his lower lip. He holds the bug-stick in front of me like it's a roasted marshmallow.

In response, I make a face. But I lean over and bite off one of the scorpion's back legs or feelers. I don't know which part I'm eating. Yet I have done more reckless things for a boy that have resulted in intense heartbreak, hospital visits, STIs, and zero college acceptances. I could have killed myself and our sevenbedroom house by accidentally backing through a garage door.

How dangerous can eating a dead scorpion be?

Doesn't the poison automatically evaporate in a deep fryer?

At least hundreds of thousands of people seem to be enjoying these creatures at the Fucheng Food Market. If I die, at least I was poisoned from attempting to be internationally adventurous.

For a moment, as I chew, my mind goes blank and I think that this is the exact moment that I'm going to die. It seems that at my eulogy and also when I give the reason for death in my afterlife, I will have to say that Iris Wang died by eating a bug. She died by trying her best to fit in. How fitting.

But it turns out that fried scorpion is a lot like devouring a small piece of extra-crispy, battered fish. Full of nutrients and protein.

"It just needs some tartar sauce, lemon, and French fries," I say.

Frank looks slightly confused. But he laughs loudly when I buy another round of deep-fried insects on sticks: crunchy tarantulas, oversize beetles, silkworms, scorpions, and buttery-tasting caterpillars.

Frank even looks majorly impressed.

"Are all Americans as spontaneous as you?" he asks.

"I don't know," I say, shrugging coyly. "Maybe? But I'm definitely up for anything involving food, drugs, sex, and fun."

Frank is gaping openly at me.

I take that as an invitation to lean in and kiss him firmly on the mouth. No tongue.

He doesn't kiss me back because his mouth is still hanging wide open from surprise when I finally pull away.

"You're pretty okay yourself, Frank Liao," I tease, popping a silkworm into his mouth.

And I don't let him say anything else, but now it's an all-out bug-eating competition, and I bet Frank that I can chow down more grubs than him!

I take a photo of us eating our dessert insects and upload it on Instagram. Forty instant likes.

"How is your family doing?" he says, suddenly looking serious. "Do you like living with your uncle Dai?"

"He's really . . . um . . . great," I say. My voice falters as I think about the huge wad of *yuan* in my wallet. Somehow, like a guilty conscience, the money seems to weigh my bag down whenever I think about it.

"Family is always complicated," Frank says knowingly. He sighs, as if he has a lot of personal experience.

"Oh my god, tell me about it," I say, picking a bit of tarantula from between my teeth. "My family has more layers and legs and wings than all these bugs combined. I mean, I honestly love all of them, but some more than others. Like I think these caterpillars are so much better-tasting than these worms, but I guess they all belong to the same family."

As I say this, I can't help but keep thinking of Uncle Dai's horror-stricken face and my grandmother's noisy tears from a few nights ago. I keep remembering her scary-strong old-lady grip and how desperate and heart-aching she looked when she saw me. My poor undead grandma who was so happy to hold me. I wonder if silkworms and caterpillars have secrets. Tarantulas and scorpions definitely do.

Smirking, Frank suddenly leans over and I think he's going to kiss me, but he just feeds me a mouthwatering beetle. Slightly disappointed, I chew and swallow extra slowly.

"Speaking of family, we should hurry back and work on some formal vocabulary for addressing aunts, uncles, cousins, and grandparents," Frank says, giving me one of his worried, sympathetic smiles. "Have you met all of your family yet in Beijing? Is Ruby your only cousin? Do you generally get along?"

"Listen, I actually need to do something important today," I say, not answering his questions. "I thought about what you said last night about not trying, and I honestly want to do better."

If I have the guts to eat a bunch of potentially poisonous bugs, why can't I disobey Uncle Dai? Why can't I meet my grandmother?

It's not like my uncle ever has to know. Since my dad lives in another time zone, when would he find out? Who would tell him? Admittedly, curiosity did kill the cat, but I'm a Tiger. It's not a betrayal of family loyalty if my insatiable need for the truth will reunite my dad with his parents. I want a full family tree, not one with missing limbs and leaves.

Visiting my grandparents will be like Ruby practicing for her creative dog grooming show.

Just another family secret.

Frank waves his fingers in my face. I barely notice.

"What's going on in there?" he asks, sounding confused. "Is everything okay?"

"Tell you later!" I say, smooching him on the cheek.

Before he can react, I race off and leave him with the tray of crispy leftover bugs.

Scanning the bustling street, I try to hail a taxi, but then I see the same old skinny dude, who grins and insists on giving me a ride on the rickshaw for free.

He wheezes asthmatically, and I feel so scared that his job is going to end his life.

"Do you need a break?" I yell as he pedals, but he doesn't understand English.

We finally stop at the Red Mandarin Hotel outside a Western-looking neighborhood called Sanlitun. I still insist on giving him a small pile of *yuan*, since he seemed to have risked his health to help me. Outside the hotel, I buy a bouquet of fresh-cut daisies and purple rhododendrons for my grandmother.

Pretending that I am a guest in the hotel, I take the key card and ride the elevator to room 33245. It's on the thirty-third floor. I knock firmly but there's no answer. I try the key, and the door clicks open, and I'm suddenly inside a large luxury suite with classical Chinese paintings and fine gold furnishings. It looks very fancy, even more upscale and modern than our penthouse in the Shangri-La.

"Hello?" I say. "Grandma?"

"Nǐ hǎo, nǐ hǎo ma?" I decide to add, in case she doesn't respond to English. What if she thinks I'm a foreign thief? I keep chorusing the greeting for a good full minute, and then I think she might actually be hard of hearing. I knock loudly on each door of the suite and then enter the room when no one responds. As I fling open each door (three bedrooms, two point five bathrooms), I call out *"Nǐ hǎo, nǐ hǎo ma,"* which is the only Chinese I can remember.

But no one is home.

I didn't expect the penthouse suite to be empty. I had a vision of me giving my grandmother the flowers and embracing her. I just imagined old people stayed home all day. For some reason, I thought she would be sitting on a couch, knitting a scarf, and maybe enjoying a cup of oolong tea. What else would she do?

Where would an old person go?

I wait.

I check my phone for English-Mandarin phrases that I can quickly learn. "Sorry, I don't understand," *bù hǎo yì si, wǒ tīng bù dǒng,* could be a very useful phrase, and so could "Wait a moment," *děng yī xià,* when I'm googling the English translations. I practice each one at least one hundred times. Due to the extreme stress of learning, I eventually fall asleep on the couch. My eyes are slowly lulled to sleep by a language that I should know, and one that I'm hopefully improving in.

Someone yelps in surprise.

I jolt awake.

It takes me a while to remember where I am.

"Grandma! Grandma! It's me, Weijun!" I say, still groggy. "I'm your granddaughter!"

I force myself to open my eyes.

But it's just a hotel maid carrying groceries. Stunned, she drops the bag and milk leaks from a plastic carton. Apologizing in half-Chinese, half-English, she immediately grabs a towel and begins wiping the floor. But there is a well-dressed and good-looking elderly couple trailing slowly behind her. The man is skeleton-thin and carrying a walking stick. He leans on the elderly lady for support.

In case they don't remember me, I say, *"Nǐ hǎo, nǐ hǎo ma,"* in a loud, extra-friendly tone so they will not feel threatened by an intruder in their home.

"Weijun!" my grandmother gasps. Then she starts speaking to me in rapid Chinese. Of course, I don't understand anything.

"Bù hǎo yì si, wǒ méi tīng dǒng." I recall the phrase from Google and shock myself by saying it in the most perfect Mandarin I have ever spoken in my entire life. *Sorry, I don't understand.*

I don't know what else to do, except run to hug my grandmother, and she slowly wraps her tiny arms around me. She's half my size, and I'm already a petite person. Sobbing like two lost howler monkeys, we sink slowly into the couch together.

The thin old man looks startled, but as soon as he hears my name, he immediately bursts into tears. He looks exactly like my father, but so much older. He actually looks like me. We have the same sharp angular features and half-moon eyelids. My grandpa, face slowly turning white like a steamed pork bun, eventually collapses beside me on the couch.

When I look at my grandparents, my eyes won't stop watering, and I don't know if it's because I'm sad or because it's the air pollution.

I literally don't have the language ability to explain myself.

That's when I know exactly what to do.

Even though I know that I will be breaking all the rules and there will be extreme anger, chaos, and consequences for me.

Nervously, I video-call my parents on WeChat. I just need real answers, and they're the only two people who can help with this emergency translation issue. Even though I know that my actions will make my dad extremely upset. Even though I know that he might never forgive me.

When they don't pick up after the sixth ring, I send them an urgent message.

WECHAT GROUP (#1WangFamily!!!)

Iris: PICK UP the phone.

Iris: Please pick up.

Iris: I need to talk to you!!!!

Iris: I KNOW GRANDMA AND GRANDPA ARE ALIVE!!!!!!!!!

After eight more tries, my mom and dad finally answer.

My parents sound utterly terrified and confused. Their anxious faces pop up on the screen and they are both wearing pajamas. My dad is wearing a green nighttime moisturizing mask and my mom is wearing a pink negligee and curlers. I realize they must have been sleeping. What time is it in New Jersey, anyway?

"What is going on?" my dad yells.

"Iris, why couldn't this wait until morning?" my mom says.

"Who told you that my parents were alive?" my dad asks. "I specifically asked your uncle not to mention it!"

"Go back to bed!" my mom exclaims.

"No," I say, crossing my arms. "A lot has been going on. I need to talk to you."

"How dare you disobey a direct order?" my dad says, sounding deeply upset.

I want to cry with happiness at seeing their familiar faces, but at the same time, I'm also so furious at them.

"First, you sent me away!" I accuse them, practically sobbing with shaky resentment and rage. "Second, you lie to me about my family, and then third, you LIE to me about Grandma and Grandpa being dead. Why would you tell me about Uncle Dai and not my grandparents? Don't you care that I've been missing two members of my family my entire life?"

Even though I'm extremely emotional and upset, I also just want to hug my shocked-looking parents through the iPhone screen. I can confront them again later about shipping me away, but it's more important to know why my grandparents seem to be the biggest secret that I've unlocked in Beijing.

"We did it to help you!" my dad retorts. "Everything we do is for you!"

Suddenly, my dad sees the older people behind me, leaning anxiously into the phone's screen. His eyes bulge, and for a second, I think I see a billion different emotions flash in them at once. It's like watching a television series in a foreign language. Honestly, it's hard to tell with his green nighttime face mask on. He blinks and rubs his eyes. He can't even speak. I'm sure that he notices the facial similarities between us three.

My grandpa, Dad, and I could be the same person, minus my long wavy hair. I can tell where I got most of my above-average looks from. It's certainly not from my mom's side of the family.

My dad can't speak.

Finally, the older man, my grandfather, starts speaking. Begging, really.

Silence.

The funeral kind.

To my utmost horror, my dad shouts in extreme anger, "WHAT IS THIS? IRIS!!! WHAT HAVE YOU DONE?!!!"

My mom starts pleading. "Jeff! Jeff! Listen to me!!!!"

My dad is making furious whimpering sounds. He sounds like an injured raccoon.

Unexpectedly, my dad hangs up on me.

I stare at my phone, shocked and confused.

My dad has never hung up on me before.

Both my grandparents react by crying loudly. In response, I start crying and hyperventilating too. I don't know exactly what happened. Why would this reunion cause such a horrible soul-crushing reaction? Yes, my dad lied to me about their existence, so shouldn't I be the one yelling and screaming at him? But what life-altering thing could have happened between my dad and his parents to make him lie about their existence?

Uncle Dai keeps talking about the importance of family, and Frank keeps emphasizing ancestors and culture and belonging. Both of them have taught me that family has no price tag, like a Ming vase from the fifth century. If you look at all of us trying to keep our shit together, family is not fun, cheap, or flimsy.

My grandmother hugs me and we start wailing and breathing loudly together. My grandfather joins in. We sound like asthmatic basset hounds. I certainly know that we are related based on our amount of caninelike distress. We're having the exact same emotional reaction.

Moments later, my mom calls back.

At first, I think she's going to apologize and explain my dad's irrational behavior. But she starts scolding me. "Iris, what game are you playing at? It's four in the morning and we thought it was an emergency. You call us and I'm in my . . . pajamas!"

I notice that she's put on a housecoat and taken her curlers out. Did she put on concealer? She must be embarrassed about the dark circles under her eyes.

"Explain to me RIGHT NOW why Grandma and Grandpa aren't dead!" I say between furious-scared-demanding tears. "I just found out that the people who are supposed to be dead are actually living in a seven-star hotel. What's going on? How can you keep lying to me?!"

I'm practically a Level 10 Audio Earthquake. I rage. I can't stop shaking with pop-eyed indignation.

"You have to call us in the middle of the night for this?"

She's right.

I completely forgot about the time difference. Is Beijing thirteen hours behind or ahead of New Jersey? I can't remember these trivial details about international time travel.

"This is a family emergency," I sniffle.

My mother sighs. "Let me talk to your grandparents."

Reluctantly, I hand my phone to my grandmother and grandfather, who exchange rapid no-nonsense-sounding words with my mother. I have no idea what's being said. All I know is that they both don't understand how the phone works, or else my mom's Chinese is cringingly shitty, because my grandmother is yelling and speaking slowly and pantomiming. She looks frustrated. Like how Frank is always trying to explain how to speak Chinese to me during our lessons. It gets worse when my grandfather tries to talk over them. It's an epic shouting match of Chinese karaoke. Everyone is fighting to speak into the phone's tiny microphone.

My mom looks seriously annoyed.

Then my grandmother finally gives me back the phone.

My mom's expression looks resigned but exhausted.

She pauses, like she doesn't know exactly what to say. Like she's wondering whether to give me the big-girl version or the happy-go-lucky kiddie version of what happens to us when we die.

Finally, she says, "Iris, your father and grandfather fought many years ago because your grandfather did several questionable things, such as having multiple affairs. When he was younger, he was a very good-looking man who loved beautiful women and men and cheated all the time on your grandmother. He really hurt your grandma. He was never home and your father had to take care of his mother.

"One day, he had a scandalous affair with Uncle Dai's mother, who was the daughter of a local shopkeeper, and she got pregnant. Your grandparents don't want me to tell you more, but I think you should know. They think you're fragile and can't handle PG-13-rated stuff."

"Go on," I say, nodding.

I feel very grown-up having this conversation. My grandfather, the former cheater, hobbles to the kitchen and brings back a plate of buttery almond cookies and honey-drizzled cakes. I grab both snacks and chew in what I think is a very thoughtful, refined manner.

"Because of China's very conservative attitude after the Cultural Revolution, your grandfather had to send your uncle to a small village to live with a distant relation to avoid bringing shame to everyone involved. When your dad found out about the affair and his half brother, he refused to speak to your grandpa and cursed him. He was sick of your grandfather's harmful behavior and he was tired of protecting your grandma. When your grandma decided to forgive your grandpa for the affair, your dad swore he would never speak to his parents again. He was furious. All these years, he has been pretending that your grandparents are dead because he can't forgive his father for never being a father to him. He didn't even want you to ever meet such a selfish man who never thought about his own wife and son."

"Are you serious?" I say. "Dad's been holding a lifelong grudge? That's not very Goatlike."

My mom purses her lips.

"Your grandma has forgiven your grandpa, but your father hasn't. She's accepted Uncle Dai and Ruby as her own. Your father is still very, very hurt and doesn't want anything to do with his parents. When the private detective and lawyer that Uncle Dai hired finally found us in New Jersey, your dad was reluctant at first, but he really wants to have a brother. And then he learned that Uncle Dai has a family, and he wants you to have a cousin. Now that your dad has had a lot of time to think about it, he knows that Uncle Dai is not to blame for your grandfather's behavior."

"Didn't he know that I would find out about Grandma and Grandpa?" I ask.

"He didn't think you would ever find out. Their side of the family is usually very good at secret-keeping. But you NEVER meeting your grandparents was a condition that Uncle Dai agreed on. He didn't want to hide it from you, but felt it was best to honor his older brother's wishes. Your grandpa just really wants your dad back in his life and asked your grandma to intervene."

"Is Dad my real father?" I suddenly ask.

This seems like the right time to finally know, since it's like we're showing each other before-and-after photos at a sleepover. Like we're confessing what we used to look like before contacts, braces, and makeup.

"What are you talking about?" my mom says. "Of course he's your dad. I would know."

"Are you sure you're my real mom?" I ask, crunching on another cookie.

"What?" she says.

"Am I adopted?" I ask.

"Where is this coming from?" she says, sounding annoyed.

"Is Uncle Dai my real dad, because I kind of look like him? Is there even a possibility at all that I was kidnapped at birth?"

"Why are you still talking nonsense?" my mom says.

After we finish our chat, my mom tells me not to call her again in the middle of the night unless I'm in the hospital.

"And tell Iris not to drink or do drugs!" My dad's voice suddenly appears from the background. "Tell her that Chinese drugs aren't FDA approved!"

Has he been listening to our conversation the whole time?

I should be angrier at him. First, for lying about my uncle, aunt, and cousin, then my grandparents. He lied about five entire people not existing! I'm also pissed at him for not wanting to explain himself when I called him. As my parent, shouldn't he be taking responsibility for lying multiple times and sending me away?

But also, I understand that the truth is really shitty, and sometimes it's easier just to leave it behind or send it away.

"Jeff, you tell her yourself," my mother replies. "I'm going to sleep for an hour before I have to get up for work."

"Iris, don't drink or do drugs!" he shouts.

"Too late," I yell back.

Quickly, I disconnect before they can ask me more questions. I can't believe that my father never talked to his parents again after immigrating to America. I can't believe that he's still furious at his father for having an affair. Is this what Ruby meant when she said that my father abandoned his family for the United States? That he never bothered to look for his baby half brother and left Beijing as soon as he could get approved for an international student visa?

The more I learn about my family's secrets, especially my dad's, the more I think that I should be designated as the mature, responsible, levelheaded adult in the Wang family. I'm the only person that I know of who isn't hiding a long-lost sibling or pretending that a misbehaving parent is dead.

Before I leave the Red Mandarin Hotel, my grandparents hug me tightly. They've been watching our conversation with looks of sorrow and shock on their faces. Poor Grandpa is literally shaking like a washing machine. Will his heart be okay? He must be a flower-heart like me. I don't know enough Chinese to ask him about cardiac arrest, and I wish I knew how to phrase it properly. He looks genuinely sorry for the past.

And yet, I don't know what to think, because he hurt my dad really badly. My grandmother has obviously forgiven him and so has Uncle Dai after being given away for adoption. But I can only imagine the messy family drama, the imploding anger, the perpetual lies, and all the manipulation. I'm already feeling so wounded by my parents for sending me to Beijing, so I can't imagine how Uncle Dai felt growing up alone in the countryside without his family. I can also see why my dad dislikes and mistrusts his own father for his selfish weakness.

Admittedly, maybe I'm more like my grandfather than anyone else in the family.

Flower-hearts cannot control their impulses.

Even though my grandparents don't understand a word of

English, they must know that my father is terribly upset at them. Because when I hug them back for the third time, my grandparents start crying loudly again. As soon as one of them starts sobbing, I can't help but cry harder. Even though our family is a real mess and I'm 95 percent probably not-royalty, I might be okay because I have people who love me. Maybe that's what family is. A safety net of highly flawed and imperfect individuals to catch you and hold on to you when you fall off a cliff.

I decide to forgive my father for lying to me, just because I want him to forgive my grandfather after so many years.

After our twentieth or two hundredth emotional group embrace, my grandpa hands me a tin full of crispy red bean pecan cookies and more Chinese cash. *5,500 yuan!!!*

I'm so lucky that my grandparents are so generous. What happened to my dad? Why doesn't he just give me money anytime he sees me? If he gave me money every time that we cried together, he'd be broke and I'd be a millionairess.

Apparently, generosity is not genetic.

What else have I inherited from my heart-attack-inducing, secret-keeping family?

As I hail a taxi back to the Shangri-La, my stomach lurches from too many varieties of bugs, cookies, decades-long secrets, and epic feelings of helplessness on a global scale. I'm extremely anxious about reconciling my entire long-lost family. Because what if I will never be able to change my dad's mind about my poor grandpa? What if my dad stays furious and heartbroken and depressed forever? How can I help him understand that forgiveness is worthy and possible when I'm still reeling from Samira and Peter?

As the nauseous feeling intensifies, I realize that forgiveness is like taking your first bite of a scorpion. You just have to believe it won't kill you and get over that funny, slightly off-putting texture. I just need to convince my dad that forgiving his father is like eating a gross-looking but highly nutritious insect. The problem is that my dad, unlike my mom and me, has always been an extremely picky eater.

Worry, like an eight-legged spider crawling inside my brain, continues to gnaw at me. I pace up and down in my bedroom for almost half the night, hatching a plan.

24

Pregnant

When you grow up with a curse, you're told to expect nonstop trouble. You're told there's nothing you can do because a Tiger girl always has horrendous luck with boys and excess facial hair. When I pluck and wax my Tiger mustache every forty-eight hours, I have sometimes wondered if there is an easy home remedy or Chinese spell to make it all go away.

Honestly, I'm sick of being told who or what I should be. And I'm seriously annoyed about being told that there is no cure for my lifelong curse.

This morning, as I keep stirring sugar in my coffee, I wonder whether I would be the same person if I hadn't known I was a Tiger or if I didn't barf all over the famous Madame Xing. I have always questioned superstitions, but I have honestly half believed them. I blame my lack of commitment to Chinese mythology on both of my parents.

My mom says "they are bullshit," but my dad wholly believes in them.

If there's one person who can change my dad's mind and get him to forgive his father after so many years, it's a famous fortune-teller. Preferably, the same one who predicted my fate. I'm certain that a professional named Madame Xing is the only person who can finally end our generation-long family feud.

All night I have searched online and used translation sites, and I have figured out that there is a Madame Xing fortune-teller and face-reader on a tour of the magical, mystical Chengdu Hot Springs. I don't know if it's the same one, but she's currently taking appointments with newborn babies and people with serious skin afflictions.

Even if it's not the same one, my dad doesn't even have to know.

"We're going on a field trip," I say when Frank shows up at the apartment for my tutoring lesson. He's the only person who hasn't lied or kept a secret from me in Beijing. So far, he seems trustworthy. Besides, he's always going on about how I don't have a worthy cause or passion. I continue, "I thought about what you said about me not making an effort, and I am going to change that. I really need your help, Frank. I need to fix my family."

I look at him hopefully.

Subconsciously, I gnaw at my bottom lip.

I nervously touch my hair, which I just washed with this amazing organic iris-infused and almond-scented shampoo that Ruby bought me as a surprise gift before she left for Milan for her costume fitting. The whole room smells like me: a sexy botanic garden in full bloom. I'm also wearing a body-fitting jumpsuit made of jungle-green chicken feathers, gifted to me by Auntie Yingfei. I look and feel like a fantastic parrot about to embark on a grand, outdoorsy adventure.

"I don't know," he says, frowning slightly.

"Come on," I beg, touching his shoulder, and he glances around, as if worried someone will see us.

"No one is home," I say suggestively. "We can do whatever we want."

My comment causes Frank to seriously blush. I giggle at his reaction.

"I'm still going whether or not you come with me," I say.

Sidling closer to him, I make my most wide-eyed, pleading face. I hope Frank is psychic and can understand how much I need his help. Also, it would just be easier if he could read my mind and we could just fool around whenever I wanted. For instance, I really want him to see me without this amazing jumpsuit on.

Frank flushes again. He looks resigned.

I show him the crumpled *yuan* from my grandpa. For once, I'm not spending it on something frivolous or even something that directly benefits me.

"You can have all this if you come," I offer. "Think of it as extra tutoring income, and you can tell me about the history of the hot springs!"

Frank's face slowly softens into a smile and he agrees.

Enthusiastically, I hug him in thanks and his body eventually relaxes into mine. After a while, he embraces me back. It's clear that this is not even a friend hug. I burrow my face deep into his shoulder, thinking wild and extremely dirty thoughts. My insides flutter nonstop. And we stay that way, inhaling the rich overriding scent of fresh irises and almonds. I wonder which one of us will step away first.

"Iris, are you sure . . . ," Frank begins in a low, low voice. I barely hear him.

"You won't regret it!" I promise quickly, worried that he'll change his mind about coming with me to find the fortune-teller who can reunite my family.

We take a two-hour taxi, a subway, and then another taxi up several bumpy, winding roads. For once, Frank isn't talking about history or discussing Mandarin, and I watch the mountainside come into full view. China's countryside is gorgeous. It's like being inside one of the calligraphy paintings at the NAMOC. I've actually never been this excited about nature before. Is this why people climb Mount Everest? To become more worldly and sophisticated?

As the car slowly climbs the mountain, it hits me that I'm really in the land of my ancestors. My father was born in a village and then he left his home so he could have a better chance of a new life. I tell myself that if I manage to find Madame Xing and get her to make my dad see reason, I'll put in more effort to learn Mandarin, whatever it takes to make my dad and his parents happy again. Whatever it takes to put my whole family together. At the end of the summer, I want to all be sitting together slurping soup noodles and wontons.

After three and a half hours of nonstop traveling, we finally stop at the Herijun Hot Spring Hotel, where apparently Madame

Xing is holding private appointments for the week. There is no cell reception, but surely the hotel has Wi-Fi.

"Where can I see Madame Xing?" I ask her assistant, who thankfully speaks English. She's a young woman with thick glasses and spiky, pink hair holding a clipboard. There are at least fifty people in the lobby.

"Do you have appointment?" she says.

"No, but can I please make one? It's an emergency."

"Sorry, we are full."

"But I just took two taxis and a really long subway ride to get here! I came all the way from the United States!"

My outburst doesn't impress the assistant. "There is waitlist for next year. I can take your name down. It's 2,500 *yuan* to hold appointment."

Frank speaks to her in Chinese, but she still shakes her head. She sees my distressed expression, and her tone becomes kinder.

"I'm very sorry," she says to me. "Madame Xing is very popular in China, Taiwan, Hong Kong, and even America these days. Everyone want her to predict their son and daughter success. You know, she can look at a baby and tell whether or not they'll go to Harvard or Oxford. That's how parents know what child to invest in. Bad facial features, bad future, as we say in China."

I stare at her beseechingly. "Please! That's why I need to see her."

"You are having baby?" she says, her eyes widening in alarm. "You are teenage mother?"

"Um . . . ," I say, patting my stomach.

It's true I've been eating a lot in Beijing and those sesame pastries at breakfast did make me gassy.

Normally I'd be upset if someone thought I was pregnant, but this is a full-on emergency. Before I can make up my mind whether or not to lie, the assistant offers, "We fit you in very early, first appointment tomorrow morning. What's your name?"

Frank is looking at me, speechless.

I barely have a moment to blink away my guilty conscience.

"Wang Weijun," I say automatically. I grab Frank's arm so he can't react. "This is the teenage father, and he's very worried that the baby will not bring him good luck."

Pretending to look incredibly worried, I learn in conspiratorially and whisper, "He won't marry me and take care of the baby unless Madame Xing approves. I need her to give me a facial reading urgently."

I try to make myself look teary-eyed and eager. I think of how sad and horrified I felt when they cut me out of Ruby's gown. I think of both my disappointed parents. I think about how upset and ashamed I really feel about not getting into any colleges. Even though I've pretended to myself that it doesn't matter, it really does. Then I think about my grandma and grandpa crying and holding me. Real tears actually trickle from my eyes at the memory. I begin sniveling nonstop because I also feel extremely shitty for lying to the girl, like my parents have lied to me for seventeen years. But I promise myself that if this helps my family, I'll work harder to learn Mandarin and study for the GED.

I look at the assistant with wide, pleading eyes, in what I hope is my most pitying canine manner.

I'm a lost dog, I keep telling myself. *Please take me home.*

For all I know, being pregnant could very well happen. I could be some young single teenage mother whose only hope is a famous fortune-teller. What would my prospects be in China? Would I have no one to take care of me?

Eventually, the assistant looks alarmed and nods sympathetically. "Poor thing! I will tell Madame Xing!"

Then she speaks to the hotel clerk and tells him that we need a deluxe room with a view. I'm absolutely shocked that this was remarkably easy.

"What did you do?" Frank asks when we are safely in our hotel room. It's not as nice and a bit outdated compared to the Shangri-La, but admittedly I'm getting spoiled. There's a comfy bed and a Western-style toilet, which makes me relieved.

"I'm going to see her tomorrow," I say, incredulous. "I can't believe it!"

"You realize that you aren't pregnant, right?" Frank says, staring at me. His expression is an uneasy blend of shock, horror, and amusement.

"Of course," I say, wondering if an actual fortune-teller will know. I glance at my reflection in the mirror and then suck in my stomach. It is a bit rounder if I stand to the right. I'll just have to slouch and cover my stomach with Frank's extra-baggy hoodie.

We have fourteen-plus hours to kill, so I suggest that we explore the rushing hot springs of Chengdu. We're surrounded by a picturesque forest, boulders, and overhanging trees. Gagging silently, I do my best to ignore the sulfurous rotten egg odor. Magpies squawk and swoop around us, and it's almost magical. Like being in an enchanted forest, away from all our problems.

We don't have any bathing suits, but everyone—tourists and locals—is practically naked anyway, so I strip down to my undies and bra and jump in! Besides, no one knows me in China. The water in the hot springs is bubbling and it feels like I'm being boiled alive in the most relaxing way possible.

Frank stands there, watching me and looking stricken. He eventually joins me, but not before neatly folding his clothes by a tree.

I splash him.

He doesn't react.

Sticking my tongue out, I make a series of super-goofy faces at him. I cross my eyes, but Frank doesn't seem to find any of it funny.

I decide to splash him again, but he does nothing. In fact, he seems distracted. Super dejected, even. Like he's just failed an important history test.

"Smile," I say, but Frank is looking way more serious and glum than usual.

Come to think of it, he wasn't particularly chatty in the taxi or subway ride, and he's being paid to teach me by the hour.

Nevertheless, I take a bunch of photos of us in the gorgeous hot springs with the pink-and-white cherry blossoms blooming behind us. It's almost movie-romantic, except for the odorous smell. I cover my nose and mouth-breathe too loudly. I try to be quieter, but my sinuses are still clogged in the countryside.

I blame my allergies for ruining a possibly romantic moment.

As I snap photos, Frank is casually turning his broad frame toward me. His semi-sad expression makes me think of pugs, classrooms, and rules. But his expression is also thoughtful and ultra-serious and for whatever reason, I can't take my eyes off him. The white fairy lights from the midday sun cause a shadow and reflect off his angular face, as if he's hiding a secret. I keep thinking about the poem he recited at the party. He's really not my type at all, I tell myself, but the voice of no self-control asks, but *what if?* What if Frank Liao is the one, but you have never dated Chinese dudes because you worried they were boring geeks? What's the difference between hooking up with a star-student poet at a top university vs. a loser pothead?

There's something charming and fascinating and also scary about the humongous difference. Frank's passion, his politics, his spontaneous confidence. I have never met anyone like him before. His intensity is dizzying. Looking at Frank is like parasailing three hundred feet in the air, dipping into the wind-whipped ocean, and being yanked back up in tandem into the blue-frosted sky.

I take a bunch of pictures of unsmiling, surprisingly sexy Frank. There are so many photogenic ones to choose from. There's still no cell signal and there's no Wi-Fi, so I'll just have to post portraits of Frank later.

"Listen," I finally say, curious, "do you like me or what? I really can't tell."

Frank still isn't looking at me. I splash water at him to catch his attention.

He says nothing, but this time, he leans in and kisses me for the longest time with tongue. For a moment, I'm taken aback. I am dissolving. Then I can gasp. Oh god. The hot springs garbage smell is truly unbearable.

Suddenly, Frank splashes me in the face.

Stunned, I shriek and splash him back. He ducks.

I almost wish someone was video-recording our interaction, because I'm sure we look extra beautiful with the exotic scenery unfolding around us. I have a theory that romantic encounters look even better to the people watching them than those who are directly involved. Getting hot water up your nose is not particularly funny or sexy.

We stand very still and close together.

Our breathing matches up in perfect sync. I'm prepared for an epic, life-changing makeout session. But then a black magpie swooping above us screeches mockingly. Something mushy, like a freshly flipped omelette, plops on my forehead. It's smelly and bitter like nail polish remover. Suddenly, hot liquid drips into my eyeball.

Frank stares at me, looking incredulous. He doesn't say anything about the bird shit raining down my face like melted marshmallow fluff. Then he bursts out laughing. He can't stop. I splash smelly water at him, and accidentally slip on a pebble, crashing backward into the white foamy toothpaste springs. This should seriously be a commercial for Colgate. Frank helps me up, grinning.

"Iris Wang, you are the strangest person I have met," he says, and I'm a bit confused until he tells me that he means that there is no one quite like me in all of China's twenty-three provinces.

"Are you saying you like me as in *like me*?" I ask, and Frank smiles sheepishly.

∽ ∽ ∽

Back in our hotel room, after scrubbing my hair fifteen times, I practically pounce on Frank and he literally has to push me off him. To be honest, I don't get the hint and it takes me a while to notice that he's trying to escape from under me. He looks utterly embarrassed. His face has turned the weirdo color of the filling in a stale red bean pastry. He has to hold me away at arm's length while we both fight over his hotel robe. What just happened to the sexy, willing Frank from the hot springs?

"Iris, we've only known each other for less than a week," he quickly says, looking remorseful. "I'm also your highly paid tutor."

"It didn't matter before," I say, confused.

"I had some time to think about it when you were in the shower."

As if I'm a slightly deranged serial killer, Frank slowly backs himself into the corner of the room. Regret transforms his face. "I'm really sorry."

This is the second time in a month I've been rejected by a boy.

Do I smell? Is there still bird shit in my hair? Is it my ever-growing Tiger mustache? I wonder if I have any embarrassing nipple hair.

I check myself quickly and I seem to be okay.

"Tell me about yourself, then," I insist. "What do you do for fun besides reciting poetry? Do you have any siblings?"

Frank looks a bit hesitant. Like he wants to talk, but some internal digestive struggle is preventing him from talking. "There's nothing interesting about me."

Astonished, I look directly at him. I cross my arms and feel like my mother, asking too many interrogation-type questions.

He averts his eyes. He looks like he's practically going to vomit!

"I'm not asking you a hard question," I say.

"I'm your tutor, Iris. And I don't think your uncle would approve."

"Then you shouldn't have kissed me," I say, thoroughly annoyed. "Why did you invite me to that party? Why did you take me to eat bugs? Do you take every girl you know to sample deep-fried tarantulas?"

"I like you, Iris, I really do, but—"

His features crumple like a fortune cookie. He looks so vulnerable and earnest. Nothing like that sneaky rat-faced Peter Hayes. We watch each other for a while, and I can't stop tracing his face with my pupils. There's a nervousness in Frank's gaze. Somehow, his extreme uneasiness about being with me makes me feel like I can trust him completely. If he is worried about the repercussions of being my tutor and fooling around with me, it clearly shows that he's one responsible dude.

For once, I'm using my brain to logic out romance.

But it's hard to do because we're standing only inches away. Barely separated by some invisible but sizzling Great Wall of China. Whatever little self-control I ever had evaporates right through my pores. Poof. Gone.

I don't care anymore.

I just know that I'm the only gourmet meal that Frank needs.

"Don't think about anything," I plead. "Just think about how you feel now. Overthinking ruins fun."

He relents and approaches me.

Eagerly, I grip his hair and pull his face toward mine, and his lips are warm and soft. He reminds me of toffee and molten lava cakes from the oven. Because Frank is literally melting into my mouth at 425 degrees Fahrenheit. Like a chocolate buffet, I just want to devour him completely. His body instinctively leans into me, all of him, and I know he feels this strange delicious attraction too. It's like I'm at a five-star restaurant, and Frank is the weird, exquisite delicacy on the tasting menu that only makes sense on this side of the world. Something that I would never try unless I was shipped to Beijing.

"I really can't do this," he finally says quietly, pulling away.

Confused, I stop touching him, and he makes a sound like deep, unfiltered regret and stares at the floor.

Abruptly, Frank exits the room, claiming that he needs to make an important phone call.

His second rejection within moments of his last one is like whiplash. Almost as painful and confusing as not getting into a single college.

Stunned, I sit down on the bed and think it would be easier if he had turned me down based on having bird shit in my hair. Honestly, I just don't understand his erratic behavior. One minute it seems that he really likes me, and the next, he's acting repulsed and running away.

Are all boys in China like Frank Liao?

Are they all like hot and sour soup?

What am I doing wrong?

I'm puzzled and really hurt by Frank's unfathomable behavior. Honestly, I thought he was really into me. But I refuse to let another boy wound me. Peter Hayes was enough. My heart is already smashed up and deeply broken. If it was taken out of me, I swear it would resemble a sloppy joe in America. In China, though, it would probably look more like a deep-fried cockroach. Shriveled on a stick but nutritious.

Hours later, when Frank finally comes back to the room, he avoids talking for the rest of the night. Desperately, I wonder if he was calling another girl. Was he even on a phone call? But he doesn't answer my questions. He doesn't even look at me. I could be the hotel furniture, for all I know.

WECHAT GROUP (#1WangFamily!!!)

25 missed phone calls.

68 undelivered texts.

IrisDaddy: WHERE ARE YOU?! Uncle Dai says you are not picking up.

Mom: You expect us to pick up your phone call in the middle of the night and you can't answer one text?

Mom: Did you lose your phone again?

Mom: Better question, how did you break your phone?

IrisDaddy: Uncle Dai is going to hire a private investigator if you don't pick up!!!!

Mom: Everyone is looking for you.

Mom: Call us back!!!

Mom: IRIS!!!!!!!

WECHAT

SuperPrincessQueenRuby8421: Did you get my email?

SuperPrincessQueenRuby8421: Hey, message me when you get my email

SuperPrincessQueenRuby8421: Okay, I'm just getting on a flight to Milan, so I won't have signal for a while

SuperPrincessQueenRuby8421: Can you call me?

SuperPrincessQueenRuby8421: The dog is waiting at the airport for you, but the monks can't seem to reach you

SuperPrincessQueenRuby8421: The spa owner has been calling you nonstop

SuperPrincessQueenRuby8421: IRIS! You promised to pick up and look after the dog!

SuperPrincessQueenRuby8421: PICK up your phone

SuperPrincessQueenRuby8421: You know how important the show is to me

25

Madame Xing

"Your baby will be a Rooster," Madame Xing says, gazing intensely at me. Her assistant, whose name is Hollie, takes a photo of me for publicity.

I stare at the fortune-teller, a little flabbergasted. I didn't know I'd be having a Rooster baby.

"Yes," she says, placing her hand on my stomach. She squeezes my belly and I wince. I think she pushed a little too hard on my bladder. Thankfully, I only had a small cup of coffee this morning. Even though Madame Xing has a heavy accent, she speaks English fluently.

"Your features show unusual strength. Are you a Tiger?" she says.

"Yes!" I exclaim. "How did you know?! Is it my mustache?"

Madame Xing slowly winks at me.

I can see why my dad has been obsessed with her for seventeen-plus years. She is a magnificent woman wearing an oversize fur coat and long fake red acrylic nails. She's also wearing the highest gold stiletto shoes that I have ever seen. Are those Jimmy Choos? She looks absolutely fantastic. Madame Xing should be performing in Las Vegas or on a five-star cruise ship. If anything, I want to be her when I grow up, except that I don't have any fortune-telling talent.

I really want to hear more about my Rooster baby, but I realize I just need to find out more about myself.

As she places both hands on my stomach again and squeezes, I'm unable to play along anymore and blurt out, "There's no baby."

She pauses, looking shocked.

"My dad says that I have a curse on me because I threw up on you when I was a baby. I am a flower-heart with no college acceptances, no boyfriend, or any friends. My dad and grandpa have been fighting for many years, and I need you to tell my dad to forgive him. He worships you."

No response.

"Please, Madame Xing, I just want my dad to be happy, and the only way is if he can have his family back together. My dad is a really proud Goat. I love my dad and even though he sent me away to China, I am starting to understand why. Sometimes people do shitty things because they think it will help the other person. Can you please help me fix my family?"

I am babbling anxiously and I don't know how to stop.

Finally, Madame Xing stares at me and then pulls hard on my nose.

"Ouch," I say, wondering if she's putting another curse on me.

There's a long, awkward pause.

Fidgeting, I don't know what to say or do.

I don't know if I should look ashamed or make up an excuse.

"You lied about a baby to see me?" Madame Xing finally says, sounding incensed.

At first, I think she's going to yell at me or throw me out of the conference room, but she starts laughing hysterically. It's a loud, booming, echoing sound. Like a gorilla. Honestly, I'm impressed by her huge auditorium laugh. Finally, she slaps her knee twice and calls her assistant to bring her a bottle of *baijiu*.

"You are very brave, persistent, and creative, aren't you?" she says, taking a swig of alcohol.

Surprised, I look at her. No one has ever said these kind things to me before. It sounds like three authentic compliments. The nicest words that anyone, including my parents, has ever said about my personality.

She laughs and eventually, I laugh too. But she doesn't offer me a drink of *baijiu*. Just a glass of water.

Humphing like some kind of farm animal, Madame Xing checks my face for unlucky moles and finds nothing. The spacing between my eyes is very symmetrical and she makes me open my mouth and checks for wide gaps between my teeth. I have many, which means, according to Buddha and Confucius, that I'll be very lucky in the wealth and fame department. She clucks a few times and then makes mysterious oohing and aahing noises.

"What?" I gasp. "What's wrong?"

Then she makes me spit into a cup and she examines it.

What kind of fortune-telling is this?

Why does my dad believe in Madame Xing so much?

It's literally like going to the dentist.

"Is there something wrong?" I practically scream as she makes her hundredth oohing and aahing sound.

"Your heart is broken because you care too much about what people think about you," she finally declares. "You have a lot of energy, *qi*, that is all over the place. You're like a storm that can't decide its direction. Pick one way and just focus, otherwise you will never get anywhere. Flower-hearts are sensitive, but they are not hopeless. You have Tiger in you to make you strong."

"But what about my dad, who is a Goat?" I say. "How can I get him to forgive his father?"

"Goats are very stubborn, yes, but they are pack animals, right? They will always need to find their family to be happy. You need to talk to your dad. You can tell him that I told you that he needs to go to Beijing and speak to his parents. Misunderstandings always happen when people live too far away from family. He can call me if he wants to talk."

She hands me her card.

"You are doing a very good thing to help your dad, Weijun. If you keep thinking of other people, you can also find out what *you* want."

"I don't know what I want," I say, suddenly sniffling. "I don't know how to make myself happy."

"You make your dad happy and then you can choose to be either a happy Tiger or a sad Tiger," she says. "It's all up to you."

"I've honestly messed up my life," I say. "Everyone back home thinks I'm a giant failure."

"Why do you always worry about what people think of you?"

she says, looking me in the eye. "Who are you, Wang Weijun?"

"I was hoping you could tell me," I admit.

She makes another loud animal-like humphing sound. It sounds like she has an excess of phlegm. "Why are you trying to be what they want you to be? Does the tiger care what the other animals in the jungle think of her?"

And I realize she's completely right.

All my life I have been one of those sad combo pizzas from Domino's, trying to be what other people want me to be. I've been pepperoni on one side and zesty ham and pineapple on the other. Sometimes I've been vegetarian or a meat lover's combo for $12.99. I've always been whatever anyone decided to order.

I'm trying to be my dad's, Uncle Dai's, and Frank's different versions of Chinese.

I've never just been my own pizza. I've never thought I could choose my own toppings. That I could be my own flavor. My own authentic brand of Chinese American pizza with lots of spicy cheeses, onions, gassy anchovies, and a few deep-fried tarantulas for extra crunch.

I've never had a strong opinion about myself. And even then, I'm only 75 percent sure. My mom always says that if I knew myself like I knew a department store, my life choices would be so much better.

"There won't be any curse if you don't believe there is," Madame Xing insists. "But you have a very good heart, Weijun."

Walking back to my hotel room, I feel buoyant. I don't have any answers, but I think that I've been put on some newfound path.

Is this how Jesus and Moses and Buddha felt 24/7? Did they feel simultaneously confused but inspired? Do all wise beings feel enlightened but extraordinary?

Whatever the solution is, I need a super-fun distraction.

As if on cue, Frank is waiting for me in the room, perched on the edge of the bed. He's staring at his hands and fidgeting. He looks nervous and way younger. More vulnerable and more like a human being. Weirdly enough, though, this makes him look unbelievably, two-dimensionally handsome at the same time. Like a cardboard cutout of the actual Frank Liao. It's like there are two conflicting personas inside him. Studious, nerdy, and serious vs. teasing, willing, and fun. Is he even a real person?

"I'm sorry for yesterday," he begins with uncertainty.

I pause, unsure whether or not I should leave the room.

This is the first boy who has ever seriously apologized to me. Not once but multiple times in the days that we have known each other. Come to mention it, he's the only person under twenty years old who has ever said a genuine "Sorry" to my face for being a little mean or rude. Is this what self-respect is? Accepting an honest and uncomfortable apology? Feeling that you deserve one at any given time, not just on major holidays like Christmas and your birthday?

As if sensing my hesitation, Frank astonishes me by pulling out a small burgundy velvet box with a swirly gold Asian floral pattern on it. I gasp. Is he asking me to be his girlfriend for the summer? Has Madame Xing already taken away my curse? Frank opens the box and I'm stunned when he takes out a very pretty purple jade pendant carved in the shape of an iris flower. It's attached to a thin silver chain.

"I got this for you at the Panjiayuan Antique Market," he says anxiously. "The flower obviously reminded me of you."

I stare at him, oddly touched.

Selfish Peter Hayes never bought me a present the whole two years we were dating. In fact, I was the one always buying all the gifts in our relationship.

"Do you like it?" Frank asks in a quiet, barely-there voice. "It's real jade, which was revered by emperors in ancient China. It signifies benevolence, honesty, wisdom, integrity, and bravery. You're one of the most courageous people I have met. You always say and do what you are thinking and feeling. I've been saving up my tutoring money so I could give this to you."

Unable to speak for once, I nod, and I allow Frank to clasp his gift around my neck. It feels smooth and cool and surprisingly light. Unlike a mall purchase, it feels like there is so much emotional value and meaning behind his super-generous and thoughtful gift.

"It's so beautiful," I say admiringly. "No one, except my parents, has *ever* given me jewelry before."

Frank grins shyly at me, and I smile widely back.

"I keep thinking about you all the time," he says. "I was going to wait until the end of summer to surprise you, but I honestly think you should know exactly how I feel now. . . ."

Madame Xing said to trust my own instincts, and I tell myself that I'm over Peter Hayes and horrendous boys who are liars, cheaters, and losers. I'm a better and worthier version of the old no-standards Iris Wang. I'm ready for Chinese Parent Approved boys who buy you expensive jade and apologize within twenty-four hours.

I'm not cursed anymore, I tell myself. *I have improved my self-esteem by at least 30 percent.*

Despite my fragile flower-heart, I might actually be okay.

Quietly, I sit beside Frank on the bed. My mom has a pair of earthy-green jade hoop earrings that her mother gave her when she married my dad. Her relatives all gave her brown, lavender, and mint-colored jade pendants, earrings, and rings during her wedding ceremony. Apparently, jade is a huge deal in Chinese culture. It symbolizes commitment, ferocious loyalty, and unconditional love because jade can never age or break. My mom never wears her jade jewelry but keeps it in a safety deposit box at the bank. "They're worth everything," she once told me when I was little, and she let me try them on once. By giving me a jade iris necklace, is Frank saying that he really, truly, definitely likes me?

Is there a possibility for a serious, authentic Beijing summer fling?

But Frank keeps staring at his hands for the longest time. For once, I decide to listen instead of talk. I let him make the first move.

"You are surprising," he eventually admits. "You are funny, unpredictable, and extremely beautiful—"

"Did you just say I was beautiful?" I say, a little shocked. Beautiful Frank Liao thinks I'm good-looking? Peter used to tell me I was "just okay."

I notice the veins pulsing in his neck. Frank's sad-somber Jack Russell terrier expression. And all I want to do is take off his clothes and touch him everywhere. I just want to push him down on the bed and lick every square inch of him like a $7.99 three-scoop Nutella waffle cone from Baskin-Robbins. How do I tell Frank all this without scaring him away?

"It's really not that simple," Frank says, turning to face me. He tucks a loose strand of hair around my ear and slowly traces the silhouette of my collarbone with his fingers. It feels wonderful. Frank feels excitingly wonderful.

"Stop making it complicated," I breathe. "Let's just have fun this summer. Forget about my uncle. Forget about tutoring me."

"Do you even know who your uncle *is*?" Frank asks suddenly. "Do you know who he is in Beijing?"

He glances away from me, and I wonder if my armpits actually smell. Maybe international travel can change a girl's romantic scent for attracting a prospective boyfriend? In America, maybe I smelled like McDonald's cheeseburgers and Sephora's top-of-the-line beauty products, but in China, I could smell like leftover soybean noodles and rotten durian fruit. What if I still smell like the interior of an airplane after a 15.5-hour flight?

What do girls in Beijing usually smell like? Exotic flowers? Tropical melons with unpronounceable names?

I sniff myself in a panic, and Frank gives me a puzzled look.

Quickly, I pretend that I'm examining the jade necklace.

I'm worried that I've just ruined the romantic mood.

What would Madame Xing say about Frank and me? What would Buddha do? These are the two questions that will fundamentally rule my decision-making from now on. Honestly, I don't know what will happen to us outside this hotel room. I don't even know what will happen tomorrow or next week. All I know is that my urgent, desperate wanting of Frank in this exact moment outweighs my intense desire for a bowl of ice-cold coconut jellies and perfectly cooked hand-cut noodles.

Frank studies me, as if deciding what to do.

I wiggle out of my top.

I unhook my bra.

Off go my pants and matching underwear. Shit. I've accidentally thrown them so far across the room that I don't know where they landed.

Frank's mouth drops.

I believe what Madame Xing meant was channeling positivity into all my interactions and showing people my true, authentic self. I tell myself that I'm a zesty delicious three-cheese pizza with extra bugs sprinkled on it. That is my updated version of Iris Weijun Wang, a Chinese flower-heart and also a ferocious Tiger who knows exactly *what* or *who* she wants.

I imagine being even more naked in front of him. I imagine Frank to be fully naked as well.

It completely works.

Because this time, Frank doesn't stop me after we hungrily kiss for what feels like the length of a long and indulgent miniseries. Our hands and mouths are everywhere. Our tongues and teeth are slow but frantic against each other's skin. Frank feels pretty extraordinary lying under me, and I just want him even closer. What happens next is completely R-rated. No hotel mattresses, furniture, or walls are broken. No one loses a limb or an eye. The act itself isn't earth-shattering, mind-blowing, or even remotely life-changing. But I do make all sorts of extra-loud, angsty jungle-animal sounds. And I only cry a little.

Honestly, it just feels super nice to be held by someone again. Anyone who is the complete opposite of Peter Hayes. Anyone who gives me expensive jewelry, uses a condom, and says that he is very, very sorry. "You're pretty incredible, Iris Weijun Wang," Frank says in a hoarse voice as we share a mini bottle of Tsingtao beer in bed afterward. We order in room service: tiny candied kumquats, delicious sugar-coated kiwi, banana and strawberry slices, sticky lotus seed moon cakes, chewy dense grass jellies, and dragon's beard candy, which is a fine, white-colored Chinese version of cotton candy.

"You're not so bad yourself," I tease, feeling my face for any Tiger whiskers. There's none for now, and I'm so incredibly pleased.

Frank swats my arm playfully. His touch still feels hot and excitingly apocalyptic. Like being too close to a miniature replica of the sun. I convince myself that I'm one of the happiest girls, if not temporarily satisfied ones, in the continent of Asia. At least within *Forbes Top 30*.

"I'm so lucky to have met you," Frank says with his usual semi-serious expression.

Smiling flirtatiously at him, I take an extra-long drink of watered-down beer before helping myself to a silver tray of candied kumquats. Then I shrug at his compliment like it's no big deal, but inside, my flower-heart thrums.

Is Frank Liao the one?

26

Naked Photos

When the taxi finally drops me back at the Shangri-
La, three detectives and six uniformed cops have taken over our
living room. Sitting on the fancy white upholstered couch, Uncle
Dai is holding his head in his hands, and Auntie Yingfei is sobbing hysterically.

Seated across from them, Ruby seems to be enjoying a matcha latte and a humongous plate of sticky mung bean cakes. She
chews delicately, like a smug little bunny.

"What's the matter?" I say brightly as I prance into the center
of the room and survey the detectives. "Who died?"

"Weijun, we thought you die!!!" Uncle Dai practically screams.

He leaps up as if he wants to hug me, but then seems to change
his mind. He sits back down and crosses his arms and legs. He
seems to remember his usual no-hugging policy at the last minute.

His face suddenly turns serious and scolding.

"We have problem with new hotel site and we think something happen to you. How could you leave and not tell us? We think you kidnap! I call police, detective, your parents fifty time. In Beijing, it is common for ransom. I even call taxi company and bus company in case you run away. Then Ruby see naked photo of you on internet and show me."

What is he talking about? Naked photo?!

I don't remember posing for any nudie photos, and it seems like something that I would remember. No matter how high or wasted I was, I would never agree to pose naked for photos on purpose.

Then I remember that when my phone started working an hour ago, I uploaded sixteen photos on Instagram, of Frank and me, with our underwear on, in the gorgeous hot springs. How are those even remotely naked photos? They're practically travel-magazine-worthy.

"Explain, Weijun!" Uncle Dai demands. "Why you naked on internet?"

"Those aren't naked photos," I protest. "They're just me and Frank."

"What you talking about?" Uncle Dai says. "No clothes! You naked!"

He shows me the photos.

I guess he has a point.

"You are KISSING boy!" he continues.

"Yes, but he's the tutor you hired. Frank? Not just any boy!"

But my answer seems to be making the situation worse.

Uncle Dai is literally covering his face with his hands. Auntie

Yingfei looks completely confused, and Ruby is staring at me while she nibbles slowly on her cakes. She looks shocked, but quickly averts her eyes when she catches me looking. And here I thought we were actually becoming friends.

Frowning at her and confused about her loyalty, I grab the plate away from her and start stress-eating myself.

The cops and detectives look at us, chat briefly with my uncle, and then quickly leave.

Uncle Dai turns to me. He also grabs two mung bean cakes himself and stuffs them in his mouth. It seems that eating in these situations is the only way to relieve the tension escalating in my stomach, throat, and nose, a stress that is also choking everyone else in the room. This kind of situation feels like a horrible ENT infection caused by the worsening air quality in Beijing. It isn't anyone's fault, right? Blame the government and the environment.

"I'm totally fine," I insist. "There was no cellular reception or Wi-Fi at the hotel. That's why I didn't call you."

My words cause Uncle Dai to almost choke on his food.

I quickly swallow my mouthful of sticky cake. These are sweet and savory and spicy at the same time. Where did the Shangri-La's kitchen get these amazing cakes?

After coughing up nearly half of his mouthful, Uncle Dai starts shouting again: "You tell no one and disappear when we already so scare with hotel. You do not text or phone or leave note. You just vanish. You not care about us!

"Your daddy send you to Beijing so we can be family, but you NOT treat us like family by not telling us where you going!

"Now we find out you take naked photo and spend whole weekend with a boy? With the tutor! I pay him lots of money to help you learn Chinese and he take advantage of my niece. You will never see him again. Weijun, I don't know what to tell your daddy."

Speechless, I stare at him.

He's right about the part where I was extremely selfish and didn't bother telling them where I was going and that I was safe the whole time. But I was just trying to unite our entire family. I can't tell him about Madame Xing. I can't tell him about how I know about the horrible decades-long war between him, my father, and my grandparents in the past.

I can't tell him that I was just trying to repair a beautiful, broken watercolor painting by searching for missing pieces.

"I'm sorry about not telling you and Auntie Yingfei," I say. "Not texting or phoning was irresponsible and wrong. But I won't apologize for Frank. He's a good person."

Uncle Dai looks at me, furious and shocked at my response.

"You embarrass family!" he says.

Is it that huge of a deal that I posted photos of Frank and me in our underwear? It's exactly like being in a hot tub, but outdoors in nature. Doesn't he admire my iPhone photography skills? There are flowers, rocks, magpies, and gushing blue-white waters. I even got 114 likes on Instagram this morning.

Why is Uncle Dai so focused on the fact that I hooked up with my tutor?

Isn't Frank better than a random person on the street?

Would he be having the same reaction if I told him that I slept with a rickshaw driver? Or a dude who operates a food stall at Fucheng Street Market?

Anyway, he's not serious about not letting me see Frank again, is he? Can uncles in Beijing prohibit modern-day Romeo and Juliet relationships? Are Chinese relationship laws based on medieval Shakespearean times?

Stunned, I turn to Ruby to ask her, but she's looking at me like I'm a mess. A centipede that she wants to skewer and deep-fry alive but won't actually eat.

Unexpectedly, Uncle Dai's phone rings and he goes into his office to answer it. Auntie Yingfei, glancing nervously at us, quickly follows him.

I turn to Ruby. "Why did you show your dad the photos of Frank and me?"

She gives me a funny, hurt expression. I almost miss her severe eye-rolling when I first arrived in Beijing.

"You were supposed to pick up the dog so my dad wouldn't find out!" she hisses. "The monks couldn't reach you, so they phoned the spa owner, who phoned Mr. Chen, and they are boarding the dog for a few days before they ship it back to the temple! Now I can't practice. My dad doesn't want me ordering any more dogs with my allowance."

"Oh my god, Ruby," I say, shocked. "I'm so sorry, I completely forgot about the mastiff."

"You promised, Iris! What type of person promises and forgets?"

She's right. I'm truly an awful person who can't remember to help her cousin when it counts.

"And guess what? I got a B-minus on the paper you looked at!" she continues. "We're both grounded for the summer."

"But that's a good mark," I say, confused. I have never gotten a B-minus on a paper before.

"I needed a high A. And congratulations. You also just lost both of our allowances."

"What do you mean? I thought your dad was joking," I say.

"You don't take anything seriously, do you?" she retorts. "No one gets less than perfect if you're related to the great Feng Construction Corp, who only builds award-winning, perfect celebrity hotels. I can't believe we are even related.

"I want my boots back," she suddenly says, crossing her arms.

I forgot that I was still wearing her beautiful gold leather boots. I wore Ruby's gift for the entire weekend in Chengdu, except when I was in the hot springs, obviously.

Can't Ruby see that her boots honestly look amazing on me?

"They make my complexion better," I tell her, before realizing that it was the wrong thing to say.

"Take them off right now," she insists. "I want them back. I shouldn't have trusted you."

I unzip them and hand them over.

"You are the worst person I have ever met," she says coldly.

Tears of horror, shame, and guilt prick my eyeballs. I feel horrible for not remembering my promise to Ruby. I can't believe that I made a commitment without even thinking about it. Does that make me a shitty friend or a shittier cousin?

My phone dings. At first, I think it's Frank, but Ruby is texting me, perched on an armchair across the room. Eyebrows bunched up as if she's about to cry, she seems unable to have a face-to-face conversation when it comes to emotional matters.

SuperPrincessQueenRuby8421: I actually thought you were okay for a while

Iris: Ruby i'm so sorry

Iris: It's no excuse but I completely forgot about picking up your dog

SuperPrincessQueenRuby8421: You don't care about anything except yourself

Iris: That's not true

Iris: I'm enlightened now!

SuperPrincessQueenRuby8421: Wtf are you talking about?

SuperPrincessQueenRuby8421: You're SO selfish

SuperPrincessQueenRuby8421: You were having fun and forgot

Iris: I'm sorry

SuperPrincessQueenRuby8421: Sorry doesn't mean anything if you keep doing it

SuperPrincessQueenRuby8421: I thought i misjudged you but you are the most spoiled and laziest person i have ever met and i know all the top 10 richest families in China

Finally, Uncle Dai storms back in, his face scrunched up and worried. "We need to move to new hotel NOW. Leave everything."

WECHAT GROUP (#1WangFamily!!!)

Mom: HOW COULD YOU BE SO SELFISH?!

IrisDaddy: How could you shame us in front of your uncle and aunt? They think we did a terrible job raising you.

Mom: You betrayed everyone's trust. You have no respect for

your elders. You didn't tell anyone where you were going. Why didn't you phone us???

Mom: EVERYONE has been so worried

Mom: We thought something horrible had happened

Mom: You need to think about other people before you disappear. We thought you were kidnapped/murdered/dead

IrisDaddy: We have not slept for 48 hours. We called the US Embassy in China

IrisDaddy: We thought Beijing would change you! Your behavior is out of control

Mom: CALL US BACK

WECHAT GROUP (#1WangFamily!!!)

Mom: NAKED PHOTOS, Iris?

Mom: Your uncle thinks you're an internet porn star!!

IrisDaddy: You spent a weekend with a strange boy?!!

101 messages.

Confrontation

"Not safe," Uncle Dai says as we exit the building with hotel security. I notice that my uncle has hired a dozen additional bodyguards, who follow us in shiny black cars. Apparently, the police think that he's being targeted by a specific group of protestors who will do anything to stop my uncle from building his new hotel.

I'm suddenly nervous. It seems incredibly serious if we have to evacuate the Shangri-La in secrecy. I'm not even allowed to bring my toothbrush. Uncle Dai won't even let Ruby leave the house with the gold boots, so she puts them on instead.

"What's going on?" I ask. "I deserve to know."

"They don't want us to build brand-new hotel," Uncle Dai says.

"Who?" I say.

"People in Beijing very angry this time. We pick site that is not accepted by everyone. Many write letter and say they want to hurt us. Someone follow Auntie Yingfei home from bank yesterday.

Feng Corp number five company in Asia and our job is to build best hotel. But people destroy hotel site last night. They think we are kicking people out of their home, but we already have many investor put money in. We make big mistake."

"What?" I ask, confused.

I stop breathing for at least a few minutes, until I feel what I think are my lungs exploding like microwave popcorn. My heart beats uncontrollably. I'm actually terrified. Nothing newsworthy like this has ever happened to me in New Jersey.

How can Uncle Dai be so nonchalant and businesslike about this problem? Is he just extra talented at hiding his feelings? Or is he downplaying his fear so we won't get scared? He seems to handle trouble better than my dad, who would be either screaming or sobbing (like me).

"Is this normal?" I ask him.

"At first police say the letter will go away last summer," Uncle Dai says slowly. "But then now many try to push car and then you suddenly missing and lots of angry people. We not worry at first because no big deal. Now we must fix problem, but we already have investor money and start building."

"Aren't you scared?" I demand, scanning Ruby and Auntie Ying-fei for social cues. They seem as uncomfortable as I am, clutching their purses but not being overly emotional. They look like they are pretending to tolerate a foreign art movie, but in reality, they have no idea what's going on. Is that how I look when I'm browsing museums? Half-constipated, half fake-frozen smiling?

"Weijun, do not worry," Uncle Dai says. "I am CEO of family and company."

"Aren't you worried, though?" I persist.

"Scare is bad for productivity," he says.

"Yes! But—"

"Weijun, enough question. Please stop talking and let me think." Uncle Dai looks deeply disturbed.

Auntie Yingfei puts her arms around me and Ruby, and we huddle together in the car. I glance at Ruby, who is no longer pouting. She glances at me without her usual snarky eye-rolling, then looks away. Is this a relatively normal situation for her? Or is this unthinkable evacuation an actual emergency for her, too?

We don't talk during the entire car ride.

I recognize the palatial structure of the Red Mandarin Hotel as soon as we near the entrance. My grandparents live here. But this time, we enter through the back with the security team at urgent, fast-forwarded speed.

Ruby and I are assigned to a suite on the thirty-seventh floor. We'll be sharing a room. Uncle Dai thinks it's better to split up, in case anyone follows him. Even Auntie Yingfei will be staying on a separate floor.

I thought that he'd most likely forget due to the stress and chaos of relocating hotels, but Uncle Dai makes us hand over our prepaid Visa cards. How can he even remember that Ruby got a B-minus in English at a time like this? For some reason, I can't find mine, which was with the secret room key that my grandma gave me.

"You not lying?" Uncle Dai asks, looking shocked. "You lose Visa card??"

I hand him my purse and wallet to search, and even he and Auntie Yingfei agree that they can't find it.

"At least I still have my passport, right?" I say. "That's important, right?"

No one says anything.

"Can I see Grandma and Grandpa?" Ruby asks.

Uncle Dai looks at me nervously.

"It's okay," I say. "I know they live here. I know what happened between my dad and you in the past."

He looks at me, incredulous.

"How?" he says, but then he changes his mind. "Forget it. Don't tell me. Tiger is very sneaky animal!"

Uncle Dai then barks orders at the security guards to take us to see Grandma and Grandpa. He assigns one guard for Ruby and me, three to Auntie Yingfei, and six for himself. He even gets to keep Mr. Chen.

"Why is Iris coming with me?" Ruby whines.

Instead of sneering this time, she has resumed her typical eye-rolling. It almost makes me feel relieved.

"You go with cousin or stay in room," Uncle Dai says. "Your mom and I go to work. We need to find way to stop problem."

Escorted, we take the elevator down and rap on the door of my grandparents' suite.

My grandma and grandpa are astonished to see us with our new bodyguard. They greet me before they hug a frowning, wounded-looking Ruby, and I fling my arms around both of them, relieved that everything will be okay.

They automatically start making us tea and feeding us cookies from tins—coconut, black sesame, almond, peanut—and red bean pastries. I grab a cookie with a crunchy walnut topping.

They keep asking questions and turn to Ruby for translation. She points at herself, but my grandparents are asking about me. As if annoyed with the attention that I'm receiving, she shrugs casually and then says something cutting in Chinese. All I understand is my own name, and I'm so pissed at myself for not trying harder to learn my grandparents' language. I have so much I want to say to them without a translator.

To my horror, Ruby pulls out her phone and shows them my Instagram photos. Me and Frank, half-nude, in a hot spring. Selfies of my arms thrown around his neck. More photos of me kissing him. I didn't think about how this might look to my parents or grandparents.

Our grandparents look at me, stunned and uncomfortable.

My photos make them so upset that they have to leave the room, where they both start shouting.

I don't know how to speak to them.

"Why did you show them?" I ask. "What did you say to them, Ruby?"

She shrugs and turns away.

In anger, I chuck a cookie at the back of her head. I don't mean to throw a cookie, but I'm so angry and fed up with my cousin's bitchy behavior. Usually, I would miss my target, but for some reason, my aim is exceptional today and the cookie lands on her head and snaps in half. I attribute it to rage, betrayal, and watching the New York Yankees with my dad.

She gasps. And whirls around. The cookie bounces off her shoulder.

We stare at each other.

"You are the most annoying and spoiled person on the planet," Ruby exclaims, throwing up her hands in aggravation. "First, you take over my life! My parents want to spend time with you instead of me. Then you torture me with all your nonstop talking. Why couldn't you just stay in America? You have gotten all these amazing opportunities in the United States and you just throw them all away because you don't care about anything or anyone."

"What are you talking about?" I say. "You're the one who is living like a Kardashian."

"What are *you* talking about?" Ruby asks, massaging her head. "Stop making up nonsense English words."

In frustration, she throws a handful of cookies at me. Luckily, she misses and they hit the wall.

"You really are a CRA! Crazy Rich Asian," I say.

As soon as it comes out of my mouth, I regret it. It's too much. I'm not a mean girl like Samira, who judges people on their behavior and IQ.

Ruby lets out a sharp, bitter laugh.

"I didn't grow up like this. While my dad was working on his company and attending school, my mom and I lived in a tiny run-down village. We didn't even have electricity or heat or running water. We practically lived in a hut with nothing to eat. My dad showed me your photos; you grew up in a nice house with a piano and tennis lessons. But you don't care about anything or anyone. Worst of all, people like you. They don't see that you're a self-absorbed brat."

Shocked, I stare at her. I had no idea that Ruby grew up in such extreme poverty. How could I have known? She seemed to be such a stuck-up princess with an unlimited spending allowance. She seemed to be so smug and comfortable with her life. Is that why she has been so mean to me?

A hurt silence escalates between us.

Ruby and I are connected by the same blood feud and long history. We love the same people, and I think we are actually on the same side of the family tree. How can we reconcile our differences?

"We're not that opposite," I say. "We both really care about family, and we want our parents to be happy with our decisions."

As if ashamed, my cousin looks down at her amazing gold boots. I stare at them too, and they instantly make me feel a little bit better. I would feel even better if they were on my feet, but I force myself to pay attention.

"Is that why you're always so angry at me?" I finally say softly.

"I guess I was incredibly jealous," Ruby admits. "When we went to that party with Frank and his friends, you just fit in without trying. You don't even speak Chinese, but you seemed to be so comfortable around people."

"But you are really smart," I say. "If I had an ounce of your brainpower, I could be running for president."

We pick up the mess of cookies silently.

I understand where Ruby is coming from. I understand that not being good at something is horrifying and scary because I am also *not* excellent in many aspects and areas of my life. But I have learned from Madame Xing that having zero confidence doesn't mean you are half a person. It doesn't mean that you are excluded from being a thoughtful, kind, and fully functioning human being.

"I really wanted you to like me," I continue. "I kept trying, but you didn't."

She laughs reluctantly.

"Give me a chance?" I ask hesitantly. "I'll make it up to you about the dog. I'm not sure how. I'll talk to your dad and explain. Right now, I just need you to trust that I want the best for our family. I was at Chengdu working on a plan to make things right."

She sighs dramatically.

"I didn't have cell reception and I honestly shouldn't have forgotten about my commitment to you. I could have asked the front desk of the hotel to call, but I wasn't thinking. Can you please tell our grandparents that it was all a HUGE misunderstanding?"

I glance nervously at her.

"Okay," Ruby finally agrees, looking at the floor.

When my grandma and grandpa come out of the other room, they stare at me with mild shock and discomfort. Grandpa is actually sobbing again and both of them are holding out *a lot* of money. I look at Ruby, silently pleading, *Please fix it.*

She speaks to them in Chinese. They look slightly relieved.

"What did you tell them?" I ask.

"I just told them it wasn't you in the photos," she says. "Everything is fixed."

"Are you sure?" I insist.

"Just take the money," Ruby whispers. "You owe me allowance money for the B-minus. Also, go along with it if someone asks you if you need money for college."

"Ruby!?" I say uneasily. What just happened? I have no idea what Ruby just told our poor grandparents. She could be endangering their lives with unnecessary stress. How many more weeks and months were shaved off their lives because I have an unreliable translator and I don't understand Chinese?

Grandma gushes something at us. Ruby glances at me and translates, "Grandma is saying that she is very happy to see us together as a family."

Her face softens like margarine.

Tearing up, I try to hug my cousin, but she backs away like she's seriously afraid of me.

"What are you doing?" Ruby says. "We're not that close."

But she's actually laughing at me. This is the first time that I've seen a genuine smile on her face. And honestly, it's like witnessing the best constipation-free miracle drug that I have ever seen.

Nodding and smiling, my grandma continues speaking rapidly to us in Mandarin. Her eyes start watering. They're like giant sprinklers.

I glance at Ruby for translation purposes.

"She's saying we're good girls," my cousin explains.

I blink, confused.

"It's her way of saying that she loves us."

"How do I say 'I love you' in Mandarin?" I ask.

"Wǒ ài nǐ," Ruby says.

"Wǒ ài nǐ," I repeat back tearfully, and it sounds 30 percent right.

My heart is full.

I hug both of my grandparents tightly.

Being with them is better than any ten-course banquet of Beijing's finest food.

For the next three hours, my grandparents, Ruby, and I spend time together, looking at childhood photos of my dad, who looks exactly like me, except for his short, cropped hair. Photos of my dad at age five riding his bike. A broken arm when he accidentally rode off a small bridge in the park. Dad eating a bubble waffle at the Beijing Zoo. Dad in his high school graduation photo in a fancy suit.

I want to know everything and anything that I can about my dad.

He's someone who has proven to be full of surprises.

On the couch, I snuggle between both my grandma and grandpa, who keep feeding Ruby and me unending stacks of sticky peanut cashew cookies and black sesame rice nuggets. If we aren't eating, my grandpa looks worried, so Ruby and I keep chewing loudly to keep him happy. I can't imagine my grandpa ever selfishly hurting my grandma and my dad. He seems to be so caring and unimaginably sweet, which might mean that a select group of people, like myself, can really change after all.

As my grandma talks about my dad when he was a kid, Ruby translates, in between bites of treats. She sits, cross-legged on the floor, looking more relaxed than usual. "Grandma says your dad was always in trouble. He has lots of emotions, so he was always falling in love with so many different people and never studied. He failed his university entrance exams."

"Dad didn't get into university in China?" I ask, shocked.

My grandma and grandpa laugh at my outraged expression.

Ruby nods. "She says that's why he had to go to college in the States. No college in China wanted him. He was a very bad student."

At first, I'm scandalized.

I can't believe my dad was such a shitty student and also didn't study yet kept pushing me toward Yale. Is that why he wanted me to go to an Ivy League university? But it makes total sense that my dad is a humongous flower-heart too. Falling in love easily and being too emotional runs in the family, like our nervous loud breathing and weird eyelid spasms!

Finally, I laugh and I can't stop laughing. My grandma, grandpa, and Ruby look confused at first, but they join in. There's nothing better than laughing hysterically with people who all sound like squawking chickens.

I still can't believe how much my dad and I are alike.

I think I understand now why he sent me to Beijing. Maybe it was to learn to be better than him.

Manis, Pedis, and Lies

After Grandma cooks us an elaborate dinner of spicy fish maw soup, crispy cashew chicken, flatbread, and lightly pickled vegetables, she suggests that we spend the evening rolling dumplings (pork *jiaozi*). The thought of touching raw meat sounds repulsive and very labor-intensive. She offers it as an alternative to studying, as Uncle Dai phoned earlier and insisted that we not waste time and work on our English and Mandarin exchange.

Honestly, our family could be in physical danger, and he's worried that we're not bettering ourselves. Being bilingual won't be useful if a mob is chasing us. They're not going to stop whatever they're doing based on how impressive our English/Mandarin pronunciation sounds. They're not going to care if I use vocabulary or grammar correctly. Saying *Nǐ hǎo, nǐ hǎo ma* to hordes of angry people is not exactly life-saving material.

Also, both Ruby and I don't want to converse with each other. I don't know exactly how I feel about her, but I understand why she resents me. To Ruby and Frank, they must think that I'm a rich American who grew up in relative comfort and luxury. They're actually right. I have never gone without heat or electricity or food. My parents have given me everything that I have ever wanted.

I have never even had a summer job.

I always just received a weekly allowance for being their daughter. It was like I was being paid for waking up in the morning, showing up for meals, and being a friendly, easy-to-talk-to seventeen-year-old girl. I could complain and moan about my mom's cooking and cleaning skills, and I would still get my allowance.

I just assumed that they loved me as much as I loved them. I never asked them what they wanted or if I was doing anything wrong.

Whether that makes me spoiled or entitled or annoying doesn't matter. Madame Xing was right. It's really up to me to choose the direction of Hurricane Iris and pick what kind of beautiful, powerful storm I want to be. Isn't the tiger, if not an empress, some kind of jungle VIP?

Suddenly, I have an idea.

Instead of cooking for hours, I think that we should pamper ourselves, especially after a very stressful day of death threats and moving. I excuse myself and go downstairs to speak with the concierge to order some in-room pedicures, manicures, and hot stone massages. After all, we are in a seven-star hotel with an award-winning spa.

I smile enthusiastically at the young woman at the front desk lobby and manage to befriend her. Soon, we are chatting nonstop and she's showing me photos on her phone. Her fiancé works in the hotel as a fitness center trainer, and they are getting married in a few months. He's a lean, muscular man with a big head and an even bigger smile. I explain my situation to her and say that I want to do something extra-extra-nice for my grandma, who I never met until this year.

"No problem," she says, grinning at me. "We give you complimentary spa service. The Red Mandarin Hotel always value its long-term guests."

She half bows at me. I half curtsy back, beaming.

SUCCESS!

"A spa evening is less work!" I say to my grandparents when I return to the penthouse apartment, and explain my idea. Surely everyone will be receptive to services that cause relaxation and family bonding during difficult times? I still wonder why anyone would find it enjoyable to spend hours folding and puckering dumpling dough. I love eating, but I don't want to make my own food. I love clothes, too, but I don't want to learn how to sew.

Raising her eyebrows in surprise, Ruby translates my suggestion. Grandma and Grandpa look horrified by my extravagance until I explain that it's all free. Anyway, I continue, my plan is way better for relaxing. It seems a shame not to use the spa in a seven-star hotel. Besides, who knows how many days or months my grandparents have left? Honestly, why would Grandma want to waste what could possibly be the last years of her life cooking? She should be calling in room service every night in her old age. She should be enjoying hot massages by good-looking dudes three times a day.

When Uncle Dai and Auntie Yingfei stop by, they seem a bit shocked, but even they smile when they are offered a massage and pedicure.

"We are taking a break from studying," I say, and Ruby nods quickly. We gesture at the textbooks that we have stacked on the floor. Ruby left the top one open, so it looks like I have done some work. In fact, at my grandparents', I have already learned three new phrases, in addition to *I love you*. I'm getting used to hearing *"Nǐ chī fàn le ma"* ("Have you eaten?") and then replying, mouth full, *"Wǒ zài chī!"* ("I'm eating right now!") and when I'm sweating like a rhinoceros and my stomach is clenching with pain: *"Wǒ bǎo le!!!"* ("I'm too full!!!") I've even managed to read two more chapters of my textbook, and I'm furiously parroting all the phrases at least a hundred times each. Somehow, learning Mandarin in real-life situations makes it easier to remember and understand.

Like overeating, wanting to be pampered runs in our family.

As the nail technicians work on my grandpa's long bony feet, even he relaxes. He smiles, then starts tearing up with what looks like happiness. Not tears of pain, I hope. My grandma excitedly chooses a burgundy polish for her hands and feet. Ruby tells me that our grandmother has never had a manicure before, and I'm shocked.

"But she lives in a seven-star hotel!" I say.

"Yes, but my dad pays for it all," Ruby says. "Until five years ago, we were all quite poor. She's not accustomed to this lifestyle."

On the spur of the moment, I decide to get bright red acrylic claws like Madame Xing. The fortune-teller has amazing, world-class taste.

Even Ruby smiles and looks like she's enjoying herself. Astonishingly, she even chats with me (shyly looking away) while she has her deluxe reflexology massage and intensive callus filing. I stare at her short wide feet. They look exactly like mine. No one has my size-five badminton-racket feet, not even my dad.

"Honestly, I really admire how you just say what you think even if it doesn't make sense," she says hesitantly.

Her defenses are down. My dad says that nothing brings people together like having their toenails trimmed and dead skin cleaned. He says that if you send Stalin and Genghis Khan and Napoleon to a nail salon, they'll come out as BFFs. I don't know who these people are, but I assume that he's talking about his high school clique.

I shrug, like it's no big deal. I never expected a compliment from Ruby!

"That's easy," I say. "I open my mouth and words just come out."

"That's a really useful skill," my cousin says, looking impressed. "You should go into business. You'd have no trouble with the networking part. Beijing success is all about who you know."

Her phone buzzes. She flushes and ignores it.

"Who are you always texting?" I ask, genuinely curious. Hesitating, I add, "But you don't have to tell me if you don't want to."

She blushes again. "I'm on this app called TanTan for online dating, where you swipe right or left depending if you like a guy. It's all good until I finally meet them. I've had thousands of matches and they all seem to run away when we meet. It's like I have bad breath or something. Is it my personality? I don't know how to talk to people, especially guys in person. It's so much easier when it's online."

My mind is blown. There's a Chinese Tinder called TanTan?

"I wish you had mentioned the dating app when I first arrived," I exclaim. "It would have made things much *more* interesting than they already are!"

Ruby laughs appreciatively.

"Don't worry, your boy problems seem to be genetic," I reassure my cousin. "All the dudes I hook up with usually run away too."

To my own surprise, I tell her about Peter and Samira, Frank, and the hot springs. Ruby giggles. She can't stop. It hurts to talk about my ex–best friend and ex-boyfriend, but somehow, I feel relieved too. Like there has been an enormous secret stored inside me. Like a bellyache, the hurt has been growing since I arrived in Beijing, even though I have done my best to ignore it.

Come to think of it, I'm not entirely sure Frank hasn't run away from me too.

"Then you accidentally backed your car through your own house?" Ruby asks, looking incredulous. "At your own party?"

"Yeah," I say. "Not my best moment."

She starts laughing, and as I think about it, it seems pretty hilarious and ridiculous too. Who wouldn't notice accidentally turning the car engine on? Only a flower-heart like me. Iris Weijun Wang, who is reckless and impulsive and formerly cursed. I'm lucky that no one was hurt. That I didn't give myself permanent brain damage or kill myself while being in the driver's seat, drunk and stoned.

I laugh but inwardly, I grimace from embarrassment and shame.

How do I even recover from the regret that is never going to leave me? It's not just a feeling that can be cleansed away with a deep pore facial or zapped away with multiple laser treatments. It feels more than a superficial film on my skin. It's a recurring blackhead, that creepy dude who follows you around the mall and won't take no for an answer.

The horrible remorse I feel for all the things I've done and did not do feels a lot like cystic acne on my insides. Shuddering, I can only imagine the damage done because I used to be a shakier earthquake of myself.

While we enjoy our pampering, Ruby's phone buzzes nonstop with TanTan messages. I try to read them, but they're all in Chinese. Her active phone reminds me of my silent one. Speaking of Frank, I wonder if he's okay?

When everyone is relaxed and chatting and drinking icy cucumber water, I sneak to the bathroom and text Frank. I have not received a single text from him even though we're supposed to have a tutoring session tomorrow. Did Uncle Dai already phone him? Did he threaten him and tell him to stay away from me forever? I need Frank to know that I'm going to fix everything. I send him a WeChat message. **What are you up to? Everything okay?**

No response.

I send him another message. **Please text me ASAP. Things have been chaotic here.**

I email him two times.

No answer.

We haven't been in contact since we arrived back in Beijing from the hot springs. It has practically been nine whole hours since we last spoke or touched each other. After we had an enthusiastic and fantastically long makeout session in the cab before dropping him off at his dorm at Tsinghua University. Frank promised solemnly that he would call me as soon as he got home. I expected at least one PG-13 if not R-rated text. We had solid romantic plans: a Chinese cinema movie, a Western-style pasta dinner, and lychee-ice dessert next weekend. He was going to take me market shopping for more jade jewelry. He promised that he knew all the vendors who sold the best, most expensive stones. We were also going to hang with his cool artist friends again.

It all seemed too perfect.

I told Frank that Uncle Dai could easily find me a new tutor or we could just continue to have fun together during our tutoring sessions, but he seemed absolutely horrified by the idea. He said that he would come up with an idea of what to tell Uncle Dai. Come to think of it, he turned toothpaste-green when I mentioned it, and looked a bit queasy.

Is he still working out a plan on how to tell my uncle? Is that why he's avoiding my texts and emails?

Sighing deeply, I turn on the faucets and keep the shower running so no one will hear me when I call him. But all I get is Frank's infuriatingly polite voice mail; no one is picking up.

Anxiously, I leave a voice message.

"Hey, it's me, Iris. I'm in trouble for leaving and spending the weekend with you. My cousin saw our hot spring photos. My uncle is super angry and he doesn't want you to see me anymore. Call me back when you get this."

I leave another voice mail. "Are you okay?"

After six additional texts and three more voice mails, I join the rest of the nail party and try to enjoy a hot stone massage. But I can't relax as the masseuse tries to work out the knots in my neck and back. It's like I've turned into a piece of furniture.

Although I am warm, well-fed, and surrounded by people who love me, I can't help but think that something horrible is going to happen.

I close my eyes and think of my red fortune-teller claws, and it only helps me relax a little.

Before bed, I check my phone again and there are zero texts, emails, or missed calls from Frank. What if he was hit by a car? Is he having a personal emergency? Maybe he's holed up studying somewhere?

Isn't he concerned that he's going to miss our tutoring session tomorrow?

Polite, overly serious, studious guys like my dad don't just ghost you after you sleep with them, right?

Jumping out of bed, I begin pacing in the humongous bathroom, careful not to wake Ruby in our shared hotel bedroom. As I tiptoe back and forth, my jade iris necklace from Frank gets tangled in my long, messy hair, so I quickly unclasp it. But in my hurry, it flies from my fingers, bounces off the marble floor, and shatters completely.

"Shit!" I exclaim loudly.

How could I break his beautiful gift of jade so soon? What would Frank think? Would he accuse me of being careless and spoiled? If the iris pendant was a test, I need to find superglue ASAP.

My stomach flips with burning anxiety.

Have I lost my chance to date a proper CPA boy???

Before I go into panic must-fix-it mode, I get an inkling that something is not right. If I try to use my brain to think about the issue at hand, my panic eventually softens. *Think, Iris, think*, I tell myself. *Wait, does jade, which is practically a cousin to the rock, actually break if you drop it?*

My mom once said that authentic jade stones last forever, which is why Chinese families always give them as gifts to loved ones at weddings and for when babies are born. According to my mom, jade stones are even inherited and passed down through multiple generations like ultra-coveted real estate.

People who give you expensive jade jewelry are saying that they cherish you indefinitely.

Confused, I examine the tiny green shards as I slowly clean up the mess in the bathroom. Did Frank know that he gave me a dud? But wouldn't Frank, who grew up in Beijing, know the real difference between cheap glass and real jade? Did he just make an honest mistake? He wouldn't be bullshitting me, would he?

Or was my mom somehow wrong about the enduring meaning of jade?

My brain hurts from overthinking.

My insides somersault again, as if I've ingested a gallon of chocolate milk in one sitting. I feel bloated with gassy and indigestible confusion. Frank wouldn't lie to me, right? He meant what he said about spending the summer together. The jade present and apology were supposed to show that he really, really liked me. I didn't expect eternity, but I was hoping to post *In a relationship for two months* on social media.

But then why does it feel a lot like I'm picking up broken beer glass the morning after one of my super-fun parties in Bradley Gardens, New Jersey?

WECHAT GROUP (#1WangFamily!!!)

Mom: Uncle Dai says you are pregnant! Your aunt sent us a photo of you in a magazine.

IrisDaddy: Is this true?????

Mom: We need to talk ASAP!

IrisDaddy: Also, American Express called and said you forgot to pay. I checked and someone has been using your credit card. They spent approx $7,000!! They even bought round-trip tickets to Paris. I'll talk to the company later. Be careful of fraud!

IrisDaddy: How much yuan do you have left?

IrisDaddy: Also, are you pregnant?!

IrisDaddy: I just got off the phone with the credit card company. You spent $7,000 on a dress, makeup, and plane tickets?!!!!!!

IrisDaddy: What is going on?

IrisDaddy: Airline says tickets are registered under your name. Who are you taking to Paris???

Mom: TEXT US BACK

IrisDaddy: CALL US

Iris: I'm okay!

29

Who Is Frank Liao?

There are no messages from Frank the next morning, and I can barely eat my breakfast. Ruby has ordered in room service. American-style, egg whites and turkey scramble, in honor of our new alliance. My stomach rumbles, but it's a different kind of uncomfortable. A sad, bitter-tasting kind.

"What's wrong?" Ruby demands, looking closely at me. "You usually eat more than everyone in my family combined."

"Nothing," I say.

I pick at a slice of overripe watermelon. I can't even drink coffee today. It's all too much, this uneasy feeling of not knowing and not understanding what's going on. Why is Frank avoiding me? I wasn't asking him to be my long-term boyfriend and I didn't even want him to be my tutor. Didn't we have fun at the hot springs?

"Are you sick?" Ruby asks, looking at the bathroom. "What did you eat last night?"

I mutter something and stare at my phone again.

"I thought you said that you wanted to be friends," she says, looking puzzled. "Tell me what's going on."

Slowly, I take a breath.

"It's Frank. He hasn't messaged me back. The weird thing is, it says the WeChat account and phone number are no longer in service. I even sent him an email. Does that happen a lot in Beijing?" I say to Ruby.

She shakes her head, looking concerned.

She suggests that we look up his name in the university student directory online, but there is no student named Frank Liao.

"Do you know his Chinese name?" she asks. "It's probably easier to find him that way."

I shake my head NO.

The uneasy feeling inside my stomach escalates.

Ruby frowns. "I know a private investigator. It was Mr. Yee who found your dad in the States. He's good but very expensive."

We don't have our prepaid Visas anymore, but at least we have money from our grandparents. Ruby agrees to give me her share. She quickly dials a number and spends a good half hour on the phone.

"He's a poet and tutor from Tsinghua University," I tell Ruby to translate to Mr. Yee. "That's all I know about him."

Mr. Yee says to give him twenty-four hours. He's confident that he can find a student called Frank Liao.

His phone call comes right before dinner.

When our bodyguard is in the bathroom, and Grandpa takes a nap and Grandma leaves for Bible study, Ruby flicks open a Swarovski-studded lighter and holds it under the hotel suite's smoke alarm. It goes off instantly. *RIIIIING!* I cover my ears and grimace.

I'm seriously impressed by her quick-thinking skills. I had no idea that she carried around a bejeweled lighter as a fashion key chain just to accessorize her gold Hermès Birkin bag. Sneaking around seems to run in our family.

Ruby grins at me as we race out the door.

Through the back elevator stairs, we manage to meet Mr. Yee, who has an address for us. He's a thin, no-nonsense man with spectacles and a professional photographer's camera. He honestly looks like a tourist instead of a private investigator. It costs all the *yuan* we have for just a name and address. Ruby speaks to him urgently, and he offers us a ride in his car.

"How did he get it?" I ask Ruby.

"He pretended to be a cop and showed Frank's photo to different students and instructors. Someone recognized him. But his name isn't Frank Liao. It's Zhou Zhifang."

"What?" I say. "That makes no sense! Why would he lie? Are you sure Mr. Yee found the right guy?"

Ruby frowns. "Mr. Yee is the best in the business."

"Is he a real cop?" I ask Ruby.

She nods. "Former Beijing secret police. My dad says he was ranked number one at torture."

Mr. Yee grins at us, revealing three fanged gold teeth. In the car, he smokes a cigar and to calm my fluttering nerves, I accept when he offers me a few puffs. I inhale gratefully because my stomach feels like a pulsating blender. I can't seem to relax or focus on any conversation.

We seem to be driving for hours in nervous silence until we get to a run-down part of the city, which Ruby says is the district of Daxing. Nodding solemnly, Mr. Yee wishes us luck and honks the horn before dropping us off. I'm horrified by the crooked assortment of decrepit buildings, and the mounds of garbage and plastic junk scattered everywhere.

A woman is standing on the threshold of a doorway. She holds up her fingers, begging for *yuan*. We don't have any left, and to my astonishment, Ruby apologizes profusely.

We follow the directions to the address and enter a dingy apartment building.

As we step into a hallway, I step on something brown and furry. Shrieking, I jump and nearly fall on it.

"It's just a rat," Ruby says, shrugging like it's no big deal. "We had those all the time when we were growing up. My mom and I would roast them when there was nothing else to eat. They're more filling than insects."

I stare at her, pity and astonishment rising in me. How can she talk so casually about seeing and then eating a rat the same size as a ladies' size-eight Converse sneaker? It makes no sense. Ruby is the fussiest, most privileged person that I've ever met. Her regular clothes vs. dog show closets could seriously fund a small village in a developing nation.

Ruby shrugs again. "We survived so we could have better. Those days are over now. I'm enjoying my life now."

We find apartment number 122. I rap three times. I wonder if anyone is actually home. As we wait, I plan whether or not to make a dramatic entry. I don't know if it would make Frank apologize for lying to me, or if it would make him retreat further from me.

But I don't have enough time to decide.

"You lied to me!" I shout as the apartment door finally swings open. I step forward, ready to confront the liar that is the impostor Frank Liao. Part of me hopes there was a humongous mistake and that it's someone else entirely. Part of me hopes that this is all a terrible cultural or translated misunderstanding. I just hope the dude who opens the door is a complete stranger. I just hope that the private investigator is wrong.

But an elderly woman, leaning on a stick, slowly opens the door. She looks shocked by my outburst. I'm instantly relieved. It's the wrong address, thank god.

"Sorry for bothering you," I say, but Ruby cuts in and demands to know where Zhou Zhifang is.

The older lady says something nervously in Chinese. I stare at her. Then I realize that she's missing a leg. One of her pant legs drags to the floor, and there is nothing where her right leg should be. I try not to stare at her missing limb. *What happened?* I want to ask. *Does it hurt?* But I know it would be rude of me. Ruby doesn't even look concerned. She just starts talking in her usual bossy way.

"Zhifang?!" the older lady finally calls out.

Immediately, Frank shows up. But it's not Frank. I remember that he has a different name.

The tutor who called himself Frank Liao looks genuinely horror-stricken and sheepish when he sees me. He tries to close the door. But Ruby is faster and jumps in the way. It's like she's used to dealing with unpleasant negotiations.

"You are going to tell us everything," she says coldly, staring down her nose at Frank.

He looks at Ruby, but he doesn't look at me.

"Iris! How did you find me?" he says, still looking at my cousin.

Ruby glowers at him for me. "We hired a private investigator. We know you're a liar."

Frank has turned a pasty gray color. His complexion matches the Beijing smog and the surrounding buildings. It doesn't camouflage him, though. He hesitates and looks as if he wants to run away.

"Aren't you going to invite us in?" I say in my unfriendliest voice.

Ruby barks something in Chinese.

Finally, shoulders drooping, he relents and lets us into a small, decrepit studio apartment with two bamboo mats on the floor. The older lady hobbles to one of the mats and collapses on it, and then I realize it's actually her chair and bed.

There's nowhere to sit, except for the unswept floor. There's not even a toilet. Just an orange bucket. The window is boarded up with tape and black garbage bags. There are stacks of books and papers on the floor, which I assume are Frank's. He introduces the one-legged woman as his mother.

She smiles at me, and I realize that she has no teeth.

"Who are you?" I say to him. "I know you're not Frank Liao. He doesn't exist."

"No lies!" Ruby warns Frank.

"I'm Zhou Zhifang. My English name is Paul."

"I don't understand," I say. Glancing around the tiny,

dilapidated apartment, I'm so shocked that anyone, let alone two people, could live here. Something furry and brown touches my hand. I squeal again. Ruby expertly catches the rat by its back paws and puts it in a lidded pot. Frank/Paul's mom smiles and thanks her.

"Why would you lie?" I demand. "It makes NO sense."

Smiling sadly, Frank/Paul says that he wants to show us something.

Confession

We follow Frank up fourteen flights of old creaky stairs, onto the roof of the falling-down building. As we climb, I huff and puff. Honestly, I can barely make it up the second set of stairs and neither can Ruby. We do not have the stamina to survive. It's a perfectly genius plan if the former Frank wants to kill us. By the time we reach where we're going, we will be too exhausted to defend ourselves.

I wish we had brought backup.

Why didn't we ask our bodyguard to come with us? What were we doing sneaking off without telling anyone?

I'm suddenly full of regrets.

Beijing has made me smarter, deeper, but also sadder overall as a person with higher emotional intelligence and multiple feelings.

For the first time in my life, I'm speechless when we reach our destination. We stare down at a slum of broken, run-down houses. Tightly packed together, they are connected into a neighborhood of concrete slabs. Grimy clotheslines and plastic bags hang out of windows, and children and stray dogs mull around. I have never seen so much poverty in real time, and it feels like a different world from my uncle's seven-star hotels.

Nervously, I blink.

Frank/Paul glances at me with a worried, scrunched-up expression on his face.

I can't look at him.

Frank/Paul begins talking in a low, urgent voice. It's almost as if he's thought and practiced what he's wanted to say thousands of times. His voice quakes like movie theater speakers; it's a familiar sound, but I can't place it. Then I understand. It's real volcanic anger. *Jurassic Park* destruction meets *Star Wars* desperation. The kind that can burn a person's insides to a crisp. Like my dad imploding when he saw my grandfather on the iPhone screen for the first time after almost two decades.

"There are two hundred fifty-seven million rural migrant workers in China," the impostor called Frank says. "I know you hate my lectures, Iris, but this is really important. Most of us don't have basic rights to education and housing. A few years ago, my mom was injured in a sewing factory accident near here and I have been taking care of her. This is our home. We have nowhere to go."

He glares at Ruby and I suddenly feel protective over my cousin.

"Iris, your uncle wants to tear our neighborhood down to build a brand-new hotel," he says, almost pleadingly.

"What does this have to do with lying to me?" I say, feeling confused. I'm hurt and angry and also shocked by his admission of having an ulterior motive.

To my surprise, Ruby shushes me. "Let him talk."

"My university friends and I have been petitioning Feng Corp for months and we didn't have any luck. Then we heard that the CEO was hiring a tutor for his niece. I speak the best English. It was Kitty's idea and we all went along with it. When we were in the hot springs, I almost changed my mind. You were nice and funny and we had such an amazing time that I felt so guilty. So I phoned Kitty and she reminded me that we were so close to making a difference. I took your hotel key and credit card when you had your appointment with Madame Xing. I'm sorry."

"My key?" I exclaim, at the same time Ruby asks, "Visa card?"

It makes sense now. Frank's reluctance and confusion in Chengdu. I had attributed it to the awkwardness of a first hookup that blurred professional boundaries. I just assumed Frank felt guilty about taking Uncle Dai's money while being involved with his niece. But Frank slept with me *after* getting the key card. Anger floods through my entire nervous system. He lied to me *and* stole from me.

Frank looks ashamed and sorry. "Kitty and our group wanted to sneak in and scare your uncle into relocating the hotel."

Scare Uncle Dai? By violence? I think back to the protestors surrounding our car. Acid rises to my throat. I want to throw up. I want to cry and scream. If I were the violent type, I'd honestly push him off the roof.

Instead, I just stare at him. I thought I knew reliable and nice and apology-giving Frank. "You were going to do what?" I ask. "Were you one of the protestors at the restaurant?"

Frank looks confused. "No, what—?"

Ruby pulls out her phone and waves it around. "I'm going to call the police!" she warns.

"I understand if you do," Frank says, looking down. He fidgets with his hands, resting them on his sides and then clasping them behind his back. "It was really horrific of us. People are protesting all over China and we wrote over a hundred petitions to your uncle's company to stop the hotel. We wanted to make a difference. Beijing is losing her culture to the *fuerdai*.

"Things have to change in Beijing and all you nouveau riche are taking over the city with your elite hotels. You don't seem to care what happens to the poor. We need housing and we need new schools. Do you know that they cram eighty migrant children in one classroom? They don't even have books and there's barely enough money to pay a teacher. What we don't need is another seven-star hotel.

"If you call the police, please don't tell my mother. She doesn't even know what I've done. I just wanted to help her, but it got out of control. She doesn't deserve this. She doesn't even deserve me as a son."

He hangs his head.

His posture slumps in defeat.

"I just care about my mother. Not what happens to me."

Horrified, I stare at him. I don't understand. Frank was just using me to get to my uncle?

I can't believe it.

How could I start to actually fall for a dude who didn't give a shit about me? How could I be so oblivious?

Frank was supposed to be a safe Chinese Parent Approved boy. Not a duplicitous user and snake.

A fury similar to Frank's anger about his horrible circumstances hits me. I want to scream at no one and everyone. Who is this monster? Are boys in Beijing just like American ones, except they are better-looking and smoother talkers?

"Iris, I'm so so so sorry." Frank is looking at me, as if he is overcome with genuine guilt.

I stare everywhere but at him, and I can't help but think about his poor mother who was handicapped by shitty working conditions. But to help her, Frank would choose to *hurt* MY family? Does it make it okay to sacrifice and deceive other people for the one person that you love?

Absolutely not.

Even though I feel for Frank, I couldn't emotionally and physically wound another living person or thing on purpose. Maybe this is because my heart has been bashed by too many terrible boys as well as my ex–childhood bestie. But who gets to choose whose individual hurts are tiny cuts or gaping wounds? No one should decide whose injury is more important.

My blood pounds like a migraine headache.

Uncle Dai, Auntie Yingfei, Ruby, and my grandparents are like having additional arms. It used to be just me, my mom, and my dad in New Jersey, but I have gained five different appendages in Beijing. On Frank/Paul's rooftop, I feel like a furious, unstoppable octopus with all-reaching superpowers. If my math is correct, I have eight magnificent limbs that I care about deeply, and I would be seriously upset if I injured or lost one.

"Wait!" I say to Ruby. "I have more questions for this liar."

Ruby stops dialing. She has gone super still. Like she's in catatonic shock. I can't even tell what she's thinking.

"Are you even a student at Tsinghua University?" I manage to ask.

Frank flushes and nods. "That's the part I didn't lie to you about. I won a full scholarship for my work in English and classical Chinese literature."

"You could have just asked me to talk to my uncle," I say quietly. "You could have just talked to Ruby and me at the party."

My words fall out so fast that even I don't believe I'm saying them. Bitterness, like a piece of tortilla chip, lodges itself in my throat. It's stuck and no matter how much I swallow, it's still there.

"Iris, I just didn't think you would understand! No one in Beijing cares about migrant workers. I really wanted to tell you at the hot springs. . . ."

"You could have just said that it was important and I would have helped you. How does pretending that you liked me make it okay? How does lying to me and getting close to me justify what you did?!!"

I'm screaming now. Tears are falling out of my eyeballs like acid rain. I can't help it. I thought I was done with liars. I thought that I had left them all behind in America.

"I honestly thought you liked me," I say, feeling foolish.

"Iris," Frank/Paul says. "I really did. I mean, I do like you!"

"You have a really WTF way of showing it," I say furiously.

Ruby is staring down at the assortment of rooftop houses,

which look like ransacked shacks. A very naked woman carrying a naked baby over her shoulder is crying. Three more naked children follow her out of the house. Someone pours something brown and liquid outside of a window above us. It falls near us, but we manage to mostly jump out of the way. But some of the brown residue splashes on our clothes. I shriek. Ruby grimaces. Frank doesn't even react.

I can't imagine living here.

I can't imagine growing up here, and hoping for change.

It suddenly makes sense why Frank has been so horrified by my laziness and inability to value the tutoring sessions that I was given.

Ruby also grew up in a shack like these while I lived in a brand-new seven-bedroom house in the suburbs.

But my mind can't get over the fact that Frank/Paul lied to me to get to my uncle. He used me to hurt my family.

My family is the most important thing to me.

They're more valuable than six designer purses and being Number 16 in *Forbes Asia*.

During our conversation, Ruby has gone super pale. Her eyes narrow. Her breathing quickens, as if she's suddenly sprinting.

I expect her to murder Frank/Paul with her eye-rolling and her signature Rottweiler sneer.

"We can fix this," she says instead. "I have a brilliant idea."

31

Emergency Meeting

Ruby texts her parents at work. This time, she labels her group message as EMERGENCY, and everyone scurries to our hotel room. Auntie Yingfei arrives first, looking breathless. She reminds me of a kindly kindergarten teacher in a flowy dress rather than a banker.

Face reddening, she doesn't even sit down before demanding that Ruby and I answer her question. She sounds as if she ran a marathon in the Olympic Games. "Is it true Weijun having . . . baby?"

She exhales the last words like she's in shock.

"What?" I say.

"Huh?" Ruby says again.

She hands me a copy of the *China Daily*, which is apparently a gossip magazine (there's me on page six with Madame Xing). I gasp loudly. I look fantastic and so does Madame Xing, who looks wise and mystical at the same time. Like she's some otherworldly beaver in her fur coat.

The hot springs must have done something to my skin, because I'm practically glowing, and then I wonder if she cured my Tiger whiskers.

I touch my lip carefully. I still have a few stubborn hairs, but much less than before.

Never mind.

"What does it say?" I ask, incredulous. "This is so exciting!"

Ruby and Auntie Yingfei look at me, both a little scandalized and horrified. They exchange looks.

"I'm not pregnant!" I finally say. "It's all a ridiculous misunderstanding."

Auntie Yingfei looks at me. "What you talking?"

"Mistake!" I say. "Not pregnant!"

Uncle Dai arrives. "Who is pregnant?" he asks, sounding alarmed. "Ruby is having a baby?!"

"NO!" Ruby exclaims.

"Good," Uncle Dai says. "Just checking if anyone hurt? We just have university students try to break in at the Shangri-La. Hotel security stop them. I need to give a report later."

Ruby and I exchange meaningful glances.

We both don't say anything.

Without knowing, Frank must have taken the Red Mandarin Hotel key that my grandma gave me. Kitty and her friends must have been trying to enter the penthouse suite of the Shangri-La with the wrong key. Suddenly, I'm so relieved by this mistake. But I'm also furious at Frank. What if Kitty and her friends had gotten into our apartment? What would they have done?! Would they have physically hurt Uncle Dai, Auntie Yingfei, and Ruby?

Auntie Yingfei asks me again if I'm pregnant.

It's my turn to apologize and explain that the emergency was a ruse.

"You need to move the building of your new hotel," I plead after a long pause.

Ruby chimes in. "Iris is right, *Bàba*. Hundreds of thousands of people will lose a school and housing if you build this hotel."

She switches to Chinese and argues with Uncle Dai.

Auntie Yingfei intervenes. I've never heard her talk so loudly.

She points at me. I smile hopefully. She doesn't react. Then she points to Ruby, who crosses her arms and sticks out her lower lip in determination.

There's more intense, rapid-fire conversation in Chinese. I really wish I was watching this on a large television screen with subtitles. I don't know what's being said or not said. All I know is that the family can't agree. Auntie Yingfei is gesturing at us, and Uncle Dai's mouth opens and closes, as if he's not sure whether to argue or swallow his pride.

Ruby and Auntie Yingfei keep talking and seem to be pointing at everything in the room.

Finally, Uncle Dai looks like he's about to yell, but Ruby steps in quickly. "What if we raise all the money to cover relocation costs? The hotel hasn't even been built yet, but how much money would we need to raise?"

Uncle Dai is staring at both of us, shocked.

"Weijun, Ruby, you are serious?"

"Yes," Ruby says. "This is the only thing I have asked you for that wasn't for me."

"Me too," I say.

It's a fact that I have never asked for money for other people. Especially for strangers.

"Plus, this would stop the protests so we could move back to the hotel and build favor with the public again," Ruby says. "It would be great PR for Feng Construction. We can call a press meeting today."

He stares at both of us. Like he's never seen us before. It's like he thinks that he doesn't know us. It's almost comical.

"What happen?" he asks. "You suddenly are friend? Ruby, are you feeling okay? Iris, you still have travel diarrhea? Is this big JOKE?"

"No joke," I say.

Ruby stands beside me so that we're linking arms. Like we're BFFs in a movie about mismatched buddies. It could almost be true, at least in this moment. I am also so proud of my cousin. I did not know that she was fiercely smart in solving real-life problems.

"You want to move hotel?" Uncle Dai says. "You want to relocate?"

"This is what Iris and I want," she says again firmly. "We also want to raise enough money to build a new school for these children. They don't even have a proper place to learn. You're always talking about how important education is for anyone to move up in this world. And we saw how poor everyone is. . . . Iris and I agreed that they really *need* a school."

Seeing Uncle Dai's deep, unyielding frown, she adds, "I'll donate my award money from the dog competitions and I'll work at Feng Corp one day a week."

I sense Ruby's nervousness and I know this is a huge-deal sacrifice for her to work at a company where she's just not interested. It's how I felt every day when I was forced to attend high school. Quickly, I add, "I'll intern too! I'll work two days a week. We'll both intern for Feng Corp and do whatever you need us to do."

I'm honestly not sure what interning entails, but I've survived a Tiger curse from birth, more than one lying, cheating boy, crunchy bugs, and Mandarin lessons, not to mention being shipped to Beijing, which is like being in another dimension of time and space. I'm pretty sure that I can handle almost anything, maybe even possibly take on the GED one day.

Everyone looks super surprised by my sudden announcement.

Then Auntie Yingfei beams and nods. "Husband, we once poor too. *Yī shì tóng rén.* Help everyone because we're family."

Uncle Dai stares at us. "You all want this?" he repeats. "My family want to move hotel and build new school for migrant? You and Iris are friend? You will both learn business from me?"

"Yes!" I agree, nodding eagerly. "We want to help."

No one says anything for a while.

Ruby grips my elbow like she's holding on to the railing of a scary ride at an amusement park. We both can't breathe. Especially me. I don't know how Uncle Dai the Dragon will react. Will he scream and burn us into crispy meat? Will he just keep frowning until Ruby's watch beeps for dinnertime?

I don't know how to contribute meaningfully to the conversation, so I begin to clap enthusiastically. Like I'm cheering for a rock band about to go onstage. I keep clapping until my hands begin to hurt. I clap right up close to my uncle's face.

Looking dazed and confused, Uncle Dai begins to clap back.

When we've finished at least three rounds of applause, Uncle Dai grudgingly agrees to figure out the numbers.

Ruby and Auntie Yingfei applaud and cheer. I whoop loudly, and everyone stops and asks me if I'm feeling okay.

32

#1 Fundraiser

My parents arrive in the hotel lobby. They rush to
hug me. I haven't seen them in over eight weeks, but it feels as if
I saw them three television seasons ago. I'm practically a completely different person now.

When I look in the mirror, I almost radiate a new authentic
kind of feline confidence. I glow, and it's not new foundation or
beach bronzer. I have never felt so incredibly proud about something that wasn't purchased with a Visa card. It's like I finally
understand my sole purpose for existing. Madame Xing was
right: I should have followed my instincts long ago.

When my parents hug me, I hug them back tightly.

I am about to apologize for my reckless behavior, but my dad
starts talking as if he's downed four shots of espresso in one sitting.

"Iris, we are so sorry about everything!" he says. His eyes start
watering and by default, mine start gushing like broken faucets
too. "It's our fault that you are having a baby!"

"What?" I say. "I'm not pregnant."

My dad and mom exchange unbelieving looks.

"I'm NOT!" I say.

No one says anything.

"Oh, we are so glad!" my mom finally exclaims in relief. She hugs me again tightly, like I'm a wad of cash. My dad joins in, and for a moment, all our confusion and hurts are temporarily stuffed away. For a moment, we are like a real American sitcom family.

After my visit with Madame Xing, I made my dad phone her for a quick chat, which cost two dollars per minute, but she did tell him that he needed to be reunited with his entire family to brush away the past like "a bad calligraphy painting."

"Talk in person is better," she admonished. "How can you see faces on small iPhone screen? How do you know what the other person is feeling? If you care, you will want to see real and bigger faces. Your daughter, Weijun, asked me to help. She knows that your family is full of flower-hearts who get cursed easily."

Immediately, my dad phoned Uncle Dai and asked him to arrange a family reunion, and my uncle told him about the planned fundraiser. At the end of July, he flew my parents to Beijing in a private first-class cabin, grinning and applauding nonstop when he told me the exciting news over dinner. "Family meeting!" he had enthused, and then ordered us a delicious bottle of Dom Pérignon to celebrate.

Before I can gush about how pleased I am to see both of them, the elevator door dings and Uncle Dai, Auntie Yingfei, and Ruby follow excitedly, with my grandma and grandpa in tow. More awkward hugs are exchanged. When my dad and Uncle Dai see each other for the first time in thirty-plus years, they grin like small, nervous children. Instead of hugging, they shyly shake hands and clap each other on the shoulder.

Then there's nervous energy between Grandma, Grandpa, and my dad.

My dad, trembling, offers his hand to his parents.

There's a scary pause that makes me think there's going to be a fight again. But my grandma starts crying loudly and then my grandpa lets out an elephant-size wail and then my dad is so stunned-looking that he can only sob uncontrollably and blink. Everyone is apologizing nonstop in both English and Chinese. Everyone is shaking hands and not hugging.

"*Duì bù qǐ!*" my grandpa shouts tearfully at my dad, and I'm shocked that I actually understand that my grandpa is begging my dad for forgiveness in Mandarin.

Trembling, my dad nods and finally embraces his father.

Auntie Yingfei jumps with excitement.

"Our family!" Uncle Dai declares, and everyone starts sobbing again.

We are so loud that hotel guests stop and watch us.

Even the manager of the hotel comes out, but then he sees all of us wailing and he goes back to his desk.

I'm crying so much that I wish I had worn waterproof eyeliner. I'm literally crying black ink like a squid. Even Uncle Dai's eye makeup is smudged. I'm shocked and touched—he wore makeup to meet his brother for the first time.

We all look like very weepy, hysterical pandas.

Not to mention, we all look exceptionally ugly when we cry.

After everyone is done greeting each other and sniffling tears, Ruby insists that we need to prep before the fundraiser starts in a few hours.

For six weeks straight, Ruby and I have been sending emails to everyone on Uncle Dai's contact list. He literally has over five thousand contacts in all of China, Malaysia, Singapore, Australia, Taiwan, and the UK combined. Ruby has been on the phone, while I have been sorting out messages and writing English advertisements. While she does most of the work that requires Chinese, I have been fetching her low-fat lattes and organizing the mail and helping book the conference room at the Shangri-La. I've even been keeping track of guests and planned the elaborate catering menu.

This is the hardest I've ever worked, and the longest that I've ever committed to a project that wasn't about my own facial hair maintenance.

Uncle Dai said that we needed over 700,000 *yuan* for him to move the hotel and build a school for the migrant workers and their children. The donations have been generous, but I'm worried that we won't have enough. Last month, I even sent a message to Mr. Chadha-Fu about our Asian celebrity fundraiser. He immediately wrote a check for 5,000 US dollars and broadcast the event to all his friends. I took the money for our cause, but I didn't want to see any of the Chadha-Fus again, especially Samira, so I didn't snail-mail their invitation to the fundraiser until it was super late. I also sent an accompanying note, apologizing for my poor planning.

Anyway, Ruby is supremely confident that we can pull it off.

But just in case, I have a secret backup plan.

All in all, we're an effective team. Despite her sometimes sarcasm and eye-rolling, she's been way nicer to me since we've discovered that we both love money. She loves investing *yuan*, and I love to spend it. We've even been taking turns sleeping in the maid's quarters, since it's only fair. Ruby keeps saying she's "the CEO" behind the event and I'm "an entry-level worker."

Actually, I've been giving her lots of advice on talking to boys in person and she's been instructing me on my Mandarin language skills. She has been working on being less scary, less sarcastic, less mean—her cover-up for being socially afraid.

"What are you really scared of?" I once asked her, and discovered we were both afraid of not being liked and being rejected. It turns out that we have opposite ways of dealing with our similar fears.

I think we can say that we are both improving, or at least practicing.

"If you have nothing nice to say about a person," I tell Ruby, "just compliment their shoes or ask them if they like dogs."

"Think more, work harder, fun later," she tells me constantly, and shockingly, I try.

We've also been spending all of our free time and weekends in the migrant workers' districts. The conditions are even worse than an outhouse at a construction site: garbage bags blanketing broken windows, and so much trash and sewage sprawled on the streets. I used to think that Bradley Gardens was the worst place on earth, but my parents' extra-large McMansion could house a family of five in each room. My walk-in closet could actually be someone's bedroom.

During our visits, Ruby and I bring containers of our grand-parents' chewy rice candies and soft peanut cookies for children, who are so thrilled to see us. I teach them to say "Hello, my name is . . ." in English, and they teach me to say "*xiè xiè*" ("thank you!") in Mandarin. It feels really nice but strange whenever someone runs up to me and hugs me. In fact, I feel a lot like a celebrity on reality TV. Honestly, I never expected that I would be regularly visiting the poorest districts in Beijing. In fact, I haven't been to a shopping mall for at least three weeks and I barely miss it.

Due to our hard work, Uncle Dai unexpectedly surprises us with formal gowns while we're getting ready. At first, I decline and say that I will just wear one of Ruby's frocks, but he insists on giving me a floor-length dress made by a celebrity seamstress, in my own size. It's a lovely lilac backless A-line gown with lace embroidery and a high-neck collar.

It's breathtaking, and I love it because it looks like a traditional Chinese dress, a *qipao*. Ruby is also given a dress in bright fuchsia with gold sequins. I love it too, but she refuses to let me try it on.

"You look like a beautiful tropical bird!" I say when I see her in it.

She shakes her head. But she laughs. And twirls in it.

I take a ton of photos of us and upload them on Instagram. Twenty-nine likes from my former Bradley Gardens classmates within two minutes. Even Samira likes my photo. Then a message from her: **Hey dude, how are things? We haven't talked in a while <3<3 <3 Heard from Dad you are still in China? When's the big fundraiser?**

At first, I ignore the message. I'm not sure whether I'll reply.

But then another message pops up: I went to the movies with Peter last night and we were saying how much we miss you. Can't wait for you to get back and the three of us can hang like old times! xoxoxo.

My eyelid spasms.

Why am I letting Samira bother me so much?

And how much does my ex-BFF value me as a human being if she can continue to treat me this way?

It seems that my friendship with Samira has reached an expiration date.

It used to be fun and fluffy, like eating an entire bag full of multicolored marshmallows. Now it's just sad and stale. Our decade-long friendship is a bag that has been shoved into the back of my cupboard, and I can't even make peanut butter and M&M Rice Krispies squares out of it.

Determined to tell her exactly how I feel, I send a quick message.

Iris: How can you pretend we're still best friends??? You've done so many shitty things.

Samira Chadha-Fu: Iris, my nearest and dearest, what are you talking about?

Iris: Goodbye, Samira. Please don't contact me again.

I unfriend her on social media. I block her number and email address.

Then I turn off my iPhone.

And nervously, I start prepping the hotel staff.

After the caterers have arrived, I stand at the front of the banquet hall with an electronic checklist on my iPad. A stunningly dressed Frank/Paul arrives early, and he watches me sheepishly. He refuses to make eye contact. I haven't seen him since he showed us his apartment. We have communicated briefly through text messages, but he has mostly talked to/through Ruby, who has been sending him mandatory fundraising updates.

We both agree that Frank/Paul is a humongous heap of steaming dog shit, but the cause is more important than whether or not we personally like and respect him.

"Zhī jǐ zhī bǐ, bǎi zhàn bù dài," Ruby told me, quoting from her all-time favorite book, Sun Tzu's *The Art of War.* "If you know both yourself and your enemy, you can win a hundred battles without jeopardy."

I didn't know exactly what she was referring to, but Ruby ordered me the English version and said that it would dramatically improve my dating life. She uses *The Art of War* to strategize all her doggy-grooming pageants.

Honestly, I'm just grateful that my cousin is like a relentless pit bull, and that she's finally on my side.

I never want to be on opposing sides with Ruby again.

"Iris, how have you been?" Frank/Paul asks.

I pause.

Then . . . finally! A group of guests have just arrived, and I dash away to check them in. I pretend that I haven't heard him.

"Huān yíng guāng lín!" I shout joyfully at a gaggle of women in couture evening gowns. "Welcome, welcome to our event."

They smile politely at me, which means that I must be pronouncing it correctly.

Excited, I practically scream *"Huān yíng guāng lín!"* fifty more times at random groups of people, including the waitstaff.

Peeking over my iPad with the guest names, I secretly observe an animated, smiling Frank/Paul. He's dressed in the bright red designer tuxedo that Ruby picked out and sent over. Of course Ruby has excellent taste in fashion, and the fit makes Frank/Paul look like a lead spy from an international thriller and a fire hydrant at the same time. The loud, garish color also reminds me of a North American stop sign. Was it intentional?

Was Ruby helping by sending me an unsubtle message?

Whenever Frank moves through a crowd of guests, there's not a chance of me missing him. The color of his suit is literally screaming STOP! STOP! STOP!, and even a student driver could see the resemblance. Frank and the danger-suit keep creeping into my peripheral vision. Should I stay away?

Doesn't Ruby know that I'm naturally drawn to lying boys and danger?

It's just a symptom of being flower-hearted.

Despite his ulterior motives and his hot and cold conversational skills, I still can't hate Frank/Paul. I *understand* why he did what he did, but I don't feel ready to face him yet. I don't feel ready to acknowledge him as a human being.

But why should I?

What do I gain by bringing him back into my life?

Don't I deserve someone who is at least honest about important things like sharing their real name?

As if on cue, all the twenty-plus journalists and media people from the *New York Times Asia* and *Vogue China* arrive, and I insist that they speak to Frank/Paul about the importance of migrant workers' rights and access to basic education. After all, he's the expert and he can speak passionately into microphones and cameras. He enjoys giving lectures and has the personal experience to back up his points.

Mostly, I'm just glad that they'll be covering our event in tomorrow's news!

Gliding over to me, Ruby triumphantly points out a few soap opera stars and minor Beijing celebrities, including a rising politician and a fifth-place pageant queen. We have 4,508 guests in total. This was the entire population of my high school. Guests swarm the conference room, greeting and hugging and kissing each other, while a professional photographer takes their photos.

"I told you!" Ruby whispers excitedly. "Didn't I say they would all come?"

I don't know who these people are, but they all seem to know Ruby, Uncle Dai, and Auntie Yingfei. They all seem to eat at the same restaurants and dance in the nightclubs in Beijing while also frequenting the same spas in Paris and ski lodges in Switzerland.

Everyone is so beautifully dressed and groomed. It's like a red-carpet night at the Oscars.

Not one but two local television stations will be covering the event and asking for more donations.

On a last-minute whim, I invited Madame Xing to do specialty face-readings at our event, and I'm thrilled when she arrives late with her assistant, Hollie. Madame Xing is also part of my secret backup plan. When she sees me and I check her name off my electronic list, I grin and flash her my extra-long red acrylic nails. She laughs and shows me hers. We match perfectly.

I finally have my own Tiger claws, filed down to extra-sharp stiletto points for protection. Whether I need them or not.

Am I destined to be as fashionable and mighty as the formidable Madame Xing? Could I be a world-class entrepreneur, if not a successful fortune-teller? I seem to be a horrible judge of character. Don't business and fortune-telling require reading the personalities of people around you?

"Iris, how is your heart?" Madame Xing asks, and I say that it's still banged up but improving.

She smiles knowingly.

"If you have a flower-heart, it can still grow back," she offers. She places her hand on my shoulder and squeezes.

I introduce her to my parents in the crowd, and my dad immediately reacts as if he's meeting a legendary historical figure. His eyes widen. He beams. He doesn't know if he should bow or shake her hand or both. It's as if he's meeting Confucius for the first time. My poor dad is practically speechless, and I can see that he wants to ask her so many questions about his past, present, and future.

As Madame Xing sets up shop in the center of the room for face-readings (65 percent of the profits will go to our cause), my dad eagerly follows her. My dad keeps pointing at moles on his face and arms and legs and asking her to explain what they all mean.

She patiently answers all his questions at first ("Good job with Tiger daughter! The Dog wife is an excellent choice!"), but after his tenth question about a raised birthmark shaped like Arizona on his lower back, she becomes seriously annoyed. In response, she smacks my dad on the back of the head.

"Sometimes a spot is just a spot," she finally says, and my mom and I start laughing. We turn away when my dad gives us a confused, shocked look.

Her answer was not exactly what he was expecting.

Nothing in China is what it seems, apparently.

When it's Uncle Dai's turn, Madame Xing peers down at his round features and massages his smooth high forehead. She counts his wrinkles: exactly twenty-four.

"You're a very powerful Dragon," she says, which causes Uncle Dai to grin.

She then closes her eyes and hums. I wonder why she doesn't make him spit in a cup.

"A high forehead means remarkable intelligence, like your daughter," she explains, pointing at Ruby. "Sometimes, though, you need to use your heart and think about what's right."

"What do you mean?" Uncle Dai asks.

"Your family will not stay together if you don't build a school," she warns. "Bad things will happen to those you love."

"More protestor?" he asks, looking serious.

"Sometimes our countries and hearts are more worth it than profit," she says, and Uncle Dai doesn't respond. He looks deeply lost in his thoughts. But his eyes water nonstop, and he pretends to check his phone, while asking Auntie Yingfei for allergy meds.

Madame Xing winks at me.

A professional photographer suddenly snaps our photo.

We gather for another shot, but this time, we pose formally and smile. I put my arms around my parents. I have honestly missed them while I have been away. No longer furious and frustrated at them, I'm just incredibly happy that they will be staying for a few weeks. In our WeChat group, we've already planned to visit Shanghai, Jiuzhaigou National Park, Zhangjiajie, and Baofeng Lake. While my mom and I shop, my dad, Uncle Dai, and my grandpa will spend some time getting to know each other and trying to forgive each other for the past.

Then Ruby and her mom will go on the Europe trip together.

Even though I would love to whirlwind across Paris, Italy, and Spain, I know Ruby wants this time with her mother. Just like I want one-on-one time with my parents. As I promised Uncle Dai, I will begin interning at the front desk at Feng Construction Corp and maybe learn about coffee making and email writing. Uncle Dai will pay me a minimum wage of 24 *yuan*/hour ($3.50 US). After talking with my initially stunned parents, we've agreed that I will slowly pay them back for my overdue credit card bill of $6,512.96.

I even spoke to Uncle Dai about allowing Ruby to continue participating in the Creative Dog Grooming Contest after her duties were finished at Feng Construction.

"She's really good!" I insisted, and he promised to go to one of her shows.

"Where else should your father and I visit in China?" my mom asks me as a waiter offers us a drink. She watches me anxiously as I grab a glass of champagne and gulp it down. I take another and finish it. Normally, she'd say something about overdrinking, but she actually looks relieved.

"You're really not pregnant?!" she asks again.

"No!" I say. "It was all a huge misunderstanding. A lost-in-translation moment."

"Oh, Iris, just try to think more before you make any decision. Not everything in life is refundable. Some things are really a final sale."

I throw my arms around my mom in a massive hug, agreeing with her for once. Finally, she is speaking my dialect of English. She embraces me tightly and then we take a step back in sync, smiling and staring tearfully at each other.

My mom is wearing a floor-length black Prada gown and gorgeous Tiffany chandelier earrings. I recognize them from the catalog that she sent my father from two Christmases back. She looks really pretty and relaxed on her holiday. I'm so pleased that I've inherited her fantastic style, even if I missed out on her extra-fast, unlimited GB brain.

"Where should we visit tomorrow?" my dad asks, joining the conversation.

"What about the hot springs of Chengdu?" I offer. "They're pretty and romantic."

Both my parents give me an uneasy look.

"What?" I say. "They're beautiful."

"Yes, we know," my mother says.

"We saw your naked Instagram photos," my dad says. "And we also see that the same boy is here."

We all swivel our heads to watch the red-tuxedoed Frank/Paul chatting to a crowd of enthusiastic reporters.

My dad glares at Frank/Paul. "Did he hurt you?" he asks.

"Yes," I admit, "but it's sort of okay now because we aren't together and he's no longer my tutor. He did some shitty things and I guess he had a reason. . . ."

"That is not 'sort of okay,'" my mom says, looking upset. "Remember, you are better than anyone who hurt you. A good person thinks about your feelings and doesn't treat you like expired milk."

"You are not rotten milk," my dad adds indignantly. "You are a luxury sports car or a multimillion-dollar company. Always ask yourself: How many iPhones are you worth?"

I realize that my mom and dad are right. Shitty, selfish people treat you like grocery store items, to be consumed and thrown away. Kind and authentic individuals treasure you. They think about your feelings, your internal happiness, as well as your overall net worth.

They are willing to sacrifice everything they have to make you a better and more beautiful and more socially acceptable person.

"I'm sorry for everything," I finally say to my parents. "I understand why you sent me to Beijing."

"We're really sorry too," my dad quickly says. "It was a hard decision, but we didn't know what else to do."

"Your parents are human beings too," my mom adds, squeezing my shoulder. "We were so shocked that you failed senior year. We thought we had failed as your parents. No mom or dad wants their child to do poorly."

I nod slowly, understanding what sacrifice means when you love someone almost as much as yourself.

As my parents watch me converse with Uncle Dai and Auntie Yingfei and make polite chitchat with investors, I feel a sense of immense pride. Especially whenever someone compliments Ruby and me for our amazing, well-organized event. Whenever someone slips us an envelope with a check, a little thrill runs through me like a first kiss.

"Xiè xiè nín!" I say politely to everyone who praises me or hands me a check. Even though my pronunciation feels clumsy, I'm so enthusiastic when I shout *"Gǎn xiè!!!"* ("Thank you!!!") at our guests, I doubt anyone will actually notice. I have been studying Mandarin dutifully with online audiobooks, and this is one of the dozen phrases that I have mastered so far. I am determined to keep going. If I manage to learn two dozen phrases or more, I might even enroll in beginner Mandarin at a language school.

After a fancy fifteen-course meal of braised sea cucumbers with scallion sauce, barley, and abalone, double-boiled fish maw broth with black garlic, spicy shark fin soup, and mango jellies over shaved ice and black seaweed, it's my turn to do the work.

Nervously, I stand up at the podium to give a speech to thank our investors. I'll be speaking in English, and then Ruby and Frank will translate after me. The easy part of collecting money and checking our guest list is over.

I stare at the bright, eager, or bored 4,508 faces, who are all looking expectantly at me.

I don't even remember who's who.

A new, irrational fear of public speaking floods my brain. How will I manage to make coherent talking sounds in front of so many people?

But at the front table, my mom, dad, uncle, aunt, grandpa, and grandma are all smiling at me, looking heartbreakingly hopeful. My parents look the most nervous. They don't know what to expect from me. I don't know what to expect from me either. But

I tell myself that this is just like giving a valedictorian speech, the one that I had imagined but never got asked to do.

I open my mouth.

But not a single sound comes out. Not even a low embarrassing moan or a squeak.

Is it possible that I have forgotten how to speak?

But whether it's because I'm sick of being considered a failure, a huge disaster, or just a formerly cursed flower-heart, I know that I cannot disappoint this time. So much is riding on our fundraising soiree. Not just for me, my badly bruised heart, my family, or even that liar Frank, but for so many people in Beijing who need a safe place to live and study.

For once, I am truly part of something bigger and so much more extraordinary than my messy thoughts. I'm part of a long legacy of proud flower-hearts, powerful Tigers, and persistent people who believe so much in me. Ancestors who originated from a small village and worked hard so their future offspring could live like C-list celebrities.

Beijing is essentially a weirdo part of me, like suddenly discovering that a hairy mole on my face is actually a supercute beauty mark.

Without my parents, Uncle Dai, Auntie Yingfei, Ruby, or my grandparents, I would have no history or family. I would have no countries or cultures to call home.

Family is what makes me the formidable Iris Weijun Wang.

I am an eight-appendage octopus of the Hudson River, the Atlantic Ocean, and more recently, the Yangtze River and the Bohai Sea.

I force myself to talk.

"Good evening, *wǎn shàng hǎo*. My name is Wang Weijun and I am Feng Dai's niece. When I first came to Beijing from America, I honestly didn't know what to expect. I thought I was being punished. I thought there was no point to learning about my cultural heritage. I blamed my parents for sending me away."

I hesitate.

My voice sounds scratchy, like I've been binge-smoking while eating way too many potato chips.

I glance at Ruby and she rolls her eyes at me to hurry up, but she nods in a somewhat encouraging manner.

"But my time in Beijing has taught me so much about family and love and sacrifice in all kinds of forms. I have learned that the city is important for everyone. . . . We have a tradition in Beijing of helping each other because we're all family. *Yī shì tóng rén.* This is a Chinese saying that I've recently learned. We must treat everyone with kindness, even if it's not convenient for us. Even if we don't want to. There are so many people who are suffering in the city while we have so much. Migrant workers are not being treated fairly in China, and they need a place to live and they need a school for their kids. This is why Feng Construction Corp has generously offered to relocate our new hotel if we can raise 700,000 *yuan*. The money will also allow us to build a brand-new school with proper classrooms and books for the students. We ask you to help by donating as much money as you can."

I pause.

I exhale in relief like an unathletic zebra who miraculously outran a lion. Ruby points at her Apple Watch and nods, gesturing at me to finish up.

"As the niece and daughter of Feng Construction Corp, we will also be matching your gifts with donations of our time. For every 20,000 *yuan*, we will be spending an hour teaching migrant children the English language. Due to lack of funding, migrant children do not receive the same educational opportunities that children in the regular public system do. We want to remedy the situation and give them a chance to learn at Feng Corporation's new school."

Emotion, like quicksand, weighs on my voice.

I realize that I'm about to burst into noisy, ecstatic tears. I can't believe that my own speech is making me cry! Last night, I had a realization that I could help collect money, but I could also give my time by teaching basic conversational English. We've already been spending a lot of our afternoons in the migrant workers' district. Ruby agreed to teach intermediate reading and writing, and I could help the kindergartners with the alphabet and read aloud Dr. Seuss. When I told Ruby my idea, she looked both stunned and also impressed by my newfound ability to think of others.

"Iris Wang wants to teach English in her free time?!!" she had asked, sounding shocked.

"Yes, what's wrong with that?" I said.

"You don't seem like the tutoring type!" she said.

"How hard can it be?" I said. "You just show up and read books with lots of pictures, right? Little kids won't know if I make a mistake."

Ruby had stared at me until we both laughed. Then, collapsing on the couch, we giggled like a pair of hysterical chimpanzees until our stomachs hurt.

After my own speech, it suddenly hits me: the humongous personal importance of collecting money for societal causes. This must be how Mother Teresa, the Pope, and people who work for charities feel every day.

Honestly, I enjoy giving gifts, sharing equally with strangers and friends. Why not work hard to give away the disposable income of extremely rich people, like my uncle? It's exactly like spending money at a high-end department store. But instead of owning a designer purse or a new pair of shoes, I'm using the money to let someone else buy a new building or food sources.

Also, by sharing my English language skills with elementary school children, I can share my internal happiness like a fifteen-course Chinese banquet, so I'm actually benefiting the world's economy! I'm donating my abundant time, energy, and joy.

At this shocking realization, I sob even more loudly.

"Yes!!!" I shout at Ruby and Frank/Paul between tears. In fact, I'm practically wailing like an extra-large hungry cat now. Both of them seem pleased but slightly embarrassed for me.

Quickly, Frank/Paul and Ruby step in to repeat my speech in Chinese.

There's a long standing ovation.

Loud applause that feels genuine and terrific. Everyone in the room is looking at us and smiling widely. Not the kind of social getting-to-meet-you clapping, but the real kind, where people actually seem proud that they are related to you.

I enjoy the moment for a while, but then I can't help but clap enthusiastically back.

Scanning the banquet room, I look for my parents, who are

both staring at me with looks of admiration and shock. I touch my upper lip to check if any stress-induced Tiger hairs have appeared. But nothing has sprouted. Am I cured? No longer cursed?

Was Madame Xing right? Was the Tiger curse all in my head?

Afterward, my mom and dad run up to me on the stage and hug me. They don't let go for the longest time.

"We love you so much," my dad says. "We're so proud of you."

"We just don't care anymore," my mom says. "You can come home and go to community college."

"We just never thought you were capable of helping other people," my dad exclaims.

"We never thought you could be so selfless," my mom adds. "What happened to our daughter?"

"Too many things," I admit, thinking of all the lying, the secrets, and the deception that I have stumbled upon this summer. How I have found five additional family members (practically a whole new wardrobe of my extended self) and another country with multiple luxury homes in four-star-plus hotels. I have discovered people, besides my parents, who love me for myself, as hokey as it sounds. I'm not even afraid of strangers not liking me anymore, because it's honestly enough that I actually *really* like who I am. Not a joke. I have a humongous crush on myself.

"I'm just so happy to see you guys," I gush, and my parents hug me again.

My dad starts crying.

As a flower-heart, he just can't stop.

Happy Ending

A week later, I meet Frank/Paul outside the hotel and we walk to the Wind Flower for coffee and pastries. I have been putting off talking to him, until Ruby became incensed by my moping and arranged a meeting. "Go see that *Dǐdo sī* before I strangle you to death for talking so much about him!" she shouted. "You're always telling me not to be afraid of talking to boys in real life!"

Mostly avoiding eye contact, we find a seat by the window and wait for the barista to bring us our order. Taro-lychee sponge cake for me with an extra-large foamy cappuccino, as well as a black coffee and Japanese matcha cheesecake for Frank/Paul.

"It worked," he says. "Your uncle is finding another location for his hotel and he's helping to build a brand-new school."

"I know," I say.

"Because of the success of the event, more businesses are pledging money to our neighborhood," he says.

"That's great," I say. "We were featured in the social pages of *Vogue China!*"

Silence.

Frank/Paul doesn't care about *Vogue China.*

I wish the barista would hurry up with our order.

"Teaching English is going great," I babble nervously. "I have a class of twenty five-year-old kids. I can repeat the alphabet backward now and I know the difference between an adverb and an adjective—"

"Iris . . . ," Frank/Paul interrupts. "I'm so sorry for everything."

"I know," I say.

"Can we please start over?" he says, looking hopeful.

The question makes me incredibly sad.

Because some part of me actually imagines us together, holding each other in the hot springs with the cherry blossoms unfurling in spring. Like some gorgeous sequel of a modern-day retelling of *Romeo and Juliet* without all the drama and lying, but most importantly, no death. Being together doesn't necessarily mean that Frank/Paul has to talk about SATs anymore. If he's no longer my tutor, he won't insist on making me study unnecessary facts and lessons. We could actually talk about movies, and the most important subject of all, ourselves.

I have so many questions for Frank/Paul. What does he like to do for fun? What are his top three (favorite) gassiest foods and most embarrassing moments? If he could be any animal, what would he be?

But the harsh reality is that Frank/Paul lied to me.

I still feel betrayed and deeply hurt.

The old Iris would immediately find reasons to forgive him, but this new me, Iris Weijun Wang of the Tiger, is stronger and more confident and takes longer to make important life-altering decisions.

What if there are other good-looking boys in Beijing who don't lie and break your heart? Even better-looking boys who don't have ulterior agendas?

What if I'm not supposed to be with anyone for a while?

What if my path has been staring at me this whole time in the mirror? What if my destiny, instead of just online dating, is collecting money from wealthy people and spending it on a variety of important causes?

I jump out of my seat in excitement.

My life purpose could be as a professional fundraiser, which is essentially a bank teller and party planner all in one.

"Iris, are you listening?" Frank asks.

"I'm sorry," I say, and I really mean it. *"Bào qiàn."* I try to apologize in Mandarin.

Frank looks a bit stricken.

"My pronunciation wasn't that shitty!" I say, trying to defuse the tension. "I just need more practice. I bought a Rosetta Stone last week, and I have been practicing. I can say *nǎlǐ yǒu xǐshǒujiān* very well now."

"Iris—"

"It's such a useful phrase: Where is the bathroom?" I say quickly, finally sitting back down. "I've used it so many times in Beijing."

"Iris, can you please give me another chance? Even just as friends?"

Frank/Paul's eyes are still hopeful. He reaches for my hand, but I pull away.

"I need to be alone so I know what I want," I say. "I've never, you know, really been without a boyfriend. Even if the dudes weren't very nice to me."

"What I did was inexcusable," Frank/Paul says. His expression looks extremely sorry.

I think I should forgive him because it's the right thing to do, but I honestly don't want to.

"I know," I agree. "But the fact is, you really hurt me. You lied to me, used me, and then you fell for me. It's too late."

The barista brings our order. Taking a sip of my warm cappuccino, I look out the window at the bustling downtown district. I eat my soft, delicious cake in three giant mouthfuls, and I notice that Frank/Paul has not touched his coffee or his cheesecake. I help myself to his piece. He doesn't look like he'll notice or say anything.

People seem to be hurrying faster despite the easiness of the afternoon.

Or maybe because Frank/Paul and I are sitting so still and quiet.

I feel like we can hear each other's thoughts. For a second, I wonder if I could be psychic. Is Madame Xing rubbing off on me?

Too much silence.

The grinding of coffee beans suddenly cuts through the room.

"Paul," I say, "what zodiac animal are you?"

He looks confused. "I'm an Ox."

"That makes sense. You're hardworking and stubborn."

"What about you?"

"I was born in the Year of the Tiger," I say proudly. "We're brave and passionate and loyal."

I finish off his cheesecake and when it doesn't look like he's ever going to drink his coffee, I add four packets of sugar and begin to sip it thoughtfully.

"Iris Weijun Wang, you're the most unique, most fascinating person that I have ever met," Frank/Paul says, looking intensely at me. "There is a reason why your uncle chose me to be your tutor. There is a reason *why* you're in Beijing. We were supposed to meet. Have you thought about what we could accomplish together?"

The question completely throws me off. Not to mention, I'm a huge sucker for flattery.

Is Frank/Paul asking me to be his long-term girlfriend/business partner?!!!

For a moment, I can't help but stare at his too-perfect profile. His chiseled statue jawline. Full lips forming a too-bright, too-dazzling, I-want-you-right-now-Iris-Wang smile. His furrowed forehead makes him look genuinely wise and remorseful. He catches me looking, and then for a second, his entire being lights up like he's starring in his own off-Broadway musical.

Despite my own misgivings, my stomach flips over like a stack of warm, gooey chocolate chip pancakes. As ridiculous and impossible as it sounds, I suddenly feel like I'm the only girl that he could ever want on this side of the Pacific Ocean.

Frank/Paul is even wearing Frank Liao's infamous blue grandpa-cardigan. But Paul isn't Frank. And Frank isn't Paul. There was never even a boy called Frank Liao who said that he liked me in a hotel room at Chengdu Hot Springs and said that I was "special."

Blinking, I break his vampire X-ray eye contact. His nerdy lying poet bad-boy spell.

I force myself to breathe. I inhale deeply. Exhale. And ignore my fast, thumping flower-heart.

Then I realize that I'm mouth-breathing way too loudly to be normal.

Attempting to focus extra hard, I finish off Frank/Paul's coffee. I don't think about what happened at the hotel. I don't think about his lips, tongue, teeth, fingers, and bare skin pressing on mine. The harsh mechanical grinding of coffee beans serves as a reminder of my present, not-so-unpleasant reality.

Even though I'm terrified of what the future will bring, I'm also secretly excited. But in order to be okay, I first need to understand myself. I keep hearing Ruby's words *Diǎo sī* in my head to describe Frank/Paul, which apparently means "loser" in Mandarin. She's a loyal cousin and thinks that anyone who hurt me is worth her hippopotamus wrath.

"*Diǎo sī*," I accidentally say without thinking, trying the phrase on my tongue.

Frank/Paul looks shocked. "Excuse me?"

"I have nothing to say to you, and I don't believe you have anything to say to me."

"Iris—" he begins.

"Please don't contact me anymore," I say firmly.

I'm honestly surprised by my own answer.

Then I stand up, pay the bill, and don't even look back.

After I leave the coffee shop, I find myself picking up a *Forbes Asia* at a newsstand and browsing the headlines. As I walk to Wangfujing Snack Street to buy an assortment of deep-fried bugs and crunchy doughnuts, I circle the Top 10 marketing companies in Asia. When

I start my internship at Feng Construction Corp, I'm going to help by promoting events for Uncle Dai's investors. I wonder if I could become a successful entrepreneur by the time I'm twenty-one. I could literally become a millionairess, since money seems to run in our family's DNA. I could even be on the cover of *Forbes Asia* and even the American *Forbes* one day. The possibilities are beautiful and infinite.

Excitedly, I begin to clap for myself. And a pigeon takes a huge shit on my head. I start to laugh and can't stop.

WECHAT GROUP (#1WangFamily!!!)

IrisDaddy: How are you? We heard from your uncle that English teaching is going well?

Iris: It's fun but hard. I'm reading the kids Archie comics and even learning grammar myself. I have to know prepositions and pronouns in order to teach it hahahahaha. My vocabulary has improved too.

IrisDaddy: Hahaha that's good.

Iris: Sometimes I read my GED book to more advanced students and we learn together.

IrisDaddy: Hahaha.

IrisDaddy: How is Ruby?

Iris: She's good. She likes teaching but is more interested in rescuing Beijing's stray dogs.

Iris: Also she tied for first place with her Miss Piggy mastiff!!!! Someone from Germany had a cool Elmo terrier.

IrisDaddy: Good for her.

Iris: We start our internship at Feng Corp next week!

IrisDaddy: Wow. Make sure you listen to Uncle Dai!

⤜ ∽ ⤛ ∽ ⤜

WECHAT GROUP (#1WangFamily!!!)

Mom: We are so proud of you.

IrisDaddy: You are doing amazing work. Uncle Dai sent us the article from South China Morning News!

Mom: You are even on the Beijing News and China Daily!

IrisDaddy: I can't believe you have been teaching English for three whole months!

Iris: ME TOO.

IrisDaddy: This is the longest you have ever done anything!

Iris: I KNOW!!!!

Mom: Did you get the box of Twix and Oreos we sent you? There's another box of Snickers for Ruby and Mars Bars for Uncle and Auntie on its way.

Iris: YUM! Thank you!!!

WECHAT GROUP (#1WangFamily!!!)

IrisDaddy: Am I talking to Iris?

Iris: It's me, Dad.

IrisDaddy: Haven't heard from Iris in a long time. Uncle Dai keeps you so busy at his company. How do I know it's you?

Iris: Umm . . . ask me a question?

IrisDaddy: Okay, what is the square root of 25?

Iris: I don't know!

IrisDaddy: Okay, it's my daughter. How did you pass your GED?

Iris: Hey, I studied hard. Ruby helped me.

Mom: We miss you. Are you sure you don't want to come home?

Iris: Yes. I love Beijing!

Mom: Dad and I are booking flights to see you at Christmas. We are so PROUD of you!

IrisDaddy: We love you so much! Can't wait, one more month before we see you. Send us a selfie when you finish work.

WECHAT GROUP (#1WangFamily!!!)

IrisDaddy: We just got to JFK. So many delays because of the snow. We have to pay extra for overweight luggage. Too many Xmas presents.

IrisDaddy: Ruby really likes those Snickers bars . . .

Iris: Hahahaha I know! She is obsessed with American candy bars.

Mom: How's it going?

Iris: Fine.

IrisDaddy: Okay, good. I heard you are dating another boy?

Iris: No boy.

IrisDaddy: Hahaha, right.

IrisDaddy: Iris always has a boy.

Iris: Guess what?!! I got into NYU SHANGHAI!!!

Mom: Are you serious?!!

IrisDaddy: Great joke.

IrisDaddy: Hahaha.

Iris: No seriously, I GOT IN!!!!!!!

IrisDaddy: Right.

Iris: You don't believe me?

IrisDaddy: LOL

Mom: Hahaha.

Iris: I GOT INTO COLLEGE!!!

Acknowledgments

Writing typically turns me into a three-headed monster. I cry, complain, and curse nonstop, and I usually dislike the entire process. However, to my shock and delight, I enjoyed working on this book immensely.

As always, I'm very grateful to have my incredible agent, Carly Watters, who is like a life coach, crisis negotiator, and financial advisor all in one. The supremely magical Jennifer Ung: a brilliant, patient, and generous editor, who took a chance on me and believed that I could bring Iris Wang to life. She made the process of book-creating nearly painless. The rest of the team at Simon Pulse: Mara Anastas, Chriscynethia Floyd, Lauren Hoffman, Liesa Abrams, Christina Pecorale, Nicole Russo, Caitlin Sweeny, Alissa Nigro, Savannah Breckenridge, Michelle Leo, Chelsea Morgan, Sara Berko, Laura Eckes for her gorgeous book design, and Jen Strada for her incredibly savvy copyedits.

The S&S Canada team, including the fabulous Felicia Quon, Arden Hagedorn, Mackenzie Croft, Rita Silva, and Rebecca Snoddon.

Much gratitude to the wonderful Marni Berger, for those dreamy long walks at Riverside Park and chatting about writing and dogs and letting me send her my manuscripts (she reads at least everything 10x and her feedback is always invaluable).

The following individuals, corporations, and animals also read drafts, fed, supported, or loved me while I displayed poor judgment during the making of this book:

The Freezer and Refrigerator of Mom and Dad

Alexis Marie

V.S. Chiu and Mr. Mistofolees

Eli the Grey Schnauzer Hughes

Cafe Bustelo

Starbucks

McDonald's

Thank you, thank you, thank you all. <3

About the Author

Lindsay Wong is the author of the bestselling, award-winning memoir *The Woo-Woo: How I Survived Ice Hockey, Drug Raids, Demons, and My Crazy Chinese Family*. She holds a BFA in creative writing from the University of British Columbia and an MFA in literary nonfiction from Columbia University in New York City, and she is now based in Vancouver, Canada. *My Summer of Love and Misfortune* is her first novel.